When a Goy
Loves a Girl

Lucas Venit

Published by
Lucas Venit
New York, NY

This novel is a work of fiction. Names, characters, places, and incidents either are the product of the author's imagination or are used fictitiously.

ISBN: 978-0-6152-1268-5

For all those in love, with love.

All Possibilities

Roughly four to five times a week I have sex with myself in the mirror. Using seductive eyes, I watch long blue veins throb beneath the skin. I grip the bar, stare intensely, and try to control my breathing as one concentrated repetition follows the next.

The Wellness Center at Presidents College is unlike any gym I've ever been to. It is a multi-story recreation center with an Olympic-sized swimming pool, squash, soccer, volleyball and basketball courts, an indoor track, and new and extensive weights and machinery. More importantly, it is packed with hot, tight-bodied, anorexic-minded girls.

On a routine Friday in March of 2003, I laced up my shoes, threw on my *Discman*, and secured my penis with duct tape. It was time to "work out."

Random Jappy Girl #1: "Like, oh my g-d, that guy doesn't even own an *Ipod*."

Random Jappy Girl #2: "That's just sad. I got like ten for my Super Sweet Sixteen."

Random Jappy Girl #1: "Me too!"

Random Jappy Girl #2: "Hey, I've got an idea."

Random Jappy Girl #1: "What?"

Random Jappy Girl #2: "Let's go back to the apartment and

bedazzle our tampons."

Random Jappy Girl #1: "Totally!"

I walked into the first room of the workout area and routinely eyed the treadmill ass buffet on my left, and the hamstring stretchers on my right, remembering to always look both ways before crossing. With my last glance I locked onto a short, skinny girl in black pants and a white tank top, but not thinking much of her, and not wanting to walk into a glass door, I looked away and proceeded into the other room where my friend Jackrabbit was waiting.

Jackrabbit was the first real friend I made at PC. He's a short guy, pushing five six on a good day, a full head of ridiculously stupid, spiked blonde hair (see Guy Fieri), and a small, athletic build. We may not have looked anything alike, but the way we thought was nearly identical. Everything a stereotypical guy would have on their mind was there, except multiplied to an immense degree.

When I transferred to Presidents College after a year and a half stint at Freeport Community College (we'll get into that later), I decided to try out for the soccer team. I was the only person to make it from walk-on tryouts, but it had nothing to do with the sun shining on my ass that day. Rather, I had been playing ball my entire life at the same, if not a higher level, than everyone already on the team. My freshman year of college I was recruited by The University of Rhode Island, but having previously played year after year after year, with no break, I burnt out and temporarily called it quits. I picked it up again when I was at Freeport, but there's a big difference between Division I Soccer and Division III Junior College Soccer. Side note; I did actually attend URI, but dropped out in the middle of the first semester (another long story we'll get into later).

So anyway, I wasn't in the best shape when I joined the team, and I had to mark Jackrabbit during my first practice. All I remember is cursing him in my head, and contemplating breaking his ankles, because that little shit could run for hours on end at a ridiculous pace. After practice though, he was the first person to go out of their way to talk to me. He could come across as a politician at times, schmoozing and shaking hands with anyone and everyone, but that was just his personality. Clearly this love story is starting to veer off in an entirely different and gay direction, so I'll just say that from then on, we were boys, and the stupid drunk stories we could tell are endless. Still, I had no idea the one he was about to narrate would introduce me to the love of my life.

"Well, somebody looks like balls!" I shouted.

"You have no idea," Jackrabbit said, lethargic and hungover.

"Rough night?"

"I might throw up on you, and I'll be lucky if I can lift the bar." Jackrabbit had a funny look on his face like he was still drunk. His feet also appeared to be cemented to the floor, so I took the initiative and weighted the bench press.

"All right, let's hear it," I said.

Jackrabbit took one of the laziest and deepest breaths I'd ever heard. "Basically..." He proceeded to yawn. "Portuguese Casanova and I sat around Crazy Hats all night and got fucked up. I take that back, Portuguese Casanova drove so it was really just me getting fucked up, while he entertained the idea."

"Any girls?" I asked.

"Nah, it was pretty dead. You should have come."

"Yeah, it sounds like I missed out," I sarcastically answered, sliding under the bar and lifting more weight than any human being on the face of the universe.

"Trust me, things got interesting," Jackrabbit laughed. "Do you remember that freshman girl I told you about the other day?"

I did not remember the freshman girl he told me about the other day. In fact, I was lucky if I remembered any. Every time I saw Jackrabbit he had a new girl to discuss. The only problem was, he wore beer goggles 24/7 and rated girls two to three points higher than they really were. When he told our friends he met a ten, which was often, we would look at each other and know she was a seven point five.

Jackrabbit was also a horny little fucker. Most guys are, but he wanted everyone to know about it. When talking about girls he literally pretended to air fuck them; pillows, legs, the corner of a table, whatever. He was like a nymphomaniac Thumper with ADHD.

"I can't say I remember her," I replied.

"She's cute, but anyway, she wasn't out last night so I had Portuguese Casanova take me to Pokehole when the bar closed."

James K. Polk Hall is the largest freshman dorm on campus. Jackrabbit was a Super Senior. That doesn't mean he wore a cape, fought crime, aced his tests and nailed his professors, but rather he used five years to graduate instead of four.

Now, because of the age difference I could have easily busted Jackrabbit's balls about going to Pokehole, but he could have easily done the same. I basically lived there during what was technically my junior year. If you saw what this place is like though, you'd literally and figuratively pitch a tent. Picture a few hundred girls, now picture the majority of them hot, now picture those hot ones drunk, factor in most of them being single and looking to get laid, and then you'll understand why I'm so bitter about being at PC for only two years.

Jackrabbit continued. "Believe it or not, the girl wasn't buying anything I said, so I put Portuguese Casanova on the line for damage control."

There's really no need to explain Portuguese Casanova. He's exactly that.

"I can only imagine what you were saying. She definitely thinks you're this creepy older dude."

Jackrabbit paused before answering. "Nah, everything's cool now. We're fine."

"*Now*. Everything's cool *now*," I emphasized, happily pointing out his slip-up. "What wasn't cool before?"

"Nothing," Jackrabbit said, trying to hide the smirk on his face. "I'm going to get a drink of water." He quickly headed for the fountain.

"I'm going to find out!" I yelled.

I could hear Jackrabbit laughing as he walked into the other room.

Minutes later, while trying to give myself another orgasm, my eyes strayed and I caught Jackrabbit talking to some girl. I couldn't make out what she looked like from such a distance, but their body language gave the impression they'd met before. Luckily, for me, they were headed in my direction. I quickly finished my set, racked the weights, and excitedly turned around to meet Jackrabbit's lady friend.

"Jon, this is Rachel," Jackrabbit introduced. "Rachel, this is Jon."

"It's nice to meet you," I said, reaching out to shake her hand.

"It's nice to meet you, too," she reciprocated.

Whenever Jackrabbit introduced me to girls, I almost felt

obligated as a friend, and an asshole, to put him on the spot and embarrass him. It was a little game we liked to play, usually resulting in the girl looking at one of us like an idiot, sometimes both, but it was all in good fun. Knowing this, Jackrabbit cleverly stuck me in a polite conversation.

"Jon is from Long Island," Jackrabbit announced.

Well played, my friend. Well played.

"Oh, really!" Rachel said, like half of PC wasn't already from there. "What part?"

"Jericho," I answered.

"I'm from Great Neck."

Let the Name Game begin!

Not so fast. I despise the Name Game. The second I saw Rachel racking her brain I cut in.

"I can't say I know anyone from Great Neck High School, North or South." I paused for effect. "Yep, I don't know *anyone* from Great Neck."

"I didn't go to Great Neck," she corrected. "I went to Solomon Schechter."

What the fuck is that?

Jackrabbit noticed my confusion and blurted out, "This one's a big Jew," as if he had racist turrets. In his defense, Rachel screamed Long Island Jew louder than Jamie-Lynn Sigler (Meadow Soprano). Having grown up in Jericho though, where the majority of the girls dress, sound, and act like characters from *The O.C.*, I've become accustomed to the persona. In fact, so much so that Rachel was exactly my type.

Most guys wouldn't say Rachel is drop dead gorgeous at first glance, because she lacks that edgy sex appeal, but to me, she was all kinds of cute. She had a cute little body, a cute braid in her brunette hair, cute brown eyes, an adorable face, an incredible amount of jewelry on for being at the gym (not so cute), and the most beautiful smile I'd ever seen. She was basically everything I looked for in a girl. Not to mention she was short, which I love. Since I'm six three that might sound a little odd, but I just can't be with a girl around my height. Don't get me wrong, I would definitely sleep with a hot six-footer, but I sure as hell don't want to cuddle with one… too prison-like. Anyway, as you can tell, the skinny girl I walked past earlier with the black pants and white tank top was making quite the first impression on a second look.

"So, what exactly is Salmon Heckter?" I asked.

"Solomon Schechter," Rachel laughed. "It's a Jewish private school in Glen Cove."

"I can't say I've heard of it."

Jackrabbit's turrets kicked in again. "Dude, I just told you… big Jew!"

Rachel pushed Jackrabbit's shoulder, instantaneously flipping a switch in my head. *She* was probably the freshman girl from the other night!

"Rachel, what year are you?" I asked.

"Oh, I'm a freshman."

I quickly looked over at Jackrabbit, who no longer wanted to sport his shit-eating grin.

I proceeded with a mild interrogation. "You look really familiar, Rachel. Were you out last night?"

"No, I stayed in," she answered.

B-I . . .

"Do you live in Pokehole?"

"Yeah."

N . . .

"How do you know Jackrabbit?"

"I met him at Food Street last week." Rachel briefly paused. "And then last night he tried molesting me."

G-O! Go, go, go!

I tried not to laugh at the, 'I just crapped my pants' look, Jackrabbit was sporting, but it was too entertaining not to.

"He didn't tell you what happened?" Rachel asked.

"Um, he gave his own rendition," I lied.

"Jon!" Jackrabbit erupted.

"What'd he say?" Rachel inquired.

"Well…" I looked at Jackrabbit for approval, even though I had no idea what or who went down.

"Jon!" he yelled again, only making himself look guilty, and foolishly playing into my game.

"He told me he went to a bar with our friend, Portuguese Casanova, called you afterwards, and that you invited him up to your room."

Rachel looked at Jackrabbit with disgust. "Are you kidding me?"

"That's not what I said!" Jackrabbit exclaimed, having a hard time keeping his composure. Of course it didn't help that I was giving him the finger every time Rachel looked away.

"Do you want to know what really happened?" she asked.

"Yes, Rachel. I would like that very much. I can never tell when this guy is being sincere." I turned towards Jackrabbit. "You're not a drama major, are you?"

"No, Jon, I am not a drama major." Jackrabbit's eyes were screaming profanities.

Rachel continued. "I did get a call from him last night, around two in the morning, but in no way did I invite him to my room. In fact, *he* was the one begging to see *me*."

"Is that right?" I instigated.

"Yep, but he was so drunk I could barely understand him. Your friend, Portuguese Casablanca, or whatever the hell his name is, got on the phone and told me that if I came downstairs and talked to this idiot, he'd wait outside and drive him home afterwards."

I spoke in Jackrabbit's direction. "It sounds like they were in cahoots."

"They *definitely* were in cahoots, because not even a minute after I signed him in, your friend took off."

I decided to take full advantage of Rachel not knowing me and throw another jab in Jackrabbit's direction. "That's pretty deceitful." I looked at Jackrabbit. "I'm actually ashamed to call you my friend right now." My performance was becoming Oscar worthy.

"I'm deceitful?" Jackrabbit laughed.

"It pains me to answer this way, but yes." I quickly continued before he could get in another word. "Rachel, I know I've only just met you, but I can already tell you're an incredible person. My advice is to turn to the little guy on your right, shake his hand, say goodbye, and then give me your number."

Rachel laughed and jokingly offered Jackrabbit her hand.

"I promise not to drunk dial you, either. I'm only twenty-one, but I think I'm too old for that kind of behavior." I almost made myself laugh with that one. Drunk dialing was as much of a sport to me as murdering is to O.J. Simpson.

"Believe it or not, that was just the tip of the iceberg."

Rachel seemed more than happy to continue.

"Do tell," I smiled.

Jackrabbit, on the other hand, threw in the towel and took a seat on the bench next to us.

"After telling him like thirty times he couldn't see my room,

I finally got him to sit down in the lobby… where I had to reject him another thirty times for trying to hook up with me."

The story in itself was starting to make me laugh.

Rachel went on. "He kept checking the security desk to see if the guard was watching us, but regardless of whether he was or wasn't, he'd sloppily throw his arm around my shoulder and try to kiss me."

"How ambitious," I said, shooting Jackrabbit a look. "I mean, maybe, *maybe*, a goodnight kiss would be okay if he took you out on the town for a nice dinner date, but clearly that wasn't the case, was it, Jackrabbit?"

Jackrabbit openly displayed his middle finger.

"You don't understand though, I was like scared for my life," Rachel randomly added. "After a while, he got really loud and was like right in my face."

Jackrabbit immediately stood up to defend himself. "Right, I was going to hit you. Are you fuckin' kidding me!"

"I didn't say that, but I didn't know what to expect. You were drunk, I barely know you, it was two in the morning, and you were practically yelling at me for not kissing you," Rachel fought back.

"Hey, look at it this way…" I intervened. "Now you guys have a story to tell the grandkids."

Rachel and Jackrabbit scoffed at the same time.

"All right, well this has been fun, but I'm going into the other room before the castration begins. You guys stay here and continue your conversation, if you can call it that."

Jackrabbit turned his back to us and walked out. He wasn't really upset, but I could see how he'd had enough.

"I think that's your cue to follow," I said. "It'd be a lot funnier if you didn't, but you probably should."

Rachel laughed. "It was nice to meet you."

"Likewise. I'm sure I'll see you around, perhaps at a lynching," I smiled.

"My favorite," she joked. "Take care."

"Bye."

Rachel went after the slow walking Jackrabbit while my eyes trailed.

We had just met, but it already felt like there was a longstanding connection. Sure, our entire "conversation" consisted of ripping on Jackrabbit, but in the process, underneath the humiliating comments, embarrassing tale, and sexual assault, there was something else, something worth remembering.

It's easy to say the future would be different if we altered the past, but it's even easier to believe in Fate. What we see as change, he sees as intent. I have no idea what I did to deserve that day, but I'm certain there was a reason for it.

After walking Rachel out, Jackrabbit returned to the weight room, smiling but ready to kill me.

"I hope you realize that's the last time I *ever* introduce you to anyone," he began.

I chose to annoyingly play dumb. "What, what'd I say?"

"What *didn't* you say!" he barked.

"She thought I was serious?" I asked, trying not to laugh too much.

"Yes!"

"That's good stuff," I whispered.

"Whatever, she'll still go out with me," Jackrabbit casually added.

"Now *that's* good stuff," I laughed again. "There's no way that girl is going to go out with you."

"Jon."

11

"Jackrabbit."

"Trust me," he insisted.

"She's pretty damn cute, I'll give you that much," I smiled.

"Get the fuck out of here!" Jackrabbit jokingly pushed me. "There are thousands of girls at PC, choose a different one."

"I would love to, but I think we shared a moment back there."

"I'll tell you what, if she doesn't go out with me, she's all yours," Jackrabbit said, disregarding the possibility. "Do you want to know what she said about you, though?"

"I don't see why not," I shrugged.

"Do you really want me to tell you?" Jackrabbit was smiling, knowing he'd just gained the upper hand.

"Sure," I said.

"You're not going to like it," he happily emphasized.

"Well, now I'm even more curious."

"Would you beg?" Jackrabbit patronized.

"Maybe not thirty times, but I'm interested."

"All right, funny man, she said you weren't even remotely attractive." Jackrabbit waited for my response before laughing.

"Fuck off!" I shouted, with complete and utter disbelief.

"I swear. Those were her exact words, not even *remotely* attractive," he repeated.

"Okay, now I know you're just fucking with me," I said.

I do have a bit of an arrogant personality, deservingly so, but the majority of the time my comments are meant for a laugh. I'm no David Beckham, but I'm certainly no schlub.

"She used the word, 'remotely'?" I asked.

"I told you, those were her *exact* words," Jackrabbit giggled.

Baffled. That was my word. I didn't know what to say or think until…

"All right, so maybe I'm just fucking with you, but you deserve it."

I immediately pushed Jackrabbit. "You cocksmoke. What'd she really say?"

"The complete sentence was, 'To me, he's not even remotely attractive, but only because he looks so Catholic.'"

As I mentioned before, I'm six feet three inches tall. I have light brown hair, sharp blue eyes, the skin tone of Casper the Ghost, but the muscular, athletic frame of an Adonis. Clearly, I am not your stereotypical Jewish guy. However, it's one thing if you're not attracted to a person, but what does religion have to do with it? I grew up in a highly Jewish populated area, know and am friends with an endless number of Jewish folk, and I've hooked up with and even dated several Jewish girls. Needless to say, I was having a hard time wrapping my head around Rachel's comment. Fortunately, Jackrabbit's turrets had good timing.

"She's Orthodox!"

Rip Her To Shreds

Like I unwillingly admitted earlier, I spent more time in James K. Polk Hall than any junior should. In my defense, I was sort of hooking up with someone.

The situation was weird; we weren't exclusive, we weren't going out, we didn't really hook up all that much, but I'd still sleep over her place a lot. She happened to be one of those hot six-footers I was talking about, but if you keep in mind our heights and the fact that we were in a freshman dorm with shitty little beds, you should understand that a sleepover was about as comfortable as squatting in a pickle patch. Girls are stupid though, stuff like that doesn't even affect them. She would fall asleep in minutes, while I'd be up all night, staring at the ceiling, trying to hold in farts. I did develop a bit of a crush, mostly because she was gorgeous and modeled in her spare time, but it was hard to get a read on how she actually felt. During Valentine's Day I tried surprising her with a romantic dinner, but ended up watching a *Ralph Lauren* runway show instead. (I can't really complain too much about that one, though.) For her birthday I got us tickets to a Dave Matthews concert, yet somehow ended up going to it with Jackrabbit. It was all very odd, but it only got worse.

About a week after I met Rachel, I was in Pokehole hanging

out with some of my friends from the soccer team. Strange Girl was also in the building, so I stopped by her room to see what she was up to.

"Hey, Strange Girl."

Strange Girl threw me a wave, barely acknowledging my presence.

"What are you guys doing tonight?" I asked.

Strange Girl's sidekick, Mivagina S. Suvagina, was also in the room.

"Um, we're not sure," Mivagina answered.

"Well, are you going out?"

"I don't think so," she returned.

Strange Girl remained silent, rummaging through her desk like she was busy.

"What are you boys up to?" Mivagina S. Suvagina asked.

"Not much. We're drinking upstairs if you want to stop by."

"Yeah… maybe," she replied, shooting Strange Girl an indifferent look from the corner of her eye.

The mood was uncomfortable to say the least. Strange Girl was acting like she'd just stepped in shit and tracked it through someone's house. Apparently, her super powers were limited to social retardation and bad acting (not to be confused with Lindsay Lohan).

"Well, all right, this was fun!" I sarcastically shouted. "Strange Girl, even though I've heard deaf mutes carry on better conversations, you're still a peach in my book."

Strange Girl finally lifted her head. "Hey, shut it. I have to organize this crap."

"I'm sure you do, and I wish you the best of luck. I'll be upstairs." Before walking out I checked the thermostat, tapping the glass to get their attention. "Seventy degrees? This thing is definitely broken."

If I had to compare Strange Girl's personality to something, it would be consistent with getting over the loss of a loved one. She was a mixture of sadness, silence, isolation, anger, regret, depression, acceptance, and intoxication. Of course, comparing someone to death isn't the nicest way to describe a person, but honesty speaks in many forms. Despite her behavior, I knew something else was up.

While back in my friends' room, drinking a beer and DJing on the computer, I noticed Strange Girl had posted an away message. Since I'm certain everyone with *Instant Messenger* does this on a regular basis, I'm not afraid to admit I read hers. However, I am hesitant to repeat what it said...

"He was like the flesh and blood equivalent of a *DKNY* dress... you know it's not your style, but it's right there, so you try it on anyway."

No fucking way! I looked it over five or six times, smiling more and more with each read.

"Dude, check this out and tell me it's not meant for me." My friend, Black Mr. Ed, who quite possibly has the most vulgar mouth you'll ever hear, leaned over my shoulder and read Strange Girl's away message.

"Yo, that shit is definitely meant for you!" he shouted.

I couldn't help but laugh with him. Even though it was classic Strange Girl behavior, it might have been the funniest thing she'd ever said or done. I called my other friends over for a third and fourth opinion.

"Read this and tell me if you think it's directed towards me," I said. "It's from Strange Girl."

Drinksandfalls went first. "Yep, you're a *DKNY* dress."

"Hey, look at it this way, at least she tried you on," Sava Shot added.

It was official; I was the flesh and blood equivalent of a *DKNY* dress. The best part about it, aside from not wasting any real feelings on Strange Girl, was down the road hearing Sarah Jessica Parker use it on television. Not only was I 'dumped' via an away message, but with a quote from *Sex and the City*, nonetheless. Classic.

Out with the old and in with the new! Several beers and many jokes later, both at my expense, I got a call from Jackrabbit.

"Hey," I answered. "What's going on?"

"Not much. Are you at Drinksandfalls'?" he asked.

"Yeah, I'm here. You coming by?" I asked, already knowing the answer.

"Jon."

"What? You can creep out more Long Island girls," I joked.

"I'm afraid my days of entering the Pokehole are over... no homo."

"If you say so," I said, playing along.

"You have to do me a favor," Jackrabbit mentioned.

"What?" I asked.

"Stop by this girl's room tonight and check her out for me. She lives there."

Within seventh tenths of a second I knew Jackrabbit was full of shit. "She could live in Bangkok for all it matters, there's no way in hell you're sending me to meet a girl for you."

"All right, fine... Rachel called," Jackrabbit muttered.

"Is that right?" I doubled-checked, rather loudly.

"Yeah, yeah, save it," he said, knowing me just as well.

"When I mentioned you guys were drinking there she wanted me to call and have you stop by her room."

It was a good thing Jackrabbit was talking to me over the phone, because the look on my face screamed, 'I told you so, bitch!'

"Wait, but weren't you two supposed to hang out?" I asked.

Of course that didn't mean I wasn't going to fuck with him about it.

"Just stop by room seven fourteen, dickbag."

"All right, All right. If I *have* to," I laughed. "Call you later."

"Cool."

"Oh, I almost forgot, check out Strange Girl's away message. You'll enjoy it."

"Why, what happened?" Jackrabbit asked.

"Dementia. I'll call you tomorrow."

Not even remotely attractive, *my ass!* As excited as I was to see what Rachel wanted, I decided not to make any assumptions, play it safe, and bring Sava Shot along for the ride.

I knocked on the door and a cute blonde girl with the cheeks of a chipmunk answered. "Um… hi," she said, wondering who the hell we were.

"Is Rachel here?" I asked.

A voice from inside called out. "Come in!"

As the door swung open, Rachel jumped off the bed and greeted me with a surprising hug and kiss. "How are you?"

"I'm good," I answered. "This is my friend, Sava Shot."

"Hey," he spastically waved.

"It's nice to meet you," Rachel said, stepping back so we could see her friends. "This is Blondie Cheeks, Blondie Glasses, and Generic. This is Jon and… I'm sorry, I forgot your name already."

"Sava Shot."

"Sava Shot," Rachel repeated. "Sorry."

After the introductions everyone got settled in and Rachel once again tried playing the Name Game. Fortunately, Sava Shot is from a very rural part of Vermont, an area unlike where any of the girls grew up, so no connections could be made on his part. I, on the other hand, just lied and said I didn't know anyone. The game soon ended, leaving a *crazy* group of kids wondering what to do on a Saturday night.

"I know!" Blondie Glasses leapt from her seat.

"What?" Rachel asked.

"We can throw stuff out the window and watch it break in the courtyard!"

You have to be kidding me?

One jar of mayonnaise, a dozen eggs and a *Snapple* bottle later, the only shattering noise I heard was the slap in the face realization that I was too old to be there. With only a few items left to break, and the 'game' quickly losing its appeal, not that it had much to begin with, another suggestion was brought to the table.

"I know what we can do!" Blondie Cheeks said, holding a bottle of fat-free Italian dressing in her hand.

"What?" Rachel asked.

"We can rate people!"

Or, you can shoot me in the face.

In case you're not familiar with how this one works, it involves paper, a writing utensil, and a few shallow minds. The way it's 'played' is randomly naming people the group knows, one at a time, while critiquing each person down to their smallest flaw. There aren't any real winners; only personal snaps for making yourself feel better by putting other people down. Sounds sweet, right? I know, and just when I thought the night had reached its peak by throwing shit out the window, those clever little cookies surprised me yet again.

"Oh my g-d, oh my g-d, what about Fucci?" Blondie Glasses asked, bringing a new name to the table.

"Who's that?" Rachel inquired

"You don't know who Fucci is? The girl on the sixth floor," Glasses clarified.

Rachel was staring at the ceiling, carefully thinking it over.

"The one with more fake bags than all of Times Square," chimed Blondie Cheeks.

"Oh, Fucci Frada!" Rachel erupted. "She's a definite member of the Three F's Club."

"She's only fucked three guys?" Sava Shot asked.

"No! Fat, frizzy, and fake!" Rachel and her evil Jewish stepsisters exploded with laughter.

"What about her beer belly?" Blondie Glasses added.

"Eww, I know," Blondie Cheeks responded with disgust. "What is she thinking wearing tight clothes? She looks like she's pregnant."

"For her birthday, let's get her a gift certificate to a maternity store." Rachel thought it was the funniest idea in the world, and her friends agreed.

"Yeah, let's get her a gift certificate to a maternity store, because she's fat, which means her stomach is big, and therefore people mistake her for being with child."

Apparently Generic's rating skills needed some work.

"What do you think?" Blondie Cheeks asked Sava Shot.

"Well, I don't really know her. I mean, I know who she is, but I've never said more than two words to her." Sava Shot wanted no part of their bashing.

The girls looked at each other like he was crazy, letting Blondie Cheeks take the reins. "Well, none of us actually *know* her."

"So then how can you talk about her like that?" he asked.

"You don't have to know people to talk about them," Rachel jumped in.

Sava Shot laughed. "I guess not, but that doesn't mean it's not fucked up."

Rachel and her friends were seemingly offended. "Are you telling me you've never watched TV and made comments about people?"

"I'm sure I have, but from instinctively not knowing any better. What you guys are doing is premeditated. There's a big difference."

Sava Shot is the type of person to always speak his mind, even if it means never getting laid for the rest of his life. I, on the other hand, enjoy vagina, so although I knew he was right, I cracked a joke to avoid confrontation.

"All right, let's just meet in the middle and say the girl has a FUPA."

Everyone looked at me like I was crazy. I'd succeeded in changing the subject, but no one had a clue as to what I was talking about.

"What's a FUPA?" Rachel asked.

"You guys don't know what a FUPA is?" I questioned in disbelief.

They simultaneously shook their heads.

"Fat... Upper... Pussy... Area," I explained.

Everyone took a second to match the words to the abbreviation, and then lost it when the joke set in.

"My high school English teacher has that!" Rachel exclaimed. "We just thought she was permanently bloated."

I'd be lying my ass off if I said I've never rated anyone, because the sad truth is, we all have. It's an involuntary reaction. Sometimes we're dicks, and our brain is simply late in catching us. However, there are those out there who are seasoned veterans, and I'm afraid breaking out a pen and paper and rating people for sheer entertainment puts you in that category. As Sava Shot said, it's premeditated. At that point, you've become shallow enough to drown in a puddle. As much as I agreed with him though, a big part of why I didn't get so worked up is because I was used to girls like the future yenta crew of room seven fourteen.

Sava Shot grew up in an isolated, rural area of Vermont, interpreted as Bumblefuck by anyone from New York. It's weird to say, but after getting just a taste of my world, Sava Shot was in awe. The particular culture shock I'm talking about can also be seen at schools like Indiana, Wisconsin, Michigan, Maryland, Syracuse, NYU, and many more. It's what I refer to as the 'Long Island Scene'. Although, in college, the nice parts of New Jersey, Philadelphia, Westchester, and a few other areas, are added to the mix.

In high school, the 'Long Island Scene' consists of all the 'popular' and 'cool' kids from towns like my own, Woodbury, Syosset, Roslyn, Wheatley, Herricks, Dix Hills, Great Neck, and others, going to the same bullshit clubs in the city. These clubs don't care about ID because the owners know more than half the kids waiting in line are going to drop a couple hundred dollars on their parents' credit card. The other weekend option consists of going to someone's mansion, regardless of the town, and treating the place like shit because the kid's parents aren't home and the party is dubbed an "open house." Of course, in both situations you have to incorporate a large amount of cocaine, Quaaludes and ecstasy, half the weed in South America, more prescription pills than a *CVS*, and an endless amount of alcohol. Throw in a few tough guys fighting every now and then, something happening to the new fifty thousand dollar car their parents just bought them, gambling on nonsense, hooking up all over the place, and basically, you get the idea. It's sad to say, but college isn't far off. Those cool kids from high school, the ones who were going to the same places and doing the same shit, are still doing it. The only difference is, now they're on their own and in a new location.

In high school, I was very much a part of *that* scene. I thought I *needed* to be there. I felt like if I didn't go where everyone else did, or at least where my friends went, then I was missing out on something socially astronomical. In the long run, those nights usually mean dick. At the time, they feel like the most important moments in the world.

In college, you realize that's not the case. You can go almost anywhere, at any time, and feel like it's the place to be. Branching out becomes a lot easier because you're not really separated into cliques anymore. You can be on the basketball team, in a fraternity, dating an Asian girl, and a member of the Anti-Sushi Club. Still, that doesn't necessarily mean you swim towards new and uncharted waters. For the most part, I stayed with the Long Island Scene while at Presidents College. And just like in high school, I remained its outlier... the kid with no money.

I shouldn't say I had *no* money, because I grew up incredibly comfortable. And I don't mean the kind of comfortable rich kids use to describe their upbringing, but rather the textbook definition of middle-class. My blue-collared parents had money, just not enough to hand out left and right. Mortgages, credit card debt, and common bills emptied their wallets, so I was lucky if they went left at all.

Going to school during the day and having endless hours of soccer made getting my own job tough, but I was also one of the laziest kids you'd ever meet when it came to working. I physically could not get myself to stay with a mind-numbingly boring and thoughtless job like serving food, ringing up clothes, or anything else of that nature. I don't mean to be offensive; my tone only resonates from briefly being in those positions and wanting to kill myself. I can't even tell you how many times I tried slitting my wrist with an ice cream scooper. We were the only place that didn't serve vanilla.

Confucius once said, and yes, you can pick your jaw up off the floor, I'm actually quoting Confucius; "Choose a job you love and you will never have to work a day in your life." It's a motto I plan on living by for the rest of my life, knowing and accepting the possibility of never achieving great wealth, but more content with constant happiness. Confooshus also say, "There's no graceful way to take a pubic hair out of your mouth." That's a whole different fortune cookie, though.

Anyway, when all the people rating and other bullshit finally came to an end, I could tell Sava Shot was in dire need of clearing his head. We excused ourselves and went back to his room.

"What the fuck just happened?" Sava Shot asked.

I had to laugh. "*That* was a little taste of Long Island."

"I thought Rachel was the only one from there?" he questioned.

"She is. The other three are from Westchester, but they're

similar areas," I explained.

"They might be the meanest girls I've ever met. Poor Fucci Frada."

"Yeah, they were pretty harsh," I agreed.

"I don't know how you're used to that." Sava Shot shook his head. "What are they majoring in, Tabloid Studies?"

Had Rachel not been in the room, I like to think I would have left after five minutes. But since she obviously was, and her adorable image was now burned onto my retina, I had to go back. I said goodnight to my friends and once again knocked on the door of room seven fourteen.

"Rachel went back to her room," Blondie Cheeks answered, knowing why I was there.

"She doesn't live here?" I confusingly asked.

"Nope."

"Hey!" Blondie Glasses yelled from inside. "Rachel's in three twenty-one. We're roommates."

"Oh, okay. Thanks."

"Wait, hang on a second," Blondie Cheeks said, stopping me before I could escape. "You have to rate someone."

I immediately knew who she was talking about, and it was either a cute elementary school plan on Blondie Cheeks' part, or just very clever improv. Either way, whatever I wrote was going to get back to Rachel. I decided to compliment her, but at the same time not inflate her ego or make it sound like I was drooling.

Rachel... absolutely beautiful, but far too critical.

I put my signature to the side and headed for the third floor. Rachel's door was open so I intrusively let myself in.

"Hello?"

"Hey," she mumbled, walking out of the bathroom while brushing her teeth.

"Are you getting ready for bed, or do you just want to make out with me?"

Rachel laughed, quickly cupping her mouth and running back to the sink.

"I stopped by Blondie Cheeks' room again. I thought you lived there!" I yelled so she would hear me over the running water.

Rachel rushed out of the bathroom. "Shhh. My roommate's sleeping."

I had overlooked the cliché hippie curtain dividing the room and apologized. "I'm sorry," I whispered. "I thought Blondie Glasses was your roommate?"

"I'm lucky enough to have one more," Rachel said, quite sarcastically.

"Well, anyway, I just wanted to say goodnight before I left."

"Did you guys have fun?" she asked.

"Um, interesting would probably be the best way to describe it. I think Sava Shot's head is still spinning. He's not used to you *ruthless* girls," I smiled.

"Ruthless, huh?"

"Vicious, evil, harsh, cruel, mean… your choice."

"Is that what you really think?" Rachel asked, with mild concern.

"Yep, you're the meanest girl in the whole wide world," I said with another smile.

Rachel playfully slapped my arm. "Liar."

"Fiiine, I'm really just afraid you're going to rate me."

"Who's to say we didn't already?" Rachel raised her

eyebrows.

"Is that right?" I wondered.

"*Maybe*," she said, smiling back.

"Well, it just so happens I did a little rating of my own," I said, allowing my eyebrows to invite her curiosity.

"You did not," she said, trying to call me on a bluff.

"I most certainly did."

"When?" Rachel asked, still doubting my sincerity.

"Just now, when I stopped by Blondie Cheeks' room."

"So, what did you write?" Rachel asked, trying not to sound too intrigued.

I shrugged my shoulders. "I guess you'll never know."

"*Or*, I could just ask Blondie Cheeks," she quickly responded.

"Damn it!"

Rachel and I were playfully flirting back and forth, whisper talking like we were on an episode of *24,* and smiling at each other like two stone cold idiots. Before calling it a night though, we kept with the third grade antics.

"I'm sorry, you want my screen name?" I mocked.

"Do you not have *Instant Messenger*?" Rachel replied.

"I do, but… " I stopped to laugh. "I'm just taken back by how aggressive you are."

"Very funny."

I walked over to Rachel's desk, wrote on a piece of paper, came back and handed it to her.

"DreidelChamp82?" she announced. "You're never serious, are you?"

"When I was in the fifth grade, this little blonde-haired kid, Billy Blonde Hair, jumped on my *Yoohoo* box thinking it'd be funny to spray chocolate milk, excuse me, chocolate drink all over the place. I pelted him with rocks until he cried. There's nothing more serious than a parched mouth, Rachel."

She could only stare.

"What? True story," I smirked.

I took the paper out of Rachel's hand and wrote my real screen name on the back.

"Thanks, weirdo."

Before the awkward silence fell upon us, I spastically rushed into a goodbye. "Well, I had a lovely evening," I said, shuffling towards the door. "And I look forward to hearing from you again, via *Instant Messenger* of course."

Rachel jokingly shook my hand. "I wouldn't wait by the computer if I were you."

"Shalom, Rachel."

"Shalom, Jonathan."

"Oh! I just remembered," I said.

"What?" Rachel asked.

"A night," I smiled.

Fine, maybe I *am* an idiot.

Hands Down

I've never been a big fan of getting-to-know-you type conversations. When you're younger, they're not that bad because everyone is more or less doing the same thing, but when you're out of college, they can be an absolute nightmare. At that point, most people are starting life in the "real world," so they think whatever it is they're doing is the be all and end all of existence. If you ever get stuck talking to one of these humps, take my advice and walk the plank. Sacrifice your drink, pretend you're getting a call, piss your pants if you have to, because it's like listening to someone narrate paint drying. Personally, I find things like music, movies, sports, or anything else that isn't work related to be more exciting, but that could also be because I'm not a very serious person. When I went out, I'd tell people my name was Reginald and I was a used car salesman, Glen and I was on the Professional Badminton Circuit, or if I was feeling extra creepy, Chester the Freelance Gynecologist. That's just me (like it or love it, those are the only options I'm giving you), but if computer software, the stock market, or even insurance is what gets your blood boiling, then so be it. Whatever floats your boat, or in my case, whoever floats your boat.

Over the next few days Rachel and I didn't see much of each other unless we randomly crossed paths on campus. Even then, one or both of us were occupied by someone else and forced into polite, robotic conversations. Talking online wasn't much different. I wish I could say we exchanged dirty innuendo and witty abbreviations, but we continued down the puppy dog trail. Nearly every day, we would stay up until two or three in the morning with our eyes and fingers glued to the computer. Most guys would call me gay before I could finish admitting that, but with every conversation, we got a little closer. Before I knew it, we moved past the point of flirting and into the sexual tension zone. That's right, I got the invite to "watch a movie," so bite your tongue, chief!

On the walk over to Pokehole I was excited, nervous, and incredibly anxious to spend some alone time with Rachel. However, I was looking for nothing more than a fun evening and good conversation (LOL). I have a penis. You're probably not going to buy that. Fine, of course I was looking to hook up, but I am being completely honest when I say a little kissie-kissie would have sufficed. It's sad to measure it this way, but that's how much I liked her. My advice to anyone in a similar situation is not to be stupid when it comes to stuff like that, especially on the first date. You heard correctly, *I* am telling *you* to be a gentleman. And ladies... don't be a whore.

"Hello, cuteness."

"Hey!" Rachel walked into the lobby looking more adorable than ever, stepping on the pant legs of her oversized pajama pants and donning a tight red t-shirt that had a pig saying, "Please don't eat me... I love you!"

"Should I sign in?" I asked, still smiling.

"Yeah. Actually, forget it. He's not looking." Rachel took off and I quickly followed, catching the elevator door just before it closed.

Ah, the crowded elevator: God's biggest test of maturity.

"Hey, Rachel?" I said rather loudly, to gain the attention of two Caucasian fellas and an Indian gal.

Rachel's eyes nervously expanded. "Yes, Jonathan?"

"Um, did you say you had a bottle of *KY Personal Lubricant*, or was I supposed to pick one up?"

Rachel's face quickly matched her tee. "I hate you," she muttered, rushing out as the doors opened.

Smiling, I threw a proud nod in the direction of the two guys, adding, "This girl knows what I'm talking about."

Since Rachel and I had been talking online so much, she knew exactly what kind of movies I liked, and therefore borrowed *Maid in Manhattan* from one of her friends. That's right, I'm an avid romantic comedy fan and I feel no need to defend myself.

Maid in Manhattan stars the voluptuous Mrs. Jennifer Lopez (a.k.a. Jenny from the Block), who works as a maid in a luxurious New York City hotel, hence the title. Hang onto your hat though, there's a twist! A rising politician staying at the hotel is duped!! He is led to believe JLo is a guest!!! I know, I know, tell me about it. JLo perpetuates the lie, eventually it's exposed, the guy breaks up with her, the guy makes up with her, the end. It's one for the ages.

The reason I put "watching a movie" in quotation marks is because that specific invitation implies you're not making it to the credits. Some doubt may arise, as was the case with Rachel and me, but if I started out by telling you I metaphorically bang myself in the gym mirror, you can imagine it wasn't much.

Now, inviting someone out to the movies, regardless of the similarities, raises several flags. In that situation you're basically picking up and dropping hints the entire night. At the end you add it all up and just hope for the best. Sometimes your math couldn't be more wrong and you're moving in for a kiss when she's thinking about ramming her head into the dashboard, while other times you're spot on and things go just as planned. Of course, if you're lucky, you could undershoot and hear or receive more than expected.

All right, so the DVD is in, the room is dark, Rachel and I are lying next to each other in her bed, we're close, we're comfortable, it sounds like a fairly romantic environment, right? Wrong. I can't even tell you how many times her friends, her roommates, her roommates' friends, Baby Daddies, Baby Mamas, and a hundred other people came and went. I hate to be racist and perpetuate the stereotype, but it was like sitting next to a group of black chicks during a scary movie.

Laquesha: "Girl, what's he doin'? What's he doin', girl?"
Monique: "He be trippin' girl, that's what he doin'."
Queen B: "Don't go in there, fool. Don't go in there!"
Monique: "Oh shit! Oh shit!"
Laquesha: "White boy got fucked *up!*"
Queen B: "For real. That cracka ain't nothin' but crumbs!"

Admittedly, our movie night was not off to the best start. It wasn't anything to get upset about, though. While Rachel hopped in and out of bed, talked with her friends and did school work, I lost myself in JLo's big ass and bad acting.

"Hey, Rachel, do you think you and Blondie Glasses could move over a drop? JLo's ass is part of the plot."

Rachel laughed, mostly to be polite, and partly because I was actually into the movie.

"A little more, please."

"You can see the whole TV," Rachel snapped, moving further away.

"A few more steps. It's a big toosh and a widescreen DVD."

Rachel looked at me like I was crazy, until she realized I was guiding her out the door.

"In or out," I joked. "We're trying to watch a movie here."

"Who's we, loser?"

"Me and my invisible date," I answered. "You don't know her, but she's also short, cute, brunette, and Orthodox. My fingers are crossed."

"So are her legs."

I could have gone back and forth with Rachel for hours, but instead I just smiled, loving the way she wasn't afraid to challenge me.

"Okay, I'll be back in a minute," Rachel said. "I have to pick up some work from Blondie Cheeks' room and then I'm all yours."

"I don't know how my date's going to feel about that, but we'll hash it out when you get here."

With about five minutes left in the movie I had Rachel back in bed and the distractions locked out... except for Gopher. Her third wheel roommate was behind that stupid tie-dye curtain again, gnawing on woodchips, growing weed, or doing some other weird shit. Neither of us cared though, because the night was winding down and moves needed to be made. Too bad the setting left "watching a movie" feel like going out to one. I needed a better read.

"So, what was your favorite part?" I asked while the credits rolled.

"Um, I'd have to say the end."

The room was dimly lit by the television, providing just

enough light for me to see Rachel's flirtatious smile.

"Yes, since that was the only part you saw, I think you would *literally* have to say that."

"Hey, I didn't miss that much," Rachel playfully pouted.

"It's okay, I'll let it slide," I said. "But only because academics were involved."

"Thank you, Professor."

"You're here for an education first. Recreational activities and socializing take a backseat to the books. That, and some people just need more time studying than others."

Rachel laughed, confident her grades were better than mine. "Is that right?'

"Don't worry, it's nothing to be ashamed of. I just don't want your gpa to drop. Then you'll have to tell your parents you chose to lie in bed with a tall Catholic boy instead of study."

"I have a 3.8," Rachel boasted, kicking my sarcasm in the nuts.

I knew she was smart, but I wasn't expecting it to be that high. Even though her gpa was more than double mine, I tried to act unfazed.

"That's exactly what I'm saying. I don't know if anyone has told you this, but your gpa is out of four," I patronized.

"Really?" Rachel entertained.

"Again, it's nothing to be embarrassed about. With age comes wisdom… with great power comes great responsibility… and with buffalo wings come handy wipes."

"So does that mean you have a 4.0?" Rachel asked, completely ignoring my ridiculous comment.

"Point two," I responded.

"You have a point two gpa!" she gasped.

"No, point two is what you get when you subtract three point eight from four point zero. I thought I'd help you with the math."

"How sweet of you." Rachel buried her elbow into my ribs. "So what's your real gpa?" she asked.

I wisely avoided numerals. "Um, let's just say it's higher than a point two."

Before Rachel could pry any further, the credits stopped rolling. Her room lost more of its light and the crappy background music vanished, along with our equally crappy repartee. The moment had arrived. You guessed it. It was time to break out my calculator watch.

1 Orthodox girl + 1 Catholic Boy − 1 Shitty Movie − 28 interruptions x 12 spoonages / 84 flirtatious moments = our first kiss.

While lying on my right side, Rachel on her left, both our bodies nearly pressing against each other, *the* awkward silence fell upon us. I'm referring to the only awkward silence in the world that can double as romantic. And then... she kissed me. Yep, *she* kissed *me*. I was so surprised my mouth didn't move. Rachel was so nervous her teeth were chattering. It was perfect.

Rachel and I eventually ended our spastic make out session, which would normally be followed by the world's second most awkward moment, but instead, we replaced it with a new comfort level. Seeing how no one in the history of the universe has ever said anything even remotely cool or suave after a first kiss, I decided to go in a different direction and recap the moment with an interview.

"So, you kissed me on the lips," I began.

"Yes, that is correct," Rachel stated.

"Were you nervous?"

"What makes you say that?" she returned.

"Nothing. I'm sure it was an earthquake."

Rachel hit me. "Hey, you were shaking, too."

"Yes, but only because I was hanging on for dear life. You were like a human tuning fork."

And there it was, the first puppy dog face of a million. I've never seen anyone pretending to be sad look more lovable than she did. I tried not to laugh as I kissed her frowning bottom lip.

"Yeah, dat's right!" Rachel joked, instantly returning to her normal self.

"Something tells me that look costs Daddy a lot of money," I said.

Rachel emphatically nodded her head. "Uh-huh, uh-huh!" She then stole the microphone. "So, were *you* nervous?"

"About what?" I asked, playing dumb.

"Kissing me, genius."

"What makes you say that?" I laughed.

"Well, let's see; you didn't make a move the entire night, you watched the movie from start to finish, and you didn't stir the pot afterwards. Are you afraid of rejection, Jonathan?"

"First of all… stir the pot?" I laughed again.

"You know what I mean, buster. Don't change the subject!"

As funny as Rachel was, I was actually surprised by her assessment of the night.

"To address your comment, I would just like to say that during the ten or twelve times you were actually in bed with me, I thought I dropped a few hints."

"Such as… ?"

"Well apparently nothing good!" I exclaimed.

"What, the leg thing?"

"Yes, the leg thing," I laughed; having no idea what she was talking about. "I'll tell you what though, this is the first time a girl has ever invited me over to *watch a movie*, and I literally *watched* the movie."

"Oh, I see, you thought I invited you over to hook up." Rachel was trying to sound appalled, but not doing a very good job.

"No, not at all," I said, grinning fully.

Rachel knew I was full of shit and waited for me to admit it.

"Okay, maybe it crossed my mind, but only because of the code. I honestly didn't plan or bank on anything more than a kiss. To my pleasant surprise, we took a trip to Firstbaseville."

"Yeah, and I drove," she happily pointed out.

"I was getting to that," I laughed. "You just beat me to the punch... again."

"Whatever you say, little girl."

"You're right, I'm very fragile. But on the bright side, now I know to bring a motion sickness bag with me the next time we make out."

"Who said there's going to be a next time?"

Rachel and I never broke stride, enjoying every second of our playful headbutts. I loved how we had our own cute way of flirting, but I loved even more the way our personalities meshed. I couldn't wait to see her again, and before leaving I worked in another kiss to help imagine the rest. Although, come to think of it, Rachel didn't show me out. So now who's the man? You guessed it. This guy!

Colorful

I'm sure every college student, past, present, and future, is well aware that Thursday night is one of the biggest and most anticipated nights of the week. However, in that unfathomable number, Jackrabbit is easily at the top of the list for most enthusiastic. Every Thursday, without fail, whether it was over the phone, in the middle of campus, at the gym, or on the soccer field, he would scream his patented battle cry, "It's Thursday!" and then follow it up with one of the most absurd dance moves you'll ever see. I always appreciated his excitement, but I'm certain it would have been less embarrassing for everyone if he'd done it without a boner.

The day after Rachel and I shared our first kiss happened to be a Thursday, so while Jackrabbit and I were discussing our plans for the evening, I thought I'd let the cat out of the bag. Even though I did nothing wrong, I felt kind of guilty. After all, he did see her first. It's a horrible way to phrase it, because it makes Rachel sound like the last beer in the cooler, but I think you know what I mean, women especially. When a girl sees a guy she likes, regardless of how long she's known him, and someone else hooks up with him, you better believe that slut, bitch, whore, skank of a floozy is going to catch shit for it. Most of the dirty work will take place behind the girl's back, but in many instances it escalates to a name calling, clothes bashing, drink throwing, hair pulling cat fight, where the guy at the heart of it all is standing in the front row, laughing and looking on with the rest of his buddies. Yep, girls are funny.

After a quick trip to the gym, where Jackrabbit grilled me for making out with Rachel, we separated our ass cheeks and got ready for the night. A shit, shave, and shower later, I headed to Pokehole to pregame with Black Mr. Ed, Drinksandfalls, and Sava Shot, before meeting Jackrabbit at the club.

Rachel and I hadn't spoken since we parted ways the night before, for no reason other than we were busy and doing our own thing. I had classes, my daily nap (taken when I had classes), gymnasium intercourse, television time, and food outings. Rachel also had classes, which she physically attended, pre-weekend shopping, lettuce and tomato outings, a mani/pedi appointment, and several other things of the girlie nature.

About an hour and a half into pregaming, I finally acknowledged the gap in time and went downstairs to Rachel's room, bringing Black Mr. Ed, Drinksandfalls, and Sava Shot with me.

"Yo, what girl is this?" Black Mr. Ed asked.

"Her name's Rachel. I met her through Jackrabbit."

Sava Shot chimed in. "Watch out, her friends are brutal. They'll pick you apart the second you walk through the door."

"What's this dickhead talking about?" Black Mr. Ed eloquently wondered.

"When we hung out with Rachel and her friends last week, they spent the majority of the time rating people," I answered.

"How so?" Black Mr. Ed asked.

"By tearing new assholes!" Sava Shot exclaimed.

Black Mr. Ed immediately looked at Sava Shot. "They must

have called you a bitch."

"Nope," I laughed. "A goofy, pear-shaped douchebag."

"Seriously?" he gasped.

Black Mr. Ed was dying. "Pear-shaped douchebag!"

"Fuck off." Sava Shot pushed Black Mr. Ed.

"I'm only kidding, they didn't say anything," I insisted. "Her friends are cute though."

"Yeah, they were," Sava Shot agreed. "I liked the one with the glasses."

"Yeah, are you gonna fuck her? Huh? Are you gonna fuck her!" Black Mr. Ed yelled, pushing Sava Shot into the wall.

"We're here." I turned around to make sure Black Mr. Ed was done beating the crap out of Sava Shot, and realized we were short one. "Where's Drinksandfalls?" I asked.

Black Mr. Ed started laughing. "Yo, I bet that bitch fell down the stairs."

I looked at Sava Shot, who shrugged his shoulders.

"Oh well. There's an elevator if he needs it," I announced.

"Hey! What's up?" Rachel heard us from inside her room and opened the door before we could knock.

I kissed her on the cheek and stepped inside. "Hey, cutie. You remember Sava Shot, right?"

Sava Shot got one last shove in before saying hello. "How's everything?"

"Good," Rachel said, confusingly. "Why are you all red?"

I quickly introduced Black Mr. Ed before he supplied an answer.

"It's nice to meet you," Rachel greeted.

"You too," Black Mr. Ed returned, looking past her and surveying the room. "Where your friends at?"

I turned around and shook my head.

"What, fucker? You said her friends were cute. I want to meet them."

Rachel laughed. "They just left. They went to Blondie Cheeks' room to get ready." Rachel walked into her closet to do the same.

"Hey, what's up?" Drinksandfalls said, magically appearing in the doorway.

"Where were you?" I asked.

"I stopped by someone's room."

"Bullshit! You fell down the stairs again!" Black Mr. Ed shouted.

"Blow me."

"Rachel, this is Drinksandfalls," I introduced.

Rachel poked her head out of the closet. "Hi."

"It's nice to meet you," he returned.

"Sorry, I'm just looking for something to wear."

"What are you talking about, you're already dressed," I said.

"Yeah, but I don't like it," she confessed.

I turned around and faced the guys. "My bad, I thought at least Blondie Glasses would be here."

"She has cute friends?" Drinksandfalls asked.

"No, they're fuckin' fat!"

I punched Black Mr. Ed in the arm for having a megaphone as a mouth. "He's never met them. You'd like one."

"Which one?" Sava Shot inquired, hoping I wouldn't say Blondie Glasses.

"Blondie Cheeks."

"Yeah, I can see that," he added, with much relief. "She has a huge rack."

"Awesome. I love big tits," Drinksandfalls openly declared. "Where is she?"

41

"I fuckin' *love* big tits!"

I raised my fist to Black Mr. Ed, causing him to flinch as well as laugh. "She's in her room getting ready," I answered.

"So then Rachel's the only one here." Drinksandfalls stated.

"Yep. You guys don't have to stay though. Actually, what the fuck am I saying? Get the hell out of here."

"Why, you gonna *bang her!*"

"And on that note, I think we'll be going." Drinksandfalls did the honors and shoved Black Mr. Ed outside. "Do you want us to get you before we leave?" he asked.

"Yeah, stop by before you go," I said.

"You got it."

"Yo, fuck her! Fuck her, Jon!" Black Mr. Ed yelled from the hallway.

I quickly closed the door and walked into Rachel's closet. "You know what?"

"What?" Rachel asked.

I paused and looked around some more. "I expected a lot worse."

Rachel laughed. "My closet is next to the refrigerator. I share this one with Blondie Glasses."

"Okay, that makes more sense," I nodded.

Rachel excitedly pulled a shirt off the hanger. "This might work." She stepped into her conjoining bathroom and changed, while I stayed where I was and looked through the crack in the door.

"What do you think?" she asked, stepping out of the bathroom and twirling.

"Um… not a fan. You looked better in what you had on."

What, you wanted me to lie? Most guys would do exactly that, but I felt comfortable enough to give my honest opinion, and generally don't have much of a filter. Plus, I wanted to see her change again… more side-boob.

Rachel grunted like an infant and jokingly stomped towards her main closet in search of something new.

"You realize you can recycle an outfit," I said. "This is the first time we're going out together."

"What are you crazy?" Rachel laughed as she stepped inside her fashion playground.

"I guess I shouldn't tell you my shirt is from high school and I've worn it a hundred times then."

"Really?" Rachel mocked. "You seem like such a jappy Long Island boy."

"Fine, you got me. Fashion is my life. I eat, sleep, and breathe the *Gucci*."

Rachel ignored me, stepped out, and did another spin.

"Well, I'm not gonna lie…" I began.

"So I've noticed."

" … your ass, in those jeans, might stop traffic."

Rachel bashfully smiled, but not for long. "What about the top?"

"I still like the first one."

"Grrrr!" Rachel loudly groaned.

"You looked really cute," I pleaded.

"Everyone says I'm cute. I want to look sexy."

"Cute *and* sexy," I corrected.

"Aww…" Rachel smiled. "… You're full of shit."

I swear, I really did think she looked sexy, but with that adorable face, and her bubbly personality cracking me up every second, it was impossible not to call her cute.

The mood was very boyfriend/girlfriend-like, and I was actually okay with it. Rachel continued picking out clothes and modeling them for me, while I threw in my two cents and laughed at how she threw it back. Eventually, while getting too involved and rummaging through one of her drawers, Rachel tapped me on the shoulder and I turned around. The smile on my face said it all.

"Really? You really like it?" she asked.

I emphatically nodded my head, beaming while short on words.

"Seriously? You're not just faking so we can leave?"

I grabbed Rachel by the waist, leaned forward and whispered in her ear. "You look beautiful."

Rachel went beet red and curled up like a two-year-old hiding behind her father's leg.

"Okay, now I just have to do my makeup."

A fortnight later, my prayers were answered and Rachel was ready. I could finally get back to drinking. Rachel and I left her room and went to Blondie Cheeks', a.k.a. the verbal slaughterhouse, where I surprisingly experienced a little culture shock of my own.

Until then, I couldn't ever recall a pregaming situation where it was just I, and an innocent group of girls two to three years younger than me. I also couldn't find anything wrong with that sentence, so I was more than up for it.

For guys, a typical night of pregaming consists of drinking games like Asshole, Kings, Fuck the Dealer, Beer Pong, Flip Cup, and many more. It's competitive, wagers are made, generally involving money or alcohol consumption, music is continuous, phone calls to girls are just as incessant, a muted sports games is on, and everyone's basically getting ripped and having a good time.

Girls pregame a little differently. They play drinking games, but no one is sure of the rules, only one or two of them are into it, and they never finish because they're too busy talking about nonsense. I know, it sounds a lot like *The View*.

Rachel and her friends are a different breed though. Pregaming with them turned out to be what I can only equate to drinking with *Dora the Explorer*.

"Did you bring the orange juice?" Blondie Cheeks hoped.

"Yeah, I put it in the fridge," Rachel answered.

"Are you guys playing any drinking games?" I asked.

"Like what?" Blondie Glasses wondered.

"I don't know, Asshole, Kings, whatever."

The girls looked at each other with blank faces, and then let Blondie Cheeks answer. "Um, no, we just take shots."

"Seriously?" Now I was intrigued.

"Yeah, we just take a bunch of vodka shots." Rachel made it sound like the norm.

"Wait, hang on a minute," I said, trying to wrap my head around what I was hearing. "The four of you, who are a combined weight of thirty eight pounds, casually sit around and knock back shots of vodka?"

"Yeah!" they simultaneously shouted.

"Okay, so then you definitely pregame for like, what, twenty, twenty-five minutes?" I asked.

"Yep, and then we go out," Blondie Cheeks added.

"Do you guys drink beer?"

Silence was accompanied by looks of disgust. "Beer's gross," Rachel answered.

If anyone walked into the room at that very moment they would have thought I saw a monkey toss Oprah's salad. Then again, I probably shouldn't have been too surprised. They were the most chaste people I'd ever met. For someone who's developed such a loving, sharing, and memorable relationship with beer though, it felt incomprehensible.

Rachel could see I was turned off by her answer, and tried her best to win me back. "Do you want to take shots with us?"

She was successful.

"Yeah, I'll take a few," I casually responded.

"Here." Blondie Cheeks handed me a shot glass with a rabbi drinking champagne and saying, 'The boobalas tickle my nose.'

Rachel took the vodka bottle from Generic and filled her glass...

"Half way?" I asked.

"Yeah, and then you fill the other half with orange juice."

My head began bobbing uncontrollably and the only words I could mutter were, "Is that right? Is that right?" I'd let Rachel's beer comment slide, but this was too much.

"What's wrong?" she asked.

"Nothing. It's just that when you said you were taking shots, I thought you meant proper shots?"

"Proper shots?" she echoed.

"Meaning you fill the *entire* shot glass with vodka. Then, afterwards, if you'd like, you chase it with orange juice. What you did is make a screwdriver... for an eight-year-old."

Rachel put her chin in her chest and made the puppy dog face. I tried not to smile, but it was impossible. I *properly* filled my own shot glass and raised it to her.

"Cheers."

Like a flick of the switch, Rachel dropped the facade and picked up her "shot."

"Mazel, mazel!" she smiled.

Our empty glasses touched the desk at the same time. "So is that considered one for you, or half of one?" I asked.

"That's one," Rachel officiated.

"Is that two for me then?" I questioned.

"No, it's still one for you. You're a giant."

I dropped my head, raised my eyes, and attempted Rachel's puppy dog face.

"Aww, I hurt the giant's feelings." Rachel pulled on my shoulders to lower me, leaned in, and softly kissed my cheek.

I wasn't sure how I entered the Orthodox Twilight Zone, but as soon as Blondie Cheeks put on the *Mamma Mia* soundtrack (featuring the music of the one and only *Abba*), it didn't matter anymore. My brain officially called it quits. Much to my delight though, the girls started imitating the way their moms dance at Bar and Bat Mitzvahs, which is easily my favorite type of choreography. After a few more giant shots and baby mixers, Rachel and I went back to her room for a final touch-up (not the kind I was thinking of). While she was in the bathroom, I answered a knock on the door.

"Hey, assbag!" Black Mr. Ed, Drinksandfalls, and Sava Shot had come back to get me.

"What's going on?"

"Yo, you fuck her yet?" Black Mr. Ed shouted.

"Asshole, you're louder than a drunk girl," Drinksandfalls said, pushing Black Mr. Ed to the side.

I called to Rachel. "Hey, are you ready yet?"

"In a minute," she yelled back. "By the way, your friend's really loud."

"Sorry. He's retarded," I announced.

"I'm retarded!" Black Mr. Ed echoed.

"Can you come here for a second?"

Black Mr. Ed started walking inside. I quickly threw him back out. "Not you, dumbass."

"You want to meet us there?" Drinksandfalls asked.

"Just wait two minutes, we'll be right out," I assured.

"Okay. We'll be in the hallway."

I went to the bathroom to check on Rachel, wondering how it was physically possible not to be ready by then.

"So, are you actually mixing the makeup before you put it on, or did someone steal your booster chair and you can't see the mirror?"

Rachel ignored my joke. "Can we talk?"

As it turns out, words *can* make you sober. Rachel was dead serious, but about what? Two thoughts crossed my mind. First, she realized I'm the coolest person in the world and didn't know how to handle having so much fun. Second, it had something to do with the night before. Last time I checked though, frenching can't get you pregnant. I was lost.

"Yeah, we can talk," I solemnly responded.

Rachel and I stepped out of the bathroom and moved towards the back of her shared closet.

"Okay, well, I'm not sure how to say this, so…"

"Jon, we're leaving!"

I came out of the closet and saw Drinksandfalls waiting for me (yeah, he wishes). "Two seconds," I told him.

"We're going downstairs to get a cab," he returned.

"Be right there," I said.

"Dude, hurry up." Drinksandfalls impatiently closed the door.

I stepped into Rachel's office again. "You were saying?"

With genuine, bashful eyes, Rachel looked at me and gave it her best shot. "I feel really stupid saying this, and I don't even know if I should, because it's not that big a deal, well it's probably not a big deal to you, although it is a big deal to me, but like, I've never done this before."

"You've never talked to someone in the closet?" I joked.

"No, stupid." Rachel took a deep breath. "I've never had a one night stand."

I took a moment to recap the previous night, double-checked whether or not I accidentally fell inside her, and then realized she was talking about our kiss.

"Like, throughout high school, I've always had boyfriends, so like I'm really used to that type of relationship, but you and I didn't talk until like three hours ago, so I have no idea what you're thinking."

And I have no idea what you're saying, Overly Jappy When Nervous Girl.

I tried lightening the mood so Rachel would calm down and it'd be okay for me to laugh at her. "Like, that's so crazy, because like, I was going to say something to you, but then I wasn't sure if I should, because like, I'm the guy, but you know, like, it's just like, well, like I thought you were using me."

Rachel punched me in the arm. I may not have successfully impersonated her, but at least she was smiling.

"Have you thought about last night?" she asked.

I paused to keep Immature Jonathan at bay, and then spoke the truth. "As you can tell by the dumb jokes and sarcastic comments, I tend to avoid serious conversations such as this, but if I must step outside myself for a moment, I want you to know I had an incredible time last night, more so than I ever imagined, and I hope we can continue watching crappy JLo movies together."

Rachel's smile lifted the weight from her shoulders. I didn't plan on saying anything like that so early, especially because it made me look all squirmy and vulnerable, but it made her feel better and that was all that mattered.

"I accidentally used some of your rouge," I said. "In case you're wondering why my cheeks are all red."

"Aww, don't be embarrassed, Gentle Giant. I feel the same way. And who knows, maybe next time we won't make it to the credits," Rachel smiled.

"My pants are vibrating."

"What!"

I took my phone out of my pocket.

"You're an idiot," she announced.

"Does that mean we're not playing Seven Minutes in Heaven?" I asked.

"What do you think?"

"I think I lost you on the vibrating pants comment."

Rachel pulled on my shoulders to lower me, leaned in, and softly kissed my lips. "Like you said, with age comes wisdom."

Closing Time

After graduating Jericho High School I attended The University of Rhode Island, lasting a mere two months before dropping out. Freeport Community College was next, where I'd spend a year and a half living and commuting from home. If you went away to school chances are you'll sympathize, because dorming with mom, dad, younger sis and grandma, driving to and from campus, and going to the same crappy bars you went to in high school, all make for a very different experience on a very sad level. Granted, I was getting my life back on track and in hindsight it was exactly what I needed, but from a social perspective, what good is that? I had friends at Gellen University (neighbor to Freeport), so despite not going anywhere new I was at least in good company, but the life I led at FCC was far unlike the one I had at Presidents College. This is helpful to remember when trying to understand the man (me), the myth (eh), and the legend (in my eyes) of Mr. Jonathan Andrew Reynolds.

During my time at Freeport Community College I had the occasional random hook-up, but the resources just weren't there. I'd wake up, go to school, sit in class, drive home, eat, go to the gym, study, watch TV, and then go to bed and do it all over again. The night before every new semester, I'd think about how amazing it would be to have at least one gorgeous girl in every class. I imagined sitting next to them and talking every day, partnering up on some projects, exchanging laughs, smiles, pleasantries and phone numbers, and then ultimately having sex with them one by one like I was operating a pornographic Ferris wheel.

Of course, the way my luck was running, I had nothing but quiet Asians, angry black men, senior citizens, and former Special Ed. students in my classes. It might as well have been the sequel to *Billy Madison*.

There were several good-looking girls walking through campus, I can attest to that, but I chose to look rather than touch. To be completely honest, as well as shallow, the short, cute, brunette, jappy Jewish type I'd become such a fan of over the years, was an endangered species at Freeport. This is a horrible way of comparing the two, but a girl from Jericho, one who is an active member of the Long Island Scene, would typically be found on a Friday night stepping out of a *BMW 3 Series*, wearing a pair of *Seven* jeans and *Prada* stilettos, a *Theory* or *DVF* top, possibly with a bra, most likely not, a *Cosabella* thong, finely applied makeup, ironed out hair, a diamond incrusted *Cartier* watch, diamond earrings, a *David Yurman* ring, a necklace from *Barney's*, and of course, a *Louis Vutton*, *Gucci*, *Prada*, *Marc Jacobs*, *Fendi*, or *Christian Dior* bag. Now, a girl who attends Freeport, one who is not a part of the Long Island Scene, would typically be found on a Friday night stepping out of an outdated *Nissan Altima* or *Honda Civic*, wearing a pair of *Abercrombie* jeans and *Nine West* heels, a shirt from *Hollister*, a *Victoria's Secret* thong, an old-school *Tiffany's* heart bracelet, a fake designer bag, an assortment of make-up, and curly, gelled hair. Again, it's a terrible way of depicting the two because I'm predominantly making materialistic comparisons, but in no way should that imply one is better than the other. In fact, if I were to make the same comparison with guys, I would easily fall into the Freeport category. As my mother used to say, I grew up with champagne and caviar taste, but beer and hot dog money. You're probably wondering what all of this has to do with Rachel, so I'll conclude by saying the build-up, in my opinion, is a justified excuse for the mistake I was about to make.

It's frightening to admit, but if I were asked to describe my relationship with Rachel after a few short weeks, I would almost compare it to the one I had with Strange Girl. Rachel didn't have the personality of a dead horse, but it was similar in regards to sleeping at Pokehole, occasionally going out together, usually meeting up with friends, hooking up here and there, and never using a label maker. No worries; that was my mentality. I loved hanging out with Rachel, I knew we'd have fun no matter what we did, but every now and again, I got the impression things were moving towards a deeper and more serious level. When that happened, in classic 'afraid of commitment' fashion, I pushed her away and implanted a buffer zone. That way, I would *technically* be free to do whatever I wanted with whomever I wanted.

The girl situation at Presidents College is incredible. What's even better is that the guy situation is not. Therefore, when you add my rambunctious (another word for horny) personality into the equation, you might understand why it was hard for me to consider settling down. I felt like my time at URI and Freeport was time lost, so if I didn't make up for it while I was at PC, I'd regret it for the rest of my life. Perhaps another chauvinistic analogy will help. To go from Freeport Community College to Presidents College, and get involved in a relationship with a little more than a year left before graduation, would be like a six-year-old walking into a candy store and only being allowed to have a *Tootsie Roll*. Despite his eyes popping out of their sockets from the vast array of mouthwatering, cavity inducing sweets, he is restricted to only one flavor, one style.

In high school, I was nearly addicted to cheating on my girlfriend, and I witnessed firsthand the damaging effects it had on her sanity. It took me a while to realize I was being a prick, but eventually, I understood that unless I can remain fully committed to someone, there's no point in being in a relationship. With that said, even though I was into my seventh month at Presidents College, I still wanted to sample candy.

Near the end of my first semester at PC, I found myself in a similar situation, but with a different girl. Her name is Grey Shoes, and she was going to be studying abroad in Australia for the remainder of the school year. For me, it was the perfect excuse to keep things on the edge of seriousness without going over. For her, we had already crossed that line. Every day she moved forward on her calendar, I moved back on mine, until eventually there was nothing to show for the relationship but a heartfelt e-mail clarifying that I was a dick. To this day, I absolutely regret the way I acted, because I'm certain she's one of the good ones. Unfortunately, that's just what happens when you're selfish and only care about yourself.

Okay, so I had my bout with Grey Shoes, and Strange Girl, but any good promoter knows you need to create a buzz around the title fight. A road trip to Loyola College, and Spring Break in Acapulco, would do exactly that. Baltimore provided a half naked make out session, while Mexico provided a fully naked fuck session. In case you forgot though, *technically,* I did nothing wrong. By instilling a buffer zone I left things up to Rachel, who never said she wanted to be exclusive, thus providing me with a free pass. She did catch me off-guard by asking about both, but I answered with honesty. It stung, but she couldn't justifiably flip out. My dating strategy actually held up!

I understand all of this might sound completely out of left field after talking about how hard I was falling for Rachel, so I ask you to keep this in mind… I'm a guy. It's not an excuse, this is just how men think and act, particularly when they're twenty-one and away at college. Sorry ladies, but a perfect man does not exist. Guys are assholes. The ones who don't want to grow up stay that way, while the rest learn from their mistakes. Eventually we get there, some just need more time than others (this guy). Now, here's where it backfires.

"It's Thursday!" Jackrabbit opened his door and dance fucked me as I walked inside.

"What's going on?"

"What's going on?" he repeated, making fun of my customary greeting.

"Not much." I began unloading a thirty pack of *Bud Light* into the fridge. "You're drinking vodka, right?"

"Fuck yeah!" he celebrated. "Brand X, six dollars a bottle."

"That shit is gross," I announced. "I don't know how you drink it." Three seconds later… "You want to take a shot?"

"Fuck yeah!" Jackrabbit repeated.

I took the plastic bottle out of his freezer, poured two shots, and set a quart of orange juice down between us.

"This is gonna suck," I whispered, holding my glass in the air.

"Cheers, pussy."

We slammed our glasses on the table and repeatedly exchanged hits of orange juice.

"All right, I'm gonna jump in the shower," said Jackrabbit.

"Hey, Drinksandfalls, Sava Shot, and Black Mr. Ed are coming over," I told him.

"Yeah, that's fine. Should I collect money from Black Mr. Ed when he gets here, or bill him for damages later?"

"Believe it or not he said he wasn't drinking," I told Jackrabbit. "The thirty is from me, Drinksandfalls, and Sava Shot."

Jackrabbit looked at me and laughed.

"Yeah, you're right," I conceded. "What am I saying?"

"Oh, by the way..." Jackrabbit started. "... Rachel and her friends are also coming over to pregame." He immediately ran to the bathroom.

I followed Jackrabbit in, the bathroom, not the shower, the bathroom, where there was a curtain between us... curtain. "I'm sorry, could you run that by me one more time?" I said.

Jackrabbit was trying not to laugh. "She wrote me online and asked if you were here yet."

"Okay, so how did that lead to her coming over?" I asked.

"I didn't want to be rude," Jackrabbit chuckled.

"Get the fuck out of here!" I yelled.

"Jon."

"Jackrabbit!" I yelled again.

"You don't want to hang out with her?" he asked.

"Not really. I mean I've seen her all week."

"So then who are you trying to fuck tonight?"

"Who am I trying to fuck tonight?" I repeated. "Who are you, Black Mr. Ed?"

"So then what, were you hoping to have a guys' night out?" Jackrabbit asked, clearly making fun of me. "Because that's great and all, I'd love to do it sometime, but it's fuckin' Thursday, Jon! It's Thursday! I'm trying to get laid, bitch!"

"First off…" I took a second to laugh. "I don't ever want a guys night out. And second, I just don't like having my nights mapped out."

"I hear ya," Jackrabbit entertained.

"If Rachel comes over to pregame it means we're going out together, hanging out at the club together, leaving in a cab together, and that's it, end of boring ass story," I whined.

"Yeah, but if you run into her there you're going to end up going home together anyway," Jackrabbit annoyingly pointed out.

"True, but at least there's a hint of unknown to the night."

"You want to hit on girls, don't you?" Jackrabbit smiled.

I laughed, but there was some truth to it. "Maybe. I'm not saying I'm going to do anything, not that I couldn't, but I do miss that new, back and forth, flirty bullshit."

"You and Rachel have only been hanging out for like a month. That isn't still there?" he questioned.

"It is, but… what the fuck am I talking about? You should know *exactly* what I'm saying!" I shouted.

Jackrabbit turned the water off. "Of course I do," he laughed. "Now give me a fuckin' towel."

I threw Jackrabbit one of his cum rags and sat on the bed in his adjacent room.

"Do you want me to tell Rachel not to come?" Jackrabbit asked.

"Yes," I quickly answered.

"Jon!"

"Call her," I insisted.

"And say what?"

"I don't know, piss off."

"Jon!" Jackrabbit yelled again, all too amused.

"Fine, we'll say I'm kidding, but I hope you know you fucked me, twatface. You fucked me!" Selling it, I hopped off the bed and trudged into the kitchen to grab another beer.

"Open up, dicklicker!"

Clearly it wasn't Rachel at the door, so I let Black Mr. Ed, Drinksandfalls, and Sava Shot in.

"Did you bring ping pong balls?" I asked.

"Yeah," Drinksandfalls answered. "Do you have cups?"

"Jackrabbit, do you have cups?" I yelled into the bedroom.

"Yeah, they're in the cupboard!" he returned.

Drinksandfalls and I set up the beer pong table (Jackrabbit's detached closet door on two kitchen chairs), filled and positioned the cups, and then quickly got the festivities underway.

"So how are things with you and Rachel?" Drinksandfalls asked, before shooting.

I unconsciously sighed. "They're okay."

"That was convincing," he laughed. "What's up?"

"Nothing." My voice... "She's awesome." Began... "We've been having a great time." To fade.

"But... " he led on.

"It just feels like the only thing for us to do from here is become boyfriend and girlfriend," I explained.

"And you don't want that?" Drinksandfalls continued.

"I'm not sure. I mean I definitely want to be with her, and I love hanging out with her, but on nights like tonight, I almost wish I were single."

Black Mr. Ed yelled from the couch. "So cheat on her!"

"Well, we're *technically* not going out so it really wouldn't be cheating," I illustrated.

"Then stop being such a pussy," Black Mr. Ed laughed.

"Is Rachel going out?" Sava Shot inquired. Adding, "I've

got next game."

"Fuck that," Jackrabbit said, having heard from his bedroom.

"We'll play doubles," I resolved. "Sava Shot and I will kick the shit out of you and Drinksandfalls."

"Done!" Jackrabbit returned.

I went back to Sava Shot's question. "Rachel and her friends are going to the same place we are. Not only that, but they're on their way over right now… no thanks to *Jackrabbit!*" I shouted.

"My bad!" he laughed.

"Anyway, I think Blondie Cheeks has a little thing for you," I said to Drinksandfalls.

"Really?" he excitedly asked.

"Yeah, a little penis!" Black Mr. Ed interrupted, making himself laugh again.

"Why aren't you drinking?" I asked him.

"I'm broke," he neighed.

"Don't worry about it, there's vodka in the freezer."

"Jon!" Jackrabbit shouted, overhearing my offer.

"Just pound it," I insisted. "Although I'm not gonna lie, it's awful."

"Whatever, I'll drink that shit!" Black Mr. Ed leapt from his seat and galloped into the kitchen.

"And… that's game." I sank Drinksandfalls last cup. "Jackrabbit, you're up. Sava Shot, let's go," I instructed.

Jackrabbit finally came out of his room. "Jon."

"What?" I asked.

"Guess?"

"Just fill your cups up," I said, ignoring his stupid ritual.

"Guess what's forever, Jon."

I shook my head, trying not to laugh.

"Diamonds, Jon. Diamonds are forever." Jackrabbit made the shape with his hands, implying I'd be racking my cups soon. He then moved it below his waist, implying I was a vagina.

If you're part of a generation older than my own, don't drink (haha), or have just had your head up your ass for the past few years, please pay close attention to what Beer Pong is and how the game is played. Do so correctly, and in no time you can be the next douchebag at the party cutting the order and challenge everyone in sight.

The rules vary depending on whom you're with, but basically you organize six or ten cups in a triangle (16oz. *Solo* cups are the preferred brand), fill them halfway with beer, play either singles or doubles (mainly doubles), and objectively shoot (worth one cup) or bounce (worth two cups) a ping-pong ball into your opponents' cups. The goal being, eliminate all of their cups before they eliminate all of yours.

Now, if your opponent tries to bounce a ball at your cup/s, by the rules of the game you are allowed to slap it away. However, you cannot do the same thing to a ball shot in the air. If you and your partner make both your shots, whether in the air, bounced, or one of each, your opponents lose their turn and your team gets to go again. Cups are racked, or condensed, at six, four, three, and two (that's how I play, it makes the games go a lot faster, but other varieties are used).

So, there you have it, the basic instructions needed to play Beer Pong. Now, set up a table, get drunk, and claim to be the best player in the world.

"Shoot your air-ball," Jackrabbit said, kicking off the shit talking.

"And... drink." I made my first shot. "By the way, you've got a little something on your chest."

Jackrabbit looked down.

"Oh, my bad, that's just your third nipple," I corrected.

Jackrabbit almost spit up his beer. "You dick," he laughed.

Sava Shot went next and made a cup. "Run that back."

"I'm sorry Jackrabbit, did you say diamonds are forever?" I mocked.

"Just shoot," he ignored.

"Let me hold this one up for you." I made another cup and held my wrist in the air like Michael Jordan.

"Just wait till we go, we're gonna run that shit," Drinksandfalls said, getting into the game. "Sava Shot's gonna miss. Miss! Miss! I fucked your mother!"

Sava Shot missed the cups completely. "Real nice, dick. Good sportsmanship," Sava Shot pouted.

"I fucked your mom, too!" Black Mr. Ed yelled from the kitchen, pouring himself another shot of Jackrabbit's bootleg vodka. "Good sportsmanship," he repeated. "What a pussy."

"Hello?"

Fuuuck!

And there they were, three of the seven Jewish Dwarfs, Shoppy, Gossippy, and Kosher.

"Come in," Jackrabbit announced, looking at me with a big grin on his face. "Come in, come in, come in," he repeated.

My mood instantly changed. Not even Kirstie Alley on all fours could have killed my hard-on faster than they did.

"Hey!" Rachel walked over to the Beer Pong table and gave me a big hug and kiss.

"Hey," I muttered.

"Is this Beer Pong?" she asked.

"No, Pao Gow."

"Huh?"

"Chinese poker." I sarcastically answered.

"Shut up, it's Beer Pong... right?"

"Yes dear, it's Beer Pong."

"I want to play!" Rachel shouted.

"But you don't drink beer," I pointed out.

"I'll use water."

I've got this one, Joey Lawrence... "*Whoa!* We'll be having none of that," I explained. "You don't want to commit your second party foul in the first two minutes."

"Second? What was the first one?" Rachel asked.

"Not bringing anything to drink."

"But we have bad fake IDs. I don't want to get arrested."

The thought of Rachel behind bars caused me to unwillingly smile. I could just picture her with a custom-made *Louis Vuitton* jumpsuit, chain smoking bubble-gum cigarettes and making fun of other girls to get their pudding cup.

"All right, so I'll let your first *and* second party foul go, but I can't let the third one slide," I said.

"Now what?" Rachel worried.

I looked her outfit up and down.

"Get out of here, punk-ass! I look good," Rachel defended, slapping my arm.

She did look adorable, but the bitterness had already set in. At times, I would look at her and melt, while other moments I couldn't help but feel like the night had been extinguished. Rather than give in to either, I held my ground... at the Beer Pong table.

Rachel's not a stupid girl, though; she could tell something was wrong. Taking a page from my immature book, she stayed in Jackrabbit's room and laughed her head off to get my attention. Not a good idea.

"What time are we getting out of here?" Jackrabbit asked, before shooting and missing.

"You mean what time are you, me, Drinksandfalls, Black Mr. Ed, and Sava Shot getting out of here?" I corrected. "I'd say half an hour."

"Jon, we can't leave them here," Jackrabbit said, lowering his voice.

"I know."

"Then what?" he asked, holding his hands in the air.

"Tell them you don't have any more comps and they should leave now so they don't get stuck waiting in line. Just say we'll meet them there," I simplified.

"Right. You mean you'll tell them that," he corrected.

"Right," I smiled.

After lying to Rachel, she and her friends didn't have much of an option but to take off. Thirty minutes later, we did the same. It wasn't until I was in the cab though when I completely made up my mind. The internal game of tug-o-war was over. The assholes won, and there would be no going back.

The club's setup couldn't have been more ideal for my situation. It was fairly big, with the majority of the people on the first floor, including Rachel and her friends, but there was also a second floor for those with a VIP stamp. This made things ten times easier for me because I was able to stay out of sight. Not only that, but I could play it off like I tried looking for Rachel but couldn't find her due to the large crowd. A classic example of how to be a dick while pushing someone away.

Operation Full of Shit had commenced. Within twenty minutes, I was taking shots and hanging out with a short, brunette, *chesty*, Jewish girl.

When I'd go out, I was a big fan of posting up, meaning I'd

spend the majority of my night with one girl. Reason being, given enough time I thought I could close anyone. Although it's funny how basically doing the same thing with Rachel bothered me. Once again, guys are assholes. Anyway, I have no idea what this girl and I were talking about, I can thank the alcohol for that, but I do remember taking a break from dancing to make out with her.

In terms of looking over my shoulder, I didn't have to. Rachel and her friends were nowhere to be found. I was in the clear with one thought on my mind, is this girl going to fuck me? Should there have been room in my inebriated brain for more, I would have realized there was a reason Rachel wasn't looking for me. Wait for it. Wait for it.

At two in the morning the bar stopped serving, the lights came on, and Ugly Betty and I headed back to, that's right folks… James K. Polk Hall! We pulled up dead center of the building, where several people were standing outside smoking cock. I mean cigarettes! Cock smoking on the inside, cigarette smoking on the outside. I sometimes confuse the two.

While stepping out of the cab, I turned my head to say hello to someone. Wouldn't you know, but during that pithy, irrelevant exchange of words, Rachel and Ugly Betty locked eyes from opposite ends of Pokehole's glass door.

I imagined the Wild West as *Queer Eye for the Straight Guy* would. Straw hats were straw yamakas. Chaps and thongs were socially acceptable. And Rachel and Ugly Betty shot razor sharp dreidels out of guns covered in *Swarovski* crystal.

Seconds later, when I adverted my attention back to Ugly Betty, the dust had settled and there was no trail of a showdown. Rest assure, for she would soon tell the tale… just not until after we hooked up.

"You didn't see her?" Ugly Betty asked, like Rachel was actually standing at the front desk in pink chaps and a thong.

"Um, no!" I erupted. "Did she see us?"

"Um, yes," she mocked

"Mother, fucker! Really?" I double-checked.

Ugly Betty nodded her head, seemingly pissed off in her own right.

Okay, so clearly I was caught with my hand in the cookie jar. Had I actually known *before* hooking up with Ugly Betty that Rachel had seen us, there's no way I would have gone through with it... I think.

Lying absolutely silent next to Ugly Betty, making her more and more uncomfortable by the minute, I came up with a *brilliant* idea. I would send Rachel a text message...

R u mad at me?

Eureka! I've found it! Tis a brain literally made of shit. And it belongs to one, Jonathan Andrew Reynolds.

There was only so long I could weird Ugly Betty out in hopes of hearing back from Rachel, so after twenty minutes I gave up and went home. During one of my more literal walks of shame, I received a little salt for my self-inflicted wound...

I'm not mad. It's no big deal. Don't worry about it.

Have you ever thought about something so much that it feels like you're stepping on your own brain? Yeah, well... Eureka!

I slept maybe two hours that night, and when I woke up, I vomited like a bulimic runway model. You see the problem with, trying to have your cake and eat it too, is that you don't realize each layer of triple chocolate goodness is laced with poison until it's too late. Your stomach turns into a volcano, you recognize the reason Rachel doesn't give a fuck is because she also hooked up with someone else, and then you spew chunks all over the place.

After regurgitating poor decisions and an entire bottle of *Captain Morgan's*, I enlisted the help of Jackrabbit, in a bar, to help figure out who hit Rachel with their lead pipe.

"You sent her a text message!" Jackrabbit was cracking up. "Are you mad at me!" he echoed. "What are you on, The Dumb Shit Diet?"

"Forget the text," I said, ignoring my own idiocy. "Something tells me that's the least of my worries."

"What else are you worried about?" Jackrabbit asked, seemingly entertained.

"Losing her," I admitted.

Jackrabbit started laughing again. "Jon, are you kidding me?"

"I know it sounds retarded, but I feel like she's out of reach now. Clearly I fucked up, but what should I do about it?" I asked.

"Dude, you guys weren't even going out," he replied.

"Right, *technically* we weren't, but I know we could have been." For some reason I was still slinging my own bullshit.

"So then why weren't you?" Jackrabbit patronized.

"Because my mother fucked my uncle and I'm a retard. I don't know, guy. I'm an asshole!" I confessed. "I took her for granted, I thought I could do whatever I wanted, whenever I wanted, with whomever I wanted, and for some strange reason she'd still be there."

"So what's your plan?" Jackrabbit asked.

"There is no plan. I'm too much of a pussy to even call her. I keep staring at my phone hoping she'll do it for me, or in the least my testicles will drop, but neither have left the starting gate."

Jackrabbit pretended to laugh.

"Did you even see her last night?" I asked. "Was she downstairs the whole time?"

"Um, yeah, she was around," Jackrabbit slowly responded.

"Did you talk to her?" I continued.

"Yes!" he spastically shouted. "She kept asking me where you were and if I could get her into the VIP room."

"You didn't tell her I was with Ugly Betty, did you?"

"No, I just kept making shit up." It looked like Jackrabbit wanted to say more, but flatlined.

I took a moment of my own and drank my beer, giving my incest DNA more time to process what it heard.

"So you never told me how your night ended," I said to Jackrabbit, slightly veering off topic. "Who did you say was the girl you made out with?"

"Some random I met on the dance floor."

"Cute?" I asked.

"Very," Jackrabbit smiled.

"Seven point five?"

"A fuckin' ten, Jon!"

"Right," I laughed.

"Get this though, when I got back to my place, there was this other girl standing outside smoking a cigarette, so I started chatting her up. We spoke for maybe five minutes until I outright asked her if she wanted to go upstairs. I was so fuckin' drunk, but it so fuckin' worked," Jackrabbit happily confessed.

"Bullshit," I said, brushing him off.

"I swear to you on my mother's life!" he insisted.

"Did you fuck her?"

"I wish. She had her period." Jackrabbit spoke with the same depressed tone every guy does when they utter that sentence.

"That sucks," I said, pretending to sympathize. "Look at you though, two girls in one night, huh?"

Jackrabbit smiled and sipped his vodka like he was auditioning for a commercial.

"All right, porn star, back to my clusterfuck of a love life," I said. "I think I'm going to call Rachel and ask her to talk, assuming she picks up. I'll just speak from the heart, my tiny, Scrooge-like heart."

The conversation went quiet again. That is until Jackrabbit's conscience saved his life.

"Rachel and I kissed last night."

Ah-ha! I knew it wasn't Colonel Mustard.

Jackrabbit quickly continued. "It was nothing though, I swear. She could tell I was lying about where you were, so to cheer her up I asked her to dance," he reasoned. Then, out of nowhere, we just kissed."

"Right, both of you missed a step and fell on each other's lips," I sarcastically returned. "With that logic I guess I should just be happy the two of you were wearing clothes."

"It's not what you think," he downplayed.

"Did you kiss her back?" I asked.

Jackrabbit hesitated before answering. "Yes, but for like two seconds."

"Bullshit! Don't tell me two seconds, I fuckin' invented two seconds."

"Dude, I'm sorry. It just happened. You were busy with Ugly Betty, and earlier in the evening you told me you wanted nothing to do with Rachel, so…"

"So you figured you'd take her off my hands," I interrupted. "I see your logic. It makes complete sense and in no way is it fucked up."

"Jon."

"Jackrabbit. Dickhead. Prick. Fuckface."

I wanted to be furious, I wanted to erupt, but I couldn't quite get there. Fine, part of me wanted to break my beer bottle over his stupid face, but deep down I knew I was the one to blame. My actions, my behavior, and my idiotic thought process had caused it, and they all effectively came back to bite me in the ass. It's nice to meet you, Karma.

"Listen," I began in a more subtle tone. "I'm not gonna lie, I'm a little pissed off, but the truth is… I still feel the same way."

"Huh?" Jackrabbit grunted.

"As much as I enjoyed your little story, nothing's changed. I *know* I want to be with Rachel," I explained.

"So then do you want to go?" he asked.

"Yeah. Fuck it!" I shouted, instantly feeling my testicles morph into cantaloupes. "Drop me off at Pokehole."

"Don't you want to call her first?"

"Oh yeah, I should probably do that," I backtracked.

"What if she doesn't pick up?" Jackrabbit pointed out.

"Shit," I muttered.

He was a penisface for making out with Rachel, but right nonetheless. I really did need a plan.

"Did you talk to Rachel today?" I asked, wanting and not wanting to hear his answer.

"Yeah."

You motherfucker.

"I called her this afternoon to tell her, that I was going to tell you, what happened," Jackrabbit said, tripping over his words.

"Wow, that's very kind of you to serve me shit, but I'll eat later. Right now, call Rachel and ask her to meet you across the street from Pokehole," I ordered.

"What if she says no?" he asked.

"She won't."

"But how do you know?" he persisted.

"Because she didn't last night," I acknowledged.

"Ha-ha." Jackrabbit faked, quickly sweeping the truth under the rug. "What do I say when she asks me why I want to see her?"

"Are you seriously asking me how to lie to a girl?" I said, raising my eyebrows. "According to the new count, you hooked up with three girls last night. And call me crazy, but something tells me you bent the truth along the way."

"So is this you mad?" Jackrabbit asked, trying not to laugh at what a wreck I was.

"No time for that. Operation Orthodox Recovery is now in effect." I threw a couple dollars on the bar, pushed in my chair, and waited for Jackrabbit to do the same. "Motion creates emotion, my friend. Let's go."

As I sat in Pizza Make You Puke, located directly across the street from Pokehole, drinking a bottle of water and nervously waiting for Rachel to walk through the door, I realized I didn't have an opening. The "plan" had worked thus far, Rachel was under the impression she was coming to meet Jackrabbit, but what the fuck was I going to say?

The bell hanging over the door loudly swung from side to side as Rachel and Blondie Glasses entered. Rachel immediately saw me and I couldn't help but smile.

"Jackrabbit went home," I spastically yelled, from the other end of the restaurant.

Blondie Glasses laughed, and then whispered something to Rachel before bailing.

I got out of my seat and cut down the distance. "I know you're expecting Jackrabbit, but he went home."

"How'd you know that?" she asked, wondering whether or not I knew more.

"I had him call you. I didn't think you'd come if I asked."

"What makes you say that?" she smirked, clearly enjoying the upper hand.

"Just a hunch," I answered.

"So then is Jackrabbit even here?"

"Again, he went home." That one had a little hatred in it.

"Then what do you want?" Rachel asked, returning the attitude.

"Um..." I didn't know where to begin so I tried buying time. "Do you think we could go somewhere else to talk?"

"About what?" she snapped.

"The stock market. I'd really like to sink my teeth into it," I smiled.

Crickets.

"Or, we could discuss what happened last night," I said, quickly returning seriousness. "I'm sure you don't want to talk about it, but there's something I have to get off my chest. What you do with it is completely up to you."

I stood in front of Rachel as a vulnerable, sincere, mysterious, yet desperate individual. Apparently it was the perfect mix, because she agreed to hear me out.

"Let's go," she sighed, turning for the exit.

Like a poodle bitch, I followed in silence.

Rachel's room was completely empty this time. Even pothead Gopher left her hippie den. Without any distractions, all I had to do was sit Rachel down, look her in the eyes, and tell her how I felt. Too bad I have the emotional range of Joan Rivers' face.

For some reason, I've never been good at verbally expressing myself. Wait, I take that back. I have no problem telling someone they suck at life, they smell like a diaper, or they're teething my penis, but when it comes to speaking sentimentally and talking about *feelings*, I struggle. Yet, if I were asked to write those feelings down it'd be a breeze. I wouldn't hesitate for a second. When the person is sitting in front of me though, like Rachel was, the words never sound the same. I'm all over the place; I'm not romantic, I babble, I leave things out, and the more I say, the worse it gets. If someone videotaped me, I'd look like shrinkage.

"So, what is it you want to tell me?" Rachel asked, initiating the conversation.

"Um, well, before I get into that I want to apologize for last night," I mumbled.

"Why?"

Rachel had no intention of making this easy for me.

"Well, I was a dick, a bit of an asshole, I ignored you, and I feel terrible… to name a few," I said.

"So you were avoiding me on purpose," she stabbed.

My eyes fell to the floor.

"Real nice."

"I know, and I'm really sorry. It's just that when you showed up at Jackrabbit's, I went into a funk."

"A *funk*?" Rachel repeated.

"I mean, I was pregaming with my friends, playing Beer

Pong, joking around and all that other crap, and then my whole mood changed."

"Because we showed up," Rachel finished. "Again, that makes me feel really good. Why didn't you just tell us not to come?"

"Right, because that would have gone over well," I unwisely said. "Basically, it felt like my night ended when you arrived. I know that sounds bad, but it mostly had to do with the spontaneity going out the window and knowing exactly how things would unfold," I added, afraid of my own honesty.

"Bullshit! You didn't want me there because you wanted to hang out with your friends, hit on girls at the club, and then if things didn't work out for you, find me at the end of the night and come back to my place," Rachel angrily stated.

"Now you're just putting words in my mouth."

"If you weren't tip-toeing around them I wouldn't have to!" Rachel snapped. "Let's put it this way, you thought you could have your cake and to eat it, too."

Transparent much?

"Okay, you probably have me with that one," I admitted. "I was also feeling a little overwhelmed by us though. Of course rather than handle it maturely, I did what I normally do and fucked it up."

"So what, you want me to forgive you so don't feel bad anymore?" Rachel asked, clearly giving me the business.

"No, not at all… well, yes, I would like you to forgive me, but it's more than that," I said, tripping over my words.

Obviously, things weren't going as planned. I was flustered and I hadn't even begun to say what I wanted to.

"I forgive you. There. Are we done?" Rachel asked, visibly annoyed with me, and my inability to get to the point.

"I don't want to lose you!"

Oh shit. Why did I just say that? Why the fuck did I just say that? She's looking at me like I'm crazy. Yep, she definitely thinks I'm crazy. Keep talking. Nothing can be worse than the constipated look she's giving you right now.

"I know you hooked up with Jackrabbit," I added.

There is something seriously wrong with me.

If Rachel was constipated before, I don't even want to tell you how she looked after that comment.

"I'm not mad," I continued. "I was a little jealous when he told me, but I just want to point out that you're also to blame."

I couldn't stop myself. It was like Missy Elliot invaded my brain and told me to put my thang down, flip it, and then reverse it.

"Even worse, you hooked up with one of my good friends," I scolded. "I may have fucked up, but there's no way I'd sink as low as to hook up with Blondie Cheeks, Blondie Glasses, or even Generic."

"First of all..." Rachel snapped, using her jappy tough guy voice. "... You might want to reevaluate who your close friends are. Jackrabbit was the one all over me, not the other way around. And second of all, I didn't think we'd even be talking again after last night."

"Wait, what do you mean, he was all over you?" I retreated.

"What did he tell you happened?" Rachel asked.

"He didn't go into details. He just said you were upset because you realized he was lying for me, and then to take your mind off it, asked you to dance. At some point during your dirty dancing session you kissed, and that was it."

Rachel immediately started laughing. I could have been mistaken, but I was pretty sure there wasn't a joke in there.

"All right then, Chuckles. Tell me what really happened," I insisted.

"Well, first of all, Jackrabbit's either the worst liar in the world, or he wanted me to know he was covering for you."

"I'm sorry to interrupt, but do you plan on counting all of your points?" I annoyingly asked. "Believe it or not I can differentiate between thoughts."

"Shut it, you." Rachel tried not to smile, even though I could tell she was enjoying the spotlight. "Basically, I knew you didn't want me upstairs, and I knew you told Jackrabbit not to give me a VIP stamp. As far as the dirty dancing goes, you're right about that. We were all over each other. He was literally grinding me."

"I like literally don't want to hear it," I said, trying to remain calm as the jealousy reheated.

"Sorry, I just don't want you to think he had nothing to do with it," Rachel said, almost smirking. Although I'm sure that's how he made it sound."

Okay, now I'm fuckin' pissed.

Rachel continued. "In some ways, he really was being a good friend, to me at least. You made me feel like an idiot, but he was checking up on me and taking my mind off it."

I'm sorry, can you move that knife over an inch. It's not quite in my heart just yet.

Rachel went on. "Jackrabbit was actually a gentleman. He even bought my friends and I shots."

That was my cue to laugh.

"What?"

"Nothing," I scoffed. "You're exactly right. He is the perfect gentleman," I laughed again, doing my part to get under Rachel's skin. "He pounced all over my mistake, took advantage of you while you were vulnerable, and fed you drinks to ease the process. Now if that's not the definition of a gentleman, then I don't know what is," I said.

My sarcasm brought Rachel right back to the pissed off party. Worse than that, she actually believed Jackrabbit was genuine.

"You can think what you want, but you weren't there," she snapped. "You were too busy with Ugly Betty. Thanks for the text, by the way."

Rachel obviously wanted to duke it out. What she didn't realize though is I had a one-two punch that would make her taste the canvas. By throwing it I'd be breaking a few "man laws," but I didn't care anymore. As far as I was concerned, those "rules" went out the window the second Jackrabbit told me he hooked up with Rachel. I waited for her to raise her fists again, and then...

"Jackrabbit hooked up with *two* other girls last night!"

Eight... nine... ten... she's out!

Apparently the distorted face of a verbal knockout actually resembles that of a physical one. As a result, I decided not to step on Rachel's uterus while she was down.

"Before I continue, I want you to know I'm not making any of this up. I just can't bear having you think Jackrabbit is this portrait of a gentleman while the wool is being pulled over your eyes," I explained.

"I prefer cashmere," Rachel joked, trying to hide her dejection. "Tell me what happened."

"Are you sure?" I asked, strictly to be nice.

"Yeah, go ahead," she insisted.

"Well, before you guys kissed on the dance floor he did the same with someone else, and then when he got back to his dorm he met another girl outside and brought her upstairs."

If we were on *BET,* someone would have yelled, "Yo, a sista got played!" Unfortunately, we were not, so Rachel just sat there looking the same way anyone else would if they got fucked over twice in one night.

"Listen." I waited for Rachel to look at me. "I know this might seem like a petty or desperate way to get back at Jackrabbit, but it has nothing to do with that. Well, that's not entirely true, it's an added bonus, but the real reason I told you is because I can feel that distance between us now and I hate it. I hate myself for having caused it, I hate myself for thinking it was okay, and I hate myself for... I don't know what else right now, but I'm sure there's more. I guess what I'm really trying to say is, there isn't a doubt in my mind that I want to be with you."

Oh my God. I did it! That wasn't half bad. I don't know where I was going with that self-hate thing, but who cares, she's smiling from ear to ear. Wait, she's not saying anything though. Is she giving me a polite smile, like when you tell someone you love them and they thank you? I hope she doesn't think that's what I was saying. Fuck! Did I say I love you? Fuck!

"If you're wondering what that means exactly, I'll elaborate and just say I want us to be exclusive."

What!

"Until the end of the semester," I quickly added. "You and I, exclusive, till the end of the semester."

Smooth.

Rachel was still smiling, but it looked more like she wanted to laugh. Hell, I did too and I was the one in a nosedive.

"Are you lost?" Rachel joked, pretending to knock on my brain.

"Just plummeting to my death," I smiled.

"Aww, don't do that, Jonathan. I want us to be *exclusive*," she mocked.

I skillfully delivered my best puppy dog face yet, and this time, Rachel broke. I wisely took advantage and kissed her.

"So is that a yes?" I asked, making sure we were on the same page.

"Yes, Jonathan. I definitely, one hundred percent, want us to be exclusive," Rachel smiled.

"Well jeez, if you're going to beg me, then fine, we can be exclusive."

Rachel hit me before giving me another kiss, most likely to prevent me from saying anything else.

There are several things I regret in my life thus far, but selling out Jackrabbit isn't one of them. I truly believe Fate is accountable for the majority of events and experiences I've gone through, and will continue to go through, so I try not to second guess myself or press the pause button. You see, from the day I met Rachel in the gym, to the nights we spoke on the computer, to the night we had our first kiss, to the early morning of April 18th 2003, when Rachel and I decided to only see each other, Fate was with me. I had no reason not to trust him.

Rhythm Is Gonna Get You

When Rachel and I decided to spend the rest of the school year together, I forgot to mention a very important question followed our newly affirmed status. So, if you don't mind, I'd like to hop in the *DeLorean* and return to that beautifully awkward night.

Rachel and I were still sitting on her bed, hand in hand, lovie dovie, exchanging kisses, and of course, exclusive.

"Okay, so there's something I want to ask you now," Rachel began.

"You couldn't ask me before?" I wondered.

"No, you were an asshole then."

"Fair enough," I laughed.

"Do you want to go to my sorority's formal with me?"

Aww, she's so cute.

"I'm sorry, I already told Ugly Betty I'd go with her."

Rachel immediately tried shoving me off the bed. I wrapped my arms around her waist and pulled her in.

"I'm just kidding," I smiled. "Of course I'll go to formal with you. Scratch that, I would *love* to go to formal with you."

"No, never mind," she ignored. "I'm taking Jackrabbit."

"Oh, that's it. Now you're dead." I laid Rachel down on the bed and planted my body on top of hers.

"Don't laugh, little one. You only have about forty-five seconds to change your mind."

"Okay, okay," she moaned. "Will... you... ask Jackrabbit to formal for me?"

Rachel started cracking up; laughing so hard her face turned into a tomato. I let go of my body weight even more.

"I'm kidding, I'm kidding," she whispered, ready to explode.

I rolled off her and sat up against the wall, pretending to be sad but having an even harder time keeping a straight face.

"Aww, look at my little baby. Come here," she said, wrapping her arms around me this time. "You're the only one I want to go to formal with."

"Promises?" I said like a two year old.

"Promises," she returned.

And there you have it, I would be attending my first college formal and I was stoked. I had previously gone to a few date parties and a semi-formal, but this already felt different, almost like I was reliving my prom (with Rachel of course, not the offspring of Satan).

At nearly all schools who entertain The Long Island Scene, there are two sororities every Jewish girl wants to be a part of, Sigma Delta Tau (SDT) and Alpha Epsilon Phi (AEPhi). It's basically like trying out for the Mets or Yankees, if they were a jappy group of girls who professionally shopped, bitched about everything, and recycled men. Oh, so it's *exactly* like trying out for the Yankees (Suck it! Mets rule!). Rachel was heavily recruited from both sides, though. Smart, good looking, religious, one third of her body weight in diamonds, meant she was easily a top ten draft pick. Ultimately SDT won out, but rumor has it they paid under the table, a lifetime subscription to

Cosmo, and a lifetime role on *Lifetime.*

Before Rachel's formal, the last suit I wore was at Bogey Lowenstein's Bar Mitzvah. With that said, my frame, not so much my intelligence, had grown since I was thirteen. Finding a suit that fit me was not going to be easy. I have long legs, go-go-gadget arms, broad shoulders, a skinny waist, and an even thinner bank account. The latter may not have been a physical attribute, but it was certainly an important one.

Rachel 'hinted', and by hinted I mean flat out told me, that every guy at formal would be wearing a suit. This left me with three options; be the only date in khakis and a button down, squeeze into my old nut hugger, or panhandle my parents. Based on the gay smile I'd been sporting since Rachel asked me to formal, the decision was a no-brainer. All aboard homosexuals, we're going shopping.

The following weekend I took a trip home, in search of a suit, but also because my brother had a soccer game against the New York/New Jersey Metrostars (known today as the New York Red Bulls). The match was a loss, along with shopping, but I didn't come back to PC entirely empty-handed. My parents hesitantly gave me one of their credit cards and trusted I wouldn't spend a fortune. Admittedly, I was tempted to dress in gold jewelry and a velour jumpsuit, but I chose not to abuse their generosity, or look like a pimp.

Call me picky, call me gay, call me what you will, but I was adamant about having my first suit as an adult look more than okay. Unfortunately, I was having the same problems I did when I looked on Long Island. If the color was right, the fabric was wrong. If the jacket fit, the pants were too big. If the pants fit, the jacket was too big. If I found one with potential, it cost too much. I was panicking. I felt like a hooker getting her period before rent's due. To make a long story short, I eventually suited up. I spent more money than expected, especially with alterations, but I looked damn good, my friends.

In the days leading up to formal, Rachel and I were closer than ever. It was too soon to say anything, but I could tell she felt the same way. And just when things couldn't get any better, Rachel placed the cherry on top.

"Should I get us a room for the night?"

"I don't know," I said, grinning. "What do you think?"

"It's up to you," she returned.

"Really? Because I feel like that should be your call."

"Well, our formal is at a hotel, so…"

"So you're trying to seduce me," I smiled. "I see your plan."

"Yeah, because I need a hotel to seduce you, hornball."

"Good point," I laughed. What are your friends doing?"

"I think Blondie Cheeks and Blondie Glasses are sharing a room."

"I'm sure their dates will love that," I muttered.

"Blondie Cheeks' date is just a friend," Rachel responded. "And Blondie Glasses and her boyfriend are on the rocks, so I doubt he'll stay over."

I could tell Rachel wanted to get the room, as did I, but there was no way I could use my parents' credit card again. I felt bad enough spending what I did on the suit.

"I could put it on my parents' credit card," I suggested.

Eh, Poppa Bear will understand.

"We're actually not supposed to let our dates pay for anything."

"Seriously?" I shouted, failing to contain my excitement.

"I swear," Rachel said, laughing at the relieved look on my face.

"Oh, well, then… uh…" I knew what I wanted to say, I just felt bad actually saying it.

Rachel could see the inner struggle and gave me a kiss. "Stop thinking like that," she said. "I promise, it's fine."

"Well, I'm not going to lie…" I slowly began. "I feel weird that you'd be paying, but if it's really not a big deal, then yes, I think it'd be cool."

"*Cool*," Rachel mocked, adding a big smile. "Because I already booked it."

Checking in!

With the anticipated day upon us, Rachel and I did all we could to handle our business early, so we'd have more time to relax at the hotel and use the pool. Too bad my tailor missed the memo, because Giuseppe didn't finish my suit until half past five. His craftsmanship saved his life, but my floaties would have to wait another day.

The lobby of The District Hotel was absolutely stunning, but the room far and away exceeded my expectations. I didn't think SDT would pinch pennies, contrary to stereotypical jokes, but they certainly outdid themselves. Our room was spacious enough to be a suite. It had a large marble bathroom, a *Jacuzzi* tub, an enormous king-sized bed, and my adorable, big fat friend, TV. Everything was perfect. Well, almost.

While Rachel was in the bathroom unpacking her toiletries, there was a knock at the door. I rolled off the bed and answered. *Now* everything was perfect. I walked back into the sleeping area and waited for Rachel to do the same. She didn't make it more than two steps out of the bathroom before freezing like a deer in headlights. A suicidal deer that is, because she was smiling from ear to ear.

"It comes with the room," I said, barely seen behind a large bouquet of red roses.

Rachel was glowing. "You bought me flowers," she gushed.

I set them down on the table and Rachel buried her nose in the petals. "Oh my g-d, they smell so good. Oh my g-d, I can't believe you bought me flowers!" she exclaimed.

Rachel was adorable. She was shy, excited, and bouncing all over the place like she had to pee. When I finally got a hold of her, I kissed her to say everything the flowers could and I couldn't.

Waiting for Rachel to get ready could be a frustrating experience, as read, but it also constituted some of our greatest memories. Sharing a sink, helping her pick out clothes, trying to keep her from putting them on, standing behind her so both of us could use the mirror, listening to music, dancing, sitting on the edge of the bed and drinking a beer, one eye on the television, the other following her around the room... those were the moments I felt like we were one. Those were the moments you couldn't paint, pay for, or replace. They were perfect.

When Rachel took that final step out of the bathroom, smiled at me and did her patented spin, the world froze. I'd never seen anything so clearly in all my life. *She* was perfect.

"Did you get these for Rachel?" Blondie Cheeks asked me, standing next to the bouquet.

"They came with the room," I lied.

"Really?" Generic said, overhearing me. "Our room doesn't have flowers. Does anyone else have flowers in their room?"

"He's just kidding," Rachel laughed. "He bought them for me."

"That's so sweet," Generic whimpered.

"Yeah, he likes me," Rachel said, giving me a big hug.

Taking advantage of my height, I jokingly shook my head in disagreement.

"Do you guys want to go downstairs?" Blondie Glasses asked, wanting no part of our public displays of affection.

"No!" her boyfriend barked, wanted no part of her.

"Let's take another shot!" Rachel loudly suggested, drunkenly cutting the tension.

Rachel was starting to display her lightweight standing. She was a two-beer-queer if she drank it, which made me wonder how much it would take to intoxicate a midget.

"Hey, tipsy, you might want to slow down," I said, very father-like. "You've got a long night ahead of you."

Rachel grabbed me by the waist. "What's that supposed to mean?" she whispered, like a drunk phone sex operator.

"Whatever you'd like it to mean," I entertained.

"That's right, whatever *I'd* like it to mean."

"Oh boy. You still want that shot?" I laughed.

"Yeah, gimme dat shot!"

The hotel ballroom coincided with the grandeur of the room, the lobby, and every other square inch, but there was one facet I found peculiar... why no one was at the party. The place was near empty! It was like we invited twenty more people to pregame with us and then rented the set of *Dancing with the Stars*.

Everything is what you make of it, though. So rather than widdle fifty sarcastic jokes, I let it go and focused all my attention on Rachel. It was her night, and I would do anything and everything to make it perfect, even if that meant posing for pictures. (Spontaneous snapshots, okay. But when someone's aiming a lens at me, making me hold a smile for thirty seconds while insisting I say something *cheesy*, I too freeze up like a deer in headlights... just one who ends up looking like they were caught masturbating.

After slipping the camerawoman a twenty to ensure the use of *Photoshop*, Rachel and I filled our plates at the buffet and sat down to eat.

"How is your pasta, Rachel?"

"Not bad. How's the chicken?" she returned.

"It is quite tasty, Rachel."

Rachel looked at me oddly before taking a bite.

"Yes, dear?" I smiled.

"Why are you talking like that?" she asked.

"Like how?" I indulged.

"Like a big fat loser on top of a big fat dork."

"This is my dinner table voice. I practice proper etiquette, Rachel."

Rachel stared at me again and then let out one of the loudest belches I've ever heard.

"Okay, that was impressive," I laughed. "I had no idea such a deafening noise could come from such a little girl."

"Surprise!" Rachel shouted, see-food and all.

It's weird to say, but I've never been so turned on by a burb. I wanted to kiss her and taste garlic right then and there. Everything she did made me smile, even when she wasn't trying to.

"So, Gassy Girl, before I try your pasta without eating it, I thought I'd point out a few gentlemen who are *not* wearing suits," I smirked.

"I knew you were going to say something!" Rachel laughed. "I'm sorry, honey. You look so handsome though." Rachel leaned out of her seat and gave me a kiss.

"It's okay. I got it from the first place I went to."

Every moment with Rachel was starting to seem better than the last. Formal was incredible, and we had a great time, but then she asked if I wanted to go back upstairs. Where was the camera lady to capture that moment? Huh? I would have blinded that girl with the smile I had going.

By the time Rachel and I got back to our room, the romantic buildup was overflowing. The only logical thing to do was get in the tub. Rachel dimmed the lights and drew a bubble bath, I mixed us a pair of cocktails, and we rendezvoused in the water. Unfortunately, for you, this is where I hang the Do Not Disturb sign. I'm a gentleman. Remember? If you need to get your rocks off, buy a *Penthouse Forum*.

I think it's fair to say the majority of us don't wake up smiling. If there's someone underneath the covers causing your eyes to open, sure, that's a different story, but for me, it was as simple as rolling over and having Rachel there. When the sun broke through that annoying crack in the curtains, and its relentless spotlight followed my face like a sniper, I opened my eyes and smiled at an adorable, sweaty little munchkin, curled up in a ball with the comforter held to her nose. It was certainly another picture for the mental frame, but sadly, some real life images don't last forever.

Checking out!

I stood next to Rachel at the counter, holding a dress and bouquet of flowers while she paid the bill. Emasculated, would be one way to put it, but the desk clerk gave me an opportunity to make light of the situation.

"Congratulations!" the flamboyant man gushed.

"Thank you," I quickly responded. "She just kept asking me, and asking me, and asking me!" I cried, mimicking his voice. "I simply couldn't say no." I smiled and kissed Rachel, who was already trying not to laugh.

"How adorable!" he exclaimed. "Uh, I love newlyweds."

Rachel signed her statement, looked at me, and then mooshed my cheeks together with the palms of her hands. "Who could resist this face?" she said, playing along. "Who?"

"Not me!" the desk clerk shouted.

"Me either," Rachel agreed, smiling uncontrollably.

"Maybe we should just stay another night then, honey." Not having any hands free, I leaned over and kissed Rachel's cheek, grinning at what she'd say under the spotlight.

"Oh, I don't know, *babe*. We have dinner plans with the Ross' tonight. You know how upset they get when we cancel."

"The Ross'!" I repeated, smiling at how well Rachel did. "I completely forget. What would I do without you?"

"Good question," Rachel laughed, looking at the desk clerk and getting him to do the same. "It's time to get this stud muffin home," she added. "Thanks for your help."

"My pleasure, sweetness... and sweetness!" he screeched, throwing a gay paw in my direction.

"Thanks a lot, buddy. You take care," I laughed.

I could hear the desk clerk giggling as we walked away.

"Bye Nick. Bye Jessica."

I Think We're Alone Now

With the spring semester coming to a close, and finals right around the corner, Rachel spent more time in the library than Madonna does pretending to be Jewish... and English... and young.

James Monroe Library is a very large, up to date, and technologically sound library, but it is also a surprisingly popular social scene. So much so that it earned the nickname, Club Monroe. Being the smart cookie Rachel is, she made the library her home for all the right reasons. I, on the other hand, am more of a lazy cookie, smart in my own right, but frequented the library with a different agenda.

The biggest problem I had with my gpa wasn't that is was a 1.36, but rather I needed to have at least a 2.0 to be eligible to play soccer the following year. I also needed a minimum of twenty-four credits. Much to my parents dismay, I could take classes over the summer and transfer them in, but raising my gpa meant I would actually have to study.

The Code Room, also known as the ADD Room (a disorder that may or may not be good for reading this book, the jury's still out) is located on the third floor of the library, and requires a special combination to get into. On the inside, it's simply divided into four private study rooms. Without anyone or anything around to catch your attention, the Code Room can be the best place on campus to study. Unless, of course, you put two love bugs in the same room, then there's likely to be a drop-off in productivity.

The second I entered Rachel's foxhole, my eligibility concerns disappeared. Learning and succeeding in life sounded great and all, but finding out more about Rachel sounded even better. Seeing how she would receive a twenty thousand dollar academic scholarship for staying over a 3.5, her attitude was a little different than mine. You can't put a price on getting to know someone, though. That's the bullshit I would be slinging.

"Hey, cutie." I took my backpack off, gave Rachel a kiss, and sat down next to her. "How's the studying going?" I asked.

"Just great," Rachel sighed.

"Stressed much?"

"I've been here for six hours," she groaned.

"I'll tell you what I'm going to do then," I resolved. "I'm going to take your clothes off, lie you down on this table, and give you a nice, relaxing, deep tissue massage."

Rachel let out a very tired laugh. "You have to let me study. I need to memorize this."

"What if I quiz you during the massage?" I suggested. "I can ask a question at each body part, and if you get it right, I'll work my magic and then move on. I get to ask as many as I want when I reach your inner thigh and buttocks though. That's just how the game is played."

"Listen to me very carefully, Giant." Rachel was trying to be tough, which always made me laugh. "If you don't let me study, I'm going to rip your penis off."

"Who gets to keep it?"

Rachel made like she was going to grab my crotch, causing

me to flinch and nearly fall out of my chair.

"Dat's right! Shut it or I take it!" she playfully yelled.

Regaining my balance, I tightly pressed my lips together and slowly leaned towards Rachel.

"What are you doing?" she asked.

I ignored her and continued forward, lips glued, eyes wide, and brow slanted.

"What, you think you're kissing me with that ugly fassa?" Rachel laughed.

The closer I got, the more she retreated, until eventually the wall served its purpose and there was nowhere left to go. Sandwiched between sheet rock and the dead weight of a weirdo, Rachel started cracking up at my creepy antics. Moving in one last time, I pressed my lips against hers, keeping them stationary while theatrically moving my head. It was easily the world's worst movie kiss.

"Wow. *That* was sexy," Rachel mocked, after being freed from my clutches. "I don't know how I'm going to study after that knockout."

"I didn't want to do it, but you made me break out the big guns." I quickly changed the subject so Rachel wouldn't return to studying. "Whatcha got in that plastic bag of candy over there?"

"Um… candy," she answered, unsure whether or not I was a ruhtard. "Why, do you want some?"

"Well, I was expecting you to offer me more than just candy, especially after that spine-tingling kiss, but I'll settle for some *Gummy Bears*."

Rachel handed me the bag. "Here. You eat, I'll study."

"What happens when I finish?" I asked, playing dumb.

"Then you also study."

"So both of us will be studying at the same time?" I questioned.

"Correct. You're a genius."

"Well that's precisely why you don't have to study. You will learn from being in my company," I smiled.

Rachel acted like she didn't hear me, silently looking in the other direction, and then sneak attacked my junk.

"Okay, okay, okay!" I cried, rather high pitched. "I'll study! I'll study," I repeated, with immediate relief.

Rachel held her now empty talon in the air and said nothing. Fearing for the safety of my frank and beans, I grabbed a book out of my bag, put it on the table, opened it, and started eating candy.

When all my chewy favorites were gone, I actually did try studying. However, when I found myself continuously rereading the same three paragraphs, I knew it was pointless. I lifted my head out of the book and stared at Rachel.

"What is this, dried mango?" I asked, taking a piece out of the bag and holding it in the air.

Rachel turned her head like she was going to kill me, but then gave in. "Yeah, you've never had it before?"

"Can't say I have," I admitted.

"It's good."

I took a bite and was less than impressed.

"You don't like it?" she asked.

"Not so much," I answered, making a yucky face. "Dried fruit in general is pretty shitty."

"Good, more for me." Rachel snatched the uneaten mango portion from my hand and ate it. Before she finished and went back to studying again, I distracted her with a new topic.

"How many siblings did you say you have?"

"Seriously?" Rachel asked, dropping her pen on the desk.

"What?" I smiled.

"Three. I have three siblings," she frustratingly answered. "An older brother and two younger sisters."

"Jews love baby making, don't they?"

Rachel looked like she was about to break, but the topic seemed to draw her in.

"There's more to it than just sex," she implied.

"Like what, foreplay?" I mocked.

"Um, try, the Holocaust," Rachel snapped.

Yikes! Where'd that come from?

I felt like I just told a racist black joke with the guy from *The Green Mile* standing behind me.

Rachel continued. "Because of the Holocaust, the Jewish population is a lot lower than it should be. We make up less than one percent of the world."

"Less than one percent," I repeated, thinking it over. "There's like six billion people in the world. Even at one percent, that's only... sixty million."

"It's definitely below sixty million, I know that much. Six million Jews died in the Holocaust, which was over sixty years ago, so you have to figure that number would be a lot higher if it never happened," she explained.

"So Jewish people feel an obligation, for lack of a better word, to have a lot of kids?" I asked.

"Some do."

"I have a feeling the girls from my high school are going to help those numbers," I joked, trying to lighten the conversation.

"You know Jews aren't supposed to have premarital sex, right?"

"Seriously?" I questioned, raising my brow.

Rachel nodded her head.

"I had no idea," I admitted. Then again, I've never met anyone who was Orthodox, so you'll have to elaborate."

Rachel paused, appearing hesitant to continue. As not to let the topic dissolve, I worked it into a question.

"Maybe this will help," I began. "If procreation is so important to rebuilding the Jewish population, then why is premarital sex frowned upon?"

The door stayed open and Rachel jumped right in. "Most Conservative Jews don't care, but for Orthodox and Hasidic Jews, it's a big deal. There are so many laws in Judaism though, it's hard to explain."

"In case you haven't noticed, we're in a library," I smirked. "I'm here to learn, Rachel."

Her eyes instantly rolled to the back of her head. "I'll just tell you about my brother, Ian. He's the same age as you, a junior at Queens College. He and his girlfriend, Heather, have been together since their junior year of *high school*, so about five years."

"Five years!" I shouted, forgetting where I was. That's crazy."

"Right, five years without sex though."

"Okay, now that's just unfathomable," I said, shaking my head.

"To most, but to them it's normal."

"So let me get this straight…" I took a moment to collect my thoughts. "Your brother has been with the same girl for half a decade, he's twenty-one years old, and his pee-pee has never been in her vajayjay?" The light bulb was starting to flicker. "Wait a minute; if his pee-pee has never been in her vajayjay, and they've been together for five years, and that's considered the norm, then he probably hasn't had sex with anyone. So your brother's still..." I went from a candle to a lighthouse. "A virgin!" I yelled, again.

"Yep," Rachel answered, immediately uncomfortable but still willing to continue her lesson. "Another reason Orthodox Jews have so many kids is because they're not supposed to use birth control. We're told that sex is meant for procreation, and therefore sperm should only be used for making babies. Sex isn't meant to be an act of gratification. On top of all that, it's only supposed to be between a Jewish man and a Jewish woman."

Have you ever seen a three hundred pound man dressed up like Olivia Newton John at the end of *Grease?* Me either, but had I, my face would have looked the same way it did when Rachel finished speaking.

"Are you all right?" she smiled. "You look like you blew a fuse."

"No, yeah, I'm fine," I rambled, the wheels still in motion. "It's just that, you know, I thought keeping kosher was the hard part."

"That's why so few people are Orthodox," Rachel laughed. "The laws require a lot of sacrifice. Compared to your friends, you probably think I'm the most religious person in the world."

"You're definitely giving the Pope a run for his money," I joked, clearing my throat before going on. "Can I ask you something?"

Rachel sensed the uneasiness in my voice and blurted out, "I'm a virgin!"

I immediately started laughing. Rachel was less than pleased.

"That's real nice, asshole."

"I'm sorry," I said, slowing the chuckles down. "It's just,

that's not what I was going to ask. I knew you were a virgin as soon as I did your brother."

Have you ever seen *Two Girls, One Cup*? No? Well look it up, you're in for a real treat. If you have though, the image of me banging Rachel's brother caused for the same disturbed face you had upon viewing such an atrocity.

"That clearly came out wrong," I laughed. "You know what I meant though, right?"

"Yes," Rachel answered, shaking her head, trying not to smile. "Tell me what you were really going to ask, gay boy."

I deservingly had myself another laugh before continuing. "Well, since you said sperm is meant for the purpose of having a child, and essentially not to be wasted on gratification, even though the average sperm count is in the hundreds of millions, then… what's the deal with oral sex?" I asked, doing my best Seinfeld impersonation.

Rachel looked more confused than disgusted this time. "What do you mean?" she inquired.

"I was kind of hoping you knew where I was going with this one," I smirked.

"Just say it. I'm not going to be mad."

I tried an obvious yet gentler way of asking my question. "You see I have this friend, who is also Catholic, who is dating this girl, who is also Orthodox."

"How convenient," Rachel smiled.

"I know, what are the odds? Anyway, he and I were talking the other day, about oral sex, and my buddy shared with me how his lady partner doesn't swallow at the conclusion of fellatio. He was perplexed as to why, but unfortunately I could shed no light on the matter. I thought maybe you could explain it to me, and then I would relay the message to him… my Catholic friend…

who's dating an Orthodox girl," I repeated.

Rachel shook her head as she laughed, feeling like she had to show some level of disapproval. "It goes back to what I was saying earlier; sperm isn't meant to enter a woman's body unless it's for the purpose of making a baby. And to quote something I heard a complete moron once say, 'Your mouth can't get pregnant.'"

I practically fell out of my chair laughing. "He sounds like a gentleman and a scholar."

"Right," Rachel ignored. "Anyway, is there really a big difference between spitting and swallowing? Does one actually feel better than the other?" she genuinely wondered.

"Again, I would have to consult my Catholic friend, but something tells me he would lean towards swallowing. He's a real creature of habit," I smiled.

"Well, you tell him that's what he gets for dating an Orthodox girl," Rachel smiled back, before adding, "And he should be happy he's getting any to begin with."

"I'll be sure to pass it on," I laughed. "I'm curious though; have any of the guys you've hooked up with confronted you on this swallowing matter?"

"Just this one idiot who indirectly asked me." Rachel pointed at me with her eyes. "And I don't hook up with random guys or have one-night stands. I have boyfriends," she clarified, holding her nose in the air.

"So are you *indirectly* saying I'm gross?" I asked.

"No, I'm *directly* telling you you're shnasty."

"So now I'm a shnasty boy?" I smiled.

"If the shoe fits…"

"Well, this shnasty boy thinks you've found yourself a hooking up loop-hole. I bet you call guys your boyfriend within a week or two of knowing them. That way it looks like you're in a relationship rather than hooking up just for kicks."

"No," Rachel said, doing a terrible job of lying.

"Right," I mocked. "Well I think I just hit the nail on the head. How many *boyfriends* are we talking about?" I inquired.

"One or two," she lied again.

Continuing to patronize Rachel… "What do you say we quit the shenanigans, put on our bathing suits, and dive right into this Olympic-sized boyfriend pool?"

"I'll tell you about the most recent one," Rachel said, pretending it was a chore. "His name is Ira Needyboy, he's your year. We went out for a few months, but I broke up with him before I met you."

"Can't say I know him. Why'd you break up?" I asked.

"I found him repulsive," Rachel quickly answered.

"Wow, I wonder what you're going to say about me at the end of the semester," I smiled.

I was only joking, but Rachel did not find it amusing. Apparently my comment struck a chord. She clearly was not going to elaborate, so I continued with the questions.

"Why'd you stay with him?" I asked.

"Obviously I didn't," Rachel barked, throwing a little attitude my way. "I just liked the things that went along with having a boyfriend more than the actual boyfriend; dinners, movies, sleepovers, stuff like that."

"So then you guys never hooked up?"

"He hooked up with me," Rachel casually responded. "But I never did anything to him, if that's what you're asking."

"Oh, so there *is* more than one way to kick a guy in the nuts," I laughed, more surprised by Rachel's calm demeanor than anything else.

"He's in therapy now," Rachel added.

"For what, his jaw?"

"Not that kind of therapy," she laughed.

"What about high school?" I asked, moving on.

"I was with someone for all of my senior year. That was my longest relationship."

"What happened with that?" I inquired.

"We broke up before I left," Rachel briefly explained.

"So it was mutual?"

Rachel shook her head, disagreeing.

"Wow, you're a little heartbreaker, aren't you?" I smiled.

"Maybe. I'm sure it's nothing you'll lose sleep over," Rachel muttered.

What the fuck? That's twice with the attitude now.

Rachel's words were like darts accurately thrown off the board. I was starting to think she had a problem with our 'pact' to be exclusive only until the end of the school year. At the risk of being wrong and embarrassing myself though, I ignored it and went back to the subject at hand.

"Something tells me the list of boyfriends continues."

"There might have been a few more," Rachel grinned.

"Okay, well I think I've already picked up on the pattern so let me ask you this, did you cheat on any of them?"

"First tell me what the pattern is," Rachel insisted.

"I would, but then I'd have to tell people *you* go to therapy... and not the physical kind."

"So you're a psychologist," she smiled. "I would have guessed a comedian, because you're so, fuckin', funny!" Rachel playfully yelled, an inch from my nose.

I smiled and kissed her before she withdrew.

"No, get away from me... a-hole."

"Does everyone laugh when you yell at them, because I've got to tell you, it's freakin' adorable. Come here, let me eat that fassa." I tried pinching Rachel's cheeks like a grandmother would, but she slapped my hands away.

"Fine, I'll go for the other ones," I said, lowering my hands.

Rachel grabbed hold of my wrists. "You wish, *Doctor*."

"All right, I give up," I submitted.

Rachel placed my hands on my lap and let go. I then closed my eyes, extended my face, and puckered my lips.

"Plant it, sugar!" I opened one eye. "Smooch me, baby. Smooch me goodl!"

"You're so shtoopid," Rachel laughed.

I closed my eyes and made my kissing face again, waiting for Rachel's lips to greet mine. The second they did, I quit the act, pushed her hair behind her neck, slid my right leg between her thighs and passionately kissed her. Every question, comment, and answer disappeared, as the moment spoke for itself.

"Okay, now I have no idea what we were talking about," Rachel smiled, visibly in a daze.

"Oh, um, I…" My brain was equally off track. "Cheating!" I remembered. "I asked if you've ever cheated on any of your one million boyfriends."

"Oh, no, never," Rachel answered, soon backpedaling. "Well.. kinda."

"No, never? Well, kinda? If this is another loophole, because I'm an expert in the category," I admitted. "What are we talking about here, different states, time zones, different guy but the same name, a leap year? What are we working with?"

"I wasn't working with any of that," Rachel said, rather disgusted. "Now I know what to ask you about though."

Way to go, shit for brains.

Rachel continued. "The summer after my junior year, I went on a Teen Tour to Israel. My boyfriend at the time was with me, but I met this other guy on the trip that I really liked. We started talking a lot, one thing led to another, and we hooked up."

"So you kissed," I insinuated.

"No, I blew him in front of the Western Wall," Rachel sarcastically answered.

"I hope that's not the note you left."

Rachel quickly punched me.

"What?" I laughed, getting right back into it. "Did you tell the guy you referred to as your boyfriend, but probably only knew for a week, that you got to first base with another guy?"

"Nope, I broke up with him and then made the new guy my new boyfriend," she smirked.

"Wow," I said laughing. "Spoken like a true guy."

"So when was your last relationship?" Rachel asked, turning the tides.

"High school," I answered.

"For how long?"

"Um, I'd say off and on for maybe a year."

"Why off and on?" Rachel grilled.

"Because I cheated on her like it was a hobby," I admitted, like a true guy.

"And you're proud of that?" Rachel asked, obviously not proud of me.

"No, but I thought I was the man in high school. I did whatever I wanted, and I didn't care if anyone got hurt," I explained.

"Elaborate, please."

I paused for a moment, hesitant to open the door to my past.

"What if I just say I was a fuck up and a bit of an asshole? Does that work for you?" I hoped.

"Nope, too vague. Out with it," she demanded.

I paused once again.

Rachel and I were very open with one another. I mean, she had just told me she was a virgin, but that was actually part of the problem, her innocence. I almost raised an eyebrow after hearing about her past relationships, but I could tell there wasn't a drop of malicious blood in her body. That, of course, meant I was going to come off looking like a complete scumbag.

"I'm waiting, dude."

I paused one more time before take off.

"All right, before I tell any stories, I just want you to know I'm no longer the person you're going to hear about. Hopefully you'll realize that on your own, but if you have any doubts, trust me when I say there's no way I'd be at PC, sitting next to you, in a library nonetheless, if I continued acting the way I did."

"Okay, now I'm excited," Rachel said, practically at the edge of her seat. "Let's hear it."

Ah, fuck it, I thought. I'd rather be called an asshole than a liar.

"Well, when I was a freshman in high school, my brother was a senior, which was awesome but also the beginning of my demise. He went to Catholic school his first three years, but left so he could play soccer with his childhood friends, at least that's what he says. He really slept with this hotshot basketball player's girlfriend, and started a war. That's neither here nor there, though. What I'm trying to get at is I partied from the get go, and it only magnified with every year."

"So you'd hang out with your brother a lot," Rachel summarized, wanting me to speed it up.

"Senior parties, drinking before school, Gellen University bars; it wasn't anything *that* crazy, but as a freshman, I thought it was the coolest shit in the world, as was I."

"Yeah, that's great and all, but get to the good stuff," Rachel joked.

"All right, I'm obviously walking on eggshells," I said. "Why don't I just throw a few at you and you can take your pick."

"I like that," she smiled.

"Okay, here we go; I cheated on my girlfriend constantly to make her feel like shit, make myself feel cool, and ultimately because I thought it was fun. My senior year of high school, I started taking drugs, which carried over to URI, which led to an overdose of cocaine and cough syrup. There was the night my friend was driving drunk and we wrapped his car around a tree at a hundred miles per hour, and at one point I essentially ran away from home and spent two weeks in the penthouse suite of an Atlantic City hotel, mooching off of my driving buddy and enjoying the occasional ecstasy trip. Oh, and I've been arrested."

Have you ever heard a potential love interest tell you they used to be an unfaithful, reckless admirer of drugs and alcohol that had to check in with their probation officer once a month? No? You've never met that guy? Well Rachel just did, and her eyes forgot to blink.

"I want to hear more about the girlfriend," she said, snapping to. "Were you in love?"

I should have known.

"Um, at the time I thought we were," I said, feeling like we reached cruising altitude. "I was young, though. I had no idea what love was. Three years later, I still don't. But I like to think I would never treat anyone I really love the way I treated her."

Well said, Jonathan.

"So how many girls did you cheat on her with?" Rachel asked.

Ladies and gentlemen, the Captain has just turned on the 'Fasten Your Seatbelts' sign. Please return your seats and trays to the upright position as we may experience some heavy turbulence.

"Like six or seven," I ballparked.

"Six or seven!" Rachel loudly repeated.

"Well, if it matters, I had a thing for one of the girls," I said, attempting to rationalize.

"Um, absolutely not," Rachel shot down.

"I told you, I was a dick. I'd like to say I admitted it because my conscience was eating at me, but that was hardly the case. I would wait until I was drunk, drugged out, and/or pissed off, and then tell her."

"Why would she ever get back together with you?" Rachel asked, rather disgusted.

I looked at her and smiled.

"Oh, g-d! Don't make me throw up."

"I don't know," I laughed. "We were in *love*, remember?"

"Right," Rachel ignored, shaking her head.

"You don't understand though, a lot of backlash came with telling her," I continued. "Crazy, fucked up, I belong in a straight coat, type backlash."

"Like what?" Rachel asked, moving forward in her seat.

"Well, getting back together didn't happen in a day, so during that in-between period, she went off her rocker. She keyed the car of the girl I had a thing for, causing her to buy all new side paneling, and later, she ran her off the road in their development. If you can believe it, they literally lived next door to each other. Well, their houses were mansions, so they weren't exactly three feet apart, but parking your car in the driveway next to your girlfriend's is still too close for comfort," I said, remembering the nights. "Crazy's mom also got in on the action. She randomly saw the girl at a Bar Mitzvah and started cursing her out with a butter knife in hand."

"Oh my g-d!" Rachel exclaimed. "This sounds like something out of a soap opera."

"Oh, there's more," I confessed. "With her preferred weapon of choice, the car, she tried hitting me on two separate occasions. The first attempt was more of a swerve, but it was close enough for my body to break the side-view mirror. The second time was in a parking lot while I was standing on the guardrail of my friend's trunk. I must have been wearing red, because she floored it at me, only to brake at the last second as I jumped and landed on the hood of her car. It was very Jackie Chan," I arrogantly smiled.

"And she was the only girlfriend you had?"

"Yep."

"I can see why," Rachel muttered.

"It's okay, that was my practice relationship. As it turns out, you're *not* supposed to cheat on your girlfriend. And now I know that," I smiled again.

"You didn't know that before?" Rachel asked, baffled by the relationship retard sitting before her.

"Um, I'd heard things," I patronized. "But you can't always believe everything you hear… unless I'm saying it."

"Whatever you say," Rachel dismissed. "Anyway, I don't want to know about the drunk driving accident, because you're just an idiot for that."

"I wasn't driving," I interrupted.

"It doesn't matter. You're just as dumb for getting in the car," she pointed out, much like my mother.

"There were actually three of us in the car, and I didn't tell you the outcome." Rachel's face went blank so I quickly continued. "I'm not going to turn this into a joke, no one died. But I don't want a lecture, either. The driver lost control, my side of the car was about to smack a tree, but somehow we spun around at the last second and hit on his side. Thankfully I had my seatbelt on, so I was able to walk out of the car with a few cuts and bruises, along with my friend sitting behind me, but the driver was knocked unconscious, pried out with the Jaws of Life, and air-lifted to the hospital."

"You guys are morons," Rachel confessed, without muttering.

"You're right, we were," I admitted. "But like most lessons in life, you learn from your mistakes."

"Can you imagine if you hit someone? Like, what if you killed a family?" Rachel brought up, too reprehensive for my liking.

"Again, I'm not looking for a lecture. I've been through every scenario in my head and I know what we did was wrong. Maybe you didn't believe me when I told you I was a fuck up, but regardless, I'd like to put the story to bed." I was visibly starting to get worked up and Rachel could tell.

"I'll drop it," she said, still disappointed with me.

"Great, because however you slice it, what we did that day we did to ourselves. It's the other shit that bothers me," I stated, with much aggravation. "I run into people from high school now, people I used to walk all over and treat like crap, and if I end up talking to them I always leave the conversation feeling like the worst person in the world. What makes it worse is these are people I probably would have gotten along with and hung out with if I wasn't such an asshole.

It was official. My ramblings had opened Pandora's box and Rachel appeared speechless.

"Now do you see why I was so hesitant to talk about everything?" I asked, fishing for a response. "I've barely open this can of fuck up and you already look like you want to bolt for the door."

"Trust me, I don't think you're a fuck up or an asshole," Rachel calmly began, already lowering my heart rate. "This is going to sound very cliché, but what's in the past is in the past. You obviously needed to make a change in your life, and *thankfully*, it seems like you have," she smiled. "Now, come here."

I leaned in and Rachel kissed each cheek, followed by her soft lips on mine. I instantly slowed down and started smiling again. In a pleasant twist of Fate, I became the one seeing her in a new and even more inviting light.

"Do you think you would have liked me if I went to your high school?" Rachel asked.

"Who says I like you now?"

I'm back!

"Yeah right," Rachel laughed. "I know you like me. Come on, admit it."

"Fine, maybe this much," I said, raising my hands and holding them an inch apart.

"More like this much," Rachel scoffed, separating them to about three feet.

"That's it?" I humored.

"Yeah, you're right." Rachel got out of her chair and made me do the same. She raised my arms and fully extended them so

I was touching opposite walls. "There," she smiled.

"Is that better?" I asked.

"You tell me."

"Nope," I said, shaking my head. "Believe it or not, my arms aren't big enough."

Before I could see Rachel blush, she stepped into my inviting hug and wrapped her arms around me. "Good answer," she whispered.

Rachel and I grew up just twenty minutes apart, yet we lived very different lives. I could name towns, parks, malls, schools, and tons of other places on Long Island, where Rachel would look at me like I was talking about a foreign country. Mostly due to her religion, it was as if she'd been living on an island within an island, and I couldn't understand how it didn't bother her. That is, until I spent two hours in a six by six room with Rachel, and realized life is always going to be about who, and not what, makes you happy.

Mother We Just Can't Get Enough

Close your books, cash them in for a dollar seventy-five, exhale, unclench your butt cheeks, stop snorting *Adderrall*, open a beer, try to get laid one last time, and then get the fuck out of D.C. because finals are over! Not only that, but Rachel and I aced every one! Straight A's for her, straight bullshit for me. She actually did extremely well, earning her academic scholarship for the following school year, whereas I did just well enough to earn eligibility for the following soccer season (pending the results of summer school). The only thing left to do was pack, and un-pact.

According to the relationship papers we signed in April, our contract was no longer valid. We had become so close since then that it really shouldn't have mattered, but Rachel and I are two very stubborn personalities. Her way of tackling the problem was to continuously drop lines and hope I'd say something, while my method was to ignore the issue and hope she'd address it.

Admittedly, a small percentage feared rejection. This is until Rachel and I went to get ice cream one night, and she told me it didn't matter whether I got vanilla or chocolate, because our relationship was over in a few days anyway. I figured I'd leave the ball in her court after that one. Besides, I had bigger gefilte fish to fry... her parents.

"How long till they get here?" I asked.

Rachel and I were sitting on the stoop of Pokehole's neighboring building, an abnormal distance apart.

"Any minute now," Rachel answered, checking her watch.

"You know, I showered today."

"What?" Rachel asked, obviously distracted.

"I said I showered today."

"Congratulations," she ignored.

"Meaning I don't smell, Rachel. Meaning I'm so fresh and so clean, clean. Meaning you don't have to pretend I'm a New York City cab driver."

Neither would admit it, but we were both fairly nervous. It was harder to tell with me because I used sarcasm and humor as a defense mechanism, whereas Rachel wore her emotions on her sleeve, but internally we shared the same level of anxiety. The roots of our concern, however, were quite different. Rachel didn't want her parents to find out I was more than a friend. If somehow they did, she definitely didn't want them finding out I wasn't Jewish. I, on the other hand, just wanted to make a good impression.

"Do your parents know I'm helping you move, or are you going to pretend you ran into me?" I asked.

"They know," Rachel said, peering down the street.

"What'd you tell them?"

"Um, a friend is going to help me move," she sarcastically answered, avoiding details.

"I meant are they aware of the benefits I receive with this position?"

"No! And you better not say anything," Rachel snapped.

"I won't, but I've got to tell you, it's not going to be easy hiding this kind of chemistry. I mean, we're practically sitting on different sides of campus and you could still cut the sexual tension with a knife."

"Clearly you're drunk," Rachel scoffed. "Although I am interested to see how you'll act around them."

"Why's that?" I wondered.

"You can cut the sexual tension with a knife. There's too much chemistry to hide. Blah, blah, blah... *bullshit!*" Rachel laughed.

"I'm sorry, was that supposed to be me?" I smiled.

Rachel stood up and relocated, practically in my ear when she sat down again.

"This confident, too cool for school, sarcastic soccer guy, is going to turn into a polite, shy, please and thank you, little boy." Rachel made herself laugh again.

"Is that right?"

"Dat's right!" she yelled.

"Well..."

"*Well*," Rachel repeated, purposely interrupting me.

I turned towards Rachel and stamped my forehead against hers. "*Well*, I think you're too scared to tell your parents about us," I said, calling her out.

"Oh really?"

"Not only that, but I think you're also too scared to kiss me right now... with your tongue!"

"Am not," Rachel said, pretending to be a preschool badass.

"Prove it," I smiled.

Rachel leaned back and pretended to yawn, glancing down the street to make sure she was in the clear.

"Smooth," I laughed.

She dove in and kissed me. Seconds later...

"Oh, shit!" Rachel pushed my chest with both hands, nearly sending me down the stairs.

Wouldn't you know it, but just as Rachel and I were getting all hot and heavy, her car pulled up directly across the street. A very large Mexican man stepped out and walked towards the meter.

"That's your dad?" I asked, very confused. "I thought you said he looks like Al Borlin?"

"That's not my dad. It's our driver, Jesús. My parents are probably right behind him though." Rachel got up and stood along the sidewalk.

"You have your own driver? That's pretty... wait a minute, his name is Jesús!" I couldn't help but laugh at the irony.

"I know, I know," Rachel said, too frazzled to deal with me, or a joke she'd heard six hundred times. "Let's go."

"Hi, Jesús. How was the drive?" Rachel asked.

"Oh, hi sweetie." Jesús turned around and swung at us with his stomach. "Do I need to put any dinero in the meter?" he Spanglished.

"No, not on weekends," Rachel answered, instructing me with her eyes not to laugh.

"Muy perfecto."

"This is Jonathan," Rachel introduced.

I reached over a mountain of a belly to shake the end of a dinosaur-like hand. "It's nice to meet you."

"Ah, so tú es el Jonathan helping us move," Jesús stated, in illegal alien

"That's me," I smiled, amazingly keeping my composure.

"Vamos while you still can. Su madre es already driving me up a wall."

Yeah, because you could get up a wall.

"I know!" Rachel exclaimed. "She's called me like twenty times since you guys left."

"So, how do you want to haga esto?" Jesús questioned, in landscaper lingo. "Yo tengo miedo to touch anything before su madre gets here. She'll chew mi cabeza off if I move the wrong thing."

That's because your cabeza is actually a watermelon, fat boy.

"Don't worry about it," Rachel resolved. "We'll bring stuff down and you can load it into the car."

"Perfecto."

Rachel and I left the piñata where he was and went up to her room.

"What do you want to say, shtoopid?"

"What makes you think I have something to say?" I smiled.

"Aside from the shit-eating grin on your face, when don't you have something to say?"

"Good point," I laughed. "However, I have a feeling this is only going to get better, so I'll wait for more material."

"You do that."

Rachel was visibly irritated.

"Would you like a hug?" I asked.

"Stop."

"What, you think he saw us kissing?"

"Yes!" Rachel growled.

"And that's why you're mad?"

"I'm not mad," she lied.

"Fine, you're like a happy Oscar the Grouch," I corrected.

"You don't understand. Jesús is the family gossip. And in case you haven't noticed, he likes talking shit."

"All right, let's not overreact. You don't know for sure that he saw us. He could have been working on his eighth chimichanga when he pulled up. Plus, you should be focusing on what's important, or at least what's funny. In a large family of Orthodox Jews, *Jesús* is the gossip!" I pointed out.

Rachel nearly cracked, but held it together long enough to continue her hissy fit.

"I'm mad at you," she claimed, attempting a storm out... then coming right back. "Can you take those bins down?"

With great amusement, I grabbed the plastic containers and met Rachel in the elevator.

"All right, I get it, you're focused, you've got your game face on, we can talk later. I just want you to know my family is as quirky as the next. I mean, look at me, how normal could we be?"

"Why, do all of you rhyme?" Rachel asked.

"Was that a joke? Did you just make a joke?" I shouted.

Rachel reluctantly smiled. "I just want this to be over."

The two of us made a few more trips between the car and her department store, unloading seasons-worth of inventory and moving at a good pace. Everything seemed to be under control, until the supervisor showed up.

"Hello?"

An older, but certainly not old, version of Rachel was standing at the door. She was dressed very prim and proper with a blouse and long skirt on, matched to a white, oversized *Louis Vuitton* bag.

"Hi, I'm Rachel's mom," she said.

"It's nice to meet you." I spastically rocked back and forth contemplating a handshake. "I'm Jon."

"Is Rachel here?"

"I'm right here, Mom."

Rachel walked out of the closet. Mother greeted her with a big hug and a kiss. It was very cute, even more so because she wouldn't let go.

"Eileen!" Rachel barked, through the arms of her mom's bear hug.

"One more minute. I haven't seen you in so long."

Rachel broke free. "I'm not four, Mom."

"Wow." Eileen was immediately distracted by the appearance of Rachel's room. "This place looks like a war zone! Jon, thank you so much for helping."

"Oh, you're welcome!" I overanxiously shouted.

"Did you finish packing?" she asked me.

"No, but it shouldn't take long. I just stuff everything in a few bags and I'm set."

"Are your parents picking you up?" Eileen continued.

I could hear Rachel stop what she was doing to listen in. "My dad should be here soon," I answered.

"Oh, okay. That's nice."

Actually, it was kind of fucked up. The only reason my dad came to D.C. was to take my belongings home, not me. A few days earlier, I told my parents I'd be staying past finals. I said I'd be crashing at a friend's apartment, also from Long Island, and we'd drive home at a later date. All of it was true; it was just a very vague version of the truth.

The "friend's" apartment I'd be staying at was Rachel's. Yes, she was moving out of Pokehole, but at the same time she was also moving in to next year's new apartment, off-campus. It's called, lying by omission, my friends. And apparently it's contagious, because Rachel did the same thing with her parents. They even drove her car down to leave at PC, because they were under the assumption she was flying back with friends. Okay, that one may have been a straight lie, and I may or may not have orchestrated this ingenious plan, but truth be told, Rachel needed it. She needed a story, she needed an adventure, and she even needed to get in a little trouble. After all, if you don't crack your shell, how are you supposed to come out of it?

"I'm sure Jonathan doesn't talk to his mother this way."

"And I'm sure Jonathan's mother isn't a pain in the ass like you are!"

It took less than ten minutes for me to see why Rachel wanted this ordeal to be over with.

"Well, maybe if you were more organized, I wouldn't have to ask so many questions." Eileen spoke in an eerily calm voice. "You can't find anything in this mess."

Rachel was not as subdued. "Holy shit! I swear to g-d, if you don't stop talking, I'm kicking you out."

"Do you see what I have to deal with, Jon? Do you hear how she talks to me?"

Awkkkkwaaaard.

I pretended to laugh, but then foolishly said the first thing that came to mind. "Rachel, be nice to your mother."

Uh-oh.

Rachel slowly turned around, spinning her head one hundred and eighty degrees and stabbing me with her eyes. I kept my mouth shut after that.

"Is Dad downstairs?" Rachel asked her mother.

"He's with Jesús."

I quickly buried my chin in my chest and tried not to laugh. Rachel saw me though, and threw an elbow at my ribs on her way to the door.

"I'm leaving. If I stay here any longer, I'm going to jump out the window," Rachel exaggerated.

"Take the elevator, honey."

I involuntarily chuckled, quickly trying to cover it up. Eileen heard me though, and smiled in my direction. "*Such* a drama queen," she added.

I pretended to laugh again and then picked up whatever was in front of me. "I should probably bring this down," I announced.

"Good idea," she said, still smirking. "Thanks again, Jon."

"Oh, you're welcome."

Rachel was standing in the hallway waiting for the elevator. I set the box down, put my arms around her, and kissed her forehead.

"Deep breaths, cutie. Deep breaths."

"She's just *so* annoying!" Rachel groaned.

"She's not that bad," I said, attempting to keep the peace. "She means well."

"Then you live with her!" Rachel shouted.

Hmmm.

Rachel quickly raised her elbow, knowing exactly what I was thinking.

"I didn't say it!" I flinched, also laughing at how cute she looked when she was angry. "You're getting worked up about packing," I said, trying to point out the insignificance. "*Packing.* Who gives a shit? You're wound too tight, cutie. You need to let things roll off your back more. Come here," I smiled. "Let me feel your toosh." I moved my hand down Rachel's back.

"No, get away from me." Rachel didn't want me to see her laugh, so she headed for the stairs.

"What? I want to see if you're clenching." I picked the box up and followed her.

Rachel yelled back to me. "You're not funny, shtoopid!"

"I don't think you can say that when you're laughing, but I do have some walnuts I'd like you to open. Can I borrow your tuckus?"

Rachel stopped and turned around, thankfully with a smile. "First, the only nuts I'll be cracking are yours, and second, how do you know the word, tuckus?"

I waited until I caught up to her to answer. "I look forward to the nut cracking, and I feel like it's somewhat of a common word. Why?" I wondered.

"Because it's Yiddish."

"Fuck!"

"What's wrong?" Rachel asked.

"My phone's vibrating. It's definitely my dad."

"You're not going to answer it?"

"I'll call back after we go to the car," I said, somewhat disappointed.

As Rachel and I made our way outside, I completely forgot I hadn't met her father yet. That is until a man bearing a striking resemblance to Tim the Toolman Taylor's sidekick approached us.

"Hey, honey." Rachel's father hugged her and gave her a kiss on the forehead.

"Hi, Daddy."

"How's everything, sweetie?"

Rachel's body language answered for her.

"Is your mom driving you crazy?" he presumed.

"Yes!" Rachel exclaimed.

"I'll come back up with you," he laughed. "Do I need to sign in?"

Um, hello? Random guy standing next to you.

"Nah, you should be fine. There are too many parents

around for them to care."

"Is there more stuff to bring down?" her father asked.

Seriously? Am I actually invisible to Jewish fathers?

"Not too much," Rachel answered. "It's mostly clothes, but Mom is making it out to be the biggest project in the world."

"That sounds about right," he added.

Maybe I'll just start saying the Our Father. Will that do it? Huh? Will randomly saying the Lord's Prayer get your attention? Okay, here we go. Our...

"Dad, this is Jon."

"Hi, how are you?" I practically yelled at the man.

"I'm well," he said, shaking my hand. "Thanks for helping."

"Oh, it's no problem," I announced, returning to a normal volume.

My pocket started vibrating again.

"Here, let me take that." I offered Rachel my barely extended hand and took the hangers she was carrying. "I'll be right back," I said, rushing to the car. I impatiently dropped everything at Jesús' morbidly fat and lazy feet, before answering my phone on its last ring.

"Hey, what's up?"

"Jon?"

"Yeah."

"It's Dad."

For reasons I cannot fathom, my dad always asks for verification when he calls. I mean I know his number, his name literally appears right next to it, and I'd like to think he's aware of both these facts, yet he never fails. It's like he thinks we're using two tomato cans and a piece of string. Better than that... conversations on *AIM*.

ThePstOfficeRcks: Jon?

ThePstOfficeRcks: Dad.

Soccerisneat24: Dad?

Soccerisneat24: Jon.

ThePstOfficeRcks: Jon? Are you there?

Soccerisneat24: Yes, Dad. Please start talking.

"Hi, *Dad*," I emphasized, hopefully ending the confusion. "Are you here?"

"Yes. I'm in front of your building. Where are you?"

"I'll be back in two minutes," I said, omitting the answer.

"I called you five minutes ago, why didn't you pick up?" he asked.

"Right. I'll be there in two minutes."

"I'm not waiting here forever," Michael Reynolds added.

"Okay. Bye." I hung up the phone, ready to cross the street again, until I saw Rachel on her way over.

"Was that your dad?" she asked.

"Yeah, he's here."

Rachel made her puppy dog face. "Please don't leave me with the big scary lady."

"Aww, you'll be fine, cutie. Call me whenever."

"*Okay*," she playfully whimpered.

I instinctively went to kiss her.

"No don't kiss me!" Rachel ordered. "Daddy's watching."

"What should I do then, pat you on the shoulder?"

"Yeah, because that won't look weird."

"Did he say anything about me?" I wondered.

Rachel hesitated before answering. "No."

"Wow, I really hope you lied better than that to your parents. Come on, what'd he say?"

"I'll tell you later," Rachel said, pushing it aside.

"Was it the eyebrow ring?" I asked, not letting go.

"Would you get out of here. Your dad's waiting."

"Fine." I quickly faked like I was going to kiss Rachel, causing her to stumble backwards. Amused enough, I left.

Less than an hour later, I stood in my empty dorm room, looking back and smiling at an incredible ten months of Presidents College. My father, who probably just thought I was high, had never seen anyone so happy about packing. I, on the hand, wishing I were high, had never seen myself so happy about a girl

I stepped into the hallway to answer Rachel's call.

"Hey, cutie. How you holding up?"

"I miss you," she whined. "Come to Food Street."

Food Street is the main dining area on campus, conveniently located just steps from where I lived.

"Are you by yourself?" I asked.

"No, I'm still with my parents... and Jesús," she muttered. "They wanted *Starbucks*. I told them I was running to the bookstore."

I sighed like it was an inconvenience, even though I would have ran to pointless New Jersey and back just to see her. "I'll meet you on the ramp."

"Yay!" Rachel cheered. "Okay, hurry. Go, go, go!"

I walked back into my room and picked up two large soccer bags. "Dad, can I get the keys?"

My father was busy taking down the television. "Here," he said, throwing them to me in classic sitcom fashion.

I hauled ass out the door and down the stairs, rushing to get in an extra minute with Rachel. When I closed the trunk, I saw her standing near the bottom of the ramp, bouncing up and down and waving. I ran to her. I mean I physically ran to her like we were filming part of a cheesy love scene. I bent down and gave her a hug, lifting her in the air as I straightened my back.

"You missed me already?" I smiled.

Rachel nodded her head and gave me a kiss.

"I missed you, too." I said, setting her feet back on the ground.

"Okay, gotta go!" Rachel faked like she was going to run away.

"That's it?" I laughed.

"Well they were already ordering when I left. My dad's going to be like, 'What'd you do, write a book while you were there?'"

Rachel's impressions always made me laugh. She used the same deep voice for everyone, while adding a Brooklyn accent to the mix.

"I'm staying at the hotel with my parents tonight, so I'll call you before we check in," Rachel said.

"Please do," I begged. "I'm going to be bored out of my mind without a television. Although the internet still works, and I do have my laptop with me, so…"

"Eww, but no time for that," Rachel dismissed. "Do you want to come to *Best Buy* with me and Eileen tomorrow? You can help us pick out stuff for the new apartment."

"What about your dad?" I asked.

"He's flying back in the morning. My mom's going home with Jesús whenever we finish."

I instinctively smiled.

"You're so annoying," Rachel said, shaking her head, trying not to join in.

"Sorry, I'm going to have a hard time with that one," I

admitted. "Anyway, don't you think your mom's going to be a little suspicious about our situation? I'm pretty sure she thinks I'm leaving today."

"Yeah, probably, but whatever," Rachel downplayed. "When you left I told her you're also staying in D.C. to hang out with friends."

"In that case, I'm in!" I was floored to see Rachel acting on impulsive. "It'll give me a chance to actually talk to your mom instead of making retarded laughing noises."

"Okay good. I call you in morning. We pick you up. Jesús go, vroom vroom, and we buy stuff," Rachel weirdly announced, sounding like a *Benihana* waitress (Pork Fri Ri? Cost you extra).

"Before you go, tell me what your dad said."

Rachel smiled. "It's nothing bad."

"Then let's hear it."

Rachel briefly rolled her eyes and then came out with it. "The second you walked across the street to put the boxes in the car, my dad just looked at me and said, 'Who's the goy?'"

"Who's the guy? That's not very funny," I stated.

"No, the goy. Who's the *goy*," Rachel repeated, getting another laugh out of it.

"I don't understand. Did he say the word, guy, but with a Hebrew accent, or did he abbreviate the word, goiter?"

"Yeah, he abbreviated the word goiter," Rachel sarcastically answered. "He referred to you as a large protrusion of the thyroid gland."

"So then he was making fun of my height?" I continued.

"No, idiot. Goy is a Yiddish word. It means gentile. You know what a gentile is, right?"

"Yeah... a tall, ugly, football-shaped gland protrusion!"

Rachel snapped, taking me seriously. "No, you idiot!"

"I'm just messing with you," I laughed. "A gentile's someone who isn't Jewish, but it's really your word for Catholic folk. Like Jesús would call me a gringo, but you'd say I'm a gentile."

"More or less," Rachel admitted. "But hey, at least Mitch and Eileen know of you now. I'm willing to bet you've never even mentioned my name to your parents."

"Names are so trivial… Rachel."

"That makes me feel better."

"I'm only kidding," I smiled. "I'm waiting until I get home to tell Jacquelyn Theresa and Michael Charles about you."

"What are you going to tell them?" Rachel asked, quickly adding, "How we're not together anymore."

All right, that's it. Give me the ball back.

"I was thinking I'd tell them I've fallen for you," I said. "In which case, I was thinking I'd tell you I don't want this to end."

Rachel curled into a little ball like she normally did when I made her blush. I had no idea where it came from, but I spoke so effortlessly, it was as if the words had been there for months.

"I have a boyfriend, I have a boyfriend." Rachel sang the words.

"Just don't make me part of the pattern," I added.

"I won't," she smiled. "Now catch me."

"What?"

"Catch me," she said again.

I held my arms out and Rachel collapsed into them.

"Very cute," I smiled.

"Since formal," she whispered.

I bent down and kissed her.

"Okay, now I really have to go." Rachel took her phone out. "Yep, that's my dad."

"Okay, go ahead. I'll talk to you later."

"By the way, what kind of car do you have?" Rachel asked.

"A blue jeep," I answered, rather confused. "Why?"

"Because your dad's been watching us the whole time."

I quickly spun around and there he was, Michael Rennie, my father, leaning against the hood of our jeep, throwing me a wave. By the time I turned back around, Rachel was halfway up the ramp, laughing her ass off.

"I guess you'll have to tell them sooner than you thought!" she yelled over her shoulder.

I was frozen. My shoes morphed into cement blocks. It had nothing to do with what was behind me, but everything to do with who was in front of me. As Rachel skipped away, I pieced together our love scene and realized this is what I've been waiting for, a love that looks and sounds like the movies.

Best Days

The first time I stepped foot on PC's campus happened three weeks after I stepped foot on Freeport's. My friends and I had a buddy who went to PC, so one impulsive weekend we decided to take a road trip to the District of Columbia. I had no idea what to expect from President's College, but truthfully, I didn't give a shit what it had to offer me as far as education and aesthetics went. All I cared about was going out, getting drunk, and getting laid... the usual. As we drove around campus though, I couldn't help but open my eyes a little wider. The housing, the parks, the girls, the monuments, the girls, even the fuckin' cherry blossoms, all led to this collective portrait of attractiveness. As we sat on the balcony of my friend's apartment, barbequing, funneling beers from the floor above and watching planes land through the sunset, I knew exactly where I wanted to be.

Two years later, I consciously found myself in that same building. I may have been looking over a different balcony, but I was doing so as a Presidents College Patriot. My days of being a *JeanCo Jean*, *Marlboro Light*, or whatever the fuck Freeport Community College called itself, were over. They undoubtedly served as my bridge, and I am forever grateful, but I stood along the edge of Rachel's new apartment smiling with optimism, smiling at how far I'd come, and smiling at how far we could go.

As expected, Rachel's apartment was stunning. She lived in a two bedroom/two bathroom on the eleventh floor, room #1111. Generic was her roommate. The views were anything but. A draw of the curtains revealed illuminated shots of The Capitol Building and The Washington Monument, while inside there was enough room to host an extravagant cocktail party. The cuisine, however, would be specific.

In case you're wondering, PC does not allow students to move off campus until after their sophomore year. But, in the wacky world of college, things happen where a student feels like their living situation is negatively affecting their social and academic experience. Against their will, they can be forced to dorm with someone who has a severe flatulence problem, masturbates chronically, menstruates abnormally, is a whore, is a manwhore, takes pictures of you while you sleep, snores like a freight train, or just plain old thinks Ashton Kutcher is funny. Complaints and requests are directed to on-campus housing, and they ultimately decide whether or not you're a whiny bitch, a bullshit artist, or someone in need of genuine help. In most situations, questioning will take place and proof will be asked for, but there is one circumstance that generally goes untouched... religion.

A tremendous part of Orthodox Judaism is keeping kosher. This particular form of dining is very important, and very specific, but when you live with those of different values, it quickly becomes difficult to maintain. Without a kosher kitchen, it's nearly impossible to happily eat the way one (Orthodox Jew) should. Taking out and ordering in become a necessity (now considered forms of Jewish cooking). Not only that, but the kosher world involves several rules, restrictions, and religious meaning. To better educate myself, Rachel suggested I drive to

127

her hometown and speak with her rabbi. I opted for the route of *Wikipedia*, but in my head the journey would have sounded like this...

Jon: "Shalom, Rabbi Knay... del... ach? Wow, that's not easy to say."

Rabbi: "Knaydelach. It's Yiddish. It means, dumpling."

Jon: "Can I just call you Rabbi Dumpling then?"

Rabbi: "Not at all. What can I do for you, Jonathan?"

Jon: "Well Rabbi, I was walking through town earlier, looking for a bite to eat... wait, how'd you know my name?"

Rabbi: "It's on your jacket."

Jon: "Oh, right. Anyway, I was walking down Middle Neck Road, craving a little Chinese, when I couldn't help notice that nearly all the eateries in town are kosher. There were kosher pizza places, kosher bakeries, kosher delis, and lo and behold, a kosher Chinese food restaurant called, Dreydl & Woks."

Rabbi: "Dreydl & Woks! Great fri ri."

Jon: "The thing is, when I sat down to order my usual dish, shrimp with lobster sauce, I couldn't find it on the menu. In fact, I couldn't find any shellfish on the menu."

Rabbi: "So what'd you order?"

Jon: "I went with some spring rolls, a nice bowl of wonton soup, and a large plate of pepper steak. The portions are great."

Rabbi: "I know, right? By the time I get to my szechuan beef, I'm stuffed."

Jon: "Rabbi!"

Rabbi: "I'm sorry, I didn't eat lunch today. Please, go on."

Jon: "I guess I'm just confused about kosher food. It didn't taste bad, but it wasn't anything to write home about, either. Different would be the best way to describe it."

Rabbi: "You see, Jonathan, in Judaism, the Torah, which is actually the first five books of the Bible..."

Jon: "Really? Get out of town."

Rabbi: "I can't, it's the Sabbath."

Jon: "That's not bad, Rabbi. That's not bad at all."

Rabbi: "If you think that's funny, you should have heard me at Steven Kirshenbaum's Bar Mitzvah. His great grandfather laughed so hard he broke his cane... then his hip."

Jon: "Killer stuff, my friend."

Rabbi: "Almost! Sorry, I'm on a challah roll. Anyway, the Torah contains six hundred and thirteen mitzvot, or commandments. Within several of those mitzvot are clear instructions on what food can and cannot be eaten. However, there are also some that are not very clear, which rabbis have made changes to over the years. Herein lies the debate over traditional and modern beliefs. Basically, keeping kosher means following Jewish dietary laws, and that includes eating the proper food, and the food being properly prepared."

Jon: "Right. I don't know if that did it for me, Rabbi."

Rabbi: "I'll elaborate. The Torah tells us which animals we're *not* allowed to eat, pig being one of them."

Jon: "No bacon!"

Rabbi: "I know. I've heard good things."

Jon: "They're all true."

Rabbi: "Now, the reason you couldn't order shrimp with lobster sauce is because shellfish is also a no-no. Fish must have both their fins and scales to be considered kosher. Before you jump in, I know... lobster!"

Jon: "Melted better. That's all I'm going to say, Rabbi."

Rabbi: "Moving on. The slaughtering of the animals has to be done according to kosher law. Someone called a shohet performs them, and the kill has to be quick and painless, meaning a slit to the throat. Hunted animals are forbidden."

Jon: "Easy, Rabbi. I just ate."

Rabbi: "In that case, brace yourself, because after the slaughter, someone called a bodek inspects the organs for abnormalities."

Jon: "Joe's Hats and Bo Derricks. Got it."

Rabbi: "*Sho-hets* and *Bo-deks*."

Jon: "I'm just joshin' ya, Rabbi. This temple's big enough for two funny guys."

Rabbi: "Save it for the church. After the slaughtering and inspection comes the nikkur, a special way of cutting the meat. Kosher butchers have to remove all non-kosher parts of the animal, which can be very tedious. There can be no traces of blood. Meat and poultry have to be soaked or salted."

Jon: "Something tells me kosher food costs more."

Rabbi: "Right you are my sarcastic gentile. We're almost done, though. On to the separation of milk and meat. This is pretty self-explanatory. Dairy products and meat products cannot be mixed, outside or inside of your body. That means you cannot eat a cheeseburger, nor could you eat a hamburger with a side of macaroni and cheese. Following?"

Jon: "I think so. That's pretty crazy though. I mean, do you switch off eating meat one day and dairy another? Like, what happens if you accidentally have a bowl of cereal on a meat day?"

Rabbi: "Seriously?"

Jon: "What?"

Rabbi: "There's a grace period between the two. As I mentioned earlier, depending on how modern or traditional you are, it can vary from one to six hours. For this reason, a kosher kitchen should have two sets of silverware, cookware, dishware, and even cups. One set is for milk, or milchig meals, and the other for meat, or fleishig meals."

Jon: "What about fruits and vegetables? What category do they fall under?"

Rabbi: "Foods that are neither meat nor dairy are called pareve, or parve. They are considered neutral, and can be eaten with either milk or meat."

Jon: "I've got to tell you, Rabbi, you're missing out on some seriously good food. No cheeseburgers, no bacon, egg, and cheese sandwiches, no ribs, no crab cakes, no shrimp, and yes, no lobster! Turf with no surf, Rabbi! That's just crazy talk."

Rabbi: "Well look at it this way, if someone like yourself, who has grown up eating as they pleased, had to make the switch to keeping kosher, I could see how it'd be difficult. But, for those of us who have been doing it our entire lives, it's not an issue. Keeping kosher requires effort, but it also forces us to stop and recognize our Jewish heritage every time we eat, shop, cook, or even look at a menu. It's this pause that makes us aware of our blessings."

Jon: "Wow, I'm not going to lie, that's pretty deep. During Christmas, Easter, and Thanksgiving, we say a prayer before we eat, but what you guys have going on is a whole other world. Like you were saying, it's different for me because I've been eating whatever I wanted my entire life, but I think if I grew up keeping kosher, I'd be very proud to have that everyday bond with my religion."

Rabbi: "Well said, Jonathan. Well said. Now, how about some ice cream? My treat."

Jon: "I'd like that. I'll meet you there in three hours."

Rabbi: "Oh, you're good. You... are... good. Steven

Kirshenbaum's grandfather wouldn't stand a chance."

Jon: "Thanks, Rabbi. One love."

Rabbi: "L'chei-im!"

With Rachel approved to move off campus, the keys to a new apartment in hand, classes complete, Jewish dietary laws understood, and no parents in the picture, it was time to enjoy our mini-vacation.

A typical day for Rachel and me consisted of waking up in the afternoon (we slept on an inflatable mattress), showering and getting ready together, walking to Georgetown in gorgeous, sunny weather, eating, Rachel shopping, visiting the monuments and other tourist locations, and going out to dinner or bringing it back to the apartment. Later, we would go to the movies or watch one on her portable DVD player, get involved in a little of this and that, and then curl up under the covers and wait to do it all over again. Love and simplicity, it doesn't get much better than that. Granted, neither of us actually said the words out loud, but on the inside it felt like we were screaming it.

In less than three months, Rachel and I had come a long way. None of it felt wrong or uncomfortable, but it was surprising how fast we were moving. Back when we first decided to be exclusive, I remember an acquaintance coming up to me at the gym and asking about our "relationship."

"Hey, what's going on?" Tool Kit asked.

"Not much," I said, seated on the mat stretching my hamstring.

"Are you going out tonight?"

"I think so," I said, looking towards the exit. "What about you?"

"Most likely," he returned.

"Cool."

"So… are you hooking up with Rachel?" Tool Kit randomly inquired.

"Um... yeah," I answered, wondering how that worked into the conversation.

"Oh, okay," Tool Kit muttered, implying something.

"Why do you ask?"

"I heard it through the grapevine, that's all. She used to go out with one of my friends, Ira Needyboy."

"Oh, okay," I imitated.

"I'm not sure you want to bark up that tree, just to give you a heads up."

I tried not to laugh because I knew exactly what Tool Kit was referring to. I wanted to hear him say it though.

"Why's that?" I asked.

"I don't know how long you guys have been together, or how serious you are, so I don't want to be a dick."

No, you're not a dick. You're a Tool, remember?

"Nah, it's cool," I downplayed. "Go ahead."

"To say you're wasting your time might be harsh, but you definitely have your work cut out for you. I just hope you're patient. She, like, never touched my boy and they were together for about five months, maybe more."

"You know what, I actually heard that... from Rachel," I snapped. "She told me he was hideous. Or did she say she found him repulsive? It was one or the other," I smiled, knowing full well I was indirectly talking to Ira Needyboy. "I think I'll take my chances buddy, but thanks for looking out."

"Yeah, no problem." Tool Kit definitely did not see that one coming.

I stood up and patted him on the shoulder. "How is your boy

these days? Rachel tells me he's in therapy," I added.

"Oh, uh, he's uh, he's fine," Tool Kit stammered, blindsided yet again.

"Cool. Send him my best."

On the last day of our little hiatus, while back in Rachel's apartment after shopping all afternoon, I collapsed on the air mattress and watched her happily change in and out of new clothes. At the end of the fashion show, before walking into the other room, Rachel ambushed me with a question of her own.

"Would you have sex with me?"

My initial response was to laugh, but I couldn't tell if she was being serious. Rachel made it sound like she wanted to know what my favorite color was, and then went into the kitchen for a bottle of water. When she returned, her demeanor was exactly the same.

"So?"

"Are you kidding?" I asked.

"No, I'm curious."

"Randomly, out of the clear blue sky, that's what you're curious about?" I smiled.

"Yep," she smiled back.

"Well..." I sat up, pausing for an abnormal amount of time. "I'm not sure."

Rachel forced herself to laugh. "Yeah right! You're telling me you wouldn't have sex with me?"

"I don't know," I said, unsure how to answer. "Your situation is different than most. I feel like it's a sensitive area, no pun intended."

"Bullshit!" Rachel erupted. "You'd fuck anything with a hole and a heartbeat."

"Hey now," I laughed. "I think maybe you need to calm..."

"I'm not saying I'm going to have sex with you, I just wanted to see what your reaction would be. Like, even if you did say yes, which you clearly did not, I wasn't going to pin you to the air mattress and fuck you," Rachel loudly announced.

"Because it would deflate?" I joked.

"You're an asshole."

"What?" I said, still laughing. "I just don't get it. Are you fishing for compliments or something?"

"Yeah, I'm fishing for compliments," she snapped. "Forget I said anything." Rachel began putting her clothes away, a task you wouldn't expect to be noisy, yet somehow sounded like a monster truck rally.

"You're obviously upset, so I think we should just drop it," I suggested.

"Wouldn't you be if it was the other way around? Don't you think it's a little insulting?"

"I guess I can see why you feel that way, but if you didn't pounce on me and throw a tantrum, I would have been able to explain myself," I said, gaining her interest.

Rachel continued moving around the room, battling stubbornness and curiosity. Eventually she gave in, looking at me with watery eyes.

"Then what is it? Are you not attracted to me?" Her voice was beginning to crack.

I tried not to smile at the absurdity. "The fact that you would even suggest that is mindboggling. I mean, when are we not all over each other? When have I ever not wanted to hold you or kiss you for every second of every day?"

Rachel was fighting back the tears.

"Honey, I don't mean to be vulgar, but I'm like a twenty-four hour erection around you. I love your body, I love being naked with you, and my penis agrees on all accounts."

Rachel was making weird noises and gyrations now. I couldn't tell if she was laughing or crying, but I continued anyhow.

"I know you think I'd sleep with any girl who rubs my leg the right way, or lets me touch her left boob, which was partially true in the past, but believe it or not, for probably the first time in my life, I'm considering someone else's feelings."

Rachel transitioned from the laugh-cry into the heavy breathing, nose sniffling phase.

"You're a virgin," I went on. "You're nineteen years old and you haven't slept with anyone. By no means is that a bad thing, but in my mind, it's a big deal. Back home in Hookerville, girls are having sex the minute they enter high school. It's crazy. You walk through the door and literally have to step over naked fourteen-year-olds having awkward sex."

The skies finally cleared and Rachel was laughing normally again.

"Come here," I smiled.

Rachel dragged her feet away from the closet and sat with me on the air mattress, wrapping her legs around my waist so we were facing each other.

"I know I don't say the things you probably want to hear, things that have to do with how I *feel*, you see, I can't even say the word comfortably, but it's because I want them to sound perfect and that only happens in my head." I wiped the tears from Rachel's face.

"You don't understand," Rachel began, taking a moment to collect herself. "To me, that's *exactly* how they sound. When you look me in the eyes, when you speak from the heart, I melt. I could hold you and be okay if they were the last words I ever heard."

Rachel immediately had me on the verge of my own tears. Before any became visible, I answered her initial question. "While we're still in the moment, I just want to let you know that if you feel like you're ready, if everything feels right and there isn't a doubt in your mind, then I can honestly say I feel the exact same way."

Rachel smiled and closed her eyes, letting a new batch of tears work their way to the corners of her mouth. I leaned forward and kissed Rachel's wet lips.

"I liked that better than shopping." Rachel used her hand to squeegee her face, slowly getting back to her cheerful self.

"If you think *that's* better than shopping…"

"*Don't* say it, shtoopid."

"Fine," I laughed. "But I have to tell you, that was not an easy conversation. There was a devil sitting on my shoulder the entire time, poppin' *Viagra* pills and lubing up his pitch fork."

"Is he still there?" Rachel asked, playing along.

"He relocated."

Rachel knew without looking. "You're hard, aren't you?"

I instantly smiled. "And you thought I wasn't attracted to you. Come on!" I yelled. "I need to tuck."

For those of you unfamiliar with the tuck, it simply involves putting your erect penis behind your belt or waistline, then covering it with your shirt.

"Well what was I supposed to think?" Rachel asked. "You said you wouldn't sleep with me."

"How about, 'Wow, that Jonathan Reynolds sure is a gentleman.'"

Rachel laughed in my face.

"Oh, shut it," I joked, laughing with her. "I was trying to be nice. Besides, I thought you aren't allowed to have sex until you're married. What happened to that?"

"I thought you aren't allowed to, either."

Rachel had a gift for turning the tables.

"Sure, the Catholic Church is against premarital sex, but Jonathan is not. Plus, you're more religious than I am. I only know the basics of Catholicism. Therefore, if we were to have sex, it'd be a bigger deal for you than it would be for me."

Oh shit. That didn't sound right.

"I'm sorry, did you just say sleeping with me wouldn't mean anything to you?" Rachel questioned, providing me with an eraser.

"No! That's not what I meant to say," I quickly backtracked. "Sleeping with you would be a tremendous deal. And I mean that in regards to how I feel about you, not because you're a virgin. Fuck! That's not what I meant to say, either."

Rachel started laughing. "Relax, I'm only kidding."

"Nice," I said, trying to catch my breath. "My right nut almost popped a blood vessel."

"Well that's attractive. Anyway, you don't follow the rules of the Catholic Church?" Rachel asked.

"I try to. I mean I've received the sacraments of Baptism, Communion, Reconciliation, and Confirmation."

"What's the one where you get on your knees in front of the priest and say you're sorry?"

"With recent molestation charges, I'm not sure that's the best way to describe it, but what you're thinking of is Reconciliation, or Confession," I answered.

"That whole thing is fuckin' sick," Rachel exclaimed, making her yucky face.

"I agree. As a Catholic though, it's a little embarrassing.

Let's just leave it alone."

"Why, did the dad touch you when you went to Confession?"

"The dad?" I repeated, looking at Rachel like she magically turned retarded.

"The Father!" she shouted. "I meant to say the Father." Rachel started cracking up.

"I am *not* liking you right now."

"What?" she said, still laughing. "I'm only kidding."

"Yeah, yeah," I ignored.

"So then explain it to me. You tell the priest you've done something wrong, he forgives you, and then you're supposed to say a bunch of prayers?" Rachel asked. "What if you've killed someone though? Do you think g-d still forgives you?"

"For some people, I think he does. When you go in the booth, or talk face to face with the priest, you're confessing your sins to God and asking for forgiveness, but meaningful forgiveness. The point is to acknowledge that you've done something wrong, feel remorseful, genuinely make an effort to right your wrong, and ask for God's forgiveness in hopes of... cleansing your soul, so to speak."

"Do you believe that?" Rachel asked.

"I do," I sincerely admitted.

"So when was the last time you went to Confession then?"

"When I was in the third grade," I shamefully admitted.

Rachel let out a big laugh. "You must believe in it a lot then."

Her comments, matched with her cynical tone, were starting to annoy me. "Laugh all you want, but I know what I believe in, and God knows what I believe in. That's all that matters." Rachel didn't expect such a serious response, especially one accompanied with an attitude.

"I'm sorry… jeez."

"I may not go to confession, but I pray every night," I continued. "When I talk to God, ask for forgiveness and thank him for all my blessings, I feel like that connection is just as strong as going to Confession. And there's no need to say, *jeez*," I added. "You could have just left it with an apology."

Rachel almost made her puppy dog face, but wisely chose not to under the assumption I'd think she was still joking around. Instead, she dropped her head into her chest and said nothing.

I wasn't really mad, because I knew Rachel wasn't purposely trying to be disrespectful, but the whole thing came across very condescending. In an overly sarcastic way, I thought I'd show her how.

"What about you guys? What's the deal with Yom Kippur?" I asked. "You don't eat for a day and your sins are *magically* forgiven? That sounds a little *out there* if you ask me."

"Yom Kippur's the Day of Atonement, jerk! Fasting is a way of *cleansing your soul*." Rachel knew exactly what I was trying to do and threw it right back in my face.

"Did you just call me a jerk?"

Rachel didn't even stop to answer. "Every year, from sundown to sunset, we're supposed to spend the day repenting our sins, free of distraction."

"Yeah, well, repent this," I said, looking down at my sleeping "devil."

"Real mature," Rachel grimaced, but only a light shade of purple.

"You see what you did? This is your fault. You can't transition from sex to the high holidays and not expect this result."

"Well, if you had said in the first place, 'Rachel, I would do anything in the world to sleep with you,' your limp penis wouldn't be an issue," she pointed out, working back to playful mode.

"Well, now it is an issue, Rachel. Your untimely religious conversation has inverted my penis. I'm going to have to birth my own genitalia. I hope you're happy," I scolded, trying to keep a straight face.

"Right, because I'm sure that will take long." Rachel started rubbing the inside of my legs.

"Wait. Wait a minute. I think I'm dilating!" I announced.

"I'll get you a doctor." Rachel was about to take her hands off.

"No! There's no time!" I shouted. "Just keep doing what you're doing, except more to the center."

Rachel tried not to laugh herself out of the moment, and instead, followed her patient's request.

"Uh-oh! I think I'm crowning! Yep, I'm definitely crowning!" I reached in my pants and gave myself an exposed tuck. "I can see the head!" I declared. "We're almost there. I need your hand, Rachel. I mean, your help. I need your help!"

Rachel pushed me so I was lying flat against the mattress, straddling my mid-section.

"You're suffocating my baby!" I yelled.

Rachel kissed me so I'd stop screaming. "I'll resuscitate him later," she said.

"Fine. Just don't forget you're his baby mamma."

"I won't," she smiled.

"You know what's kind of funny though, other than pretending to give birth to your own penis?"

"What?" Rachel hesitantly asked.

"How we can't argue normally. It's a sarcastic comment here, a sarcastic comment there, twelve more after that, both of us turning the tables and trying to gain the upper hand, and then we laugh and make out. I love it. There's no real or unnecessary drama."

"We argue!" Rachel yelled.

"Are you trying to argue with me about arguing?"

"Maybe!" she yelled again.

"You're too cute," I smiled.

"Fine. You're right. Gimme dat keppy."

"What? Give you a cupcake?"

"No, your *keppy*," Rachel laughed. "It means head in Yiddish."

"Oh, definitely. I'd love some keppy."

Rachel climbed up my body and kissed my forehead. "Such a putz."

I nodded my head in agreement. "So… do you really think you're ready to have sex," I asked, once again returning to the initial conversation.

"Well, I know it's only been like three months, which is why I can't believe I'm saying this, but yes, I'm ready," Rachel smiled.

"What about the religious issue?" I double-checked. "Not to mention your first time would be with a goy. I bet you didn't see that one coming."

"I definitely did not," Rachel laughed. "But like you were saying, my religious beliefs are my own. I don't follow or agree with every law of Judaism, but that doesn't make me a bad Jew. I have my own connection with g-d just like you do, and I feel like if we slept together, it's not something I would ever feel guilty about. There would be no repenting," she smiled.

If Rachel weren't mounting me, I would have been the one to curl into a shy little ball.

"Plus, I figure it's better than what my aunt told me," she continued

"And what was that?"

Rachel smiled. "Not to buy a car without test driving it."

After a short nap, a sushi dinner, and another interesting packing session, Rachel and I made our way back to the inflatable bed to watch a movie.

Rachel set the mood by lighting four candles and placing one at each corner of the bed. I did so by lying handsomely in my boxers. For nearly two hours, I rested Rachel under my arm while balancing Patrick Swayze on my stomach. As we watched this rugged yet sensitive soul from the wrong side of the tracks, find love with an innocent, silver spooned, country club sweetheart, I couldn't help but ponder how if these two dirty dancers could face adversity and come out on top, then why couldn't we? That, and nobody puts Rachel in a corner. Nobody!

There are very few moments in my life I am incapable of writing about, but that night is definitely one of them. It is simply impossible. The words do not exist. However, if for some paranormal reason I were able to look into the future when I was fifteen years old, and see that very night, two things would have happened. First, I would have masturbated. But second, and more importantly, I would have waited another six years for Rachel. Something like that is obviously easier said than done, but I am certain now of the same thing I was certain of back then... I loved her.

City Love

When I transferred to Presidents College I planned on becoming a doctor. And I don't mean a doctor like Dr. Dre., Dr. Doolittle, or a dentist, but an actual physician working in the medical field. With a 3.7 gpa out of Freeport, being accepted to PC, and my newfound passion for learning, I was more than optimistic. I genuinely thought I could do it. My mother is a Hospital Pharmacist, and my uncle a Pediatric Cardiologist, so keeping medicine in the family was my golden ticket to the proud parents factory. Too bad Chemistry's cousin is an asshole.

Dear Organic Chemistry,

I hate you. I hate you from the depths of my soul, to the clenching fists I'd like to beat your face in with. Never in my life has anyone made me feel as stupid as you have. Every week, for hours on end, you would stand in front of the class and taunt me while your gay sidekick, Periodic Table, looked on. The two of you would laugh at how I failed to name chemical compounds, and even made fun of my carbon chains. While everyone else looked like they were solving Rubik's Cubes, you watched me struggle to open a banana. You took my pipe dream, shit on it, and complimented the defecation with an 'F.' While down and out, I looked to the advice of my mother. She said, "When the going gets tough, the tough get going." I am no pussy, Organic Chemistry. I am a tough S.O.B. I adhered to the quote and got going... far and fast in the opposite direction. Carbon compounds may form the basis of all life processes, but you, sir, do not control mine. Eat a dick, O.C.

- Me -

Clearly, it was time for a change, a major change. Since writing is something I've always enjoyed, along with movies and television, I figured why not do one for the other. Unfortunately, PC did not offer Creative Writing as a major back then. I was forced to minor in it, switching and pretending my concentration was in English. I never fancied reading the way I did writing, but since they're conjoined twins, who was I to ax the ugly one that looked like a fetus. I stuck with it and read Shakespeare, Renaissance poetry, the Romantics, American Literature, Irish Literature, English Literature, and several other littoral genres. Yet, much like the twin with half an ear and seven toes, they stole days from my life. Every piece we looked at was picked apart and dissected so extensively, I started hearing authors from beyond the grave.

James Joyce: "Say, Shakespeare."
Shakespeare: "Yes, Jimmy J?"
James Joyce: "How many times do I have to tell you not to call me that? Huh? How many freakin' times?"
Shakespeare: "Jeezie Chreezie, take it easy, my neezie."
James Joyce: "Again, just because you sounded like Snoop Dog in the seventeenth century, doesn't mean you get to talk like him now that you're dead."
Shakespeare: "Quiet down a minute. Little Mrs. Nipples Are

Showing just said I named Romeo after Rome, Italy, because the city's like *so romantic*."

James Joyce: "How did you come up with the name?"

Shakespeare: "Do you know Margaret Cavendish, the biddy with the apple bottom?"

James Joyce: "Of course."

Shakespeare: "Well, I was getting blackout drunk in the pub one day, when I overhead this guy named Romeo telling a crazy sex story about he and some married lady. While listening further, the chickenhead he's talking about turns out to be none other than Margie Cav! I figured anyone who can tap that ass, and tap it the way he did, deserves mad respect"

James Joyce: "Margie Cav... a lady in the cobblestone streets, and a freak in the bed."

Shakespeare: "Yeah, yeah!"

Don't get me wrong, the classics and their authors are to be admired, but they inspired me about as much as a hobo. However, if I changed my major again before the start of my senior year, I would have had no shot of graduating on time. Therefore, I took the bad, discussing three paragraphs of *Moby Dick* for two hours, with the good, writing an original screenplay, and ran with it.

As previously explained, to complete my eligibility requirements for soccer, I needed to transfer in credits. I shit you not, but I chose to enroll in four summer session classes at Yeshiva University, where I would also be living. I registered for Spanish II and III, 20th Century Irish Literature, and Topics in British Literature. My parents were less than pleased with the cost, but since my stellar play on the field earned me scholarship money towards my senior year, and Freeport's cumulative tuition totaled four dollars and twenty-eight cents, Michael and Jacquelyn graciously emptied their wallets. Oddly enough, I had to do more convincing with Rachel than I did with my parents.

When Rachel and I came home from our D.C. hoopla, the circumstance in which we returned raised several eyebrows and generated even more questions. Neither of us told our parents how serious things were, nor how fast they were moving, but we said enough for them to know we were more than just friends. What Rachel didn't tell Mitch and Eileen was that I'd be living in one of Yeshiva's dorms for the summer. The reason being, it allowed her to also enroll at YU.

Having waited until the last minute, Rachel only got into the second summer session. Sadly, this meant seeing each other during the month of July would no longer be easy as waking up. Monday through Thursday I had classes, seven hours a day, and Friday night to Saturday night was the Sabbath (or Shabbos, the weekly day of rest and observance), which Rachel's family spent at their summerhouse in the Hamptons. Our only option was for her to drive into the city. That may not sound like a big deal, but if you've never driven by yourself at night, or a distance exceeding twenty miles, there's bound to be some apprehension (I drove Rachel's car home from PC).

Between laughter and amazement, I found out Rachel's father disallowed both while she was in high school. Needless to say, a solo trip on the Long Island Railroad was also out of the question. Rachel's father was very protective, as most fathers are, but that seemed a little over the top. His reasoning, given through Rachel, was equally inflated.

"It's dangerous."

"What is?" I asked. "Driving alone, or driving at night?"

"Both!" Rachel shouted. "What happens if I have to stop at a red light?"

"Do you not know where the brake is?"

"Someone could run up to the car and shoot me!" she exaggerated.

"Sure, but that could also happen during the day. The chances are extremely slim, especially where you live, but if for some reason a stranger did approach your car, I'd like to think you'd run the light," I said, mocking her.

"What if I don't see him coming until it's too late?" Rachel continued.

"Are you assuming he's black, or that he's a ghost?"

"Stop! I could get a flat tire and someone could pull over and rape me!" Rachel yelled, pitching the plot to a low-budget horror film slash porno.

"Again, you're assuming the worst," I pointed out. "How do you know the person isn't trying to help you? Why do they have to 'R' you?"

"Because there are sick fucks out there!" she returned.

"Right, but the situations you're describing are rare, particularly on Long Island. I know it sounds crazy, but people do drive at night. I promise you, other cars will be on the road. Your *Lexus Jeep* might be one of the nicer ones, which I'm sure factors into your reasoning, but I highly doubt there are gun slingers waiting for you at every crosswalk."

By presenting all the bad things that could happen, as unlikely as they were, her father implanted a fear I doubt she would have developed on her own. If she continued to avoid that fear, it would only magnify and spill over into other aspects of her life. Bottom line, you should never intentionally put anyone in harm's way, but you shouldn't lock them in a force field either.

After almost two days worth of encouragement and coaching, Rachel finally believed she was capable of driving into Manhattan at night... by herself! (I know, it could almost be another JLo movie). She lied to her parents about whom she was seeing, and where she was staying, but that part I understood. Little legs take baby steps.

The only condition I had to adhere to was staying on the phone with Rachel for the entire ride.

"All right man, I'm doing it. I'm doing it, man. I'm in the car. I just pulled out of the driveway. It's dark out. The sun has gone to sleep. The moon is following me. I'm a freakin' badass!" Rachel yelled into her speakerphone, giving a play-by-play I hoped would not continue.

"Are your lights on?" I asked.

"No, I'm holding a flashlight out the window."

"It's nice to know Mitch didn't scare away your sense of humor," I laughed.

"Oh stop it. He's just worried about his little girl. Are you telling me you're not going to be the same way if you have a daughter?"

"No," I lied.

"Bullshit!" Rachel shouted, calling me out. "I can only imagine how protective you and Chris are of Nicole."

"Maybe a little, but she's our sister. That has more to do with a guy hurting her and us hanging him upside down by his balls," I casually explained.

"Do you think Nicole has had sex yet?" Rachel annoyingly asked.

"Eww, eww, and eww!" I shouted, nearly vomiting.

"What's the matter?" she laughed. "You're the one who said Jericho girls start early." Rachel was purposely trying to get a rise out of me.

"Stop, you're going to crash," I said, trying to get off topic.

"No, I'm fine," Rachel ignored. "But if your sister hasn't had sex already, she's eventually going to"

"That doesn't mean I *ever* want to talk about it. Do you want to talk about your brother having sex?" I asked, turning the tides.

"Oh, you mean Ian, my virgin brother, who has never had sex before. Sure, we can talk about him."

"I hate you," I muttered. Rachel had me there, but I stayed with it. "Your brother may not be having sex, but he and Heather have been together since high school. That's a whole lot of oral."

"Eww! You're freakin' gross," Rachel yelled into the phone.

"What? You don't want to picture your brother lying in bed, naked, spread eagle…"

"Stop talking!" Rachel interrupted. "Stop talking, stop talking, stop talking."

"Yeah, that's what I thought!" I gloated. "You don't want to hear it either."

"You're graphic though, you sick bastard."

"That wasn't graphic," I laughed. "If you'd like, I could go into detail about how Heather licks…"

"Gotta go!" Rachel cut me off again. "I'll call you when I get there."

"But I thought we were going to talk the whole time?" I patronized, smiling from my end of the phone.

"Yeah, well, not anymore, loser."

"Fine," I laughed. Call me when you get out of the Midtown Tunnel. I'll meet you by the parking garage."

"See you soon."

"Wait!" I shouted, catching her before she hung up.

"What?"

"I just want you to know that even though your brother and Heather may not be having sex, that doesn't mean Mitch and Eileen aren't slappin' each..."

"Goodbye, jerk! I hope you're wearing a cup when I get there."

Rachel's big adventure may not have been on the level of Pee-wee's, but I was proud of her nonetheless. Even she stepped out of the car beaming with confidence. It doesn't seem like much, but that little hurdle was another stepping-stone towards independence. Rachel realized she could handle these "obstacles," and as a result, we were able to see each other more often. She even stopped lying to her parents, unless of course she was sleeping over. If they weren't okay with Ian and Heather sleeping in the same bed, I sure as hell had the red light.

With July coming to a close, and two classes successfully under my belt, it was time to kick off the best summer of my life! Although, any good romance will tell you, there's rain before every rainbow.

"We have to talk."

I nearly dropped the phone. Before my legs buckled, I sat down at the desk in my dorm room.

"I don't know how to say this, but do you remember last Saturday, when I went out with my friends in the Hamptons?"

My heart shifted gears and the brakes cut out.

"Well, there was this guy there, not a random guy, he's someone I know, but regardless, we were dancing and drinking all night, one thing led to another, and before I knew it... I..."

Holy shit, she cheated on me. I'm going to die and the autopsy will read heart attack instead of filthy whore of a girlfriend.

"I... I'm... *kidding!*" Rachel erupted with laughter. "I

definitely got you. Come on. Admit it. You were scared," she laughed again.

I couldn't feel any sense of relief, only anger. Before I heard another stupid comment come out of her mouth, I hung up the phone and didn't answer her incessant calls until it was time to go out with my friends.

"What?"

"Are you really mad at me?" Rachel whined.

"Are you really an idiot?" I returned.

"I was only kidding."

"And in what way was that funny?" I asked.

"I'm sorry. I didn't think you'd get upset."

"You didn't think I'd care if you cheated on me?" I rephrased. "That's good to know."

"I didn't mean it," she pleaded. "I'm sorry."

Rachel was the one sounding scared now. She knew she fucked up, but I had no intention of telling her it was okay. I had a different agenda.

"Well, I'll tell you what…" I began. "… you did a fantastic job of sending your boyfriend out extremely pissed off. I hope you enjoy your night now, wondering what I'm doing and who I'm doing it with. And, if you're lucky, maybe your little joke will come true."

Rachel was in tears. "Jon, stop. Please don't do this."

It hurt me to hear her cry, but my anger was in control. "I have to go," I said, closing the phone and silencing Rachel. Within seconds she called back, but again I didn't answer. I ignored all her calls and voicemails until four thirty in the morning when I decided we *had to talk*.

"Hey." Rachel answered her phone on the first ring and it sounded like she never stopped crying.

"Hi," I whispered.

"You just get in?"

"Yeah."

"How was your night?" Rachel asked, trying to stay calm and carry on a normal conversation.

"It was cool," I returned. "I had a good time."

"Are you still mad at me?"

I paused before answering. "No, not really."

Rachel was immediately suspicious, but she worked around the real question to avoid sounding indicative. "That's good, I guess, but you were pretty upset before. Any reason you're fine now?"

I paused again, even longer this time. My silence was the equivalent of Rachel's, "We need to talk," and I could feel her heart sink as she tried to speak without crying.

"Did something happen?" Rachel was clinging to the phone in painful anticipation.

The window of opportunity to lie was open just as wide as the one to tell the truth, but my hesitation to answer caused Rachel to insinuate the worst. She completely broke down and all I had to say was, "I'm sorry."

"Who was it?" she sobbed.

"Some random girl,"

"What'd you do?"

Silence.

"I'm going to throw up!" she yelled. "You fucked her, didn't you?"

Before I could respond, Rachel loudly intervened. "Don't answer that! I can't stop shaking. It feels like my heart is punching through my chest."

Rachel was hysterically crying. It was painful to hear, but

even more gut wrenching to know I caused it.

"Please stop crying. I didn't sleep with her."

The wailing briefly subsided.

"I didn't even kiss her," I added. "She doesn't exist."

I quickly continued before Rachel could process what just happened. "I only wanted you to feel what I did before. I didn't mean for it to get this carried away."

Rachel didn't say a word, just more tears.

"The thought of you hooking up with someone was beyond crushing, as I'm sure you could say the same, but that's no excuse for me being a petty asshole and pulling the same stunt. I'm truly sorry, honey."

Bawling followed by sniffling.

"Please say something. Listening to you cry and not being able to hold you is killing me. You have no idea…"

"I love you."

In a choked up, heartfelt and tearful voice, Rachel whispered to me again. "I love you."

There was no mistaking her that time. I heard everything I ever wanted to in those three little words.

Through the tears, Rachel continued. "You don't have to say it back, but I can't hold it in anymore. I've wanted to tell you for so long now, but I was worried I'd scare you away. I still am."

I tried holding onto my own tears, but they silently escaped. "I love you, Rachel. I love you, I love you, I love you. If I had to make up for all the times I said it in my head, we'd be on the phone for months. Still, I'd mean every one the same… with all my heart."

I could feel Rachel smiling on the other end, as I was doing the same. For as many times as I wanted to tell her I loved her, I never actually imagined a plan for doing so. It happened in the strangest of situations, over the phone nonetheless, but it felt perfect. Everything about it felt right. Three unbelievably powerful words melted our souls and molded them together.

Life with Rachel at Yeshiva University was a replica of how we spent our time at Presidents College, except it was in kick-ass New York City. We were openly in love, hand-in-hand, day in and day out, with skyrockets in flight, and afternoon delight. We couldn't get enough of each other. If I were going to spend the night at Rachel's dorm, she'd have dinner waiting for me; we'd eat together, study, watch a movie, and if her roommate was gone, most definitely sex it up. Almost every Thursday, she would pack a bag and we'd walk over to my building. We'd pick up food and alcohol, eat, drink, be merry, be in towels, be naked, go out on the town, come back to my room, and most definitely sex it up. In every way, shape, and form, life was incredible.

With Rachel's independence then reaching Kelly Clarkson status, she started feeling more and more comfortable using my name around her parents. So much so, she openly invited me to her aunt's surprise thirty-fifth birthday party at *The Plaza Hotel*. It was time for me to *really* meet the parents.

"Hey," I said, answering my phone.

"Guess what?" Rachel shouted.

"What?"

"Daddy said you could come to the party!"

Rachel waited for me to match her enthusiasm.

"What's the catch?" I asked, not quite there.

"There's no catch, shtoopid. You're coming."

"Do I have to wear a yamaka or fake peyos'?" I joked.

"*That* I would love to see, but we'll save it for the bedroom. You just need a suit."

"Not this again," I said, thinking back to formal. "And

before I forget... gross."

"Relax, you can wear your new suit, your only suit," Rachel laughed.

"Hey, shut it, rich girl. That's not the problem. The party's tomorrow, right?"

"Yeah, at *The Plaza*. We're telling everyone to get there before eight," Rachel informed.

"Okay, that makes two problems then. First, my suit is at home. Second, by the time I get back from classes, shower, change into something and take a cab to the hotel, I'll be there just in time to ruin the surprise."

"Why is your suit at home?" Rachel asked, sounding annoyed.

"Well, last time I checked, Spanish III and British Literature aren't formal affairs," I pointing out, adding a little sass.

"Do you have any ties?"

"Yes... at home, next to my suit. Inviting me the day before the party probably wasn't the best idea."

I was starting to get annoyed in my own right. Rachel had told me about the party days before, but at that point she said she couldn't take me because her father thought it would create problems. The "problem" being, my religion. He felt it would be easier on everyone if Rachel brought a girl, or any Jewish guy on the face of the earth.

"Why are you giving me an attitude?" Rachel asked.

"It's just frustrating, degrading even."

"Oh, stop it. He said it was fine, so what are you getting all worked up about?"

"I'm curious as to what changed his mind," I said.

"Um, I might have cried to Mommy and she might have yelled at Daddy," Rachel admitted, also being the only one to find it funny.

"Sweet, I got a pity pass," I said. "Do I need to hand that in at the door, or will the unworthy look on my face be enough to get me in?" I was laying it on pretty thick, but only because I was bothered by my religion being an "inconvenience."

"Listen to me, you little pain in the ass. I told my mom you're the only person in the world I want to go with, and if I can't take you, then I'm not taking anyone. I also said you're a huge part of my life now, so Daddy better *lock it up!* Then I told her I love you."

I ripped through the phone with laughter. "Yeah, right! Did you forget who you were talking to?" I asked, still laughing. "I'm willing to bet that wasn't even a fraction of the real tantrum you threw at your mother."

"Verbatim!" Rachel yelled, laughing at her own lie.

The chip on my shoulder quickly disappeared, and making Rachel happy rightfully took its place. "All right love, you got yourself a date."

"Yay!" Rachel briefly cheered. "Do you at least have dress pants and dress shoes?"

"That I have," I unavoidably smiled.

"What about a jacket you could match to the pants?"

"Nope, I left my blue blazer on the yacht."

Rachel loudly grunted. "Grrrr!"

"Sorry, dude. I can buy a tie between classes tomorrow, but I don't think I'll have enough money for a jacket," I admitted.

"All right, don't worry about it. I'll talk to Eileen and see what she says."

"Ya' gotta love the Eileen!" I shouted.

"You say that now," Rachel laughed. "Wait until you eat dinner with my family and meet all my relatives. First impressions are everything."

"Wait, are you being serious, or you're just trying to make me nervous?"

"Sweet dreams, honey. I'll talk to you tomorrow!" Rachel hung up the phone, having a little fun at my expense.

The following night, as I sat in the back seat of a slow moving cab, dress shoes glued to the floor and tieless shirt untucking in the back, I contemplated a last minute ditch. I imagined everything and anything going wrong. I saw myself ruining the surprise in classic sitcom fashion. I pictured myself as the most underdressed outcast at the party. I heard myself bombing with Rachel's family and relatives, and worst of all, I saw a look of utter disappointment and regret on Rachel's face. I don't sweat like a fat man walking up stairs though, so at least I had that going for me, but the real reason I didn't call in a sporadic case of West Nile Virus is because I had the perfect opportunity, at the perfect time in our relationship, to overshadow any preconceived notions of me or my religion, and it'd be as simple as being myself.

I called Rachel the second I stepped out of the cab. "I'm outside."

"Come to the third floor," she instructed. "I'll meet you in the hallway."

"Is your aunt here?" I asked, carefully eyeballing every woman in a fifty-foot radius.

"No, they said she's running late. Avoid all blonde women just to be safe."

"Tonight or in general?"

"Both," Rachel laughed.

"Got it. See you soon."

Before stepping foot in *The Plaza Hotel,* the only

preconceived notions I had derived from what I'd seen in *Home Alone 2: Lost in New York*. According to Rachel, it was one of the nicest and most famous hotels in all of New York. She couldn't have been more right. It was elegance, refinery, and *Grey Poupon* at its best. I thought the hotel we went to for formal was gorgeous, but compared to *The Plaza,* it was the Daniel Baldwin of the family.

When the elevator doors opened, I moved down the hallway and hid near the restroom, nervously waiting for Rachel to meet me with one of her brother's ties. That is until, all of a sudden, like being thrown in the middle of a science fiction movie slash porno, a floating pink object drifted my way. I immediately rubbed my eyes, thinking perhaps my nerves were getting the better of me, when the image stood within arms distance in the form of an angel; an actual angel, in a stunning pink dress, looking more beautiful than anyone or anything in the whole wide world (yes, even you Molly Ringwald). The crazy part… she bore an exact resemblance to Rachel. I was so hypnotized I didn't hear a word she said, but an awakening kiss revealed I was in a fairy tale.

"Wake up, shtoopid!"

"What the…"

"Here." Rachel handed me a red *Hugo Boss* tie with diagonal white stripes.

I may have snapped out of my trance, but I still didn't know what to say.

"What?" she asked, matching her smile to mine.

"Do you have any idea how unbelievably beautiful you are?"

"Of course," Rachel shrugged. "Now, go change."

Before I could finish laughing, Rachel kissed me again.

"I'm just kidding. Thank you, honey. You look very handsome," Rachel smiled. "But you'd look even more handsome with that tie on."

"All right *Push-pop*, all right. I'm going. You'll be here when I get out?" I asked.

"Yes, I'll wait for you, little girl."

"Yeah, well... we'll see who the little girl is tonight."

Rachel's eyes instructed I close it.

"Sorry, I had nothing."

I walked into the bathroom and squared up with the mirror. My hair was too short, I had a noticeable blemish, the tie was the nicest part of my outfit, and my eyebrow ring had been unwillingly removed. I wouldn't have asked my reflection for an autograph, yet my nerves were subsiding. Just seeing Rachel was enough to put me at ease, while the smile I wore convinced me the night would be incredible. After all, I'd be with the best looking girl at the party. It's too bad everyone else was led to believe otherwise.

"You ready?" Rachel asked, as I stepped out of the men's room.

I raised my arms and held them at my side. "This is as good as it's going to get," I sulked.

"You're such a dork."

"What?" I smiled.

"You know what," Rachel laughed. "You're quoting *The Princess Diaries*."

"*The Princess Diaries?* Never heard of it," I lied.

"Right. So you *randomly* told me you have a crush on Anne Hathaway the other day?"

"A mere coincidence," I smiled again.

Rachel and I continued down the hallway and into the

ballroom.

I was Waldo, but easier to find. I was a black man at a KKK rally. I was a white man at *The Source Awards*. I was a homeless man at a real estate auction. I was an Asian in the *NBA*. I was a Jew in the *NBA*. I was a redneck in the White House. I was a toe thumb.

Immediately overwhelmed, I let Rachel lead the way. Here a yamaka, there a yamaka, everywhere a yamaka, yamaka. We initially planted ourselves in an empty area of the room, but it soon filled up.

"Hey, sweetie. Hi, Jonathan."

"Hi, Mrs.... Eileen," I corrected, saving myself. "How are you?"

"I'm very well, thank you. I like the tie," she smiled.

"Oh, this old thing?" I joked, like a corny douchebag.

Eileen politely laughed while Rachel amusingly looked on.

"Thank you very much for having me," I politely added.

"Anytime," Eileen suggested. "You're more than welcome."

I think that depends on who you ask.

Eileen turned to Rachel. "Have you seen your father yet?"

"Mom, we came together. Stop drinking."

"I'm not drinking," Eileen laughed, while holding an empty wine glass. "You know what I mean. Go say hello."

The Eileen Hour ended earlier than I would have liked, and it was time to hear from The Mitch. Acting as a human periscope, I located Rachel's father and led the way.

"Dad," Rachel interrupted.

"Ra-Ra! Are you having a good time, sweetheart?"

"Yes, it's very nice, Daddy."

"Do you remember my friend, Dateline?" Mitch asked Rachel. "We grew up together in Brooklyn."

"Oh, yeah," she lied. "Hello."

Dateline shook Rachel's hand while I stood in the shadows. "It's nice to see you again, Rachel. You look more beautiful than ever."

Easy, Dateline. That's my line.

"So how old are you?" he asked.

Really? That's your first question? Stick to the Internet, pal.

"I'm nineteen," Rachel uncomfortably answered.

"Well I'd say that's old enough to hear some stories about your father then, don't you?" Dateline nudged Mitch with his elbow. "Huh? What do ya' say, big guy?"

"Oh, that's all right," Rachel broke in, rightfully creeped out by Dateline's predator-like persona. "I've already heard my fair share."

Dateline paid no mind and went on. "Don't tell Mom, but your dad was quite the playboy back in the day. Although I shouldn't give him too much credit. *I* was actually the one who introduced your parents."

"Really?" Rachel exclaimed, like she gave a shit.

"This crazy guy actually dated your mother!" Mitch added.

I did? Oh, you meant Dateline. That's right, no one's acknowledged my presence yet. Carry on.

"They were pretty serious, too," Mitch continued.

Dateline raised his near empty glass of scotch and shouted, "I could have been your father!"

Rachel couldn't help but inquire. "So what happened?"

Dateline happily took the lead. "Your mother and I eventually parted ways, but being the good friend I am, I set your dad up with her. A few weeks later... they're engaged!"

"That's funny." Rachel pretended to laugh, and then used me to change the subject. "Dad, you remember Jon, right?"

"Of course," he said. "How are you, Jonathan?"

"I'm good," I responded, shaking his hand. "Thanks for having me."

Mitch turned to Dateline. "Jon's a *friend* of Rachel's from school. He's living in the city for the summer, so she invited him to the party."

Downplay it anymore Mitch, and we'll all be in China.

Dateline also shook my hand. "It's great to meet you, Jon."

"Likewise," I lied.

"Hey, maybe later I'll tell you a story about me, this guy, and enough rocks to fill up a playground," Dateline boasted.

Unless it's the kind of rocks you can smoke, I don't want to hear it, Dateline.

"I'd love to hear it!" I lied, yet again.

"I think its time to go in the other room," Rachel announced, clearly exhausted with the conversation. "We'll see you in there."

"Bye, sweetie."

"Bye, sweetie," Dateline repeated.

Rachel and I once again shuffled through the crowd. "There's another room?" I asked.

"This was just the cocktail hour. We're going in there in a second."

As if Rachel was wearing a microphone, she pointed to two heavenly doors and they opened on cue. Everyone soon filed into the dining area. It was even more lavish than the first room. There was a large kosher buffet filled with an assortment of food, tables set and decorated so delicately they could have been in a wedding, and a chandelier so enormous and extravagant, it looked like there were diamonds dripping from the ceiling. Before I could soak in the grandeur, the doors closed behind us in anticipation of the guest of honor.

"Surprise!"

Rachel's aunt immediately began to cry. She was shocked, happy, impressed, ecstatic, so on and so forth. Enough about that thunder thief though, let's get back to my night.

I stood next to Rachel on the buffet line, side stepping slower than the elderly and nervously piling food on my plate. The kosher butterflies were hungry, as the make or break portion of the evening had arrived.

After spooning my final portion of sweet potatoes, I had no choice but to head to the main stage and perform for Rachel's parents. During what I could only imagine is exactly, precisely, and identically similar to the walk inmates have to make when facing their death row sentence, I looked back on all the times in my life when I too had killed. I'd murdered with my personality, strangled with my charm, drugged and date raped with my smile, and even ran over a few people with my good looks. Still, I was determined to add a new method to my list. That night, I would kill a Jewish family with kindness.

"Jon, do you like the Mets or the Yankees?" Rachel's youngest sister Emily asked, as if she'd been told to do so.

Knowing Rachel and her family were Yankee fans, I unfolded my napkin into my lap while answering, "I'm a Mets fan."

"Islanders or Rangers?" she tried again.

"Islanders."

"We're Islander fans, too!" she yelled.

"I'm a Mets, Jets, Islanders, and Knicks fan," I announced, figuring I'd cover them all at once.

"Us, too! Except the Mets," Emily pointed out again.

Rachel's mother changed the subject. "Jon, do you have any

brothers or sisters?"

"I have an older brother and a younger sister," I answered. "Nicole is seventeen and she'll be starting her senior year at Jericho in September, and Chris is twenty-four and he plays professional soccer for the Chicago Fire."

"That's the MLS, right?" Rachel's brother Ian asked.

"Correct. This is his first year with the team," I explained. "The previous three he was living in Minnesota and playing in the league under the MLS, the A-League."

"Isn't Chris Armas on the Fire?"

"Yep, he's on the team," I supported.

"What position does your brother play?" Ian continued.

"Goalie. Right now, he's second string though. The starter, Largely Overrated, has been with the team for years, and is surprisingly playing well, so my brother's stuck waiting in the wings."

Heather, Ian's girlfriend, joined the conversation, also asking questions she already knew the answer to. "You play soccer at PC, right?"

"Yes." My fork and hand felt like they were levitating at this point.

"How's the team?" she continued.

"We had a good year. We won our conference and got an automatic bid into the NCAA tournament. Unfortunately, we lost to Maryland in the second round, but we should be contenders again next year."

"That's great! Congratulations!" Heather excitedly shouted.

"Thank you," I smiled.

"Do you guys remember when Rachel used to play basketball?"

Knowing or unknowingly, Mitch got me out of the hot seat.

Any more questions like the ones I had just answered and I'd butcher with boredom before I even had a chance to kill with kindness. Thankfully, the thought of Rachel being athletic was enough to liven the table.

"That's right, I was the next Michael Jordan!" Rachel announced, trying not to laugh at herself.

"Yeah… the short, white, Jewish girl who sat on the bench and gossiped with her friends was the next Michael Jordan," Mitch patronized, causing everyone including myself to laugh.

"I remember going to one of your games with Heather," Ian added. "You had a double-double. You painted ten fingernails and ten toenails, all from the sidelines."

The table erupted with laughter again.

"Hey, shut it! I played point guard," Rachel corrected.

"Yeah, you pointed at people from the bench and yelled, 'Hey, guard them!'"

Everyone continued to have a go at Rachel. The jokes were sprinkled with Parmigiano-Reggiano, but they effectively lightened the mood. Eventually, I was relaxed enough to embarrass Rachel with one or two witty cracks of my own. Despite being torn a new one, Rachel was smiling at the end of the meal. I knew a large part of that had to do with how I got along with her family, but only time would tell how much ground I covered. For the moment, I wanted to look at some different steps. My all time favorite steps in fact. It was time to pay homage to the art of Mom Dancing.

Without question, Bar and Bat Mitzvahs are my favorite type of party. They are downright, across the board, fuckin' fantastic! They're great when you're young, and they're great when you're drunk/older.

There are sport themes, movie themes, music themes, state

of the art interactive games, and wacky pictures you can put in even wackier frames. There are signing boards large enough for a thruway, complete with embarrassing photo and enough mazel tovs to last a lifetime, and you can even take home a cheap t-shirt with a catchy saying, like, "I had a ROARING good time at Jake's Bar Mitzvah" (jungle theme). You can also eat all the shrimp, caviar, spring rolls, and blackberries you'd like during cocktail hour, and then later, hold another plate in front of a man slicing the ass off a cow. Still, if none of that tickles your fancy, the candle lighting ceremony is sure to entertain.

Catholic folk, picture your thirteenth birthday. Now, instead of having your cake brought to you with all the candles lit, imagine a more exciting way of lighting them. How, you ask? Well, by using Dr. Seuss-like rhymes and catchy dance music, of course! For example…

Ike: "This next person holds a special place in my *heart*,
    You have been by my side from the *start*.
    On my fourth birthday you bounced me on your *lap*,
    And on my eleventh you taught me how to *rap*.
    Because of you my rhymes are so *tight*,
    Grandpa Mortechai please join me on my special *night*."

DJ Dustin Diamond: "Grandpa Mortechaiiiiiiiiii, come on down and light candle number five!"

…Cue the spotlight on the eighty-year-old man struggling to get out of his chair, and DJ break me off with a little Will Smith.

DJ Dustin Diamond: "Na na na na na na na. Na na na na na na, Grandpa Mortechai! Na na na na na na na. Na na na na na na,

Grandpa Mortechai!"

If all that still doesn't make you want to sew on a yamaka and start reading backwards, then you simply had to wait for the parents to hit the dance floor and the magic to begin. There would be arms swinging around like kites, leg kicks rivaling a *Riverdance* show, toes tapping, fingers snapping, and necks moving about like bobblehead dolls. Add a few husbands to the mix, all with the same Chubby Checker twist move, play a little *Shout* through the speakers, and you've got your very own Jewish Animal House.

To my own surprise, Mom Dancing isn't limited to just Bar and Bat Mitzvahs. It's universal. The second Rachel saw me eyeing down the dance floor with a ridiculous grin on my face, she knew exactly what I was thinking.

"No! Please no," Rachel said, trying to curb my enthusiasm.

"Ra-Ra! Come on," I smiled, not forgetting to use Rachel's family nickname. "Just look at the lady raising the roof and the guy next to her doing the Cabbage Patch."

Rachel spun her body around the chair and immediately started laughing.

"Now, look me in the eyes and tell me you don't want that to be us."

Rachel slid to the edge of her seat, put her hands on my knees, and looked me dead in the eyes. "J-dog, I *do not* want that to be us." Rachel tried holding her stare, but the smirk on my face made her crack.

"Nah, I don't believe you," I laughed. The time has come." I stood up and offered her my hand.

"Promise me you'll be good." Rachel would not accept my offer until I agreed.

"Good? I'm going to make Usher look like my bitch."

Rachel tilted her head, waiting for the real answer.

"Fine, dance Nazi. I'll behave."

Rachel got out of her seat, appropriately hit me, and then led us out to the dance floor.

I thought I could do it, but the second I felt the electricity around me, I turned into a dancing mixed tape. I sampled everything from the Sprinkler, to the Shopping Cart, to the Roger Rabbit, and even the Robot. I mowed the lawn, threw a lasso, went fishing, and even rolled some dice. But then, as if *Barney's* announced a fifty percent off sale, everyone left. The first slow song of the night came on and myself, Rachel, Mitch, Eileen, Ian, Heather, and two other couples, were the only ones left on the dance floor. It had taken most of the night, but I was finally able to hold Rachel without feeling like I was doing something wrong. I wrapped my arms around her hips, her hands barely making it around my neck, and we swayed from side to side, never leaving each other's eyes. I could feel another set burning a hole in my back, but I paid no attention to it.

"Pup..." I whispered in Rachel's ear. "I love you."

Rachel pressed her head against my shoulder so no one would see her cry. After using my shirt for a tissue, she rested her chin against my chest and looked up at me with watery eyes.

"I love you so much," she whispered.

As I looked out onto the party, purposely distracting my own tears, it was obvious all returning stares could tell Rachel and I were more than just college friends.

That moment was single-handedly the best moment of my entire summer, and I will carry it in my heart forever, a constant reminder that true love can never be hidden.

Different People

"Who do you think you are, God's gift to the world?" Well... yes. As a matter of fact, I am. Growing up, I would hear this question often, despite presuming the answer was obvious. Yet, it wasn't until I met Rachel when I discovered my name actually means, "gift of God." You see, Rachel's a lot like the father from *My Big, Fat, Greek Wedding,* except she finds words rooted in Hebrew or Yiddish. Instead of using *Windex* as the solution to her problems, though, she uses cream cheese. Got a bunion? Shmeer a little cream cheese on it. Cut your finger? Vegetable cream cheese. Black eye? Cream cheese with lox.

By now, it should be obvious that Rachel and I shared very little in common other than attending Presidents College, growing up on Long Island, and being madly in love with each other. We both had brown hair, a driver's license, and could count to three, but we were true opposites of attraction. She was an innocent, wealthy, jappy girl too embarrassed to shop at a *Macy's* or stand in line at a *Taco Bell*, and I was a beer drinking, party-going, do-as-I-pleased, bad-ass motherfucker! I'm sort of kidding, but you get the point. Religion was our most palpable difference, but underneath the surface, it always begins with history.

Rachel's grandpa on her father's side is a Holocaust survivor and immigrant of Germany. Her grandmother is also of German descent, but sadly they both passed away before she was born. Rachel's grandparents on her mother's side are from Russia, and they currently reside in an elderly community on Long Island.

When Rachel's grandfather came to the United States, he began working at a tiny deli in Brooklyn, New York. After several years of labor, he saved up enough money to buy ownership of the store. With good business and continuous profits, he began purchasing and renting apartments in the area. He then used the steady revenue to start a fabrics company, which over time blossomed into a manufacturing conglomerate. It's another incredible story of The American Dream, and not just because of his financial success, but because this is someone who survived imprisonment in a Nazi concentration camp, where he lost both his parents and younger brothers, immigrated to another country, started and raised a family of his own, and worked his heart out to provide for them. I wish I could have met Rachel's grandfather, although I don't know how welcomed I would have been if he knew I was dating his granddaughter, but it would have been an honor, nonetheless.

With the passing of Rachel's grandpa, her father and uncle inherited the business. At that point its success was astronomical. I hate to be tacky, but Rachel's family doesn't have to worry about money for the rest of their lives, and many generations thereafter. That's with the company split in half, too. It's crazy, but when I watch these rich and famous shows like *MTV Cribs* and *Vh1's The Fabulous Life,* narrated by the fabulously gay Robin Leech, I can't help but laugh at how Rachel can shrug her shoulders at nearly everything she hears.

The real difference between Rachel and the majority of the talentless chodes who appear on those shows is class. She is the wealthiest person I've ever come in contact with, and probably ever will, but she'd never wave it in your face. Yes, her family lives extravagantly, but if they really wanted to they could imitate royalty. Thankfully, her family understands the importance of being humble, and they've done an incredible job of not turning into spoiled little assholes. What's even more admirable is how they share their money with those less fortunate.

While strolling through town one day, shopping for menorahs, koogle, change purses, and other things of the Jewish nature, Rachel's father came across a family trying to raise money for their ill daughter. The little girl had a rare disease, potentially curable with surgery, but barely covered by insurance. After talking with the parents, finding out more about their daughter, her illness, and the operation, Rachel's father graciously made out a check, consisting of five figures. What's more commendable than the dollar amount is was how he refused to accept any kind of recognition. The family wanted to inform the media, host a party in his name, or anything else to let people know what he was doing for their daughter, but Rachel's father happily declined, content with knowing he helped. His mitzvah was their miracle.

After 9/11, Rachel's father made an enormous donation to the families affected by the tragedy... six figures. He's also made tremendous contributions to the state of Israel, Rachel's high school, their community, numerous temples, and several other organizations I have no idea about. This is why when I see people with far more money than they know what to do with, acting like stuck up, obnoxious, penny pinching fuckfaces, I want to slap the shit out of them until their head spins. That way, they can watch me repeatedly kick their ass.

As I mentioned earlier, Rachel has three siblings. Her oldest brother, Ian, is my age, and really just a spitting image of Mitch. Their appearance, personality, mannerisms, and humor are hauntingly similar. Amanda is eight years younger than Rachel, and easily the shiest of the bunch, while Emily is ten years younger than Rachel, and an off the wall firecracker. She will gladly perform a spot on rendition of Fergie's *My Humps,* and definitely knows far more than she should. Simply put, Rachel's family is great. Each personality shines through in its own way, but it is obvious they are one. I feel the same way about the compilation of my family, but our ancestry was sculpted very differently. I'll begin with the juicy and scandalous tales.

My great-grandparents on my father's side are immigrants of Ireland, who grew up in a Pennsylvania miner's town. My great-grandfather was in fact a miner, while my great-grandmother kept house and tended to the thirteen children. I repeat, thirteen children. How do ya like dem apples, Jew Crew? You guys aren't the only ones with *Slip and Slides* for vaginas. As the story is told, according to my grandma, her father used to frequent the town bar after work with his buddies. However, there was a female bartender there who may or may not have been more than a friend. My great-grandma believed this woman was trying to break up their family and run away with her husband. The details of whether or not anything happened remain a mystery, along with his death.

One random workday, my great-grandpa came home from the bar feeling abnormally sick, so e went upstairs and got into bed. My great-grandma assumed he drank too much, until my great-grandpa randomly started calling his children in one at a time to say his final goodbyes. Left to raise thirteen kids on her own, my great-grandma angrily searched for answers to her husband's bizarre and unexpected death, only to come up with a hunch... the bartender poisoned him.

Life went on, and several years later, one of those thirteen children, my grandma, met, loved, and married Michael James Reynolds Senior. My grandparents quickly abandoned Pennsylvania, relocating to Forest Hills, New York in anticipation of Michael Charles Reynolds Junior, their first and only child. While in their retired years, they moved to Jericho to be closer to our family, but sadly, my grandpa died of lung cancer when I was just four years old. My mother continuously tried getting him to quit, but the consequences were merely noise. On the day she gave birth to Nicole, my grandpa was being treated in the same hospital, literally on his deathbed, fighting to stay alive. As soon as he got word that his daughter-in-law and newborn grandchild were healthy and in good spirits, he let go. Years later, after living in an empty house and taking care of herself, my grandma became very lonely and moved in with us. We converted our garage into a small apartment, where she still resides today, now in her young nineties.

So, that was one *A Current Affair*-like story, now onto the other. My great-grandparents on my mother's side are immigrants of Lithuania. They came to the United States with their three daughters, my grandma being the youngest, also to set up home in Forest Hills. For over a year they lived in a tiny one-bedroom apartment of the shabbiest conditions, struggling just to put food on the table. Then, out of the clear blue sky, their lives changed forever. It had nothing to do with money though. In the most cowardly of ways, my great-grandpa packed his bags and went back to Lithuania, leaving his wife and three daughters to fend for themselves. How they survived and came out the way they did is a testament to all, and I couldn't be more proud to have their bloodline.

My grandma and grandpa met in Forest Hills where they fell for each other, drove each other nuts, and loved every minute of it. My grandma was the best. Some of my favorite memories include the way she forced my grandpa into taking in a new dog or cat every time she saw one in need of rescuing, how she controlled what and when he ate, how she spoiled all her grandkids, slipping us money under the table for eating our vegetables, how she stressed the importance of God and family, and how she emphatically believed in angels.

When I was eighteen years old, my grandma had a stroke. She died when I was twenty. From the day she entered the hospital, to the time she was moved to a nursing home, to the second she passed away, my grandpa was there. Day in and day out, he stayed by her side, holding her hand, talking to her, joking with her, taking care of her, and loving her, the same way he'd been since the day they met. My grandpa has never left though. He continues to visit her grave every day, and will continue to do so until it's time to be with his angel again. My grandma and grandpa are the definition of true love, and if I can have even a fraction of what they had, I know I'll be in for a lifetime of happiness.

My parents obviously grew up in Forest Hills, living fairly close to one another, but attending different high schools. Mike Rennie went to public school, while Jackie Urbonas spent her days at an all girls Catholic school. They met through mutual friends and fell in love at a young age, marrying at twenty-two and twenty-one, respectively. Shortly after, they moved into their own house. Mike worked as a mailman (*Newman!*) while Jackie began her nursing career at Jamaica Hospital. On April 28, 1979, my brother was born. Three years later, just past five in the morning on New Year's Day, yours truly entered this world. Four years later, I went from riding my *Big Wheel* down Metropolitan Avenue, to the burbs of Jericho, Long Island. On top of that, our sister Nicole was born. The year was 1986, the Reynolds family was complete, the Mets won the World Series, *Mr. Mister* and *Starship* rocked the airwaves, Ferris Bueller took a day off, and Tony Danza was the boss.

Over two decades later, the Mets are wearing the same World Series ring, Justin Timberlake and Kanye West have taken over the music world, Harry Potter rules the box office, and Tony Danza's fame lasted long enough for a self-titled talk show (and a vicious sex move). On the Reynolds forefront, Michael remains an employee of The United States Postal Service, but as the Postmaster of the Hicksville branch. He's lighter on top, rounder in the middle, anxiously awaiting retirement, and utterly obsessed with soccer. Jacquelyn continues her drug trade position at Jericho Hospital, but she now serves as Department Head. She's also made her way onto the soccer bandwagon, heavily enjoying the sport, but mainly keeping Mike in check.

Chris might as well have soccer balls for testicles (the little ones you juggle with, not the size fives you use for a game). In high school, he was one of the top goalkeepers in the nation. He set records, won awards and championships, was an All-American, and was voted one of the top ten college recruits in the United States. He accepted a full ride to the University of California, Santa Barbara, while playing for the United States Under-20 National Team as well. After his freshman year, he transferred to Fordham University, on scholarship again, playing two much more successful seasons, but then left in the middle of his junior year to play professionally in Minnesota. From there, he moved to Chicago and "played" two overshadowed seasons in the MLS. After ending his playing career, he got married to the only girlfriend he's ever had, whom he met in Minnesota. She's a native Minnesotan, six years older than him, half-Mexican, half-German, obsessed with nutrition to the point of controlling both their eating habits, and controlling to the point of having him by the balls... I love her. They currently reside in Charleston, South Carolina, where he works as Head Coach for a top college soccer program, while Katherine does administrative work at a local high school.

Last but certainly not least is Little Nicki. Nicole turned twenty-one on February 15, 2007, and is still finding herself through the adventures of college, similar to those of Bill and Ted. She's a miniature Jackie, which scares me plenty. She's worked all throughout high school, excelled academically, continues to do so at Wisconsin, and is undoubtedly the golden child of our family. There's nothing more precious than your mother asking you why you can't be more like your younger sister. Good times. Little Nicki can do no wrong, but she deserves all the praise and then some, because no one works harder than she does. She's generous, caring, looks after her older brothers, and I love her. All I have to say is good luck to the guy she brings home.

Our family's financial situation is obviously nowhere near what Rachel's is like. Jacquelyn and Michael both have good, stable jobs, making slightly above average money, but raising three children in Jericho is far from easy. Our house is small, with three modest bedrooms, and one and a half bathrooms (plus another half bathroom in Grandma's apartment), but because of its location, it will sell for at least three quarters of a million dollars. There are so many places in the United States where a house valued at the same price would mean living in a mansion, but my parents wanted to provide us with the best they could afford, even if it meant barely staying afloat. They have sacrificed a great deal, and worked incredibly hard to give my brother, sister, and I all the opportunities in the world. Their work ethic and family values are ones I wish to instill in my own children, but when it's all said and done, after all the grief, gray hair, and stress, all I really want is for them to be as proud of me as I am of them.

So there you have it, Rachel's a female sheep, and I'm God's gift to the world. She's an innie, and I'm an outie. Penis... vagina. Our families are uniquely different, on and off the surface, but who's to say they wouldn't go well together? I'd contend the last combination worked out just fine, wouldn't you?

Overkill

All good things must come to an end, as did our summer of love at Yeshiva University. It was time to head back to Presidents College for another year of academia.

For my senior year, I would be leaving behind the raggedy conditions of Hoover Hall, and literally moving on up to the east side. Since my new athletic scholarship covered housing expenses, I was now in a comfortable one-bedroom with my friend from the soccer team, HGH. Our apartment, as I liked to call it, did not even compare to Rachel's, but it far and away met my standards. We had furniture, which is always nice, a big screen TV, cable, Internet, a decent-sized bathroom, a new kitchen, a living area large enough for Beer Pong, our own closets, and a bedroom that could easily fit two full-sized beds. I'm afraid that was the only downside to the apartment. Some people need coffee to wake up, I simply had to roll over and see HGH's hairy ass crack five feet away from my face.

My freshman year at Rhode Island, I quit the soccer team the day before I was supposed to report to school. My sophomore year at Freeport, our "preseason" was just three days long, and hardly demanding. And my junior year at Presidents College, I walked onto the team late, avoiding preseason all together. This leads me to my senior year, where I had to train in ninety-five degree weather, four hours a day, six days a week, for two weeks straight. Had I not been playing grabass-kissieface all summer, preseason might not have been so bad, but the juice was undoubtedly worth the squeeze. I would have endured a year's worth of physical hell if it meant spending another summer like I had with Rachel.

When the soccer season and academic year got underway, Rachel and I fell back into place like we never skipped a beat. I spent so much time at her apartment I might as well have paid rent. If HGH and I didn't share a room, I think the time would have been divided more evenly, but what can you do. Limited funds, limited square footage.

By September 2003, Rachel and I had been together for just over five months, meaning we officially reached our comfort level plateau. In my opinion, there are certain obstacles you have to get past before you can reach relationship Eden. Different couples find different issues easier or harder to overcome, but they are usually your standard, potentially embarrassing, nerve-racking hurdles. In the beginning, it's something as simple as eating in front of each other. Most girls are aware of what foods are good to eat on a date, while guys don't realize it until they've gone through their eighth napkin and half a chicken is stuck between their teeth. Then, there is the constant raising and lowering of forks, both spastically unsure when to eat and when to talk. Girls are careful not to eat too much and look like fatty-boombatties, not to eat too little and look like skinny minnies, and not to purposely order the most expensive items on the menu and look like, well, inconsiderate assholes. I don't think there's a cute name for that one. From here, you usually move on to the first kiss. Does my breath smell? Why's he eating my face? This is awesome! Should I grab her ass? Why's he grabbing my ass?

If the kiss lasts long enough, your mind will continue asking questions and making comments, but if the chemistry is there, the voices will eventually fade.

The same thing goes for when you venture beyond kissing and move into sexy time. Being completely naked is just another step towards the Promise Land. If you're able to look at each other with the covers off and the lights on, take another step. Are you confident and comfortable enough to hook up in the shower though? What if there's a shortage of hot water? Are you secure with your manhood? Do your boobs hang low? Do they wobble to and fro? Can you tie them in a knot? Can you tie them in a bow? If all of these concerns and more aren't really concerns at all, then keep climbing the ladder. When it's time to take the entering course, there are enough steps to rebuild the Empire State Building. However, depending on the girl, access to all "floors" isn't always granted. When you and your loved one have accomplished all this, and you feel like you're holding on to the top of the mountain, there is still one more push needed to get you over the edge.

When Rachel and I got to the point where I could lie in bed with her, fart, and pull the covers over her head, I almost shed a tear, and not from the smell. Stereotypically, guys are the ones with the flatulence problem, yet we view it in a different light. When a guy farts, he celebrates it like it's an accomplishment. He'll bask in the glory of its odor, applaud its roaring thunder, smile with relief, and encourage others to share in his achievement. Women, on the other hand, are like farting terrorists. They disguise their farts, showing no change in facial expression nor giving any warning signs. They creep up on you like stealth ninjas, drop their silent but deadly bombs, and then flee the scene faster than O.J. Simpson. Here's the kicker; cute, adorable, sweet, innocent little Rachel, is a hermaphrodite in the farting world. At first, I thought she was just unloading months worth of backed up cargo, but after a while, I was hit with the shocking realization that my girlfriend's ass is a time bomb. Never in a million years would I have expected odors far beyond nostril tolerance to come from her little bum. Her friends actually dubbed her the Poomsie Queen, poomsie being their code word for fart, just in case you had trouble cracking that one, Robert Langdon.

From here, I think it's obvious what came next. The expression, "Don't shit where you eat," did not apply to Rachel and me. What did, however, was dropping deuces whenever and wherever we pleased. Holding in a fart is one thing, but holding in a shit is like your ass' version of a brain freeze. Rachel and I were actually so disturbingly close with one another, that if she had to dump out and I wasn't there, she would call me while sitting on the toilet.

"J-dog?"

"Yes, love?"

"Guess what?"

"You're taking a shit," I answered correctly.

"How'd you know?"

"Because you have that half constipated sound in your voice."

"Hey... I do not," Rachel moaned.

"I love how talking to me on the phone helps you…"

"Gotta go!" she yelled. "Doodie time!"

Rachel and I may have gotten back into a relationship rhythm, and our comfort level may have been soaring at new heights, but the toll of a time-consuming soccer season was starting to take affect. When we first met it was springtime, and although a short season was in place, I didn't have to take part. My coaches instructed me to stay off the field, live in the classroom, and concentrate solely on raising my gpa. I adhered, to some extent, but their orders were really just a free pass to spend all my time with Rachel, which I did.

In the fall, however, when the soccer season was at its peak, I had to try balancing my life like the mature adult I was not. Non-conference games were scattered throughout the calendar, meaning we could travel to George Mason in Fairfax, Virginia on a Wednesday, fly to San Jose, California for a tournament over the weekend, and then play a home game against Towson University on Thursday. When conference games got underway in October it became more of a routine, playing every Friday and Sunday. But if we were on the road, that meant disappearing from Thursday to Sunday, sometimes early Monday. Factor in practice days, classes, studying, eating and sleeping, and you're left with maybe fifteen minutes to try and get your dick wet. Having a girlfriend provides some comfort, but if you're someone who *loves* to go out, *loves* to drink, and *loves* to party, you quickly miss it.

Making matters worse, our couch implemented new team rules. They included a dry season and game night curfews, agreed upon by contract. This may have been the direct result of a Halloween incident from the previous season, involving myself, Jackrabbit, Sava Shot, Drinksandfalls, Black Mr. Ed, and HGH, but why ruin a good thing? We won the school's first conference title in men's soccer. That's like writing *The Bad News Bears,* and then writing *The Bad News Bears Go to Japan.* The team quickly became divided between goody two-shoe scrubs, and fun loving starters. Not wanting to lose my scholarship and cost my parents any more money, I was forced to toe the line and act discreetly, if at all. I'll tell you who no longer gave a fuck about going out and living it up though… Rachel! My innocent little chicky emerged from her shell in full force, feeling like she had some catching up to do.

"Are you going out tonight?" I asked Rachel, lying down in her bed

"Yeah, I think so," she said with her back to me, rummaging through the closet. "Do you have a game tomorrow?"

"Yes, tomorrow would be Friday. Why don't we stay in tonight and go out tomorrow?" I reasoned.

"Because all my friends are going out tonight and Fridays are usually dead." Rachel quickly and wisely added, "Plus, tomorrow is Shabbos."

"Right," I chuckled. "Tomorrow is Shabbos. Funny how that wasn't your first excuse."

"The only reason I go out on Shabbos is because of you," Rachel snapped, now wanting to make eye contact.

"Well that's far from the truth, but with your logic I guess that means I'll be *forcing* you to go out tomorrow, too."

Rachel rolled her eyes and shook her head. "You don't get it. I *don't* like going out on Shabbos. I *never* do it at home, and I *only* do it here because we're together."

Rachel's crap was finally beginning to match her volume.

"And I suppose this *pressure* I put on you is so extensive that it carries over to the weekends when I'm away and you still go out on Shabbos? That's all me, right?"

"That's bullshit!" Rachel snapped.

"Right, I'm making it up. I can't believe *I* am trying to convince *you* to stay in with me," I laughed, still keeping my composure.

"Oh, so you mean like all the times over the summer when *I* wanted to stay in with *you* and got dragged to the bar. Because I love watching you get drunk with your idiot friends and ignore me."

All right, that one admittedly packed a bunch. I muted *Sportcenter,* sat up against her headboard, and got right back into it.

"I love how much you *need* to be a part of that scene now," I said, purposely smirking. "You're trying so hard it's obvious you never were. Have fun though."

"What the fuck are you talking about!" Rachel yelled. "You go to these parties, too."

"Yeah, I went when I was single, because they're guaranteed ass, but I could give two shits about them now."

"Now *that's* a pile of shit!" Rachel scoffed.

"Okay, fine, I still go on occasion," I backtracked. "But let's keep in mind how little I have to spend. You're there because you want to feel like you're part of the *in* crowd. This is exactly what happens when people like you, ones with no high school stories, come to college. You act like if you go to where the hot shots are, you'll be considered one of them."

Rachel was fuming and I loved every minute of it. Her face was red, she kept stomping in and out of the closet, and with any luck, she'd throw something.

"Stop saying I *need* to go! Rachel barked. "I go because that's where my friends want to go, and I have a good time there. I don't go to feel cool, asshole!"

"Admit you care," I arrogantly smiled. "You know you do."

Rachel was about to yell again, but lowered her voice when a light bulb went off. "First of all, I don't care. But you're right; you don't have to spend a lot of money at these places. Yet, you still manage to do so. What I find funny is how you complain to me that you're broke, and then buy all your friends shots at the bar."

That one wiped the smile off my face.

"I'm sorry, I'd rather spend the little money I have doing something fun, rather than waste it on going to dinner. Although, I guess when Daddy's footing the bills neither is an issue."

Rachel silently told me to go fuck myself… by giving me the finger.

"You're good though," I patronized. "I have to admit. For someone who has no idea what they want to do with their life let me suggest law school. You do a fantastic job of flipping every argument we have."

"You make it easy," Rachel confessed, proudly smirking.

"Well, I'll continue making things easy for you," I said, making my way to the door. "Have fun tonight. Wear your nicest *Prada*, match it to your most expensive *Louis Vuitton*, dance around for all to see, and don't come to my game tomorrow, not that you would have anyway."

As the season continued, so did the arguments. Rachel and I were lashing out at each other and meaning most of what we said. The annoying part was, we were fine for half the week. We'd have our sleepovers, cook dinner together, go to the gym, watch our shows, everything we loved to do and had already been doing, until the extended weekend rolled around. Then we were back at each other's throats. It was as if we were in a mini long-distance relationship, failing when we couldn't be together, and succeeding when we were.

My college soccer career came to an end in mid-November, with a loss to the University of Virginia in the first round of our conference tournament. As I entered early retirement, I immediately looked back and wished I'd taken the sport and my team more seriously, genuinely applying myself and discontinuing my pattern of half-assing everything. It's the classic case of not knowing what you have until it's gone. Of course that's time you can never get back, so there's also no point in dwelling on it. This was the same thought process I had for time lost with Rachel. But unlike soccer, our relationship continued. The opportunity to rebuild and get back to where we were still existed. Yet, I didn't try.

I had never loved anyone the way I loved Rachel, and therefore I had never contemplated my future with anyone but her. Still, the good, the bad, and the in between were fucking my brain sideways. Come winter break, they were raping me.

New Year's 2004, my twenty second birthday, was celebrated with Rachel and friends at a rented bar in New York City. It was absolutely one of the best birthdays of my life, sharing champagne kisses and bodily fluids. Our resolution... never stop loving each other. One week later... die, fucker!

By the time Rachel and I returned to Presidents College for the spring semester, my last and final semester at the school, three reoccurring thoughts were playing a game of tug-o-war. Graduation, a long distance relationship, and religion were battling it out with love. Being completely outnumbered and seeing the odds, I had to wonder if love was enough.

One random Thursday afternoon in early March, Rachel and I lay in bed at my apartment, ready to take a nap before classes.

"What time should I set the alarm for?" I asked.

"Four fifteen." Rachel took her pants off under the covers and threw them on the floor. "Okay, shluffy time," she said, rolled over and kissing me.

I stripped to my boxers and spooned Rachel. "Let's make a baby."

Rachel laughed. "I'm on the pill, dude."

"What about tushy sex?" I smiled.

"What about it?"

"Let's be the world's first couple to have a back door baby."

"You're an idiot," she sighed.

"What? We won't know unless we try," I said, poking Rachel's butt with my erect penis.

"Jon!"

"We can call him Dookie," I laughed. Or Poopette, if it's a girl."

"Poopette?" Rachel repeated. "You want me to name my daughter Poopette? Like adding the 'ette' at the end makes it sound cute."

"Would you prefer, Craparella?"

"I prefer not having a butt baby we have to name after shit," Rachel confessed.

"What would you name our vagina babies then?" I asked, still laughing.

"For a boy, I like Hunter or Blake. For a girl, I like Madison or Dakota."

"Wow," I said, loosening my grip on Rachel's stomach. "I don't mind the trendy, Hollywood, I'm a *cool parent* name for girls, but no son of mine will be called Hunter or Blake. It's been scientifically proven that names such as those will stunt their growth, strip their athleticism, and encourage incessant blazer wearing."

"Yeah, but they'll be smart, good looking, and get all the girls," Rachel countered.

"They'll get their asses kicked, smoke a lot of weed, and only get jappy Long Island girls."

"Fine," Rachel ignored. "What names do you like then?"

"I'm not crazy about any guys' names yet, but for a girl I like Emma. Emma Faith."

"Eh."

"Eh, your face!" I shouted.

Rachel reached her hand around me and slapped my ass.

"I love that *and* I love the name," I declared. "I also like Isabella, because then we can call her Bella for short."

"All right, that one's cute," Rachel admitted.

"Come on, just picture little Emma and Isabella running through the house in party dresses, drinking apple juice from sippy cups, and dancing around to the *Sponge Bob Square Pants* theme song. Tell me that's not adorable," I said, smiling at the thought.

"Yes, it's very cute, honey. Just like you." Rachel kissed the back of my right hand, and then tightened my arms around her stomach again before drifting off to sleep.

I lay awake. Not because I don't ever want to be touched when I'm actually trying to sleep, but because I was trying harder than ever to convince myself our relationship had promise.

When Rachel and I spoke about our future, as rare as that was, she acted like it was a game of imagination. I couldn't hear any truth or sincerity in her voice. For me, the following year would involve having to work full-time and establishing myself in the "real world." For Rachel, it would mean coming back to PC for her junior year, studying abroad in Florence for the half of it, and enjoying the carefree, partying lifestyle of college. In my mind, it was obvious why she didn't care; she was on the winning side of a shitty situation. The more I thought about it, the more I believed our relationship was destined to fail. At the same time, just the idea of not being with her made me sick to my stomach. It was an obvious catch-22. I could stay with Rachel for as long as possible, best case scenario until she went to Italy for five months, or I could break up with her now and spend the rest of my days at Presidents College single, living it up like I had been before she came into the picture.

"Wake up, cutie" I pulled the covers down and kissed Rachel's moist cheek. "It's four fifteen."

"No," she groaned. "More shluffy."

"Sorry, dude. Shluffy time's over. You have class."

"You're not going to yours?" Rachel croaked.

"Nah, I think I'm done for the day."

"Jonathan." Rachel rolled herself over, trying to act motherly but too tired to really care.

"It's all right, I've only missed a few," I lied.

"Did you sleep?" she asked.

"No, but you need to wake up. Someone has to do well and support our butt babies."

Rachel laughed herself into a moaning stretch. "Why didn't you sleep?"

"I tried, but once I start thinking about things, my mind takes over and I can't relax."

"What were you thinking about?"

"Nothing special," I lied, again.

"About graduation and stuff like that?" Rachel wondered.

"That was part of it."

"What were the other parts?"

"Um…" I was hesitant to talk about it, but more worried my head would explode if I kept it in. "I thought about us."

"What specifically?"

"Let me ask you something," I began. "After I graduate and summer is over, what do you see happening to us?"

Rachel wasn't sure how to answer. "I don't know. I haven't really thought about it."

"You haven't thought about it?" I repeated.

"I mean, I try not to," she rephrased.

"Any reason?"

"Because I don't know what's going to happen that far down the road. I'm happy right now, and I *know* that's because of you. The idea of being apart makes me upset, so I don't even let it enter my mind," Rachel skillfully explained.

"You see, I can't do that," I admitted. "No matter how hard I try, I can't act like we're not going to hit a road block."

"What road block?"

"I just don't see how things can work next year."

"Why? Because you think I'm going to be going out every weekend and hooking up with random guys?" Rachel insinuated.

"I hope not, but who knows."

"I know!" she barked.

"Okay, so you'll continue your pattern of finding a new guy, very quickly I'm sure, start hooking up with him, and in turn convince yourself you're better than everyone else because, as you say, you don't hook up with random guys."

The notion of it actually happening was more than enough to bother me, and in turn, I started blaming Rachel for a hypothetical.

"You're being an asshole," Rachel correctly pointed out.

"Maybe, but I hate how I'm getting the shit end of the stick, and I hate the way you're downplaying it."

"What, you want me to drop out?" Rachel patronized.

"Don't say it like you'd even consider it, no one's buying your bullshit. A little concern is all I ask for."

Rachel angrily got out of bed and put her pants on. "Maybe

I'm not as concerned as you because I thought we'd be able to handle it. I guess I was wrong."

"Look at how we were during soccer," I said. "Are you seriously telling me you think we can handle a long-distance relationship?"

"I don't think it'll be easy, but you make it sound like we'll be thousands of miles apart."

"If we make it till spring, we really will be. Then what?"

Rachel's eyes left mine. "I don't know," she whispered.

"Exactly," I retorted.

"How do you expect me to answer these questions?" Rachel returned. "Like I know what's going to happen in the future."

"Obviously you can't answer them, so maybe just understand where I'm coming from," I frustratingly pleaded.

"It's almost like you're looking for an excuse to break up," Rachel added. "Why can't you just be happy now and worry about the other stuff when we get there."

"Once again, it's a hell of a lot easier to say that in your position."

"Oh really? Would you?"

My eyes left Rachel's.

"Exactly!" she yelled. "If things were reversed, you wouldn't even consider having a long-distance relationship and you know it."

"You sound like a politician, saying the right things aloud while saying the honest ones in your head. Sure, you're happy now and you'd be happy staying together till the end of the school year, but maybe that has more to do with you not wanting to see me with anyone else."

That one struck a nerve.

"So that's what this is about. You want to hook up with

other girls," Rachel angrily assumed.

"If I wanted to hook up with other girls, we wouldn't even be having this conversation. I'd just go about it on my own."

That one didn't make it any better.

"I'm leaving."

I quickly continued so Rachel wouldn't walk out. "It seems a little convenient for you, that's all. You say you want to stay together, you believe a long-distance relationship wouldn't be an issue, but I think it's because you don't want to deal with our break up right now."

Tears were streaming down Rachel's face. "Maybe it's because I love you. Did you ever think of that one, asshole! I lost my virginity to you in three months, why do you act like you're not important? Why do you act like you're not different? Never before have I felt even a fraction of what I feel for you, yet you sit here and tell me I'm insincere, our relationship doesn't mean anything, and we're going to break up. You're right, I guess I should start thinking about the future."

Rachel grabbed her shoes and stormed out of the apartment. I stayed in bed and let her go.

The problem with stubborn people is that we don't actually think we're stubborn, we just think we're right. Despite our argument, I knew Rachel loved me with all her heart, as I did her. Still, I was eventually going to have to answer my own question... would love be enough?

Walk Away

June 6, 1944 will forever been known in American History as D-Day, the day American and Allied forces stormed the beaches of Normandy and cracked the Nazi grip on Western Europe. What most people don't know is that D-Day, in military terminology, is simply the day on which an operation is set to begin. When operations are determined, their exact dates and times are not always known. If a mission is to be carried out a day earlier than D-Day, it becomes known as D-1, and if it is to be carried out a day later, D+1. This was actually the case in the invasion of Normandy. D-Day was originally planned for June 5, 1944, but was delayed due to inclement weather. The military also uses the terminology, H-Hour, for the time of day at which the operation will take place.

I couldn't tell you the day or time in which I broke up with Rachel, but I could tell you my plan of invasion. I mapped out every scenario I could think of, mentally placing myself in the moment, preparing for her response, and then cautiously approached it with the element of surprise. Normally, this war tactic would provide a strong advantage, but love is a different kind of battlefield, Pat Benetar. The more I thought about it, the more I realized I'd be the bearer and recipient of a double-edged sword. I hoped being prepared would lighten the wound, but real life can never duplicate the masterpiece you've created in your head. Reality will always be counterfeit.

I closed the door behind me as I walked into Rachel's bedroom.

"What's up, big pup? You hungry?" she asked.

"Nah, I'm okay. I just had *Subway*." I walked across the room and sat at Rachel's desk.

"I want *Subway*. I want the veggies, the multi-grain, and the vinaigrette dressing. That shit is fuckin' good, man. It's fuckin' good!"

Unfortunately, Rachel was in a hyper, playful mood.

"Why are you cleaning?" I asked, briefly distracted by the extraordinary.

"The maid never showed up." Rachel walked into her bathroom. "Poota!"

Okay, when she comes out, just sit her down, grow a pair, and do it; like ripping off a band-aid.

Rachel came out of the bathroom holding several products and dropped them on her bed. "Look at all this crap. I've never even used any of it. You want a bottle of mousse?" she joked.

I was so nervous I couldn't speak. When Rachel didn't hear a sarcastic comment come out of my mouth, she looked over and immediately read my face.

"What's wrong?"

We have to talk.

"Can you stop looking at the floor and tell me what's wrong?" Rachel insisted.

We have to talk. Just say it; she'll know what it means.

My eyes were glued to the carpet. "Can you sit down for a minute?"

Rachel was practically pacing back and forth now. I could

feel the panic building inside her, as if in the back of her mind, she knew this was it.

"Please sit down," I said again, softening every word.

Rachel walked over to me and put her hands on my face. She tried lifting my head, but I wouldn't let her. The guilt was too heavy, and I knew I'd fall apart the second I looked into her eyes.

"Please," I whispered.

Rachel was afraid to let go. She knew the moment she sat down, our relationship was over. She painfully loosened her grip, walked backwards to the side of her bed, and helplessly waited for me to break her heart.

"So?"

My mouth was drying up faster than my heart. I raised my eyes, looked Rachel in hers, and let my tears speak for me.

"You're breaking up with me," she said, not asking.

I nodded my head.

There was no lightening of the wound on either end. It felt like I drained every ounce of life from her body as she sat there staring at me with dying eyes. Her body was shaking, she was crying uncontrollably, but her eyes wouldn't let go. They were pulling me into her heart, forcing me to feel every agonizing rhythm.

My head fell to the floor again while Rachel collapsed into her bed, burying her face in the pillow. As I sat there listening to her cry, I began hating myself more and more. Rachel deserved far better than a few tears and a nod of the head, so I took a chance and tried exposing my own heart.

"Rachel." It felt like the first word I had ever said. She didn't move an inch. I wanted to get up and sit next to her, hold her and cry with her, but I knew if I did, I'd never be able to say what I had to.

"You don't have to talk," I started. "I just want you to hear what I have to say, maybe understand where I'm coming from, and hopefully realize it absolutely kills me that things have to be this way." I waited for any kind of a response.

Rachel picked her lifeless body up and leaned it against the headboard. She grabbed the box of tissues off her nightstand and rested it between her legs, taking one and blowing her nose.

"I think you and I both know it was only a matter of time before this happened," I continued. "Still, I think neither of us wants it to. You've become my life. You've become my heart. I think about you day in and day out, but no matter how hard I try, I can't think about you without thinking about the future. More than that, I don't *want* to think about the future without thinking about you."

I was doing all I could to swallow the tears so I wouldn't cut short what I had to say. Rachel was still crying on the bed, following my eyes and feeling the emotion behind every word.

"This might sound crazy because we haven't even been together for a full year, but I don't need time to tell me what my heart already knows. I want to spend the rest of my life with you, Rachel. I just wish you wanted the same."

"Who says I don't?" Rachel sat up even more, wiping her eyes with another tissue.

"Fine, your words may agree, but your religion and your father certainly do not," I added.

"Obviously he'd be upset, but it's not his choice who I marry," Rachel quickly returned.

"So then you'd marry someone who's Catholic?" I asked.

"I don't know." Rachel slowed down. "You don't understand. It's complicated."

"You're right, I don't understand. I don't understand how if you're in love with someone, if you feel like they're the person you're destined to spend the rest of your life with, if they make you happy, treat you like a princess, love you unconditionally, more than any spoken or written word, every minute of every day, for the rest of your lives and thereafter, I don't understand where religion comes into play. What does it matter if our beliefs our different? The fact that I'm Catholic didn't keep you from falling in love with me, and I guarantee you it's not what makes you fall out of love with me. I'm afraid that's going to be on you."

I didn't want to get upset, but her outlook was beyond frustrating. I understood how important religion was to her and her family, but I couldn't fathom how God wouldn't want her to be happy, even if that meant being with someone who wasn't Jewish.

"So you're telling me it wouldn't bother you if you married someone who wasn't Catholic?" Rachel countered, as expected.

"If I was in love with them, it absolutely wouldn't make a difference," I said, not lying in the least.

"But I know you want to raise your kids Catholic," she added.

"Sure, if it was up to me, I would like to raise my kids Catholic, but that's not what I think about. Relationships are about compromise, and I'm sure marriage magnifies that tenfold. Yet, I would be more focused on raising a happy and healthy family and taking care of my wife and kids, than I would be on whether or not to plan for a Bar Mitzvah or Confirmation."

"So then why don't you convert?" Rachel asked, still working me at the stand.

"I wouldn't convert because I've already established a

strong relationship with God, a relationship that means far too much to just give up on. I feel strongly about what I believe in, and I don't see how I could adopt different beliefs even if I tried. With that said, I still wouldn't have a problem raising my kids Jewish, because I think religion in general instills good morals, teaches respect, and provides structure, faith, and hope. Let me ask you this, did you choose to be Orthodox?"

Rachel angrily looked at me like I was patronizing her at entirely the wrong time. "Obviously not," she answered.

"Right, because most people inherit their religion from their parents. You didn't just walk into the kitchen one day and tell Mommy and Daddy you wanted to be Jewish, they told you and that was it. When you're young you believe everything you hear, thinking it's right, thinking it's normal, especially when surrounded by those of the same faith, but at a certain age there comes a point where you should see the world differently, and hopefully not live *exactly* by the book."

I wasn't sure if any of that sank in, as Rachel quickly fired back. "So then you don't think you're here for a reason? You think you were born into this world to just have a few laughs and then be on your way to afterlife?"

"I think that's part of it," I said, shrugging at the truth.

"Well, we believe that life is a gift from g-d that's not to be taken for granted. While we're here, we should live by his laws, practice and preach his religion, procreate and instill that faith on our children, and hopefully, we'll be welcomed into heaven for doing so. Jews don't believe in an afterlife," Rachel pointed out.

I no longer was the only one feeling that frustrated sense of anger. All tears were put on hold as the debate between love and religion continued.

"I believe a lot of the same things you do," I said. "Still, the way you explain it sounds like you already have your life mapped out, like you *know* what God's plan is."

"In a way, I think it is mapped out," Rachel agreed.

"Right, but you can't honestly believe you have any idea how? They may sound the same, but God or a GPS aren't going to tell you what direction to head in for the rest of your life. I'm afraid you're going to have to discover some of that on your own. And truthfully, that's the fun part."

That one sank her battleship. Without an immediate response, I continued.

"I do agree with part of what you're saying, as sometimes I think I'm here to write and tell stories that will impact people's lives. But, I'm also good with kids, so maybe I'm here to work with them and have a positive influence on their lives. Yet, maybe, just maybe, I'm here to love you Rachel, every day, for the rest of *our* lives."

Painfully tears began filling the room again. "Then why are you breaking up with me?" she cried.

"Because I don't think you realize how hard it's going to be if we stay together until that inevitable point. As much as it kills me, and you have no idea how much it does, it's the best thing for me. If I can get through this while I'm around you, then adjusting to it while you're away will be ten times easier. It's that instant separation I won't be able to handle," I explained.

"And you don't think you're going to be a mess right now?"

"I already am," I whispered.

"Then why not be with me for as long as you can?" Rachel pleaded. "Jonathan! Please don't break up with me."

I didn't know what else to say. Her tears were contagious and I couldn't bear looking at her anymore. Completely and utter drained, I swiveled my chair in the other direction. My head was throbbing, my heart was aching, and just when I thought I couldn't handle any more, Rachel did what she always does and threw me for a loop.

"No! No! I don't care what you say." Rachel sprung off her bed like she found the solution. She turned my chair around and sat in my lap, locking her hands behind my neck.

"I'm not letting you break up with me," Rachel announced, dripping endless tears on my cheat. "I love you too much. I love you so, so much!" she yelled, kissing my cheek with her quivering lips. "I'm not giving up. I know how much you love me, and I *know* you don't want this."

"You're right," I lowly admitted.

"Then don't do it, Jon! *Please.* Please don't do this."

Rachel was holding me tighter than ever before. I could feel her trying to squeeze new life into me, new hope. She was fighting for us with every bit of her heart, and I sat there, lifeless, empty.

"Look at me," she ordered.

I didn't move.

"Look at me!" Rachel shouted, gripping my face and turning it towards her. "You can't break up with me. Do you know why?" she asked. "Do you know why you can't break up with me?"

I slowly shook my head, ready for a bullet.

"Because I'm your heart," she cried. "You tell me all the time, 'Rachel, you're my heart. You're my heart, Rachel.' Well, how are you going to live without your heart?"

I kissed her wet lips, tasting her tears, hiding mine, and generating more. "You're always going to be my heart, Rachel. Until the day I die, you will be what has kept me alive."

Concrete words were taking effect and I didn't know how

much more I could take.

"I really do think about marrying you," Rachel said, bailing me out. "I think about it all the time. When I told my friends that, they thought you were giving me drugs."

I couldn't help but smile. Seeing this, Rachel quickly went on.

"I love talking about what our kids would look like, I love giving them names, especially Hollywood ones," she smiled. "And I love picturing us as a family. Every bit of it makes me the happiest girl in the world, because in my mind, I can have the perfect life."

"But in real life?" I interrupted.

"In real life, it's perfect now." Rachel wisely added, "But that's not to say it can't be the same way in the future. Don't you think I wish religion wasn't an issue? Don't you think I wish my parents were okay with this?"

"I wish *you* were the one without the concerns," I confessed.

"It's not that simple."

"So I've heard." I tried standing up, but Rachel wouldn't let me.

"No! You're not leaving," she cried.

I lifted us out of the chair and placed her feet on the ground. She instantly wrapped her hands around my waist.

"It just kills me," I whispered, lightly shaking my head over hers. "It absolutely kills me."

"What does?" Rachel quietly asked, looking up at me with bloodshot eyes.

"It kills me that I've found the missing piece to my puzzle, the one and only piece that will complete my picture and make sense of it all, but as I literally hold onto it, I know it doesn't matter anymore... it's already been framed."

There is nothing in this world that compares to love; it's as simple as that. The emotions that come with it, the joy, the pain, the lessons learned, the memories shared, every aspect of it, or lack thereof, molds us into who we are. However, love lost will always break you down. It's where the expression 'a broken heart' comes from. That's not to say there aren't two options though... repair, or start fresh.

Fighting For My Love

Rachel and I ironically broke up around the most religious time of year. She spent Passover in Florida with her family, while I celebrated Easter on Long Island with mine.

Passover, or Pesach, a.k.a., the Festival of Unleavened Bread, honors the time in history when Jews were freed from slavery in Egypt. The Pharaoh believed Jews were becoming too powerful, and thus ordered all male Jewish babies to be killed. Getting word of this, one couple, Jochevad and Amran, tried saving their infant son by putting him in a basket and floating him down the river. He was in fact rescued, except by the Pharaoh's daughter. She took him in and named him Moses, meaning taken from the water. Later discovering he was Jewish, Moses wanted to help free his people. The Pharaoh refused.

G-d then sent ten plagues to Egypt; blood, frogs, lice, beasts, cattle disease, boils, hail, locusts, darkness, and slaying of the firstborn. The murdering of his offspring is the one that got him, as he then freed the Jewish people. They immediately fled, taking only their belongings and unleavened bread (this is why matzah is eaten during Passover). Realizing you don't know what you have until it's gone, the Pharaoh changed his mind and ordered his army to retrieve his slaves. Not agreeing with this, g-d parted the Red Sea for the Jews to cross, and then closed it on Pharaoh's soldiers, killing them all. The Jews were free. Of course they spent some time wondering the desert after that, but what's forty years of sand compared to four hundred years of slavery.

Passover is an eight-day celebration. The first two days and the last two days are major holidays, while the days in between, Chol Hamoed, are festival days. Seders are special dinners that take place on the first two nights. During Seders, the story of the Exodus from Egypt is told, using a special text called the Haggadah. The Haggadah is divided into fifteen parts, and four cups of wine are consumed during the narrative. Seders are also filled with questions and answers, mainly to spark an interest and curiosity in the children. There's even a miniature scavenger hunt. A piece of matzah is hidden, or the afikoman, the last thing eaten at Seder, and whoever finds it is rewarded with a prize, usually money.

In middle school, my friend invited me to his Seder, but I had no idea what he was talking about. I was hesitant at first, but when you're eleven years old and your friend describes it as a party with lots of food and money, you're in the car before it's started. This was pre-Bar/Bat Mitzvah era though, so I was very confused. When they handed me a yamaka, I thought it was a shoulder pad, when they spoke Hebrew, I thought they were choking, and when they showed me a jar of gefilte fish, I thought they were out of their minds. When it was time to search for the afikoman, I laid low and sat in the kitchen, partially because I was uncomfortable, but mainly because I had no idea what I was looking for. When I reached across the table for a macaroon, I noticed a piece of matzah in someone's bag. I assumed it fell in there accidentally, because no sane woman is going to walk around making a mess of their *Louis Vuitton*, so I took it out.

"The Catholic kid found it! The Catholic kid found it!" Before I know what's happening, I'm standing in front of the Seder's Don Corleone, exchanging unleavened bread for twenties.

Rachel's family celebrates Passover a little differently. They spend it at a five star hotel in Miami, Florida. Hotels, resorts, and even cruise ships all across the United States revamp their establishments, making them kosher for Passover, in hopes of attracting families to week-long vacations. It's basically an eight-day, Jews only, *Star Trek* convention. Her parents stay in the penthouse suite where their Seders and other meals are catered, while the kids and one of their housekeepers, usually Shama Lama Ding Dong, are split up in regular rooms around the hotel. Passover follows a lot of the observances of the Sabbath, so to better accommodate their guests, the hotel adds amenities like goyim elevator operators, twenty-four hour on-call rabbis, and a converted ballroom where you can, Pray With The Stars!

There are also recreational activities for everyone. Matchmaking and the ancient art of yenta are big amongst the mothers, while their younger counterparts enjoy hours under the sun and in the spa. When the men are not davening in shul, they can be found splashing around in the pool. This usually means a lot of wet payus', chest and back hair, but if you're Jewish and adopted, heard of but never met your uncle, have only seen pictures of your relatives or just want to put together the family tree, head on down to Florida and dive into the Jewish gene pool, you're bound to come up with answers... or hair in your mouth.

Rachel, however, was shopping for clues elsewhere. She solicited the help of her mother to find them.

"This is cute," Eileen said, taking a shirt off the rack.

Rachel turned around. "Eww... Mom... gross."

"What? I think it's cute." She held the shirt against her chest and looked in the mirror. "Maybe I'll get it."

"Please don't," Rachel muttered.

Eileen placed the shirt back on the rack. "So how are things with you and Jon?"

Rachel turned and shot laser beams from her eyes.

"You know what I mean," Eileen said. "How are you handling it?"

"Just great," Rachel sarcastically answered.

"Have you spoken to him since you broke up?"

"A few times over the phone. So far I've woken up Amanda, Emily, and Heather."

"From crying or from arguing?" Eileen inquired.

"I don't want to talk about it." Rachel put her head down and continued shopping.

"Sometimes it's good to talk about it. Go ahead, get it off your chest."

"Don't worry, everything rolls off my chest," Rachel smirked.

"At least you haven't lost your sense of humor," Eileen laughed.

"Yeah, just Jon."

"Aww, Ra-Ra," Eileen whimpered.

"Did you tell Dad?" Rachel wondered.

"Of course. He's my husband."

"I bet he's happier than ever."

"Honey, no one wants to see their child upset," Eileen said, doing a good job of avoiding the real answer.

"Bullshit," Rachel snapped. "You know he doesn't want us to be together."

"Is that why you guys broke up?" Eileen continued prying.

"It didn't help!" she yelled.

"Sweetie, you're twenty years old. You're still very young."

"You were engaged at twenty-one."

"Yes, but things are different now," Eileen reasoned. "There are so many guys out there, right here even, who are better suited for you. Why don't you let me set you up?"

"You're ridiculous," Rachel scolded.

"Ra-Ra, we only want the best for you," Eileen pleaded, with ulterior motives.

"It's funny how you think you know what that is." Rachel stormed out and walked back to the hotel.

Easter is the most religious and celebrated holiday in Christianity. On what is known as Good Friday, Jesus Christ, the only son of God, was nailed to the cross and died. Three days later, he rose again, commemorating Easter Sunday.

Easter also marks the end of Lent, a forty-day period of fasting, repentance, and moderation, which begins on Ash Wednesday. Jesus died for the sins of others, but through his death, burial, and resurrection, he offers eternal life for all who believe in him.

Over two thousand years ago, in a stable in Bethlehem, Jesus was born (Christmas!). He grew up in Nazareth with his father, Joseph, and mother, Mary, where he later became a carpenter. Jesus saw the people of Palestine suffering under the rule of Herod's sons, and the Romans, and decided to wander the land with twelve disciples, preaching religious reform and telling of God's love for his people. The Pharisees, or Jewish scholars, strongly disagreed with his teachings. The commoners did not, as they looked at him to be the Messiah. Unfortunately, the more recognition he got, the more Jewish and Roman authorities suspected him of being a revolutionary. Jesus faithfully followed his religious customs though, including Passover, traveling to Jerusalem one year to celebrate. The real Jerusalem that is, not to be confused with where Rachel grew up.

Jesus was greeted with great praise when he arrived, which angered the Pharisees even more. They decided it was time to get rid of Jesus, and with the priests and Romans they planned his arrest and execution. Days later, Jesus celebrated the Feast of Passover with his twelve disciples, more commonly known as The Last Supper. During the meal, he told his disciples that before the night ended, he would be betrayed by one of his own and handed over to those who wanted to kill him.

John, the disciple sitting next to Jesus, whispered to him so no one else could hear, "Lord, who is it?"

Jesus whispered back, "It is the one to whom I shall give a piece of bread after I have dipped it in the dish." Jesus later reached across the table and handed the bread to Judas. Towards the end of supper, Judas left, but before doing so, Jesus said to him, "*You dirty rat.*" I mean, "Do quickly what you have to do." At the end of the meal, Jesus broke unleavened bread and handed a piece to the eleven remaining disciples saying, "Take this, all of you, and eat it; this is my body which will be given up for you." He then passed around a cup of wine and said, "Take this, all of you, and drink from it; this is the cup of my blood, the blood of the new and everlasting covenant. It will be shed for you and for all so that sins may be forgiven. Do this in memory of me." These words are better known as The Words of Institution, and are used to bless the Eucharist (better known to Jews as the *Nilla Wafer*). Jesus spent the rest of the night praying; knowing that before morning, Judas would betray him.

When Judas left the table, he went to meet with the High Priest of the Temple, selling his boy out for thirty pieces of silver. The next morning, Judas led the High Priest, Pharisees, and Roman soldiers to Jesus, but to assure them they were arresting the right person, Judas embraced Jesus with a hug (That's some fucked up shit right there; in the world of *The Sopranos,* if Judas tried pulling that shit with Tony, he'd take one between the eyes). Eventually, Jesus was sentenced by Pontius Pilate and the Roman governor to death on the cross. However, three days after his death, when a group of women went to put fragrant herbs in the linens covering his body, they discovered an open tomb, and two angels sitting where Jesus' body once lay. The angels told the women not to fear, for Jesus had risen from the dead.

Jesus was a real person, there is no doubt of that, but very little is known of his life other than what his followers told and wrote. There isn't, nor will there ever be, enough thorough, definitive, or factual evidence to support or refute these stories. Therefore, the story of Jesus, Moses, and many others, are only true based upon belief. Unfortunately, some people can't believe without seeing.

Easter on Long Island wasn't as glamorous as Passover in Florida, but it's a tradition I look forward to every year. I love going to church and seeing springtime via pastel shirts and flower dresses. I love seeing families come together while envisioning my own. I love how my grandma still makes Easter baskets for her grandkids. I love how my mom still makes us an Easter egg hunt. I love even more how we've transitioned from hiding chocolate covered eggs to hiding plastic ones with money inside. I love listening to my grandpa's war stories. I love the ham my mom makes, and I most definitely love the chocolate mousse. I love our traditions because they strengthen our memories, but what I love most is my family. Still, that doesn't mean you always love hearing their advice.

"It's probably for the best. Don't you think?" Jacquelyn said, busy layering a tray of lasagna along the kitchen counter.

"Why's that?" I asked, seated at the table.

"Well, don't you think Rachel being Orthodox would create problems down the road?"

"No, not really," I shrugged.

"So then you'd give up your religion?" she inquired.

"No, not at all."

Jackie and I have a weird way of discussing personal issues. Rather than openly say what she's thinking, she asks a series of questions in a fake weatherman's voice. What Jackie doesn't realize is it's completely obvious, and indirectly she's giving me her opinion.

"Dou you think Rachel is allowed to marry someone who's not Jewish?" my mother continued.

"I'd like to think the decision is ultimately hers," I responded. "Obviously religion is a big issue, but I think love and happiness are overwhelming factors."

"Do you honestly believe her father would let her marry you?"

"Again, I'm sure he'd be far from happy, but she's old enough to make her own decisions," I pointed out.

"Don't you think you're setting yourself up for a lot of complications? How would you raise your kids? Would they celebrate both holidays? Don't you think that would confuse them? Where would they go to school?"

Here's where Jackie's tactic backfires. Eventually, I reach a point of frustration where I purposely disagree with everything she says, regardless of whether I believe it or not.

"I think *you guys* are the ones who make everything

complicated," I snapped. "I think *you guys* are the ones who make it like we're doing something wrong, like our relationship is a bad idea. Rachel, unfortunately, has a harder time fighting that pressure, whereas I could give two shits if you don't like who I date."

"I never said I didn't like Rachel," Jacquelyn retreated. "You know I think she's a nice girl."

"That's great, Mom. Good to know. But you could hate her all the same and it wouldn't affect how I feel." I paused to calm myself down. "You just don't get it."

Jacquelyn walked over to the kitchen table and pulled up a chair. "Explain it to me," she said.

Without hesitating I got straight to the point. "I love my religion, I'm very proud to be Catholic, but you're never going to fully understand or feel the relationship I have with God, just like you won't understand or feel the relationship I have with Rachel. I also don't think God is going to be mad at me for being happy, for marrying the girl I love. Do you? Because I don't see that happening."

"Okay," Jackie patronized. "So then why aren't you guys still together?"

Down goes Reynolds!

"I don't want to talk about it." I walked out of the kitchen like a little kid refusing to believe he had lost. In reality, I knew a lot of what she was saying was right, but deep down it wasn't the conversation I was upset about losing.

Family and religious obligations eventually came to an end, as Rachel and I separately returned to Presidents College. Once again confined to a small perimeter, it was nearly impossible not to see her. I tried, I really did, but sometimes sticking to your guns can feel like shooting yourself in the foot.

I missed Rachel. I wholeheartedly missed her. I missed holding her, I missed kissing her, and very simply, I missed us. A day wouldn't go by where something didn't remind me of her. Everywhere I went, I saw her. Sometimes literally, sometimes figuratively, but I definitely could not get her out of my mind. She was my magnet, and it had nothing to do with having buns of steel.

Slowly but surely, Rachel and I reverted back to old ways. Monday through Wednesday we would act as if we never broke up, falling into our routine, and then the extended weekend rolled around and I wanted to party. Alcohol eased my conscience, but what it really boils down to is I was acting like a selfish asshole. There's no other way for me to say it. I was fucking with Rachel's emotions. When it was time to stay in, I needed her; I wanted to be with her, I couldn't push her away. When it was time to go out, I needed to be independent, I wanted to clear my head, I had to move on. I was your typical, schizophrenic, prick of a guy. What makes it even worse is I was as aware of it then as I am now. The only difference being, I believed my own bullshit back in the day.

Meanwhile, on the other front, Rachel was an emotional mess. On nights she stayed in and I went out, she cried till all hours of the morning. Sometimes not answering her calls was just as bad as picking them up. There were nights where I couldn't bear being without her and would go back to her apartment, while other nights, I would purposely ignore her and go back to my own. On nights she'd go out, I made it an issue to go somewhere else, and if for some reason *I* stayed in for the night, well, take a guess where I spent it.

I believe in Karma as strongly as I do Fate. However, when I think about Fate, I'm optimistic, whereas when I think about

Karma, I'm just scared. There is such a thing as Good Karma, but he tends to be overshadowed by Luck. The Karma I know is that creepy bastard lurking over your shoulder, whispering, "You can run, but you can't hide." He's Dog the Bounty Hunter. He's the bullied kid making a 'list.' He's Justin Timberlake singing, *What Goes Around.../...Comes Around*. Karma is ultimately the balance beam of the universe, but what frightens me is his waiting game. Sometimes he'll put your plan on layaway and let you think you're getting off scot-free, while other times, he won't wait more than ten minutes to punch you in the face.

Another college night out, about halfway through my final semester at Presidents College, my friends and I went to a bar in downtown Washington, D.C. I was hesitant to walk into The Long Island Scene, because Rachel would most likely be part of it, but with soccer recruits in town we needed an eighteen and over party. Simply put, if a high school kid goes on an official visit where he goes out, gets drunk, and hooks up with a college girl, he's more likely than not going to attend the school. After that you just have to hope he doesn't suck it up on the field.

While waiting in line with Drinksandfalls, Black Mr. Ed, Sava Shot, and three eighteen year olds, I noticed Polka Dot was working the door. Polka Dot is native Long Islander. When I transferred to PC, a friend from high school introduced the two of us. She's short, cute, brunette, and Jewish, so obviously I was attracted to her. She also has an identical twin, which is always great. There's the obvious sexual fantasy, but then there's the comfort of knowing that if you strike out with one, you're guaranteed another at bat. Polka Dot was also a lot of fun and our personalities instantly clicked. The fact that she was exactly my type was just icing on the penis cake. Every time she worked a party she would take care of my friends and me, but that was honestly as far as it went. When I was single, she had a boyfriend, and when she was single, I had a girlfriend. I was a square peg and she was a round hole. We got along, but we were aware of the obvious, so neither of us tried anything. That night however, technically, *technically*, we were both single. Even though I was destined not to fit, we tried forcing it.

"Polka Dot."

Polka Dot lit up when she saw me. "Hey, what's up!" she exclaimed.

"Not much," I said, giving her a kiss on the cheek.

"Where've you been? I haven't seen you in a while."

"I've been around," I smiled. "Waiting for you, mostly."

"Yeah, yeah," Polka Dot smiled back.

"Are you coming in later?" I asked, hoping she would.

"Yeah, I'll be in for a drink."

"Cool."

"Are you with all these guys?" she asked, looking over my shoulder and making a face when she saw The Jonas Brothers.

"Well you know Drinksandfalls, Black Mr. Ed, and Sava Shot. The Hanson brothers are soccer recruits in for the weekend. You can charge them double if you want."

"No, it's fine," Polka Dot laughed. "Just make sure they go in as eighteen."

"Anything for you."

"We'll see," she smiled.

Seconds upon entering, my friends and I posted up near the bar like we normally do. The crowd was exactly what I expected, different ages and variations of jappy girls and douchebag guys. The only good part about it was I could continuously talk to new girls without having to move around.

"Hey, Rennie."

"Plum!" I shouted. "What's going on?"

Plum was a girl on the track team, long-legged, blonde and innocent. She was nice, not necessarily my type, but every now and then I'll have a crush on a blondie and she was it.

"How's everything?" she began.

"Everything's cool. Who are you here with?"

"Your girl, Lady Conan O'Brien," she laughed.

"Yeah, we're practically engaged," I joked, while my stomach turned.

"That's what I hear."

Plum was staring at me with a huge grin on her face.

"You're never going to let me live that one down, are you?"

"Nope," she laughed.

"In that case, we'll try erasing it with alcohol. Your memory or mine, it works either way."

Plum and I took a shot at the bar and eventually broke off. The night carried on that way, exchanging conversations and shots with friends and females. Eventually, the one I'd been thinking about came out of nowhere and tapped me on the shoulder.

"Are you ready?"

"Polka Dot! You're done working?"

"Yeah, I couldn't take it anymore. I told them I was going inside."

"You missed me that much, huh?"

"How'd you know?"

"Just a hunch," I smiled.

"You ready to start drinking?" she asked.

"Start? You ready to catch up?"

"Something tells me that'll be hard…"

Too late.

"… But I'll try," she finished.

Polka Dot and I walked three steps to the bar.

"All right, so we'll go two shots my choice, two shots your choice," I said. "Deal?"

"Two shots each?" she questioned.

"Huh?"

"Are we doing two shots each during your round and then two shots each during my round, or just two shots total, per person?"

"Um...

What the fuck is she talking about?

"What's that?" I asked.

"Never mind. Just order two shots *each*, four *total*," Polka Dot said, like I was a three-year-old alcoholic.

The nameless and faceless bartender popped up out of nowhere. "What can I get you guys?"

"Um, um, I would like…." I counted on my fingers then held up four, "This many shots of *SoCo* and lime, please."

Polka Dot hit me on the shoulder as the bartender walked away.

"What?"

"Nothing," she smiled.

The bar was quickly reaching capacity, which meant Polka Dot and I were practically on top of each other.

"You look cute tonight."

"Thank you. You look…" Polka dot leaned back and gave me the once over.

"The same as usual," I answered for her.

"Good," she smiled, again.

"That'll be twenty-eight!" the bartender shouted, placing the shots in front of us.

"I got it." I took my dwindling funds out of my pocket and paid the bartender. "You ready?" I asked Polka Dot.

"Yep."

Polka Dot and I each picked up a shot.

"Cheers."

Polka Dot and I each took down a shot.

"Do you want a lime?" I asked.

"No, I'm good," Polka Dot casually answered.

Me too, I suppose.

"Are you ready to go again?" she rushed.

Nope.

"Of course." We touched glasses and knocked down the second shot.

Polka Dot kept her foot on the pedal. "All right, it's my choice now."

"What are you going with?" I asked.

"*Jameson.*"

"*Jameson?*" I repeated. "You want to take shots of *Jameson?*"

"Yeah, I love *Jameson.*" Polka Dot made it sound like she was talking about apple juice.

"No girl likes *Jameson,*" I declared. "Not unless she's two hundred and forty pounds, covered in leather, and rides on the back of a *Harley.*"

Polka Dot laughed at my disbelief. "I swear, it's one of my favorites."

"Oh, so then you're the coolest girl in the world?" I smiled.

"Pretty much," she returned, flirtatiously smiling back at me.

Polka Dot slid in front of my cock and leaned over the bar. "Four shots of *Jameson,*" she loudly ordered.

"You know you don't have to impress me." I looked down

and checked out her ass. "We're way past that."

"I know. I'm just trying to get you drunk so I can take advantage of you."

The bartender returned with our shots as I neared shooting something else. "That'll be twenty-eight!"

Before I could even get my hand in my pocket, Polka Dot paid for the drinks.

"What?" she asked, wondering why I was looking at her like a mirage.

"Nothing," I lied. "I was just thinking."

"Uh oh. We can't have any of that. Quick, drink this." Polka Dot handed me a shot.

I raised my glass alongside hers and we took them down. I quickly reached for a lime.

"You look like you're struggling a bit," Polka Dot smiled.

"What makes you say that," I mumbled, keeping the lime in my mouth.

"Just a hunch."

I took the lime out and put it in the empty shot glass. "Listen, Polka Dot, while you were busy standing next to a door tonight, soberly crossing names off your grocery list, I was busy perfecting my Beer Pong game. One of us clearly has their priorities straight, and I think it's the person training for the Beer Pong Olympic Team."

Polka Dot paused and raised her eyebrows at me. "Are you done?" she asked.

"Well, Beer Pong isn't actually an Olympic sport, but in the event that it does become one, I'll be ready to take the world by storm."

Polka Dot continued staring at the village idiot.

"There's no point in stalling, is there?" I asked.

Polka Dot shook her head. "Nope."

She handed me the other shot then picked up her own. I reached for another lime, sliding in front of her and sticking my ass out like she did earlier.

Polka Dot started cracking up. "Oh, so that's how you like it."

"Be gentle," I whispered.

We touched glasses and drank our final shots.

"How good is that?" she asked.

"It's delicious." I took a quick bite of the lime. "Although if you genuinely like the taste of that, I'm curious to know what else you think tastes good."

"Whatever do you mean, Jon?"

"Nothing. I was just…"

"Were you thinking again?" Polka Dot interrupted.

"Maybe," I grinned. "Although it's hard to tell with only nine brain cells left."

"Now what did we say about thinking?" Polka Dot reprimanded, like a grade school teacher to her Special Ed. students.

"Um, not to?" I played along.

"That's a good boy."

Polka Dot gave me a kiss on the cheek. "I'll be right back. I'm going to say hi to my friends."

It was official; Polka Dot was a Cool Chick with a Hot Ass. A CCHA if you will. As I stood there, watching her walk away, Drinksandfalls came over and quickly slapped the grin off my face.

"Rachel's here," he announced.

"What?" I casually surveyed the room.

"Yeah, she just walked in with Blondie Cheeks, Blondie

Glasses, and Generic."

"Fuck!"

"I don't know if anything's happening with you and Polka Dot, but I just wanted to give you the heads up," he said.

"I'm not even sure what's happening with us, but something tells me it's over now. I appreciate it though."

"No problem. I'll talk to you later. Let me know how it works out." Drinksandfalls had a smirk on his face, trying not to laugh.

"You're leaving?" I asked.

"Yeah, we've got to get the recruits out of here before they get into some shit. One of them is already running his mouth."

"That sucks," I said, not really caring. "I'll talk to you tomorrow then."

"Cool. Have fun," Drinksandfalls said, fully laughing now. "Although I should probably be wishing you luck."

Great. Now what?

I scanned the bar again to see where Rachel was. I couldn't find her.

"Hey, handsome."

Oh shit.

"Don't tell me you're back for more *Jameson?*"

"Nope, more Jonathan," Polka Dot smiled.

Oh shit.

"So I heard something very interesting," she began.

"What's that?" I asked.

"A little birdie told me you and Rachel broke up." Polka Dot quickly realized it wasn't a very flirtatious subject. "We don't have to talk about it though."

"It's fine. You can ask whatever you want." I figured the conversation might be shorter that way.

"Did you break up with her, or she broke up with you?"

"I broke up with her," I returned.

"Any reason?"

Yeah, I thought it'd be a good April Fool's joke.

"Um, it was just something I had to do. We were going to break up eventually, so I figured it made more sense to do so now, rather than the day before she came back for her junior year."

"That's right, she's a only sophomore," Polka Dot said, stating the obvious. "I see what you're saying though. I'm sure it's hard now…"

Not any more.

"But that kind of immediate separation would be even harder if you're on Long Island and she's here. When did you break up?" she continued.

"Just before Passover."

"And how are you handling it?"

Katie Couric is not a CCHA. I appreciated the role-play, but I appreciated Polka Dot's tight ass rubbing against me even more.

"I'm good," I said, answering her anyway. "I think you healed me."

"Is that right?" she smiled.

"Yep, you have a gift."

Polka Dot quickly regained her flirtatious ways.

"Well I'm not sure what I did, but I'm glad I could help."

"You're a Jewish Mother Theresa," I joked.

"So I'm the ugliest woman in the world?"

"Far from it," I laughed, sinking a gimme.

Polka Dot blushed, but not for long. "In that case, I have another gift for you."

"What's that?" I asked, playing dumb.

Polka Dot leaned in.

I know what it is! I know what it is!

The moment our lips touched, my brain officially shut down (not to say it was working well before). Ironically, I adhered to Polka Dot's advice and actually stopped thinking. If you ask me most guys would have done the same thing if they were in my shoes, but that's far from an excuse. I hold only myself responsible for walking in, and not walking out, of the situation.

So there we were, right in the middle of the bar, French, French, Frenching for all to see. God only knows how many eyes were upon us, but there was only two that really mattered. Unfortunately, they had front row seats.

"What the fuck are you doing!" Rachel forcefully ripped me off of Polka Dot. The three of us stood there in a triangle, frozen, as if we'd simultaneously sharted our pants. Luckily, for me anyway, Rachel unleashed her wrath in the other direction.

"Are you fuckin' kidding me!" Rachel shouted.

Polka Dot was still in shock and didn't know what to say.

"What?"

Bad choice.

"*What!* What the fuck do you mean, *what?*" Why the fuck are you kissing him?" Rachel erupted.

"I uh, I thought you guys, uh, I thought you were broken up," Polka Dot stammered.

Technically we were, so *technically* I didn't do anything wrong, but technicalities don't mean dick when you see the person you love making out with someone else.

"That doesn't mean dick!" Rachel screamed, casing my point. "You don't know what our situation is, so stay the fuck out of it!"

Rachel was an angry little F-Bomber. I'm not gonna lie, for the first time, one of her tirades was actually pretty scary.

"All right. I'm sorry," Polka Dot tried.

"Yeah, I'm sure you're *real, fuckin', devastated!*"

Polka Dot was desperately looking for a lifesaver. At one point her eyes were blinking so much I thought she was sending distress signals. Tiptoeing out of there and leaving Polka Dot with the fiery Orthodox certainly crossed my mind, but I knew what I had to do. Saying my prayers, I stepped in the crossfire.

"I don't understand, are you such a fucking *whore* that you hooked up with every guy in here and now you have to go after mine? Huh?" Rachel asked, still tearing into Polka Dot. "Answer me, whore!"

Okay, maybe I pumped the brakes, but I'd get it on the second attempt.

This is going to hurt.

"Rachel, please calm down," I said, hearing my voice crack. "We're both at fault."

"No shit, ASSHOLE! You think I don't know you have a crush on this *whore*. This stupid fuckin' *whore!*"

Polka Dot shoved me aside and finally stepped to Rachel. "Call me a whore again. See what happens, *bitch!*"

Oh no. Bad idea.

At the top of Rachel's lungs... "WHORE, SLUT, BITCH, SKANK, WHORE, WHORE, *WHORE!*"

Polka Dot and Rachel were face-to-face, stiletto-to-stiletto, handbag-to-handbag. In my best announcers voice, I mentally read the tale of the tape.

"In this corner, wearing the *Diesel Jeans*, standing at five feet five inches, a hundred and eleven pounds, hailing from

Merrick, New York, with a record of 22-0, eighteen by way of bitch slaps, connecting one win after another, the undisputed, reigning Cat Fight Champion of the South Shore... Polka Dot the Punisher!"

"And in this corner, wearing the *Seven Jeans*, standing at five feet three inches, a hundred and four pounds, residing from Great Neck, New York, with an impressive record of 17-0, fifteen by way of verbal and mental abuse, the North Shore's reigning Cat Fight Champion... Rachel the Soul Crusher!"

The brief thought of two sexy women fighting over me was enough to finish going through puberty, but I used the extra testosterone and deepened voice to do the right thing, step back in the middle, and have sex with both of them. I mean separate them! I stepped in the middle and separated them.

"Enough!" I shouted, trailing off as soon as I felt the intensity of the lion's den. "Could we please just end this?" I descreetly lowered my hands to protect my junk.

"You know what?" Polka Dot said.

"You're a whore?" Rachel answered.

"I'm going to be the bigger person and walk away."

"You're definitely bigger." Rachel impressively worked in a fat joke.

I looked at Polka and thanked her with my scared expression.

As soon as Polka Dot left, Rachel's anger left with her. Tears replaced the red in her eyes, but there was nothing I could say to substitute the pain. Rachel broke down and practically ran out of the bar crying. Once again, my cake tasted like shit.

I stayed at the bar after Rachel left, walking around in a daze and drinking myself into an even bigger one. I was a complete mix of emotions, but before I could collect a thought, the lights came on and it was closing time. I didn't bother saying goodbye to anyone, nor did I care to. I didn't see any of my friends, nor did I care to find them. I drifted outside, stood by the curb, and waited for a cab to end my night.

"Hey."

A metrosexual hobbit appeared out of nowhere and started talking to me.

"What's up?" I said, being polite.

"Are you waiting for a cab?" he asked.

No, I moonlight here on weekends.

"Yes," I answered.

"Me too."

"Um, cool?"

I didn't know if Butt Baggins was looking to jerk me off or share a ride. I wasn't looking for either though, and both were making me uncomfortable.

"You know, I appreciate the conversation, it's great and all, but I'm not looking to share a cab," I explained.

"Me either," he returned.

"Is there any reason you're standing so close to me then? We're not exactly in a crowded elevator."

"It's a free country."

Right then and there, I knew exactly what Butt Baggins was trying to do. "It's a free country," is what every pussy and every douchebag, from sea to shining sea, says when they're too afraid to really speak their mind. It's somewhere between, "I'm rubber you're glue," and, "I know you are but what am I?" That's not to say I wasn't going to be a wiseass.

"Okay, I get it. You're not trying to fuck me *in a cab*, you're trying to fuck me *out of a cab*," I said, getting under his skin.

Butt Baggins didn't answer. Instead, he shot me an adorable, I mean, terrifying look.

"I have to tell you, if your plan is to stand a foot in front of me and flag down a cab, I don't recommend it. I've killed for less," I added.

Butt Baggins didn't care for my sarcastic tone. "You think you're fuckin' tough, don't you?"

Are hobbits allowed to curse?

"I'll stand wherever the fuck I want!" she shouted. "How about that?"

I guess they are.

I immediately laughed in his face, knowing it would piss him off, but also finding his tough guy act comical.

"Keep laughing," he threatened.

I did.

"You realize you're the ugliest kid I've ever seen," Butt Baggins fires at me.

"I know," I smile. "It's very disheartening. Your girlfriend makes me put a brown bag over my head when I fuck her."

Butt Baggins stepped into me and that's when I no longer found him amusing.

"What are you going to do?" he said.

I flipped the psychotic switch. "All right you little fuck, now you're done talking. Be smart enough to know I will open your *fuckin'* head up all over the concrete… and laugh about it."

"Yeah…" Butt Baggins cleared a little space before continuing. "Sure you will."

"Looks like someone's going to the emergency room," I announced.

Still towering over Butt Baggins, I waited for an excuse to pour blood out of his face.

"We'll see, buddy." Butt Baggins wisely started backing away. "That's all I'm going to say. We'll see."

B. Baggins turned around and left, while I stayed at the curb adding violent anger to my list of emotions. As I continued my search for a cab, an unexpected gust of wind hit me in the face. That is until I saw Butt Baggins hopping up and down in the middle of the street and realized he "punched" me.

"All right, now you're fuckin' dead!" I yelled.

"Bring it, bitch!"

I instantly walked between two cars and into the middle of the road. Yet, due to the long line of parked cars, I didn't see seven of Butt Baggins' friends standing behind him.

Great, here we go.

"Yeah, you're not so tough anymore, are you, *dickhead?* What are you gonna do, bitch? Huh, what are you gonna do?"

Butt Baggins didn't seem to have a problem running his mouth anymore. He'd come a long way since, "It's a free country," but he knew he was even further from a one-on-one fight.

"That's what I thought," he continued. "You're not going to do shit! You're going to stand there like a little pussy and take it. How'd that punch feel?"

I started laughing. "Are you serious? Did you bounce off of me or just run into the street?"

Butt Baggins stalled on a comeback. "I'm waiting on you, bitch!"

"Are your boyfriends waiting for me too, because I've got to tell you, I'm not into the gay frat brother shit?"

I should have known Butt Baggins was part of PC's homosexual buddy system, a fraternity by the name of, APES (Alpha Pi Epsilon). They were strikingly similar to AEPhi and

SDT in that they loved fashion, wine coolers, and Ryan Seacrest, but much like the *American Idol* closet-case, they refuted these claims and tried to be something they weren't... tough. They would often get into fights, but I've never seen or heard of one where the numbers were even. I guess when you spend so much time doing each other in the ass you feel compelled to have each other's backs.

"Let's go, pussy!" Butt Baggins continued his hobbit-like tirade.

"That's right, I'm the pussy. Not the midget hiding behind seven of his friends."

The biggest guy in the group, Cock Gobbler, stepped forward. "This is your last chance, pussy. You can either show everyone what a pussy you really are, or you can take the beating of a lifetime. It's your choice, pussy."

"You know, for guys who love dick so much, you use the word pussy a lot. And just to clarify, this beating you're talking about is going to come in the form of punches, right? You're not going to gang bang me, are you?"

"You see what I mean, bro?" Butt Baggins said to Cock Gobbler.

"Bro, he's pissing his pants," Cock Gobbler returned. "He's not going to do anything. Ain't that right, *pussy?*"

Typically, people who are stubborn are also very strong in pride. Playing sports my whole life has made me into an extremely competitive bastard, and being successful at them has turned me into an extremely arrogant one. If I'm physically and mentally capable of doing something, regardless of who it's against, whether they're better than me or not, I always believe I'm going to win. The only downside to this is not being able to walk away from a challenge. If you question my ability, if you doubt my tenacity or underestimate my heart, whether it's a game of checkers, basketball, or a fight, when pride is on the line, I never walk away.

Having heard enough, I snapped back into psychotic mode and went straight for Cock Gobbler. I slowly walked towards him, silent, looking for nothing but blood.

Goodnight.

In one fluid motion, while within three feet of Cock Gobbler, I raised my hands, turned, and knocked out the ever-living shit out of Butt Baggins. Seconds later... fists began saying hello to my face. Shortly after that, I joined Butt Baggins on the pavement. I curled up in the fetal position, using my forearms to blanket my head, and took blow after blow. Thankfully the shots came in the form of punches, not semen, but a few did catch my mouth, splitting my lower lip wide open.

Fights always feel longer than they really are, so I had no idea how long I played the part of a human punching bag, but at some point two guys from the soccer team came outside and recognized I was the one getting his ass kicked. They ran over to the pile and started pulling guys off. Not to my surprise, that's when the crazy APES scattered. My friends flagged down an untimely cab, but it wasn't all misfortune. Butt Baggins was still there, just coming to, trying to get his legs underneath him. I helped by kicking him square in the face.

"I'll see you in the hospital, fucker!" I hocked up a wad of bloody phlegm and spit it on the back of his lifeless body, laughing my way into the cab.

My teammates and I got dropped off at another friend's apartment, where Drinksandfalls, Black Mr. Ed, Sava Shot, and the recruits were hanging out. When everyone saw my battered face they obviously wanted to know what happened, so I grabbed some paper towels for the bleeding, a beer for my troubles, a glimpse in the mirror for my own good, and then ran through the abridged version of fight night.

After story time, I went back into the bathroom for another look at my wounds. I wasn't hurting, mainly because I drank enough alcohol to kill a horse, but I had two cuts inside the bottom of my mouth that looked pretty bad. Seeing how Drinksandfalls had had a few mishaps of his own since we met, I deemed him the expert of the group and asked him to take a look.

"What do you think?" I mumbled, holding my lip down.

"Yeah, you need stitches," he said, pointing at one of the cuts. "I don't know about the other one, but this one is pretty deep. It's split in two. It looks like you have a mini vagina in your mouth."

I laughed. It hurt. I stopped. "All right, I'm going to walk to the hospital."

"You want me to go with you?" Drinksandfalls asked.

"Nah, it's cool. I was thinking I'd call Rachel."

"Are you kidding me?" he laughed.

"I know. It sounds retarded, but I figure this is my best chance to talk with her," I said, still drunk.

"I guess, but do you really think that's going to happen tonight, in the emergency room nonetheless?" Sober, Drinksandfalls was trying to be the voice of reason.

"It's a long shot, but even after what happened with Polka Dot, I know Rachel would never want to see me physically hurt."

"You just need a few stitches," Drinksandfalls laughed again.

"Yeah, but she doesn't know that," I said, writhing with pain as I tried to smile.

"So what are you going to say?" Drinksandfalls asked.

"I don't know." I took my phone out and dialed. "I'll wing it."

"Well, once again, I wish you luck," he said, very amused.

"Wait, hang on a second." I stopped Drinksandfalls at the door of the bathroom. "I might need your help."

"What if she doesn't pick up?"

Four rings later...

"What do you want?" Rachel was less than pleased to be hearing from me.

"Hey. How are you?" I opened.

"How do you think I am?" she snapped.

"Sorry, force of habit."

"Can you just tell me what you want so I can cry myself to sleep and forget you ever existed?"

Okay, not the best start. Time to throw it out there.

"I have to go to the hospital," I blurted.

"What! Why?"

"I kind of got jumped outside the bar, and I'm kind of bleeding all over the place," I embellished.

Drinksandfalls was shaking his head, while Rachel was trying not to sound too concerned.

"Where are you now?" she asked.

"Iceland and England got me in a cab and took me to Alaska's."

"That's great." Rachel quickly lost interest.

"Iceland and England left though, Alaska's passed out, and Drinksandfalls, Black Mr. Ed, and Sava Shot have to take the recruits home."

Rachel didn't answer. I felt like I was losing her so I sank to a new low.

"Here, if you don't believe me, talk to Drinksandfalls before he leaves."

Not wanting to, but knowing he was my last chance, Drinksandfalls got on the line.

"Hello?"

"Is he lying?" Rachel got straight to the point, as she was in no mood to deal with any more of my bullshit.

"No, he's not lying," Drinksandfalls answered.

"Because if he's lying, tell him this is the last time we'll ever speak."

"Rachel, I'm looking at him right now. He has to go to the hospital." Drinksandfalls turned his head away from the phone and shot me a look, as if to say, "Are you not entertained?"

"How bad is it?" she asked. If I come over there and he has a little scratch, I'm killing both of you."

"He's pretty messed up," Drinksandfalls assessed. "The bottom of his mouth is split open in two places so he'll more than likely need stitches, but he got hit in the head a lot, so they might give him a CAT Scan to check for internal bleeding."

What!

I looked at Drinksandfalls and whispered, "Really?"

He nodded his head.

Well that sucks.

"Tell the asshole to wait there," Rachel ordered. "I'll be over in a few."

"Thanks." Drinksandfalls hung up and handed me the phone.

"So? Is she coming?" I asked.

"Yeah, she wants the asshole to wait here... that's you," he laughed.

"Sweet."

"I don't understand though, are you trying to get back together with her?"

"I'm not sure," I said.

"I mean you did make out with someone right in front of her," Drinksandfalls annoyingly pointed out.

"I know. I'm just hoping she'll give me a chance to apologize. I can worry about the other shit later," I explained.

"I hear ya."

"All right, I'm going to grab some ice and wait for her outside. Thanks again," I told Drinksandfalls.

"No problem. Let me know what happens, with Rachel and your vagina mouth."

Rachel and I barely spoke in the emergency room. I told her what happened with the fight, but she completely ignored the Polka Dot issue. She was physically and emotionally drained, fed up, pissed off, and hurt. Still, she was there for me. She filled out my insurance forms, spoke with the nurses, and when it was time to have my mouth stitched up, stood by my side and held my hand.

I wanted to tell Rachel how much I loved her, and especially how sorry I was for treating her the way I did. I wanted to tell her she was the best thing that ever happened to me, and that I wanted her in my life forever. I wanted to say so much, but I couldn't. Someone literally had their hands in my mouth. Instead, I let my eyes talk for me, and when Rachel raised my hand and used it to wipe the tears from her face, I knew she heard every word.

The following morning was one of the biggest wakeup calls of my life. It was also one of the most painful. My body ached with every movement, and I looked like Bubba from *Forrest Gump*. None of that mattered though, because all I cared about was Rachel's well-being.

The odds were stacked against me that morning, the night before, but really since the day we met. Dating Rachel was like holding the winning lottery ticket and not being able to cash it in. But how could I throw it away? What if? What if there was a way to make it work? I loved Rachel, and when we were together, I was happier than ever. Yet, clearly, my logic was *not* working out. I decided it was time to look at our relationship from a different perspective... Rachel's. If she still wanted to stay together, for as long as that may be, then so did I. I would start a new timeline, and every day she spent in my arms would be its own victory. We would carve the past in stone, bury the future, and together, celebrate the present.

Just Not Fair

Academically, I peaked in the fifth grade. When I graduated elementary school, I was awarded a certificate of academic excellence. I know it doesn't sound like much because it's grade school and the merit of the award was based on how well I played the recorder, my high score in *Oregon Trail*, and my exceptional rope climbing ability, but out of the entire graduating class, they chose me and only me.

I remember the ceremony like it was yesterday. The gymnasium was split down the middle with parents, friends, and relatives on both sides. Every boy was paired with a girl based on alphabetical order, and we walked down the aisle to the sound of gushing moms, camera crazy dads, and confused grandparents who thought they were at a wedding. We sang *A Whole New World* from the *Disney* classic *Aladdin*. The Superintendent of Jericho School District was in attendance. Our principal and teachers spoke inspirational words, and even our class president, Snoochie Booches, my first kiss, my first girlfriend, my first ex-girlfriend (dumped her for the fully developed Dee Cups), got in on the action and addressed the audience with a killer speech of her own. But, before it was time to hand out our diplomas and, "embark on a new chapter in our lives," my teacher graciously spoke of one particular student with a tremendous passion for learning. She described a student with great enthusiasm, a real knowledge sponge, someone who demonstrated achievement, embodied success, pissed excellence, and shit on mediocrity. Two minutes into her speech, I made my predictions and whispered to the twirp on my left the names of a nerdy Asian boy who always got picked on, a quiet Asian girl who spoke no English, and an Indian boy who may or may not have already been a doctor. By the time I finished pronouncing their names, the speech was over, the audience was clapping, and the person sitting on my right was pulling at my sleeve. She had called my name. *I* pooped on mediocrity.

The award is easy to joke about, but in all seriousness, I am, and always will be, proud of my achievement. I was just as surprised as everyone else that day, practically pinching myself in disbelief, but when I look back on it now, it's obvious why they chose me. I wasn't the most well behaved kid, but I did want to be the best. I never wanted to be average. Despite doing very well academically, that was how I felt. My teachers used the award to instill confidence. They recognized my potential and wanted me to achieve it. As great as that was, what really meant the most was that they believed in me. *That* is why the award still means so much, because later on in life, people like them no longer existed.

I was written off by my senior year of high school. Everyone who knew me, or knew of me, already labeled me. I was an asshole, a dirtbag, an athlete, a basketcase, a princess, and a criminal. I may have brought most of it on myself, but these preconceived notions killed the fifth grader in me. I didn't know who I was anymore. Thankfully, my parents never let me forget.

Even after all I put them through, after all the pain I caused, after the embarrassment, the disrespect, the grief and the disappointment, they still looked me in the eyes and said, "We know you can do this. We believe in you." At a time when I dropped out of college, was working at a yogurt shop, and completely stopped believing in myself, that was all I needed. Those simple words meant the most, and not necessarily because of what they said, but because of who was saying them. For a year and a half I went under the radar at Freeport Community College, proving to no one but myself and my parents that I was more than capable. Two years later, the labels didn't exist, because I refused to hear them. Instead, I put on my cap, wore my gown, waved to my family, and graduated from Presidents College.

Peroxide couldn't have wiped the smile off my face that day. After the ceremony, everyone poured into the campus streets, scurrying to find their loved ones. I located my parents with ease. They were the ones glowing. Of course that could have been the sun reflecting off my dad's head, but regardless, when I hugged them it brought tears to their eyes. For the first time in my life, I could look at my parents and *know* they were proud of me. It was one of the most rewarding moments of my life, and as much as I wanted to revisit every shit talking, confidence-killing doubter and *literally* brand them with my diploma, I took a page from their book and wrote them out of my life.

After Karma kicked me in the ass, it took a while to earn Rachel's trust back. The decision was out of my hands, but I made it clear to her that she was the only girl I wanted to be with, for as long as that may be. I decided to do the opposite of everything I thought was right. Instead of distancing myself, I stayed by Rachel's side. Instead of thinking about the future, I concentrated on the present. Instead of going out with my friends, getting drunk, ditching Rachel, and flirting with other girls, I left the weekends up to her. Most importantly, I stopped acting like an asshole, I stopped walking all over her, and instead, I went back to treating the love of my life like a princess.

They say that behind every great man is a great woman. Without Rachel, I was far from any level of greatness. With her by my side, I was at least scraping the surface.

Forgiveness did not come easy. Rachel is a ballbuster by nature, so I deservingly took a shot to the nads every now and again. I couldn't blame her though. If the situation were reversed, I would have used her ovaries for speed bags. With that said, our love was real, and far too strong for a random kiss to ruin it. The wound healed, and Rachel was back in my arms once again.

People always ask, "How do you *know* you're in love?" Well, I'm convinced now that those who ask have never truly felt it, and those who answer will never say the same thing. To me, love isn't a moment. Love is a recurrence.

Every time I saw Rachel, she made me smile. If I spotted her from a hundred yards away, I smiled with every closing step. If I woke up next to her, I started my day with a smile. If I went to bed next to her, I smiled in my sleep. I smiled at the way she said, "Thank you, *so much*." I smiled at her endless collection of *Juicy* velour jumpsuits, and how she always matched the top to the bottom. I smiled at how she'd undo her pants like Al Bundy when she was gassy, and I smiled at the way she smiled. When I looked at Rachel, I *saw* love.

Graduation had passed though, another summer as well, which meant Rachel and I would soon find out if an old assumption was about to become a new reality.

We spent our last night of the summer in Great Neck. It was

fairly typical of us, dinner and a movie, but I couldn't tell you where we ate or what we saw. I was going through the motions, and slower than ever, in hopes of somehow prolonging the inevitable. For almost an entire year, I had the mindset where even though I loved Rachel with all my heart, and there was no one else in the world I'd rather be with, we were destined to go our separate ways. But for the last four months, I had been living in the now, and stopped dwelling on the future. Sadly, at some point, one always catches up with the other.

Rachel and I both had our cars that night. When the movie let out, we thought we were going to say our gut-wrenching goodbyes then and there, but the parking lot did not allow for much privacy. Rachel led the way and I followed her into a neighborhood not far from her house. During the drive, I tried bracing myself for the heartache I was about to endure. It was pointless. I learned my lesson when I had tried preparing myself for our break up. Your mind cannot feel what your heart does.

I parked my car behind Rachel's, the only vehicles along a quiet and secluded road. The orange street lamp provided enough light to see through her back window, as she appeared even more hesitant to step out of the car than I was. When she did, in continuing fashion, I smiled. I couldn't help it. Even at our greatest breaking point, she made me glow. Rachel lowered her head so I wouldn't see her smiling back, and then adorably captured sulkiness like she was in an amateur acting class. She dropped her shoulders lower than my grandma on a rainy day. Her feet scrapped the pavement as if lifting them were a chore. Arms out like a zombie, Rachel bear hugged my waist.

"Well that was a frightening glimpse into the future," I laughed, Rachel still attached to my body.

The second I heard her nose sniffling, I knew she was

crying. I was hoping the mood wouldn't turn somber so quickly, but the puddle forming in the middle of my shirt said we were getting right into it.

"Hold me tighter," Rachel whispered from the side of her mouth.

"Any tighter and I'm going to puncture your lungs."

"Tighter," she ordered.

"Okay, but don't blame me if you miss bingo night," I joked, lamely trying to keep my guard up.

Rachel let go and took a step back. "Please," she whispered again, tears rolling down her face.

My wall instantly came down, as Rachel's saltwater eyes made me weak. I stepped towards her and engulfed her body, holding her so close that my right hand reached my left elbow. I rested my chin on top of her head, closed my eyes, and inhaled.

I was back in room 1111 waking up on an air mattress. The sun opened my eyes, but the angel lying next to me kept them that way. She was the most beautiful girl I'd ever seen, adorably holding the comforter just under her eyes. She didn't snore, but every so often, she'd exhale like she was blowing into a tissue. I was smiling ear to ear until I could bear not kissing her. Feeling the moistness of her forehead, I laughed, and Rachel woke up.

"I can hear your heartbeat," she whispered.

"What?"

"Your heart, I can hear it," Rachel repeated.

I opened my eyes and really kissed Rachel's forehead, tasting the salt from my own tears. "What's it saying?" I asked.

"It's telling you to never…"

Rachel stopped and swallowed the rest of her words. I clenched the muscles in my arms and kissed the top of her head. I was doing everything in my power not to completely breakdown. Hope only looked as strong as I did, whether it was false or not. I let go of Rachel and wiped the tears from my eyes as I reached behind my back to pry her hands apart.

"No, please don't," Rachel said, tightening her grip.

"I need you to look at me," I whispered.

Rachel paused for a moment. I could feel her eyes shut as she clutched my body with every bit of remaining strength. When her arms gave out, I reached around my back again and took her hands into mine. I placed them in between our chests and waited for her eyes.

My entire body quivered when they met. If I swallowed any more tears, I was certain I would drown. I quickly looked towards the sky to collect myself. It was pointless. Rachel brought me back to Earth like she always did. She was my gravity.

"For the rest of our lives, you could never say a single word to me…" I pressed Rachel's hands against my heart. "And I will always hear you."

Crying, I leaned into Rachel and kissed her, tears forced to go around our lips.

Rachel gently whispered in my ear, "I love you."

My entire body was ready to crumple. I physically wouldn't be able to stand much longer. I closed my eyes, kissed her again, and let those three little words echo into my soul.

White beams of light shot at our feet from the chandelier. We were dancing slowly along the hardwood floor, but perfectly enough to miss every one. Nothing could steal me away from that moment. Nothing could steal me away from Rachel's eyes. Her friends, family, relatives, and half the Jews in Manhattan, faded to black. We were the John Hughes script of the twenty-first century.

Rachel and I were pressed together so tightly I could feel her phone vibrate. We both knew who it was, but only one of us could ignore it. Rachel pulled away and answered her father's call.

"I'll be home in a minute." Rachel spoke softly but abruptly, using anger to hide her sadness. Mitch, on the other hand, had a booming voice, so I could easily hear him through the phone.

"Blah, blah, blah, it's dark out. Blah, blah, blah, driving. Blah, blah, blah, late. Blah, blah, blah, Jonathan. Blah, blah, blah, say goodnight."

"Okay, Dad."

"Blah, blah, blah, Catholic."

"Goodbye!" Rachel aggressively snapped her phone shut with two hands. Her frustration was evident, but not enough to vanish the reality that our time was up.

Rachel moved in for another hug. "I can't believe how hard this is. I'm afraid to walk away," she sobbed.

"Trust me, watching is going to hurt a lot more." I held Rachel with all my heart and all my soul, having no idea when or if I'd ever get to hold her again. I closed my eyes and kissed her one last time.

My face felt like it had been hit with a shovel. I was beaten, battered, bruised and drained, but the anguish on the outside didn't even compare to the pain on the inside. I closed the car door and broke down. At one point, I was crying so hard, I started laughing. My emotions took over and I didn't know how to control them. I couldn't have imagined a worse time or place to find out what it's like to be pregnant. As I watched Rachel drive out of our dead end, I truly felt what it's like to lose someone you love. Fate giveth and Fate taketh away.

Lying Is The Most Fun A Girl Can Have Without Taking Her Clothes Off

Webster's Dictionary doesn't define an open relationship, but Jonathan's does.

Main Entry: **open re-la-tion-ship**
Pronunciation: [oh-p*uh* n] [ri-ley-sh*uh* n-ship]
1. A "relationship" where both partners are allowed to hook up with other people.
2. A fantasy world.
3. An excuse.
4. Bullshit.

It didn't take long for Rachel and I to reach dating's most absurd status. Three weeks into the fall semester of her junior year, I got a phone call explaining the logic.

"I'm not saying I want to hook up with other people, that's not how I feel, but if something were to happen then…"

"Then there wouldn't be any ramifications?" I interrupted, adding, "*Technically*, you wouldn't have done anything wrong, so *technically*, I couldn't be mad at you." The familiarity of those words only emphasized my hatred towards Karma.

"You make it sound like I'm going to purposely hurt you," Rachel said, like it was so far fetched.

"It's just another loophole. It's a way for you to have your cake and eat it, too," I pointed out, nearly choking on my own words.

Rachel continued her political, I'm full of shit façade. "I don't *plan* on hooking up with anyone. I can't even picture myself touching another guy for that matter. But I also don't think it's healthy for either of us to have restrictions when we're not boyfriend and girlfriend anymore."

"I don't know what to say. I mean you're right; we're not going out anymore so there's really nothing I can do about it," I admitted. "But just so you know, even though you don't *plan* on hooking up with anyone, that doesn't mean it's not going to hurt like hell when you do."

"Like I'm not going to cry when you hook up with someone?" Rachel returned. "The thought alone makes me nauseous."

"Allow me to help settle your stomach... the ball is entirely in your court," I said.

"So you're only going to hook up with someone if I do?" Rachel clarified.

"Pretty much."

"But I don't want to talk about that stuff with you."

"But we're in an *open relationship*, Rachel. That doesn't just apply to your legs."

Life after college was neither a disappointment nor a fulfillment. I was unemployed and living at home, but I didn't have any real expenses. I was fed, given shelter and transportation, and surrounded by two loving parents. Then again, I was penniless, lacking privacy, and surrounded by two loving parents. It was what it was. When most people think about their future, they factor in a career. It tends to play a big part in other aspects of their lives. I, on the other hand, only thought about Rachel.

Main Entry: **the re-al world**

Pronunciation: [*th uh*] [ree-*uh*l] [wurld]

1. An expression for the physical and mental realities most experience in their daily lives.

2. The stage in life after the completion of formal schooling, usually college.

3. An *MTV* reality show.

4. A cock block.

For weeks on end, I did all I could to busy myself and make the most of my days. I spent time at the spa (singing/showering in the bathroom), I went to the gym (push-ups and sit-ups in the basement), I utilized my library's resources (*Newsday's* classified ads and online job search engines), I wrote in my office (whichever room was the quietest), and I sharpened my culinary skills with delicacies like grilled cheese sandwiches and salads. I also collected some "me time" in front of the television with educational programming (*Desperate Housewives* and *The Amazing Race*). If all that wasn't enough, I went the extra mile and slept two hours more than the recommended eight. Still, as impressive as my rigorous schedule was, it didn't put any money in my pocket. Eventually I woke from my hibernation and knew what I had to do. I would go back to school and accumulate thousands of dollars in debt earning my Master's Degree in Physical Education.

For the most part, I managed to cope with my slow and uneventful life, but there was one particular aspect that felt like torture. In college, my social life was on cruise control at a hundred miles per hour. There was always something to do, and always someone to do it with. Post-college is another story. The real world eventually enters your mirror like an annoying cop car, forcing you to slow down. With every day she gains more and more ground, until eventually, she's right on top of you, riding your ass the entire way. Her lights are flashing, her siren is blaring, and before you know what's hit you, you're parked on the side of the road awaiting a very long and expensive ticket... marriage. Okay, I may not have been at that stage yet, I think that was my midlife crisis talking, but the tides had certainly turned. Once again, I was on the shit end of the stick. Unfortunately, Karma was just warming up.

There have been many times in my life where I've seriously considered the possibility that I'm psychic. I don't actually believe anyone can truly see the future, I think ESP is a sliding scale somewhere between carnival gypsies, old Asian woman, and the *Zoltar* machine, but I do think some people have a "gift" where they get spontaneous intuitions that are accurate and consistent. My powers, for example, successfully tell me who is calling just from a ring of the phone. They also tell me when a baseball player is going to hit a homerun from the second they step into the batter's box. I'm yet to discover a way to benefit from these premonitions, but I do believe it's a sixth sense, rather than lucky guesses or assumptions. There's no real way for me to explain it, something just clicks inside and tells me the cable guy is calling, or David Wright is going to knock one out of Shea. Annoyingly, I have a third psychic ability that tells me when Rachel is hooking up with someone else.

It didn't take long to feel the same discomfort and anxiety Rachel did when I went to the bars without her. I did all I could to distract myself, but I was in mental prison. Television, movies, poker, and even alcohol, were mere time killers. I couldn't escape her. Even as I lay in bed one night, for hours on end, painfully staring into the darkness, knowing at that very moment Rachel was with someone else, I refused to disconnect.

The next day, I waited for Rachel to call (knowing of course which ring indicated it was her).

"Hey, Ra-Ra."

"Hi."

"What's up?" I cheerfully asked, pretending nothing was wrong.

"Not much. Sorry I didn't call you back last night. I got home late and didn't want to wake you."

"It's okay. I was up though."

Rachel's somber mood was only perpetuating my gut feeling.

"What'd you do?" I asked.

"Um, we went out downtown."

"You have a good time?" I continued.

Rachel hesitated before answering. "Not really."

I could tell she was battling her conscience, so I decided to help her along.

"Is everything all right? You sound sad."

Rachel paused again. "I am."

"Any reason?"

"Yes," she said softly.

"You hooked up with someone, didn't you?"

Her silence was my answer.

I stopped pacing around my room and leaned against the

wall to catch my breath. Despite my intuition, it hurt more than I ever imagined. I needed to know more though. I needed to know every little detail otherwise my mind would invent scenarios far worse than those envisioned the night before. I let go of my body, slid to the floor, and like a third grader doing a current events assignment, asked five very painful W's.

"Who was it?" I began.

"Um, do you know Drinksandfalls' friend, Unimportant?"

"Yeah."

"His best friend, Pelican," Rachel answered.

"What'd you do with him?" I asked.

"Can we not talk about this, please?"

"Trust me, I don't *want* to hear any of this, but I have to. What happened?" I continued.

"We kissed."

"That's all?"

"Yes!" Rachel was insulted by the insinuation.

"I'm sorry, but I'm going to need more info than that. Where and when did this take place?"

Rachel took a deep breath, and then slowly began hammering my heart. "When we were at the bar, he was talking to me, like the entire time, but nothing happened. Afterwards, I had planned on going home, but Unimportant asked Blondie Cheeks and I back to his and Pelican's dorm. At first, I was completely against it, but then Blondie Cheeks said something that changed my mind. She said I would never know whether or not I was ready to move on if I didn't try."

"I had no idea Blondie Cheeks was nailing Dr. Phil," I said, hiding my anger. "Small world."

Rachel rightfully ignored me. "Anyway, we were all sitting in the living room area until Blondie Cheeks and Unimportant went into his bedroom."

"And?" I interrupted.

"And Pelican and I made out on the couch."

"Who kissed who?"

"He kissed me."

"For how long?" I asked, like middle school props were on the line.

"A little bit," Rachel answered, avoiding honesty.

"In minutes."

"I don't know, half an hour," she muttered.

"Half an hour!" I loudly repeated. "You clearly generalize time like a fat immigrant named Jesús. Did anything else happen?"

"No. He tried taking my pants off, but I didn't let him."

I nearly dropped the phone. The anxiety was eroding my stomach, but I couldn't stop the infliction. I wanted to overdose.

"Were you in his pants?" I asked.

"No!" Rachel yelled again.

"So who ended it?"

"Blondie Cheeks, when she came out of Unimportant's room."

"Oh, so then really you just ran out of time. That's good to know, fuckin' *Ra-Ra*." The sarcastic anger kept building.

"Nothing else happened because it was weird, uncomfortable, and I didn't like it," Rachel confessed.

"Well, don't give up just yet, I'm sure you'll find someone you have more chemistry with."

"It was weird and uncomfortable because it wasn't *you!*" Rachel shouted, having enough of my remarks. "I didn't like it because it wasn't *you!* I cried about it then, and I'm crying about it now. Is that what you want to hear?"

It was, but I chose to exhale rather than answer.

"I miss you," she whispered.

I was starting to get choked up myself. In an instant, I went from wanting to beat in a man's bird face, to just holding Rachel.

"I miss you, too."

I had one more question to ask, but I was too afraid of the answer. I didn't want to admit it, but Blondie Cheeks' 'you'll never know if you don't try' pep talk, actually made sense. The end result of Rachel's kiss may have worked out in my favor, but I didn't know if it meant she didn't want to move on at all, or if she wasn't ready to move on just yet. I remained Optimus Prime for as long as I could, but eventually, my insecurities got the best of me, and I followed through on my open-relationship guidelines.

Halloween 2004 fell on a Sunday, so my friends and I celebrated it the day before with an eighties theme party. Let's just say that when it comes to everything eighties, my adoration for Mom Dancing doesn't even compare. Not enough? Fine. If getting molested by Michael Jackson meant being on the set of *Thriller*, I would have turned my head and coughed.

The party was in Long Beach at a friend's house, but due to the lack of females in attendance, we moved the festivities to a bar down the road, costumes and all. Sadly, few people were matching our Halloween spirit. Needless to say, when Hulk Hogan, Madonna, Bruce Springsteen, Cindy Lauper, Boy George, an eighties prepster, rocker, go-go dancer, Prince, and a painted black version of Mr. T walked through the door, heads rolled. If you can comfortably embarrass yourself in public, you'll have fun doing anything though, including tonguing down a random thirty-year-old for all to see.

The scoreboard was tied up. See How I Feel Rachel and

Petty Jon were even at one apiece. Rachel's reaction to my lip locking adventure was no different than my reaction to hers, but despite our different reasoning, they managed to briefly bring us back together. Rachel finished her fall semester without anymore "experimentation," which meant I also refrained from Frenching random skanks. Before I knew it, winter break had arrived. Rachel was back on Long Island, and the two of us would happily celebrate my twenty-third birthday and the year 2005. Having her in my arms again was ecstasy, without the glow sticks. I rediscovered my smile, my genuine, sincere, legitimate, daily, Rachel smiles. That is until Cupid took his finger off the pause button, spring semester began, and Rachel flew to Italy for five months. I shouldn't complain too much though, because before she left, we did get to have another super duper fun, not at all annoyingly repetitive, 'where do we stand' talks.

"So... Ray-dog."

"Yes... J-dog."

"While you're *studying* in Florence, and by studying I mean eating, sleeping, sightseeing, and partying, do you think you're going to be able to find time in your busy schedule to reach out to little old me?" I

"I'm certainly going to try, but I don't know how often I'll get through. I hear the jealousy lines get tangled a lot."

I tried not to laugh, but Rachel had me pegged with that one. I brushed it off and continued our seriously nonchalant conversation.

"Question number two," I stated.

"Yes, dear?"

"Hypothetically speaking, let's say you're in a relationship, a relationship of any kind, open, shut, ajar, whatever, how do you see it working out during your time abroad?"

252

"Well, *hypothetically speaking...*" Rachel emphasized. "I would have to say going abroad would change the relationship a great deal, *but* as long as both parties are mature about it, I think there's a chance for light at the end of the tunnel."

I obviously did not want to get into another intense, emotionally-filled discussion, so as always, I continued using sarcastic humor to substitute what I really wanted to say.

"Are we talking about a drive through tunnel like the Lincoln or Midtown, or are we talking about an underground tunnel for slaves? A guaranteed point A to B, or an unknown shot in the dark?" I playfully asked.

"Well, if I have to use your retarded analogy, I would say it's more of an unexplored path," Rachel answered. "I have no idea what being overseas will do to this *hypothetical* relationship, time will answer that, but what I do know is I would like to experience freedom throughout my journey."

I tried not to laugh too much. "Freedom, you say?"

"Yes, freedom, I say."

"That's an interesting choice of word," I mocked. "Are you using it to continue with my retarded analogy, or would you have expressed it regardless?"

"Regardless," Rachel answered.

"Well, that certainly is fascinating then. I could be wrong, but last time I checked, being away at school, living in a ridiculous, rent-free apartment, driving a *Lexus*, not working, and having enough credit cards to color coordinate them to your outfits, doesn't exactly border along the lines of slavery."

Rachel remained calm, knowing it would annoy me. "I think you know what I mean."

I did, but since my only option was to respect her wishes, I almost left it alone.

"So, how excited are you to hook up with little Jewish boys in blazers?"

"I can't wait," Rachel entertained.

"It sounds that way," I returned.

"Jon."

"Yes, dear?"

"I'm not going there to hook up. I obviously can't predict what, if anything, is going to happen, but I hope you know that's not my purpose for studying abroad."

Quick, cough and say bullshit.

"For the past, I don't even know how many years, I've had a boyfriend," Rachel began.

Damn it! Too late.

"I've never actually been single, and I think that's something I need to experience. And I'm not talking about the aspect you're thinking of, I'm talking about other aspects."

"The freedom aspect?" I patronized.

"Yes, the freedom aspect."

I tried not to laugh again, but Rachel sounded like a jappy, girl version of William Wallace.

"You can take my virginity, but you'll never take, MY FREEDOM!"

I refused to admit it, as always, but I knew exactly what Rachel was talking about. She was twenty years old and she could link her love life in succession, never breaking the chain. To me, that's not living. In the same instance, I was extremely bitter about the timing of her realization. I could have asked a dozen questions beginning with why, but they wouldn't have changed a thing. Rachel would still be going to Italy, and I would still be visiting her in February. Until then, all I could do was hang on to as many smiles as possible.

As soon as our semesters got underway, mine at Gellen University, Rachel's at *Pizzeria Uno*, the two of us basically stopped talking. I had an eighteen-credit course load. Rachel had some classes, mixed in with sightseeing and partying, plus the six-hour time difference, the expense of calling (for me), and of course, the constant echoes reminding us we're both "single." We'd occasionally talk online if she made it into an Internet café, but that wasn't the only infrequency. Rachel was yet to hook up! With two weeks to go before my visit, I decided to take advantage of one of those sporadic phone calls and ask Rachel to curb her hormones until I got there.

"Okay, bella, I'm going to go out on a limb here and basically ask you for something I probably shouldn't."

"If it's anal sex, don't even bother."

"It's not anal sex," I laughed.

"Good, leave my tuckus alone," Rachel joked.

"Probably not, but anyway, seeing how you've gone thus far in your freedom journey without hooking up with anyone, and I'm coming to see you in two weeks, for eleven days, ten nights, I thought it'd be a good idea if neither of us, specifically you, hooked up with a third party."

"Wow, you have a little trouble with that one?" Rachel teased.

"Sure, mess with the vulnerable guy," I laughed.

"Oh, I'm only kidding."

"I know, but seriously…" I said, getting back to the matter at hand. "If you want to give me your whole, 'I don't *plan* on hooking up with anyone' speech, that's fine, I could recite the rest if you get tired. However, if we keep things the way they are right now, untainted we'll say, then it should make for an unbelievable trip, and I say that with both of us in mind... always."

"Aww, how cute are you?" Rachel whimpered. "I love stammering, exposed Jon."

"That's right you love exposed Jon!" I announced. "Now, are you going to keep your pants on so I can take mine off? Or, am I going to have to put my chastity belt on when I get there?"

Rachel laughed at the thought. "Are you saying that if I hook up with someone you're not going to sleep with me?"

"More or less."

"Will I at least get a spanking?" she mocked.

"You wish. You'll be lucky if you get a kiss on the cheek, and that's when I'm drunk."

Rachel confidently chuckled.

"Laugh all you want, but that just means I'll have to find Italian romance elsewhere."

"You'll have to find a new place to stay as well."

"Touched a nerve, did I?"

"Do you want to see *me* hooking up with someone else?" Rachel asked.

"Not really. I don't feel like straining my neck."

"Me either," she returned.

"Hey! Not funny."

"Come on, that was good."

"*Fine*. I'll give you that one," I laughed. "But seriously, and I don't think I've ever used that word twice in the same conversation, let alone a week, what do you say?"

"I definitely agree, cutie. I'm waiting on you."

I was instantly smiling on my end. "Perfect. Now I can give you the code to unlocking my pants. It's your hands."

"Please, I knew that one a long time ago," Rachel scoffed. "Add a few drinks and it's your own hands."

"Wow do I miss you."

"I miss you too, J-Dog! I'll talk to you soon."

"Ciao, bella."

With Rachel's reassurance, the only part of the trip I had to worry about was the flight. I've been on a plane several times in my life, to various locations and even continents, but as I got older, my fear of flying was the only thing I felt when climbing to thirty thousand feet. I'm not a fan of heights in general, but it's more than that. Statistically, the chances of a being involved in an automobile accident heavily outweighs that of a plane crash, but how many times has a plane gone down and the result's been a dent to the side door? The adjectives alone are enough to make me worry. I can't say I've ever listened to the news or opened the paper and read about a plane *accident*, because when a plane makes unwanted contact with the Earth, the funeral business profits. Miracles do exist, and sometimes tragedies are averted, but the idea of putting my life in the hands of two complete strangers, who could be two complete jerkoffs (aside from Bush and Cheney), on top of trusting a machine I've never used, nor know anything about, makes it beyond unsettling. Trust is a part of life though, and sometimes people will come through and comfortably bring you to safe ground, while other times, they'll go against their word, hook up with someone when they said they wouldn't, and leave you to crash and burn.

Not long before our Italian rendezvous, my misfortunate ESP kicked in. Once again, I was regrettably right. The next day's phone call was far and away more painful than the original, and the anger coincided. I felt completely betrayed.

Never in a million years would I have guessed Rachel had it in her, particularly when she started blaming alcohol.

"You don't understand. I drank so much I can't remember half the night," she pleaded.

"Yeah, *I* don't understand. I've blacked out more times than your power, but please, tell me what drinking too much is like." It was a stupid thing to argue about, but I was pissed off enough to hate every word of every sentence, and eagerly pounce on all of them.

"He was just being nice," Rachel continued. "I could barely walk so he got me in a cab and took me back to his place."

"Why the fuck didn't he take you back to *your* place?" I asked.

"He wanted to smoke," Rachel explained, like it made perfect sense.

"Of course, the gentlemanly thing to do. How trashy of me to forget."

"I didn't smoke though."

"That's my level-headed girl, always making good decisions when faced with bad ones," I angrily patronized. "So I take it this was a consensual date rape?"

"You're not funny," Rachel snapped.

"I'm not trying to be. I'm only trying to understand how you think going back to a random guy's house, by yourself, while obliterated, is a good idea. And that has nothing to do with how fucked up it is in regards to our situation," I added, with blind yet partially subdued rage.

"First of all…"

"No, don't even bother giving me that first of all, second of all bullshit. Talk!" I yelled.

"Not if you're going to be an asshole," Rachel barked.

"Right, I'm the asshole. I apologize. Please, carry on. Tell me about how you couldn't wait two weeks because you just had to hook up with this *dreamboat*. Tell me all the juicy details. I'm dying to hear every one. Oh, and keep using alcohol as an excuse, hold *Zima* responsible."

After backing Rachel in a corner, she started firing back. "*First of all*, he wasn't a random guy. It was Blondie Cheeks' best friend from home. She was the one who introduced us."

"A therapist and a pimp," I interrupted.

"*Second of all*, I *was* really drunk. I'm not using it as an excuse, or the cause for what happened, but it did play a part. And the whole 'not hooking up with anyone before you visit' thing was completely your idea. I went along with it, but what was I supposed to say?"

I quickly responded. "Um, you could have been an adult and said what you were really thinking. Or, you could have *fuckin'* honored it!" I yelled again.

"Right, because I'm sure you would have been real happy hearing the truth," Rachel threw in, purposely fueling the fire.

"Obviously not, but I think it's funny you couldn't wait two weeks when after my visit, you have over two months to be a *whore*," I emphasized. "You hooking up isn't what kills me though, it's that you lied and acted like I'm a fuckin' nobody."

"Okay, now you're being an asshole and blowing things out of proportion."

"Did you fuck him?" I asked.

"Um... no... not really," she muttered.

Rachel was acting like she didn't want to tell me, but I knew she was pissed off enough to want to disclose everything.

"What does *not really* mean?"

"We had dry sex," she answered.

I let out a loud, fake laugh. "You dry fucked? What are you, in the third grade?"

"That makes no sense."

"You're right, it doesn't. Why the fuck would you mime sex?" I asked.

"He liked it," Rachel quickly returned.

"No one *actually* likes dry sex. It's just a nonverbal way of hinting you want to fuck."

"Well, he came, so he must have liked it."

This time I really did laugh. "He came! That's like something out of an *American Pie* movie," I said, still laughing. "Let me guess though, he's short, maybe an inch taller than you, two if he's wearing his spiffy dress shoes, Jewish, as strong as a ten-year-old, and most definitely rocks a blazer."

"What's your point?" Rachel ignored.

"Aside from being able to read you like a book, you're officially no different than every other jappy Long Island girl who goes for the same jappy Long Island guy. I'm sure SDT is very proud. You're now an official clone."

"I'm done talking. You're now an official asshole!" Rachel screamed into the phone. "Why don't you do me a favor and not visit. That'd be great."

"Are you crazy? I can't wait to see you!" I exclaimed, still mocking her. "In fact, I want to see you *so* badly, these next two weeks are going to be sheer torture."

"You're going to have a tough time finding me, seeing as I look like everyone else," Rachel annoyingly joked.

"Nah, I'll be fine. After all, it's Italy. I'll listen for the girl going, 'Like, oh my god, like, look at my new *Prada* shoes. They're like *so* hot!'"

"Tell Paris Hilton I say hi."

"Don't be cute," I ordered. "I hate you right now. I deserve to be angry when I hang up the phone."

"Okay." Even more annoying, Rachel transitioned to her puppy dog voice. "Before you go, I just want to tell you I'm sorry, and I still can't wait to see you."

I was frustratingly running out of mean, so I quickly used whatever was left in the tank and spitefully said goodbye. "I wish I could say the same, but I think we both know you just ruined that. I honestly don't know what I'm going to do, but you take care."

I ended the call, genuinely hurt, extremely pissed off, but eventually ready to recover the only way I know how, with a tall, strong glass of revenge, served on the rocks.

Knowingly or unknowingly, Rachel made the mistake of telling me about her passionate night of friction on a Friday, one of two days during the week when I attempted to have a social life. Before calling my friend Italian O, I took a moment to think about the last time I hooked up for retaliation. Yes, it leveled a hurtful playing field, but that type of quick fix fades fast. Then all you're left with is the guilt of having purposely hurt someone you care about. At the same time, I also remembered a passage Rabbi Knaydelach read to me. It came from the second book of the Torah, Exodus 21:23-27, and famously referenced, "An eye for an eye, a tooth for a tooth." I decided irony such as this could only be a sign from above, 'G' dash 'D' style, and therefore met Italian O at Jericho's local watering hole, ready and amped for a good ole vagina vengeance.

Read Between the Lines is conveniently located within walking distance of my house, and thus I've frequented there often from my younger to older years. It's not necessarily a dive bar, but it's not exactly at the top of *Zagat's* list either. It's simply a great place to get drunk, hang out, listen to some tunes, and if you're lucky, hook up with one of the random girls who walk in. It's usually slim pickins, but like I said before, I had a higher power on my side. As a result, I was not surprised when a short, cute, brunette, Jewish-looking girl in glasses, popped up at the other end of the bar.

"Go ahead," Italian O said, smiling at me.

"What are you talking about?"

"Don't play dumb," he laughed. "You know what I'm talking about."

"What? Her?" I said, looking down the bar.

"Please," he scoffed. "Stop being a pussy and go talk to her. You said you're on a cootchie quest, right?

I almost spat my drink in his face. "Vagina vengeance," I corrected.

"Cootchie quest, vagina vengeance, same shit," Italian O eloquently explained. "Either way, press start, Zelda."

"Zelda!" I loudly repeated, having another laugh.

"You're acting like a fairy, aren't you?"

"I suppose, but I'm pretty sure the princess' name was Zelda."

"Fine, so you're a girl," he reasoned. "Again, we're splitting hairs here. Get going."

Italian O was cracking me up, and it helped just to laugh at stupid shit for a while. What happened with Rachel was still in the back of my mind, but for the moment, it was time to play the game.

"I like your glasses." I opened, saying the first thing that came to mind.

The girl at hand turned around and thanked me, then immediately faced the bar again waiting to collect her drinks. I took her spot after she stepped out, ordering two drinks of my own and discreetly gesturing for Italian O to join me.

"Here." I handed Italian O a beer.

He snatched the bottle out of my hand and started shaking his head. "Pussy."

"What? I like light beer," I said, trying to cover up Italian O's loudness.

"You know what, Zelda."

"All right. All right," I laughed.

I had no idea why I was acting so shy, but I decided to listen to Italian O and stop caring. There's no real science to picking up a girl anyway. Truth be told, if she thinks you're cute, and you stay in bounds with what you say, you're in. How far you go after that is usually up to your personality, which in my case meant, well…

"So, am I the first person tonight to tell you you look like Lisa Loeb?"

She turned around and smiled this time. "No, I'm afraid that big guy over there said it earlier."

"Butt Punisher," I said, like I knew the guy. "My friend Italian O thinks he's cute."

"And you don't?" she asked, playing along.

"Well, I was going to say I think you're cuter, but now that I'm up close and personal, it's a tighter race than I thought."

I waited for her to finish laughing and introduced myself. "I'm Jon."

"Drywall," she returned.

"It's nice to meet you. This is Italian O." I opened my shoulders and let him into the conversation.

"Drywall," she said, leaning forward to shake his hand.

"I'm not gay," he stated. "Just so you know."

"What's wrong with being gay?" I asked, putting Italian O on the spot.

"Nothing, I just don't want her to think I'm okay with Butt Punisher giving me the business."

"So then you want to give *him* the business?" I rephrased.

"Yes, you got me. I want to make Butt Punisher my bitch and fuck him like an inmate."

"Graphic," I announced.

"Yes, quite," Drywall added, joining the fun.

"So, what brings you to the glorious RBL?" I asked, changing the subject.

"I'm here for a friend's birthday," Drywall answered.

"Is this her?" I motioned to the girl standing next to Drywall.

"No, not her. Believe it or not, we just found out the birthday girl isn't showing up."

"Well that's fucked up," I confessed.

"I know, but she's a cunt."

Hey now!

"This is my friend, Jessica Simpson (look-alike)," she added.

Jessica Simpson (look-alike) turned around. "Did you call me?"

"Yeah, this is Jon and his friend Italian O," Drywall introduced.

"It's nice to meet you," I said.

"Yo."

"Nice to meet you," she returned. "Are you guys from around here?"

"Yeah, we live across the street," I answered. "You?"

"I'm from New Rochelle, and Drywall lives in Minneola."

"New Rochelle!" Italian O shouted.

"It's only like an hour away. I'm staying at Drywall's tonight."

Jessica Simpson (look-alike) was about to steal the spotlight, so I focused all my attention on Drywall and let Italian O handle the blonde.

"Where'd you go to school?" I asked Drywall.

"Binghamton. What about you?"

"Um, I went to a few," I began. "I started out at The University of Rhode Island, came home and went to Freeport Community College, transferred to Presidents College where I graduated, spent a summer at Yeshiva University, and now I'm getting my Master's at Gellen University."

"Is that all?" she joked.

"For now."

"What are you getting your Master's in?"

"Phys. Ed. I'm going to be a gym teacher," I said, stating the obvious. "At least that's the current plan. I tend to stray off path and seek change."

"I'm sure your girlfriend loves that."

I had to laugh. "Look at you, subtly checking my status."

Drywall flirtatiously smiled. "Whatever do you mean?"

"Right," I smiled back. "Well, I only have an ex-girlfriend, and there's no reason to worry about what she thinks."

"Ouch. That was a little harsh."

It might have been, but I decided not to get into it. "I take it you're also single?" I inferred.

"You... take it..."

Drywall's thoughts got tangled so I jumped in. "We went over this already; Italian O takes it in the butt, not me."

"I was trying to say you're right about me being single, but my mind *strayed off path*," Drywall mocked.

"You see, now that's the sarcastic flirtiness I enjoy."

"So you think I'm flirting with you?"

"I don't want to put words in your mouth, but…"

Drywall quickly pounced on my opening. "Then what *do* you want to put in my mouth?"

"Hey now!" I shouted.

"What?" Drywall smiled, acting all sexy and coy.

"I didn't know we were flirting at an R-rated level," I said.

"Aww, are you too young?"

"No, *meanieface*, I am not. I am a twenty-three year old man who may or may not live in the basement of his parents house."

"You live with your parents?" Drywall repeated, sounding like I just punched her ovary.

"Correct," I sadly admitted.

"Um, I guess I'll let that go," she hesitated. "But only because you're back in school. I had no idea you were such a youngin'."

"I'm not *that* young. I mean, I don't use training wheels anymore."

"How adult of you."

"Tell me about it. Pretty soon I'll be eating without a bib. How old are you?" I asked, wisely turning the tides.

"I'm twenty-six," Drywall answered.

"Twenty six!" I mocked. "Holy shit! Does the nursing home know you're out?"

"Nope, I'm a sneaky one," she laughed.

"I'm sorry, how rude of me." Slowly shouting in her face I asked, "DO YOU NEED ME TO TALK LOUDER?"

Still laughing, Drywall answered her question with a question. "Did you say *I* was the one flirting *you*?"

"Well, you're certainly not, not flirting," I quickly returned.

"Huh?"

"Give it a minute," I said. "At your age the brain's not what it used to be."

Drywall and I continued flirting until the bartender announced last call and we found ourselves at the awkward, end of the night, 'where do we go from here' crossroads.

Drywall huddled with Jessica Simpson (look-alike), leaving me second-guessing myself. After a delay of game penalty, they broke and Drywall invited me back to her apartment. The only thing left to do was convince Italian O to make the drive. Mineola is about twenty minutes from Jericho, but his house is less than one. Therefore, I was forced to do the only thing I knew would work, lie and tell him Jessica Simpson (look-alike) wanted to play with his balls. The fact of the matter is, when a man is presented with even the slightest chance of hooking up, he'll drive from Long Island, to The University of Rhode Island, at five in the morning, after a drunk night out, and then upon arriving, fall asleep while getting head. Just saying.

With Italian O onboard, the only task at hand was getting rubber penis gloves. Drywall was riding with Jessica Simpson (look-alike), but she had a few drinks in her, so to play it safe, we followed the advice of *Supertramp* and took the long way home. At our forty-seventh red light, I called Drywall and told her we needed to stop for gas, despite having enough to fuel an Ethiopian village. It was right around this time when I felt like the big guy in the sky went to bed. It had nothing to do with fellatio; he's just a lightweight.

The first gas station we pulled into was closed. The second didn't have a convenience store, so we said the pumps were broken. The third was just right. Too bad Jessica Simpson (look-alike) parked her car in front of the bodega's glass window, forcing us to bail on the mission with nothing more than fifty cents worth of gasoline.

In my eyes, there was still no way I wasn't getting laid. She seemed like the kind of girl who shopped for condoms at *Costco*. After all, she was three years older than me and I met her at the RBL. If you bring someone home from Read Between the Lines, or they bring you home, you're almost guaranteed sexual intercourse. It's an unwritten law. The other one is that if you stay past closing the female bartender will fuck you. But I've "heard" that one's a myth.

As it turned out, I was right. I didn't have to worry about condoms at all. The moment the four of us sat down in her living room and started watching *The Next Kid*, sex was a moot point.

At around seven in the morning I pulled Italian O off the couch, exchanged numbers and more french kisses with Drywall, and then headed home.

Ironically, my night with Drywall is what I imagined Rachel's to be like with Preemie, minus the softcore sex. However, I assumed Rachel's fun only lasted one night, whereas in the period between meeting Drywall and leaving for Italy, she and I hung out almost every night.

I wish I could say the reason I saw Drywall so much before Italy had everything to do with general interest and nothing to do with trifling jealousy, but then that would imply I had morals. You see, if Rachel's one night stand turned out to be more than that, which I planned on investigating at some point during the trip, then I now had ammunition to fire back with. Sounds juvenile, right? Well, you don't conquer your cootchie quest and then just lock it in the vault. That's not how it works.

My flight to Italy was direct into Rome, but since eight hours of continuous paranoia is more than enough for me, I took a train from Rome to Florence. For the hour and a half land based ride, I stared blankly at the Italian countryside. For ninety minutes, I listened vacantly to *The Killers.* Vineyard, after vineyard, after mountainside, after sheep, Rachel would not let go of my mind.

It had been about two months since I last saw her, but even two days felt like too many. I was ecstatic, yet hesitant. I was elated, yet tentative. I was floating on cloud nine, yet worried about a storm. Above all, I was bitter. Had Rachel not hooked up with someone before my arrival, leaving me feeling like I was stabbed in the back, those secondary feelings would not have existed. What should have been a peaceful and scenic train ride, felt more like an emotional rollercoaster.

Florence, Italy turned out to be a lot how I envisioned it, as far as the landscape goes, with old, attached, mid-story walk-ups, narrow cobblestone streets, quaint eateries and cafes, piazzas, gorgeous architecture and historical culture, and of course, *Vespas*. It is the most laid-back, easy-going environment, and certainly the most romantic. Italy is by far the best place I've ever vacationed, and possibly ever will. Sadly, when I'm asked about my time there, I talk more about the beauty of the country itself then what I did with the beauty I went to visit.

As always, any resentment Rachel and I shared never surfaced when we first saw each other, as was the case in Italy. The moment my suitcase touched the floor of her apartment, I had a much lighter and cuter type of baggage in my arms. I held her in the air, feet dangling from the ground, and out of habit, kissed her the only way I knew how, with my heart. Every feeling of hesitancy, mistrust, and anger I felt on the train was instantly thrown under the tracks.

After napping on a twin bed, Rachel and I showered,

separately, and then went to dinner. To this day, I'm convinced the food in Italy is made with *Viagra*. Every time we ate, regardless of whether it was at a walk-in deli or a fancy sit-down restaurant, I had a boner. In fact, the conversation during our first meal, if you can call it that, consisted of me continuously blurting out, "This is *so... fuckin'... good!*" while Rachel laughed at my happiness and amazement. Still, the delicious cuisine wasn't the only thing staining my underwear. The wine was equally exceptional. It was *so... fuckin'... good* that I brought two jugs back to Rachel's apartment. My plan was for us to pregame before going out, Italian style, but Rachel had another idea.

"Do you have any cards?" I asked.

"Yeah, on my desk."

I grabbed the deck and returned to the bed. Rachel and I lay in opposite corners facing each other. "What drinking game do you want to play?"

"Umm…" Rachel's face lit up, smiling instead of answering.

"I don't know what game that is," I said, hoping for words. "It would help if you spoke."

"You know the game," Rachel said, continuing to smile. "We've played it before."

She was right. I knew exactly what game she was talking about, but I chose to fake it. "Strip poker?" I asked, heightening my voice.

"*Maybe*," she shyly answered.

I involuntarily laughed at her cuteness. My brain did not like this. He immediately brought up some of those reoccurring feelings from the train ride. Seeing the wheels in motion, and in fear of ruining a great night, Rachel quickly changed the subject.

"Do you still want to go out?" she asked.

"Um, I don't know," I said, distracted. "It's your call."

"Well, I'm not sure what's going on yet, but we could just go to a bar, if you'd like, then figure it out later. We could also stay in and watch a DVD if you want to relax."

"What happened to strip poker?" I asked.

"That's *your* call," Rachel said, trying not to smile.

"Well, I think I'm ready to gamble with you," I admitted.

Rachel and I were flirting like we had just met. The bitterness still existed, but like Rachel, I didn't want to ruin the night. I really couldn't have pictured a better start to the vacation, so with every fiber of self-restraint, mixed with a lot of wine, I kept my mouth shout about Preemie, Drywall, and anyone or anything else that would have killed the moment. On top of that, I ignored the pact I had made with myself about not sleeping with Rachel. Hey, a gorgeous girl getting naked in front of you piece by piece can make a man quit a lot of things. Hell, I would have quit breathing if she asked me to (as long as it was during sex). The way I looked at it, in Eastern Standard Time, I lasted a solid twelve hours! That's half a day and a half a medal in my book.

For the next three days, Rachel and I took in the sights, the sounds, certainly the food, and even some more of each other. We walked through the Duomo Cathedral, one of the most breathtaking and enduring symbols of Italy. We saw the David, Michelangelo's larger than life statue in the Accademia Gallery. We checked out the most famous and accomplished museum in Florence, the Uffizi. We took a train to Pisa to see the leaning tower. We continuously shopped, Rachel at *Prada, Louis Vuitton,* and *Gucci,* myself at every soccer store, t-shirt stand, deli, bar, and piazza we came across. I even went to one of her art classes, where we masterfully sketched the profile of Saint Peter. To top it all off, we walked hand in hand along the most romantic bridge in the world, the Ponte Vecchio, sharing a kiss above the River Arno and later dining at what I like to call God's restaurant. Still, no one knows better than the Italian great, Bruce Springsteen, that you can't start a fire without a spark. So, when Rachel and I were at the bar one night, and Preemie walked in, then soon walked out, all it took was a glimpse of his sharp hemming to ignite the beast.

Almost twenty-four hours passed where I miraculously didn't say anything to Rachel, but fittingly, after the only subpar meal of the entire trip, I got heartburn and began shooting fire from my mouth.

"So, did you have fun last night?"

From the condescending tone in my voice, Rachel knew exactly what I was implying. "It was okay. You looked like you had a good time."

"Is that right?" I asked, pissed she was immediately trying to throw me under the bus.

"How long were you talking to that girl?" Rachel blamefully inquired.

"For a bit I answered," quickly correcting... "I mean, thirty minutes."

"Sounds familiar," Rachel smirked.

"Yeah, well, regardless of the actual time, she saw us together in your art class and wanted to say hi."

"Great. She and I aren't friends," Rachel pointed out.

"Like that means anything to you," I muttered.

"What's that?" Rachel loudly asked, having already heard me.

"Don't blame dumb. You saw me talking with Blondie Cheeks last night."

Rachel slowed down a bit. "And?"

"*And*, as it turns out, when you hooked up with Preemie, you *knew* he and Blondie Cheeks shared a past."

"Oh please," Rachel said, waving her hand in the arm to downplay the situation. "They're just..."

"AND!" I yelled over her. "When she introduced you she wasn't doing it to set you up, she was doing it to be nice. Of course that wasn't the version I got from someone else. You made it sound like Blondie Cheeks threw this guy in your lap and the rest drunkenly fell into place. Lo and behold, it was *you* acting like a drunken *whore*, throwing yourself all over the place."

The fire-breathing dragon was out of his cage and in full force. I could have flame-broiled burgers from across the pond.

Rachel attempted to join the argument. "That's pretty funny, because..."

"No, actually it's not!" I interrupted. "You fucked over one of your best friends, who's clearly mad at you, you fucked me over, and I think it's no surprise how I feel, and when I spoke to your new group of friends, the ones you're supposedly so close with, they told me you asked them if you should hook up with Preemie before I came to visit, and they said it'd be a mistake. How they felt though, along with everyone else, meant nothing."

"You don't know what you're talking about," Rachel said, dismissing everything she heard.

"I know exactly what I'm talking about!" I erupted. "So much so that your drunk, bullshit story means nothing to me, because the whole fuckin' thing was already thought out."

"What do you want me to say?" Rachel asked, not even attempting to match my intensity. "We're not going out anymore. Who I hook up with is my own business, not anyone else's, and I'm old enough to make my own decisions."

With that sentence, Rachel extinguished the fire. For the first time since we met, I saw her in a new light, one illuminated solely by disappointment.

"I guess you're right," I admitted, trying to slow my heart rate down. "There isn't much to say, and you obviously hooked up with Preemie more than once."

Rachel happily tilted her head in agreement.

"Well, you've certainly come a long way from the innocent girl too afraid to drive at night, drink a beer, or kiss a random guy, that's for sure."

"Thanks."

"I'm not trying to be mean. This is just life, I guess. You live, you love, and you learn."

Rachel put her head down, but whispered loud enough for me to hear. "That's what I'm trying to do."

For the remainder of the trip, my conscience slipped in and out of sanity, resulting in the usual highs and lows for Rachel and me. The immediate days following our argument were the worst, especially after revealing my own fling with Drywall. Rachel called me a hypocrite so many times the Italians thought it was my name.

Luigi: "Hey, Ipocrita, why does-a the little one-a yell-a so much?"

Jon: "I'm not sure, Luigi. I think she's deaf in one ear."

Luigi: "So then she is-a trying to make-a me dead, too? What do I-a ever do-a to her?"

Jon: "Deaf, Luigi. Not dead... deaf."

Luigi: "No, I mean-a dead. If I have to listen to-a her anymore, I'm-a gonna kill myself."

Rachel and I did manage to salvage some of the trip, spending the last two nights at a hotel in Rome. I think being caught up in the excitement of the city, with so much to see and so much to do, helped us put aside our bitterness and enjoy the moment. However, when it came time to say yet another goodbye, it was the worst one of all. I still looked Rachel in the eyes, kissed her and held her, but even with our bodies pressed together, our hearts felt silent, distant. Perhaps not the size of the Atlantic Ocean, but if flying over it for ten hours could help me realize that time created an enormous gap in the world, then it could certainly create a gap in our relationship.

The Ghost In You

People say luck happens in threes, but I believe the translation was lost somewhere and luck is a set of three. There's Good Luck, Bad Luck, and Just Plain Luck. Since the beginning of their existence, they've always been a close-knit group, looking after one another like triplets. Therefore, it shouldn't be any surprise that when one shows up, the other two are sure to follow. However, as in my case, the Luck Family spread out their arrivals.

Just Plain Luck was the first to make his way on the scene, unexpectedly and in the form of a brand new, black, 2005 *Kia Spectra*. When my parents picked me up from the airport in a car I'd never seen before, nor heard of, and my dad tossed the keys to me like I was Corey Haim in *License to Drive*, I was confused to say the least.

"I don't get it?" I said, staring blankly at my father.

"What, you don't want to drive your new car?" he smiled.

"Right. My new car," I slowly repeated.

Mike Rennie kept his smile going while inviting me into the driver's seat.

"Okay, I get it," I announced. "We're just stealing shit now. Right? That's what this is?" I asked.

"Jonathan, get in the car!" my mother yelled, through a crack in the backseat window.

I looked at my dad with sincerity. "You didn't really buy me a car, did you?"

"Well, it's not a microwave, buddy."

"Get the fuck out of here!" I shouted, beyond excited.

"We're trying to," Mike returned, walking around the front bumper to the passenger seat. "Get in the goddamn car already."

With a year's worth of commuting to and from Gellen University ahead of me, work on top of school, both my parents needing their cars, and a very large student loan taken out in *my* name, Mike and Jacquelyn Reynolds felt like a third car was necessary and deserving of their son. After such a turbulent trip, the only thing I was really looking forward to was seeing my parents. A gesture like theirs only made it more obvious as to why.

Good Luck was next to show. The day after returning, I was thrown right back into the academic world. At the time I was less than happy, but eventually it proved to be the best thing for me. Before, and certainly during my time in Italy, my mind was caught in an emotional whirlwind, Rachel being the eye of the storm. After Italy, my mind was engulfed in my studies. I attended every class, took notes, listened intently, offered my opinions, participated, and actually tried. Granted, being in a Master's program these contributions should be expected, but by finally putting in a full effort I achieved genuine pride and passion in my future career.

For one of my classes, we were given a project to create a unique, fun, and age appropriate activity station, involving some type of skill (spatial awareness in the case of my group), for kindergarten classes within the area. The event was held in Gellen University's Fitness Center, and it was the first time I ever worked with kids of such a young age. Prior to the event, I thought, how hard could this be, they're five years old and less than four feet tall? That notion was quickly erased the second I saw over a hundred, crazy-eyed midgets. Nerves running around like they were, I briefly lost confidence. Organized, educated, and smiling, that insecurity also disappeared. The kiddies didn't want to leave; parents and teachers were complimenting and thanking us, our fellow classmates were impressed, our professor applauded us, and as if all that wasn't already enough, we received an 'A' on the project.

The decision to go to graduate school remained incomplete until I could decide between Physical Education and English. Seeing how I received my Bachelor's in English, it made sense to continue with the discipline, despite not learning very much. Phys. Ed easily came into the picture because I had been playing sports my entire life, and trivially it was the subject I had the most fun with when I was younger. However, in terms of social status, Gym Teacher is near the bottom of the list. Dickheads say, "Those who can't do, teach, and those who can't teach, teach gym." To them I say, "Those who are insecure, driven by money, power, and fame, have a small penis." To each their own (interpretation). What it really boiled down to was choosing an occupation I would be happy doing, and when working with kindergarteners for a mere two hours left me with an overwhelming sense of reward and accomplishment, I knew I'd made the right decision.

Good Luck didn't stop there. He was operating on The Snowball Effect. A friend of mine set me up with a catering job, which meant I fell in even higher graces with my parents. It's not that Michael and Jacquelyn are huge fans of finger foods and serving trays, just paychecks. As long as I was working and not asking them for money, I could pretty much do no wrong. To most, having your parents like you, working, and doing well in school wouldn't be considered gifts from Good Luck, but to me, the combination of all three was unfathomable, so it had to be. On top of that, for the first time in my life, I was actually on a career path. Yet, I found it ironic that I didn't reach that point until I distanced myself from Rachel.

Bad Luck was the last one to arrive, late but in full force. More specifically, a brand new, silver, 2005 *Volvo C70*, which Rachel's parents surprised her with upon returning from Italy.

With the completion of Rachel's junior year behind her, and summer underway, it had been months since Rachel and I last saw each other. We spoke maybe a handful of times, online and over the phone, but neither of us seemed concerned with the circumstance. We were preoccupied with ourselves. The distance and time apart created a void, one I couldn't do much about, but returning home brought Rachel back into the picture. Seeing her and talking to her was no longer a chore. That alone was enough to fill some of the emptiness. It was also enough to make me fuck my brains out, contemplating whether or not I should try plugging the hole. Fortunately, Rachel did it for me. Unfortunately, it didn't feel very good.

"I think we should just be friends," Rachel began.

"Wait, are you eating bullshit or halibut?" I asked.

"Very funny."

"It's not bullshit?" I asked again. "I could swear I'm smelling bullshit."

"You know what I'm talking about," Rachel insisted.

"Obviously, but you're out of your mind if you think that could ever work." Truthfully, I was only partially surprised by what I was hearing.

"So you'd rather not have me in your life at all?"

No, I'd rather have you in my life always.

"I just know I'll never be able to look at you as only a friend," I explained.

"What about after I get married?" she asked.

"Then I'll see you as the one who got away."

Rachel blushed and dipped her head into her shoulders.

"And my wife as the one I'm settling for," I added.

"Don't say that," Rachel laughed.

"It'll be a magical eight months," I joked. "We'll almost have a child together."

"You see why I want this? You're like my best friend," Rachel said, leaning into the corner of the booth.

"I know, it's just…" I didn't know how to answer. I didn't want to hurt Rachel's feelings, I didn't want her out of my life, but in no way whatsoever did I want to enter the friend zone.

"Pals?"

Okay, NOW I know how to answer.

"Sure, I'll be your friend, Rachel," I said with a fake smile. "But I should warn you, my friends and I talk about everything. Nothing is out of bounds. Sex stories are our favorite!" I exclaimed.

Rachel displayed an unsettling face.

"Are you *sure* you're not eating bullshit?" I asked one more time.

Rachel finally answered. "Its halibut, idiot."

"Great. Well anyway, since you're *just a friend* now, one of the gang, I can tell you what the sex was like with Drywall."

Rachel was blindsided even more, and no longer curled up in the corner. Plus, since *she* was the one who wanted to travel down the friendship road, it was hard for her to be mad at me.

"I'd rather you talk about that with one of your other

friends," Rachel admitted.

"I like keeping everyone in the loop... *pal*."

"Well, now we've talked about it, so let's change the subject." Rachel said, clearly upset.

"What! We haven't even scratched the surface." I, on the other hand, didn't let up.

"You're being obnoxious," Rachel correctly pointed out.

"That's not what my friends would say," I smirked.

"Fine, you want to talk about it? Let's talk about it," Rachel said, angrily giving in. "Did you fuck her?

"I just told you I did."

"Did you fuck her before you came to Italy?" she elaborated.

"Before and after," I answered. "And you already knew that."

"How many times then?"

I signaled two in the pink, one in the stink with my right hand, two in the goo, one in the pooh with my left hand, added a thumb and answered, "Seven."

Cringing, Rachel followed up. "Was it good?"

I happily smiled.

"Great," she said, already trying to forget. "Are you still seeing her?"

"Oh, no, I heaved the ho."

Finally hearing something she wanted to, Rachel ended the interview. "Better?"

"I guess," I responded, tilting my head. "I can't say I felt any genuine interest, but your effort won't go unnoticed."

"Good, now we can talk about me and Preemie." Rachel had a smirk on her face like she was some kind of diabolical genius.

"The Adventures of Rachel and Preemie," I announced, nearly choking on my penne. "Sounds like kiddie porn."

"It was definitely X-rated," she returned.

"Really? Did you actually fuck him after I left?"

Please say no. Please say no.

"No..."

Sweeeet.

"But basically everything else."

Eh, you can't win 'em all.

"Sounds like fun." I put my head down and continued eating.

"Sounds like fun?" Rachel mocked. "That's it? You don't want to hear any *intimate* or *juicy* details?"

"Nah, I'm good."

"Where's the effort, *pal?*"

Rachel was somehow making me smile, but I hated how we were being our usual, playful selves with such a gut-wrenching topic.

"Do you realize now why being friends won't work?" I revisited.

"Then what do you suggest?" Rachel agreed without saying.

I took a long sip of water to buy time. It didn't work. A solution seemed out of reach. Rachel and I hit a point where we ran out of relationship titles, and were merely clinging to the word.

Our dinner date ended that night in the restaurant parking lot. We made out in the backseat of Rachel's new car (I didn't want to defile the *Spectra's* cloth interior). The outcome wasn't a baby, but rather an unspoken agreement to live our lives, still keeping the other person involved, all while keeping our emotions in check.

In the days to follow, our saliva held the imaginary contract together. Rachel and I were all around copacetic. Whenever either of us had the urge to see the other, we did just that. If something was on our mind, we called and spoke about it. If nothing was on our mind, we called for the sake of calling. If Booty called, we answered. We didn't harp on outside affairs. Very simply, we had fun.

Rachel would be going back to Presidents College at the end of the summer. Instinctively, I thought, if what we have carries into her senior year, and at least some of it stays alive until she graduates, then maybe, just maybe, it really is meant to be.

In the days following the previous days, a lot changed. Our imaginary contract faded faster than Marty McFly's family. Copacetic downgraded to pleasant. The main reason; I started work at a basketball camp, and Rachel moved into the city to intern at a top law firm.

I chose not to enroll in graduate courses over the summer. It was a huge relief. In comparison to living in New York City, for free, in a ridiculous apartment, while working two days a week, well, it didn't. As usual, Rachel was in a better position. Seeing her once again become an arduous task. We soon reverted to talking less, seeing each other less, and mattering less. I could feel Rachel loosening her grip.

After weeks of continuous digression, Rachel and I made plans to meet up one Saturday night.

"Hey, cutie, what are you up to?" I asked over the phone.

"I'm in the Bronx?"

"Yankees game?" I assumed.

"You know it, dude! They're playing the Red Sox."

"What about Shabbos?" I wondered.

Rachel laughed. "Look at what a little Jew you've become."

"You wish!" I laughed

"I do," she returned, joking with honesty. "We celebrated

Shabbos in the city at my aunt and uncle's. We only missed the first two innings."

"What's the score?" I asked, not really caring.

"Three nothing Red Sox."

"Is Derek The Douchebag Jeter in the lineup?"

"Zip it," Rachel ordered, defending her team. "He's hot."

"Right," I ignored. "Are you coming back into the city tonight?"

"Yeah, Jesús is driving me. Are you coming in?" Rachel wondered.

"I sure am."

"What are you doing?" she asked.

"I'm going to K-Rock's apartment to pregame, then out somewhere."

"Do you want company?"

"*You* want to go to the bar with *me*?" I joked.

"*Maybe*," Rachel flirtatiously answered.

"Drinks and gay dancing like the old days?" I inquired.

"*Maybe*," she answered again, with even more excitement.

"Well fuck me!"

"Careful," Rachel laughed. "I'll be back around midnight, one the latest."

"Okay. Call me when you get in," I said. "I'll let you know where we are."

"I will."

"Talk to you soon." I quickly yelled into the phone before hanging up. "Go Sox!"

I'd been looking at my watch all night, stapling my right hand into my pocket to make sure I'd feel my phone vibrate. Both remained silent. Two thirty rolled around and I hadn't heard from Rachel yet. My morale plummeted, my blood alcohol level skyrocketed, but at least it didn't look like I was playing with myself anymore. After singing an angry rendition of an already angry Alanis Morissette song, I made the drunk decision to dial Rachel.

Two rings... straight to voicemail. Never before had I felt so disposable. Rachel had officially let go, and I was a tampon. I rode the train home that night absolutely crushed, wondering whether or not she even cared. I pictured Rachel looking at my name and number on her phone, dismissing it in a matter of seconds, and then returning to whatever or whoever she was doing, unfazed. A small part of me felt like I was overreacting, like she didn't owe me anything because of our current situation, which may or may not have been true, but the following day, when I received an apologetic text from Rachel, minus an explanation, our history told me I deserved *a lot* better than that.

They say it's better to have loved and lost than to never have loved at all, but in my heart and in my mind, I know true love cannot disappear. It's immortal. Rachel and I had lost each other, but that's not to say we couldn't find our way back... eventually. For the time being, I owed it to myself to see what else was out there. Rather, *who else* was out there. Doing so would involve temporarily shunning Rachel, but it was a necessary part of the process. I stopped calling, I stopped seeing her, I stopped *IMing*, I stopped texting, and I stopped responding. It was absolutely my biggest and most painful test of self-restraint, but before I knew it, Rachel became the ghost of relationship past.

New Shoes

I met someone. Not just anyone though, a short, cute, brunette, CATHOLIC girl! Hallelujah, hallelujah! Give thanks to the risen genitalia. Hallelujah, hallelujah! Give praise to her fine ass.

One summer Saturday, while floating face down on a raft in my friend's pool, I heard the penis tickling sound of female voices. One belonged to Pookie, a friend of mine from high school, but the second was unfamiliar. Hungover and nearly glued to the plastic floatation device, I gathered whatever lazy strength existed and used it to lift my head.

"Reynolds!"

Pookie was standing at the edge of the pool, accompanied by her friend.

"Hey," I groaned.

"What are you doing?" she asked, wondering why I was alone.

"My taxes."

"Right," Pookie laughed. "Are you hurting from last night?"

"Sure am," I admitted.

Sympathizing… "Well that sucks."

"Sure does."

Pookie turned in the direction of her sidekick and then back at me. "This is my friend, Basket," she introduced.

Basket waved. "Hi."

"It's nice…" I cleared my raspy throat so I could finish. "It's nice to meet you," I said, feeling like my eyes just swallowed a dose of ibuprofen.

"Same here," she reciprocated.

The only way Basket could have been more my type was if she was having sex with me. From head to toe, I liked everything about her. She had thick, yet straight, shoulder-length brown hair, an adorable face, incredible lips, a chest, a vagina, a skinny waist, nice legs, and a perfect bubble butt. On top of that, I loved her style. She was wearing a pair of aviator sunglasses, a plain white tank top, tight jean shorts that cut off at the top of her knee, and a pair of low top *Converse.*

After making the uneasy decision to move on from Rachel, I thought it'd be a good idea to try new things and bring change into my life. I took up the guitar, rocked my hair in a mohawk, and I too laced up some *Converse.* I used to think they looked like bowling shoes, but after my first pair I was hooked. I bought them one after the other; high tops, low tops, different designs, different colors, basically whatever I saw and didn't already have. More importantly, I found skinny girls who wore them to be incredibly sexy. An added bonus; Rachel hated them.

I remained in isolation for the next hour, floating around and checking out Basket like a horny Tom Sawyer. My cock did she look good. Dinner was making its way to the table though, so I punctured the float with my erection and went to see if this girl was more than meets the eye.

"I go to C.W. Post," Basket said, answering my friend, Sir Tucksin Shirtsalot.

"What are you studying?" I asked.

Everyone at the table immediately stopped what they were doing. Knives and forks fell to the ground. I'm pretty sure the stereo skipped a beat. Eyes fired in my direction, brains faltered, and then simultaneous laughter covered the backyard.

"The fuckin' dead guy can speak!" Italian O yelled, continuing the hysterics.

I could only laugh with them. I looked like hell on Earth and had spoken maybe six complete sentences since I'd been there.

"I was saving my breath for the guest of honor," I said, getting back in the rhythm of words.

"What are you gonna do, blow her?" Italian O wrongfully asked.

"Hello!" I shouted, partially surprised by his comment.

Sir Tucksin Shirtsalot threw a dinner roll at Italian O. "Take it easy, Dice Clay."

Italian O picked the roll out of his lap and ate it.

"Oh, Italian O," Pookie adored.

"*Anyway...*" I shouted, trying to regain Basket's attention. "You were saying?"

"I'm an English major," she answered.

"Oh, that's cool. I was an English major, too," I said, subdued only by the effects of last night's alcohol.

"Where'd you go to school?" Basket asked me.

"Presidents College." I could see she'd never heard of it. "It's in D.C.," I added.

"Oh, okay."

"Are you from Long Island?" I wondered.

"Yeah, I live in Atlantic Beach."

"Are you still in school?" I asked.

"I was."

"How old are you?" I questioned.

"I'm twenty-two. I took some time off to work in the city, but I think I'm going back to C.W. Post in the fall."

"What do you... do?" I slowly finished, finally realizing I was being an annoying twit. "Actually, you don't even have to answer," I said, interrupting myself. "I sound creepier than a homeless rapist."

"It's okay," Basket sort of laughed. "I don't mind."

"I do!" Italian O jumped back in. "Would you shut the fuck up already?"

"Jerk!" I laughed. "Go eat another sausage."

"I don't want anymore," he smiled, happily listening in.

"Then just go eat, fat boy."

"I'm full."

"Then what do you think is next?" I asked.

"I hate you," Italian O joked, picking up his empty plate and leaving the table.

"You'll be missed!" I shouted.

Italian O gave me the finger before going inside. I gave my attention back to Basket.

"He loves the cock," I said, breaking the silence.

I might have still been drunk, or happily getting back to that point, but either way, I was being my normal, unfiltered self, and Basket didn't mind at all. In fact, she was extremely receptive. As our sidebar continued, the rest of the table vacated. Better than that, I found out we had more in common than majoring in English and wearing *Converse*. Basket also liked to write. She was also obsessed with music the way I am, sharing several of my favorite bands. And she even had the exact tattoo I'd always wanted, yet never spent the money on (an outlined cross on the inside of her wrist). On paper, Basket didn't look like the perfect rebound. She looked like the perfect girl.

The next night, my friends and I went to a local bar. With Basket having been the only thing on my mind since we met, I decided to resort to middle school antics and ask Pookie for her number.

"What's up, Pookie?"

"Reynolds! What's going on?" she asked.

"Not much, just hanging out, drinking a bit. Oh, and I'm in love with your friend," I casually added. "Tequila?"

Pookie laughed. "Yeah, I'll take a shot of Tequila."

I yelled to the bartender leaning against the cash register. "Can I get two shots of *Patron?*"

"Thanks," Pookie said, lighting up a cigarette.

"So... does Basket smoke?" I asked, grinning through my real thoughts.

Pookie didn't seem interested in talking about Basket, despite knowing how interested I was, but thankfully gave in.

"She says she doesn't, but I've seen her smoke."

"That's okay. I tell people I'm not smart, funny, or good-looking. Here I am though, choice D, all of the above."

Pookie knew me well enough to know I was joking, but there are many out there who would have looked at me like a narcissistic penisface.

"So then you like her?" Pookie asked.

"I think so," I admitted.

"After meeting her once?"

"Sometimes that's all it takes."

"Interesting," Pookie muttered.

"I think she is," I said, making sure I got in the last word.

"Great. Well, I don't want you to get your hopes up."

"Why's that?" I asked.

The bartender interrupted us. "Twelve," he said.

I handed him fifteen dollars, slid the shots in front of Pookie and me, and then quickly returned to the subject at hand. "So, why shouldn't I get my hopes up?" I inquired.

"She's just in a weird place right now. I don't want to see you get hurt."

"Well that was vague," I announced. "But I've only known her for a day, so I don't think that will happen." Also adding... "And she's in a weird place like what, Canada? The Special Olympics? Explain."

"No, *retard*. Like she just got out of a three-year relationship and is a complete mess." Pookie frustratingly inhaled half her cigarette.

"Oh, well that's all right. I just got out of a relationship, too," I said, still excited.

"Yes, but you're functioning like a normal human being," Pookie assumed.

"Maybe on the outside, but on the inside I'm Britney Spears, I joked. "Besides, Basket seemed fine to me."

Pookie took another drag of her cigarette. "That was the first time she's been out in months."

That one caused me to slow down a bit. "What's she been doing then?"

"Decomposing," Pookie chuckled, rather cynically.

"She's just been sitting around?" I asked, not fully believing what I heard.

"Yes!" Pookie snapped. "She's being doing nothing but lying around, crying her eyes out, and starving herself. She actually got really sick and had to go to the hospital, which is partly why she's been bedridden for so long."

Pookie was planting a completely different image in my mind than the one that was already there, yet I had to wonder how much of it was true. She had a crush of her own. It was on me. A regular Jerry Springer love triangle was in the works.

The night before I first met Basket, Pookie and I were out again at a bar. When it closed, she drove me close to home. We ended up in a parking lot talking and listening to the new *Coldplay* CD. Nothing happened, except we passed out and woke up with the sun... like normal twenty-three year olds do. To me, the night wasn't anything more than a story. To me, Pookie had a different interpretation. I had no desire to uncover the issue, though. I left it alone, never brought it up, and went back to discussing the person I was genuinely interested in.

"My intuitive genius tells me he broke up with her," I said, not allowing the conversation to get too serious.

"Good pick up, Einstein."

Jealous. J-E-A-...L-...O-U-S! Jealous.

"I appreciate you looking out for me, Pookie. I really do..." I paused for effect. "But I think I'll take my chances."

"Bad choice," Pookie muttered.

Ignoring her I asked, "Can you text me Basket's number?"

"Sure," Pookie responded, quite coldly. "Just don't say I didn't warn you."

Pookie was so over the top, I thought Stallone was going to walk into the bar. Still, it was hard to *completely* ignore what she said. Therefore, I took her advice, and my shot, with a heavy grain of salt.

I allowed an entire week to go by without calling Basket. I wasn't trying to play it *cool*, or follow any unwritten dating rules, but rather, I felt slightly uncomfortable asking her out after speaking only once. Oh, the fact that I got her phone number through a friend didn't help either. Believe it or not, a shy side exists. Thankfully, Sir Tucksin Shirtsalot bailed it out. He called and asked me to his father's house in Montauk.

I got the invite around five in the afternoon on a Saturday, so I was initially hesitant to drive two hours and then come back the next day. Pulling me in the other direction was wanting to experience a new and infamous part of Long Island. I had spent time in the Hamptons before, but all I knew of Montauk was it had a big lighthouse, it generated bumper stickers that read, "The End," and my parents liked going there for their anniversary (gross). As mentioned earlier, men will travel to the end of the Earth if there are girl's there. I had no idea whether or not Basket was actually waiting for me, but I only had to drive to the end of Long Island to find out.

Sir Tucksin Shirtsalot greeted me at the door, drunk and extremely giddy. "Hey, hey, hey!" he shouted, giving me a hug. "Welcome, big boy."

"Thanks," I said, weirded out by the big boy comment.

"Thank *you*," he echoed.

Smiling, I pointed out, "You're shitfaced."

"You've got a lot of catching up to do," Sir Tucksin Shirtsalot declared. "We've been ripping shots and sipping champagne for the past two hours. Oh!" he remembered. "You have to see this."

"What?" I asked, ready for a present.

"You'll see," he said, skipping up the steps to the second floor.

When we reached the top I saw my other friend, Rabbison, mixing concoctions in the kitchen.

"Reynolds, get over here," he instructed.

"Yes, Rabbison."

"Hurry up with that," Sir Tucksin Shirtsalot ordered, before disappearing into the other room.

I walked into the kitchen and took a shot off the tray Rabbison was holding. "Where are the girls?" I asked.

"They're right in there…" He pointed down the hallway. "Showering."

"Seriously?" I double-checked.

"Yep. We all are."

"Naked?" I asked, unsure whether or not to be excited.

"Pookie had her top off," Rabbison explained. "But that was it."

I threw back the shot and put the empty glass on the counter. "Lead the way, big boy!" I thought I'd try it out. Very gay was the result.

I followed Rabbison down a hallway, around a corner, and true to his word, there was Basket, Pookie, and Sir Tucksin Shirtsalot, laughing it up behind a foggy glass door.

"Who wants another shot?" Rabbison yelled over the water.

"I do!" Pookie saw me as she turned around. "Reynolds!"

"Pookie!" I returned.

The shower door opened, hurling a cloud of steam around the bathroom. Pookie stepped out and gave me a big, wet hug.

"Let's take a shot!" she exclaimed.

"Okay!" I yelled, trying to match her enthusiasm.

Rabbison placed the tray next to the sink and the three of us picked one up.

"L'chei-im!" Rabbison cheered.

We touched glasses and knocked 'em down.

"Hey, what about us?" Sir Tucksin Shirtsalot cried.

Pookie took two shots off the tray and carried them into the shower, handing one to Sir Tucksin Shirtsalot and one to Basket.

"I'll make some more." Rabbison grabbed the shaker and went back to the kitchen.

"Reynolds, get in here!" Pookie yelled.

"Rabbison said you were topless," I called back.

Pookie lifted her bikini top and pressed her firm chest against the glass. "Better?"

Faster than a speeding Preemie cumming in his pants, I stripped down to my boxers and joined the potential steam shower orgy.

"Hey Basket," I said, very nonchalant, like my penis wasn't brushing her thigh.

"Hello, Jon." Basket raised her hands to her head, combing wet hair out of her eyes.

"No *Converse?*"

"Not at the moment," she smiled, brining her arms and breasts back to their starting points.

My penis moved before I said it. "Well, you look fuckin' great."

Basket confidently smiled again, soaking it all in. "Thanks."

"For the moment," I quickly added.

"Hey!" Basket slapped me on the shoulder. "Not nice, big boy."

There it is!

"You're right," I smirked. "Now do it again and let's get this fantasy underway."

Because of my late arrival, I only experienced the end of shower happy hour. Like they kept telling me, I had a lot of catching up to do. I obliged, binge drinking for an imaginary trophy. Upon reaching a drunk, level playing field (complete oxymoron), everyone dolled up and got ready for our night on the town.

Sir Tucksin Shirtsalot acted as our tour guide, starting us at a restaurant on the water for more drinks and apps, and then relocating everyone to an indoor/outdoor bar.

In general, the East End of Long Island is one of the most relaxing and serene places I've ever been. There are gorgeous ocean views, stunning beaches, crisp, clean air, beautiful sunsets, and bright, star-filled skies. The Hamptons and Montauk are both consumed by an incredible amount of wealth (more so in the Hamptons), but if I had to distinguish the two, in terms of Spice Girls, the Hamptons would be Posh Spice, while Montauk would be Sporty Spice. They're both great in their own right, but Montauk is a little more my zig-a-zig ha. With that said, I wasn't at all surprised at the fun I was having. The bombshell was Basket.

While at the house, Basket appeared to be the same fun, normal girl I'd met a week ago, better even, but when it was time to go out, she flipped a switch and instantly turned into the conflicted person Pookie had described. She put up a wall and shut everyone out. I assumed her vagina was bleeding.

"What's going on, Basket?" I sat in the chair next to her.

"Nothing."

"You seem a little down," I pointed out. "Did you lose something?"

Perhaps your personality?

"No, I'm okay. I didn't lose anything either."

I was seeing Basket, but hearing Ben Stein.

"Are you sick?" I asked.

"Not that I know of."

"Hungry?" I continued.

"Nope."

"Tired?"

"Not really."

"I think I know what it is then." I got up, walked to the bar,

296

and quickly returned with two *Coronas*.

"Here." I placed one of the beers in front of Basket.

"Thanks," she responded, half alive.

"If you start feeling weird, don't worry about it. I happen to know firsthand you can mix beer, roofies, and *Midol*."

Basket continued staring into space. "I bet you do," she muttered from the corner of her mouth.

And I bet you eat children.

I gave it one more try. "I know what the real problem is, and it's completely understandable, but you shouldn't beat yourself up about it." I dialed down the sarcasm to gain Basket's curiosity.

"What's that?" she entertained.

"Do you really want to have this conversation here?" I asked.

"I don't know what you're talking about."

"All right, if you're going to act coy, I'm flopping it on the table," I threatened.

Basket looked at me like I was out of my mind, or like I was going to take my penis out.

"You're in love with me," I smiled.

Unsuccessfully hiding it, Basket did the same. "How'd you know?"

"Isn't it obvious?" I acknowledged. "When I got into the shower earlier there were tears of joy streaming down your face."

Basket took a sip of beer to keep from laughing.

"And then tonight," I continued. "My God! If you hang on me anymore I'm going to be put in a closet."

Basket finally submitted to laughter, but those brief chuckles were as far as I got. The wall stayed where it was, despite what I deemed panty-dropping material. Eventually, I gave up. I was losing interest in her, and not wanting to lose any more of the night. It was time to relocate.

After a short walk, Sir Tucksin Shirtsalot led us to an awesome dive bar. The place was exactly my type. The atmosphere was great; there were a lot of people our age, it wasn't overcrowded, everyone was friendly and outgoing, drinks were cheap and easy to order, there wasn't a bathroom line, and the kicker... live cover band. Within minutes, I was having fun again. Within a few more, Debby Downer wanted to go home. Rabbison bit the bullet, so thankfully Pookie, Sir Tucksin Shirtsalot, and me were able to enjoy Montauk till the wee hours of the morning.

Hangovers feel a lot like what I imagine getting fucked in the ear would feel like. Unfortunately, no one defiled Sir Tucksin Shirtsalot, so he was up at ten a.m. ready and roaring to go. I, on the other hand, felt like balls (which could be where the expression comes from). We weren't coming back to the house though, so I packed my bag, used a Q-tip, and schlepped out the front door.

I spent the first hour at the beach in a sand coma, not to be confused with a dead Iraqi. After the heat discontinued my heavy slumber, I curiously wanted to find out which Basket was in attendance. I took a dip in the ocean long enough to wake me, short enough not to shrink my penis, and then asked Basket if she wanted to go for a walk.

"Yeah, I'll take a walk along the beach," Basket agreed. "I remember reading something about that on your *MySpace* page."

"A joke?" I laughed. "I think you cured my hangover."

"Believe it or not, I'm actually a lot of fun," she declared.

Basket and I began our stroll. "Hey, you don't have to tell

298

me," I said, building sarcasm. "I witnessed it last night. You were a regular social butterfly."

Basket took it seriously. "Not cool," she said. "You can't judge me based on last night. I wasn't myself."

I had to laugh. "That's kind of what I've been wondering."

"What?" Basket asked.

"Who you really are," I proclaimed. "I'm not trying to be mean, but you seem to have a bit of a Jekyll and Hyde complex."

Sarcasm led to seriousness.

"It's complicated," Basket declared. "Rather, I'm complicated. Actually, going one step further, I think I'm crazy." Basket held a straight face, but it sounded more like a sales pitch than an honest confession.

"We all have problems," I reasoned. "But that doesn't necessarily make you crazy."

"True, but no one else experiences my problems. They may be able to relate to them, but they don't actually feel what I feel, and they especially don't handle them the way I do." Basket interrupted her own train of thought. "Does that make sense?"

"More than you know," I laughed. "Basically, you and another person could share the same problem, say getting dumped by your boyfriend, but she won't feel what you feel, you won't feel what she feels, and you'll both recover differently. She could be fine in three months, while you could take three years, never get out of bed, not eat and harm your body."

Basket was about to continue, but stopped when she realized I was talking specifically about her.

"Pookie told me," I hesitantly admitted.

Basket didn't say anything, but I could see her mind at work.

"Don't be mad. I was curious about you, interested even. She didn't walk up to me and expose your personal life. If anything, I pried it out of her," I said, trying to recover.

That may have only been half true, but I didn't want Basket bringing it up to Pookie.

"It's okay, I'm not mad." Basket left an awkward pause at the end of her sentence.

"Are you sure?" I double-checked. "Because if you are mad I could let you drown me a bit, get out some of your frustration."

Basket gave a half-hearted laugh to amuse me. "Really, I'm not mad. I was actually wondering what you thought."

"Well, I really don't know very much," I said. "I only got a vague summary, enough to get the gist that it was a bad break up."

"That far from describes it," she muttered.

"Do you want to talk about it?" I asked.

"Um..."

I continued before Basket could give her answer. "Here's my suggestion; it's obviously very therapeutic to get things off your chest, and I'm sure you've talked about it plenty of times before, but maybe this time, if you want, talk to yourself. Listen to your own story. Maybe at some point you'll say or realize something that will help."

Basket took a moment to think it over. "I guess."

"Cool!" I exclaimed, not expecting Basket to agree so easily. "I'm won't say a word until the very end, but I'll be listening the entire time... unless it's really boring."

Basket nudged me with her elbow.

"Kidding!" I laughed. "At some point you may feel like a crazy old lady, because you're talking to yourself, but remember, as far as I'm concerned, that title needs to be earned."

"Thanks," Basket ignored.

"Wait, you don't have any cats, do you?"

Basket pushed me. "You're a very focused therapist, let me tell you."

"Okay, no more," I said, slowing down my laughter. "Are you ready?"

"Sure."

"Is your game face on? Because it doesn't look like your game face is on?"

Basket swiped her hand past her face, changing a smile to a somber stare. "My game face is on, Jonathan."

"Well now you just sound like a robot, but who cares. Let the healing begin!" I copied Basket's emotional magic trick and waited for her to start.

Basket didn't say a word.

Oh crap, I ruined it. Why do I have to turn everything into a joke? I should stop saying shit for my own amusement. Sure, people laugh sometimes, but other times they're probably thinking...

"My ex-boyfriend's name is Rubber Room and he's a stupid, fucking, dickhead!" Basket yelled,

Wow! That's not quite what I was going to say, but preach on, girl.

Basket did just that. "Three months ago, after having been together for over three fuckin' years, he broke up with me. His reasoning was the biggest copout I've ever heard. The guy has no fuckin' balls!" Basket shouted.

Well, I think it's obvious who's playing the white trash angle on Springer.

"He told me he couldn't be with me anymore... because I was too good for him!" Basket scoffed. "He said he didn't deserve me. What the fuck kind of stupid fuckin' reason is that?" Basket eloquently wondered. "Even if it was true, which it's not, who dumps someone for being too good to them? Oh, and then, as I'm thinking everything is great… *BAM!* I get blindsided by a cocksucking, mother fucking, asshole!"

Basket was blatantly giving her ex the business. It was frightening in a *Carrie* sort of way, and I was extremely relieved she didn't agree to the drowning idea.

Continuing… "After it happened, I basically fell apart. I would uncontrollably go back and forth between anger and sadness, never having that epiphany where I tell myself I'm better off without him. Eventually, I couldn't function at work, so I started taking days off. I would cry my eyes out when I was home, while repeatedly watching *Eternal Sunshine for the Spotless Mind*. I was so sick to my stomach that I stopped eating. I ended up with kidney stones, which hurt like a motherfucker, and they kept me in bed even longer, which kept me thinking about him even longer."

I was starting to understand what Basket meant about switching between anger and sadness. She went from a penis butcher to a mourning widow in ten seconds flat. I was going to say my piece before any tears, or lives were lost, but Basket flipped the switch yet again.

"I just don't understand it from his point of view," Basket said, shaking her head. "I don't understand why I can't be normal. You know what really gets me, though?"

Pickle jars?

"That piece of shit coward calls me, while I'm lying in bed, sick and in pain, *because of him*, and tells me he needs time to get his life together. Once again, what the fuck is that!" Basket shouted. "He lives in the city and works in real estate. What the fuck is he going to do, quit his job, move to Indonesia and find inner peace?"

I hear it's lovely this time of year.

"Second of all, I thought I was too good for him, what happened to that? Now he just needs time to himself? I'll tell you what it really is; he wants to go out with his friends, be young, hook up with random girls, and then two or three years from now, when he's ready to settle down, he wants to bring me back into his life. Well, that douchebag has another think coming if he thinks I'll be waiting for him."

Amen!

"He's a fuckin' moron for breaking up with me, an even bigger idiot for believing he'll have a chance with me in the future, and I'm happy I cheated on him... twice!"

Oh... my... God. It just keeps getting better, and better, and crazier, and crazier.

Basket and I reached a large bed of rocks dividing the beach, thus ending her therapy session. I was flabbergasted to say the least, but my period of silence had expired. It was time to deposit my two cents.

"So... that was interesting," I said, trying not to laugh.

"I told you I was crazy."

"Um, you're definitely a little emotional, I'll give you that, but I don't know if I can hand you the crazy crown just yet."

Basket let out a deep sigh, trying to unwind.

"Are you sure you're not PMSing?" I asked.

Quick, take it back! Take it back!

"I'm sorry, I'm an idiot," I apologized. "I actually own that title. Three years running, Idiot of the Year. My parents are very proud."

"You're on your way to a fourth," Basket replied.

"More than likely, but anyway, how do you feel?" I asked. "Did listening to yourself help?"

Basket took a second. "Yeah, maybe a little. I don't think I discovered any underlying event or moment that would provide reasoning for what happened, but it did feel good just to vent."

Basket was speaking softer and seemed to have a lighter, calmer aura about her. Then again, that's usually what it's like before a storm.

"So, now do I get to hear what you think?" she asked.

"You most certainly do. I just need a second to collect my thoughts. You gave me a lot to process."

I didn't need to collect a thing. The trash was bagged and ready to be taken out. I just had to decide how much of it I wanted to dump on her.

"I guess I'll start with the first thing that popped into my head." Smiling I asked, "Did you used to work on the docks, Johnny?"

Basket started laughing. "I know. It's bad. Both my mom and Bon Jovi tell me I should be driving a truck."

"Yes, you have quite the potty mouth, young lady."

"Go fuck yourself!" Basket joked.

"Aww, listen to you. You're like a delicate flower."

"A regular rose," she smiled.

"That's because you've seen *Titanic* so many times."

Basket bumped into me with her shoulder. "*Eternal Sunshine*, jerk."

Basket may not have found happiness after her breakup, but at that moment, I felt like she was spelling it. It was too early to tell whether or not she'd finish, or get it right, but I thought I could help her sound it out.

"Are you ready for my diagnosis?" I asked.

"I can't wait."

"I'm actually going to be completely serious, because

there's a very simple explanation for how you've been feeling and acting."

"Which is…?" Basket wondered.

"You have a broken heart."

I didn't know if Basket was expecting to hear something stupid, or if she was just expecting to hear more, but either way, she seemed disappointed.

"I kind of knew that already," she responded.

"Right, but it's that simple. You were in love, and he broke your heart."

"Again, something I already know," Basket sassed. "You're like the illegitimate, yet retarded love child of Dr. Phil and Dr. Ruth."

Oh! So THAT'S what it sounds like to use humor as a defense mechanism. I must really piss a lot of people off.

"Hey, I told you it was simple, but sometimes the simplest things are lost on people," I said, returning my own friendly attitude.

"Maybe you can break it down for me then. After all, I, just, am, be, an, uned... uned... un-ed-u-ba-cated wittle girl."

Okay, my material is way better than that.

"Pay attention, Forrest, because here it comes." I took a deep breath and then aggressively ran through my summary. "Your heart is broken, you're angry, you curse your ex to the high heavens, you're hurting, you're sad, you can't find a balance between the two, and you're searching for an explanation. They're all normal and understandable reactions, but there has to come a point where you decide what it is you really want. If you think he's the guy for you, if you can picture spending the rest of your life with him, despite what he did to you, then fight for him. If he continues to push you away, then he probably isn't the right one, but at least you tried. However, if you think you want nothing to do with him, then you have to actually convince yourself of it. As sad and cheesy as it is, you should look back on the good times, but carry them with you as you move forward."

I couldn't believe what was coming out of my mouth. I was giving Basket advice, but talking to myself. I was clearly enrolled in my own therapy session.

Continuing… "A few weeks ago, I made up my mind that I was going to completely stop talking to my ex, Rachel. For about a year and a half, our relationship was incredible. We had the occasional rough patch like most couples, but the good heavily outweighed the bad, and I fell more in love with her than I ever thought possible. I was absolutely certain she was the one, the girl I was supposed to marry and spend the rest of my life with. But then I graduated, and all of a sudden, things started deteriorating. We hardly saw each other, she went abroad to Italy, which only made matters worse, and then this September, she's going back to PC for her senior year. I'm rambling, but the point I'm trying to get across is, if you don't make up your mind, you're never going to find closure."

"So you've found closure by ignoring your ex?" Basket patronized.

I'm still on the clock, jerk. Zip it!

"No," I admitted. "For me, and apparently you as well, it's too early. Like I said, it could take some people as little as three months, while it could take others as long as three years. However, I think the longer you wait, the more harm you cause yourself, especially if you're not even trying."

"I'm sorry to interrupt again, but it just seems like you're not practicing what you preach. I mean it's good advice, but it's so much easier to speak about it than it is to actually do it." Basket smiled at her accusation. "Have *you* reached that fork in the road, the one where you have to make up your mind, choose a path and go with it? Do *you* have a plan for closure?"

Holy shit, is she still sassing me? I think she's sassing me.

Apparently, my advice pinched a nerve. I didn't think I was being condescending, but Basket felt like I acted in possession of all the answers, which was hardly the case (I know, try not to shit your pants, I just admitted I don't know everything).

"Well, *Basket*, believe as you may, but I've been traveling down that road for weeks now."

"Is that right?" she asked, still mocking me.

"Oh, that's right, *big boy!*"

Count it!

"But honestly, I shouldn't gloat," I added. "Unfortunately, at some point in the future, my road is going to split."

Basket had no idea what I was talking about.

"I'll elaborate," I said, taking a moment to gather my thoughts. "The reason I'm not talking to Rachel is because it'll help me move on. She's already done so, and I need to do the same. Maybe I'll meet someone, maybe I won't. Hypothetically speaking, let's say I do though. Let's say I fall madly in love with a girl, want to marry her, start a family, and have lots of little Reynolds' running around. All of that should be more than enough to provide closure. Now, let's turn the tides and say I don't meet anyone. That right there is going to raise a Chinese flag, and I'm going to be convinced Rachel is the girl I'm supposed to spend the rest of my life with. Which would mean…"

"You'd have to win her back," Basket finished.

"Correct! How, you ask?"

"I didn't."

"Well, I'll tell you how," I smiled. "When I decided to stop talking to Rachel, she didn't exactly make it easy on me. She would call, leave messages, text, *IM*... basically everything shy of stalking. I didn't know how to handle it, at first. Self-restraint isn't exactly my forte. I was constantly in and out of my head. While on the verge of cracking, I randomly sat down at the computer one day and started writing. I wrote about how we met, how we broke up, our highs, our lows, how I felt and everything in between. Pretty soon, what started out as a means to empty my thoughts, took the shape of a book." I paused before the finale. "When I finish, I hope to surprise Rachel with it as a birthday present. It may be the last one I ever give her, and maybe nothing will change, but at least she'll always know how much I love her. And *that* is all the closure I need."

Basket was smiling, impressed it seemed, and maybe even a shade of red. "*That* is pretty romantic," she said.

I looked at her and purposely batted my eyes. Overdramatic and not being able to resist a cheesy comment, I responded, "*That* is true love."

Basket immediately started laughing. "Okay, now that was just gay."

As we neared the end of our walk, it felt good to see Basket returning with a smile. That little stroll down the beach, our joint therapy session, made my trip. The next step was breakfast, but after that, it was time to get back on the road.

F.O.D.

Jonathan Reynolds' Six-Point Plan for a Successful First Date

1. Be Old-School, But Not A Senior Citizen.

- Act like a gentleman. Open her door, let her go ahead of you, pay for everything (if you can't afford it, don't do it), keep your eyes on her, and always give her first choice. At the same time, don't unfold her napkin, don't buckle her seatbelt, and don't try holding her hand, because then she'll just think you're a pussy.

2. Find A Balance Between Not Giving A Shit And Trying Too Hard.

- If your date is going to consist of lunch and a walk through the park, don't dress like you're going to a Bar Mitzvah. At the same time, don't just slip into a tank top and sandals, the beach and the park are two entirely different places. In other words, dress accordingly. Shower before the date, but not in cologne (I don't care if you're Puerto Rican). Don't try to impress her with money, but don't staple it to the inside of your pockets. And when she's in your car and you're on the road, don't get nervous and turn into your great uncle Albert, just relax and drive normally. However, no smoking J's in the back of the *Benz*, and no driving fast like Jeff Gor-don. Save that shit for Nelly.

3. Literally Leave Her With Something To Remember You By (STDs Excluded).

• At some point during the date, whether it's the beginning, middle, end, or any combination of the three, buy, win, make, or desperately steal without getting caught, something your date can keep to remind her of you and the time you spent together, assuming all went well (if you bombed, it'll be in the trash faster than your phone number). Don't overdo it though. Cruise tickets or a tandem bicycle will creep her out, *or* bring her back for the wrong reasons. I ain't saying she's a gold digger, but you don't always have to call a spade a spade, or a whore a whore. Sometimes actions speak louder than words.

4. Compliment Her Without Drowning Her.

• Sometimes, too much of a good thing isn't good at all. Occasional and subtle flattery can go a long way, but constant adoration will get old fast. Even if you actually believe everything you're saying, it's going to look like you're trying too hard. Depending on how far you go, it might even look borderline pathetic. Worst of all, your words will lose their meaning. All girls have insecurities. Most are overstated and unwarranted, but that means there's enough where at least one will present itself. My advice is to wait for that moment to give her your most sincere compliment, and then deliver it like the fuckin' Gettysburg Address. If you have to lie, it's probably a tell tale sign she's not the right girl for you, but do so anyway, because in the least, she'll feel good about herself, and maybe even tone down the crazy for the next guy.

5. Don't Not Bet On It.

• Find a way to turn one or two parts of the date into a competition, and then make a reasonable wager on them. Don't ask her to fuck you on the skeetball machine or give you head behind the waterfall of the mini golf course, but rather, use good judgment based on how well the date is going. Come up with something light-hearted or entertaining enough to make her laugh, but in no way should you do anything to embarrass her. If you can keep the game close every time, do so, but remember, just because you can beat her, doesn't necessarily mean you should. You may benefit more from a loss.

6. Remember Your CC!

• The most important thing to have with you on a first date is your commonsense and confidence. Without either, you're dead in the water. If you can apply both to the previous steps, you should be platinum. Work off of her reactions, don't over think everything, and relax. If all goes well, you should be on your second date in no time. If it falls through, don't beat yourself up, vagina isn't going extinct. Try to be perfect, but remember, in the dating world, where Fate's pitching, you can bat a thousand and still strike out.

I parked in front of Basket's house and left the car running while I walked to the front door. Barely making it past the sidewalk, Basket skipped out of her house and eliminated any chance of meeting her parents.

"Hey!"

"What's up, smiley?" I gave Basket a kiss on the cheek.

"Not much. You ready?" she cheerfully asked.

"Yes, but first I have something for you." I held up a brown paper bag.

"Aww, you got me a forty," Basket gushed. "Who told you I love malt liquor?"

"Doesn't every girl?" I laughed.

"More than diamonds!"

I opened the bag and took out a large plastic container with *Ralph's Italian Ices* written on the outside. Basket's smile grew even wider.

"No way!" she screamed.

"Peanut butter and jelly," I announced, putting the tub back in the bag.

"Get the fuck out of here! How'd you know my favorite flavor?"

"You mentioned it the first time we spoke," I said, laughing at her ladylike etiquette, and handing over the goods. "Believe it or not, I have a good memory. Don't think I didn't just store that malt liquor comment."

"I'm like the happiest girl in the world," Basket smiled.

"I was hoping you'd say that at the end of the date, but I'll take it."

"I'm sure you'll hear it again," she added. "I'm going to put this in the freezer. I'll be right back."

Basket bounced up the stairs and back into her house, more elated than I'd ever seen. Granted I'd only seen her twice, but still, it felt great. Within seconds, she duplicated her cheerful exit and we pulled away from the house.

"All right, so I know I should probably have something planned, being the guy and all, but with the exception of the beach and a few bars, which we've already done, I don't know anything in the area."

"Wait, you're the guy?" Basket double-checked.

"Yes, for today, I'm going to be the guy," I entertained.

"Okay, I was just curious. I can't believe you got me Peanut Butter and Jelly from *Ralph's!*" Basket was still glowing.

"Wow, I think I could have ended the date back there and still made a good impression."

"Definitely. I'm happy you didn't though, and we can do whatever you want. I'm up for anything."

Restrain yourself, idiot. We're only a minute into the date.

"Well, even though I didn't necessarily plan anything, I did have some ideas," I announced.

Basket excitedly slid up her seat. "Let's hear 'em."

"To start, we could go to the place with the thing," I said.

"Nope, they closed down," Basket cleverly responded, not skipping a beat.

"I guess that rules out our second option, the guy with the balloon, since they were affiliated and all."

"Yep, he's dead. Anything else?" she asked.

I pointed to the *Hooter's* restaurant on our left.

"Too chesty. Everyone looks at mine like they're birth defects."

"That's it!" I exclaimed.

"What?"

"Golf," I said.

"Yeah, I'll golf," Basket laughed. "There's a driving range like fifteen minutes from here."

"If you'd rather play mini golf, we can do that," I suggested.

"Why, because I'm a girl?"

"Well, we already established that I was the guy."

"Right, which is why I want to hit some *balls!*" Basket

playfully yelled. "No cups or holes for me."

The driving range was a triple-decker. Basket and I went to the third floor. That way, we could say we hit every ball in the air, regardless of whether it traveled up or down.

"How you doing over there?" I turned my head around to look at Basket, who quickly discontinued her backswing.

"Hey, you're not allowed to watch," she scolded.

"You realize I'm standing right next to you. I can see where you're hitting."

"You can see over three hundred yards?"

Basket kept a straight face, but I cracked. "*Right*, because, 'This is fuckin' bullshit!' is the usual response for a plus three hundred drive."

"The sun was in my eyes," Basket said, with her aviators on.

"Of course it was. Could you do me a favor though and turn the fan down?" I pointed beyond Basket. "The back of my neck is getting cold."

Basket turned around. "I don't see a fan."

I moved my finger in front of Basket and waited for her to turn around again.

"You see, now I'd be really scared," Basket warned, realizing I was talking about her.

"Of what, catching pneumonia?

"More like a nine iron."

Basket and I continued challenging each other, along with golf, until both lost their appeal and it was time for something new. Just up the road from the driving range was a large shopping center with a movie theatre, *Border's Bookstore*, and a *Dave and Buster's*. Neither of us were in the mood to sit through a movie, but we did want a little down time, so we pretended to stimulate our minds with literature.

"Do you read a lot?" I asked.

Basket took a book from the fiction section. "Not really, but I'd like to. You?"

"Hardly."

"What's the last book you read?" Basket asked.

"*Goodnight Moon*," I answered.

"I've never heard of it."

"It's an American classic," I said, trying not to laugh. "What do you have there?" I pointed to the book Basket was holding.

She lifted it up and showed the cover.

"*Mrs. Dalloway*," I announced. "Written by none other than the happy-go-lucky Virginia Woolf. Should I call the suicide hotline now, or wait for you to read the first chapter?"

"Why, is it depressing?" she asked, not knowing.

"Let's just say I couldn't finish it because the paper cuts on my wrist were getting too deep."

"That's quite the review," Basket laughed. "But I doubt it's as bad as you're making it out to be."

"You're right. Virginia Woolf suffered from depression and mental illness, had a failed suicide attempt followed by a successful one in a river, so she probably wrote about kittens and rainbows."

Basket didn't care. "Well, it sounds interesting to me."

Yes, it's the perfect read for someone who just spent three months wallowing in bed.

"Are you sure you wouldn't prefer one of those *Calvin and Hobbes* calendars?" I asked.

"Yes, I'm sure."

Basket seemed to be entertained by the idea of darkness and morbidity. I was starting to get the impression she actually enjoyed indulging in self-pity. That, or it really was out of her control.

"I'll be right back. I'm going to look for a book." I broke away from Basket, and in my own twisted way, tried cheering her up.

When Rachel and I were together, and she told me she'd never heard of *The Giving Tree*, my favorite childhood book, I went out and bought it for her. In exchange, Rachel got me *Goodnight Moon*, her favorite childhood book, because I'd never heard of it. We would leave both copies on the nightstand of her D.C. apartment, and read to each other before going to bed. We usually changed the words around to make the stories dirty and funny, but it just became one of our cute rituals that we loved. Yet, there I was, standing in the parking lot of the shopping center, surprising Basket with my old memories. When she saw that *Goodnight Moon* was a children's book, she laughed and became all smiles again, but for me, the gift of giving didn't feel so good this time around.

For the third leg of our date, Basket and I walked next door to *Dave and Buster's*. The place is tremendous. It's like a *Chuck E. Cheese* on crack. There were three large bars, different dining areas, flat screen televisions at every angle, pool tables, a bowling alley, and several other sporting and arcade games. Basket and I quickly dipped back into the competitive spirit, playing a few racing games and a best of three air hockey series. Against my own advice, I didn't let her win. Again, I'm a competitive prick, so it's hard for me to swallow pride. Basket was a good sport though, and she accepted her final defeat by performing for me on *Dance Dance Revolution*.

After what looked like a seizure, Rachel and I ended our rivalry, joined forces, and used the remaining points on our game cards to win tickets, redeemable for prizes. Our strategy was simple... kiddie games. The two of us followed around everyone under four feet tall with a game card and more tickets than their greedy little hands could hold, and then hovered over them like Lurch and the world's tallest female midget. Most would quickly get uncomfortable and walk away (although some ran in fear of a kidnapping), leaving Basket and I free to drain their Automated Ticket Machines. That was until we met the baddest kid East and West of Route 110.

"Back up."

"I'm sorry." I bent down and turned my ear towards the little fella.

"Back... *up!*" he yelled.

"Wow, that's quite the temper, young man." I looked at Basket, who was trying not to laugh. "You sure he's not related to you?"

The boy turned around again. "She wishes."

Basket lost it, as did I. "What's your name?" she asked.

"For you, Billy. For him, None of Your Business." Billy turned around and swiped his card, activating the machine.

I annoyingly lingered over his shoulder and asked for an explanation to the world's simplest game. "What do you have to do?"

"Concentrate."

"I think you're supposed to stop the light on the highest number of tickets," Basket added, playing along.

"Brains and beauty. What the hell are you doing with this guy?" Billy rocked his thumb at me like he was hitchhiking.

"*Now!*" I yelled, startling Billy. "Do it... *now!* No, wait. Take your time. You go when your... *now! Now!* Not now, hang on, *now!*"

Billy accidentally pushed the red button at the wrong time,

earning an abysmal two tickets.

"Billy, didn't you hear what Basket said? You want to stop the light on a *high* number," I mocked... a child. "If you count on your fingers, you'll notice that two is actually a very *low* number."

Billy smashed his hands against the machine and shook his little fists like he was having his own baby seizure.

Startled, but still amused, Basket and I laughed at the same time. "Well, it was nice to meet you," I said, almost out of breath. "We're gonna take off. Chin up, buddy."

"Wait!" Billy slowly turned around, elevating his head to give me the evil eye.

"Is something wrong?" I asked.

"Yeah, something's very wrong... with you."

"Tell it to my therapist, Bill."

Basket was pretending to be scared, but really cracking up behind my shoulder.

"Little Willy, how old are you?" I asked. "You're quite the strawberry shortcake."

"I'm nine, pinhead."

Using a stereotypical gay man's voice... "Well somebody's not eating their vegetables."

Billy ignored me and got all up in my thigh. "You messed up my game, doodiehead. Now you're going to pay."

I reached into my pocket. "Gum? I know you're not supposed to take candy from strangers, but it's sugarless."

"Tickets!" he barked. "I want all your tickets and I want them..." Billy took another step towards me and pressed something against my leg. "*NOW!*"

Billy started his life of crime at a *Dave and Buster's* in Rockville Center, hiding a six shot cap gun in the pocket of his

Teenage Mutant Ninja Turtles vest, and robbing two immature adults. His age and his size took Basket and I by surprise, although not necessarily his intellect, because he didn't search her purse and there were plenty of tickets in there, I'm talking enough left over to buy *Fun Dip*, bracelets made of lanyard, and even *Crazy Straws*, but Billy's daring life of crime made him a legend in his time, East and West of Route 110.

When Basket and I left *Dave and Buster's,* the sun was setting and we were famished. Nothing takes it out of you like a nine-year-old sticking you up. We figured it would be uncomfortable to eat at the crime scene, so Basket navigated us to a quaint Italian restaurant near her house.

"My name is Over Excited and I'll be your server this evening!"

A vivacious older woman with dark black hair placed two menus on the table.

"How are you this evening?"

"Not great," I answered, pretending to be sad.

"I'm sorry to hear that, precious. What's wrong?"

"We were just held up at gun point," I sobbed.

"My Lord!" Over Excited gasped. "Are you okay?"

"We're coping. I mean he was nine, and it was a cap gun, but there's a lot of emotional damage happening."

Over Excited had no idea what I was talking about, and I couldn't tell if Basket was amused or embarrassed. I let it go.

"I'm just kidding, Over Excited."

"Oh, you joker you! He's a joker, isn't he?"

"He's a joker," Basket echoed.

"So, can I get you guys something to drink?"

I looked across the table and whispered to Basket, "Malt liquor?"

Basket laughed as she ordered. "I'll have a *Diet Coke*."

"And for the joker?"

"I'll have a *Coke*, please."

"You got it. Back in a jiffy!"

Over Excited hopped away on her Pogo Stick, returning seconds later with our soda pop. After placing our order, and replacing our regular straws with crazy ones, I filled the empty time by asking Basket about her family.

"So, I remember you saying you're an only child... how's that going?" The subject of family can be a sore spot for a lot of people, so I figured I'd open with idiocy instead of curiosity.

"Terrible. I have no one to play catch with, color with, or watch cartoons with." Basket pretended to pout and blew bubbles with her soda until they reached the top of her glass. "All I do is read Virginia Woolf." She proceeded to fake cry.

"Well, at least you get to swim," I added.

"Good point," she laughed.

"That was actually my way of asking about your family, in case you were wondering."

"I noticed. You're smoother than a baby's bottom."

"In that case, let's have it," I said.

"Well, oddly enough, I met my half-brother the other day."

"So you're not an only child?" I asked, somewhat confused.

"Technically, I'm not. My dad had a kid with his first wife, but I'm the only child between my father and mother."

"Did you know you had a half-brother?" I asked.

"I knew of him, but nothing more than his name. After the divorce, he and my dad's ex moved to Arizona, so they never really established a relationship."

Basket didn't sound uncomfortable or appear fazed, which only made it easier for me to ask more questions.

"Who recognized who?" I proceeded.

"Believe it or not, we were in the same subway car and he recognized me from pictures. He works in the city, so we exchanged numbers and might do something next week."

"How serendipitous."

"I know. It's almost as crazy as these straws." Basket took a sip of her soda.

"What about your mom? Multiple marriages?" I asked.

"Yep, she's also on her second. No kids with her first husband though."

"What do your parents do?" I wondered.

"They're retired now, but my dad was a lawyer and my mom was a school librarian."

"So did they retire early or have you late? Although I guess they could have retired early and still had you at a fairly young age."

"They're old," Basket answered, knowing what I was getting at. "My dad's sixty-five and my mom's fifty-nine."

"So you probably have a small family then. Any grandparents?" I continued.

"Just my grandma on my mom's side."

"Who ordered the chicken parmigiana!"

After telling Basket about my own family, the conversation changed, but never fizzled. There were no awkward pauses, and there was never a point where we got tired of talking to each other. The clock was still ticking though, despite feeling the opposite, so I paid the bill, tipped Over Excited some *Ritalin* money, and drove Basket home.

The date was a success, and nearly perfect in my mind. The only part I beat myself up about was not giving her a goodnight kiss. I dropped the ball, my testicles so to speak. Based on how the date went, I felt like I was sitting in front of a green light, but for whatever reason I became more hesitant to drive through it than Helen Keller. I didn't dwell on it though, because the one thing I was completely confident about was seeing her again.

For our second date, Basket and I went for a walk through Central Park and dined on Madison Ave. For our third date, we saw a movie and ate sushi. For our fourth date, we went bowling and sat at *T.G.I. Friday's*. The dates continued, but we also hung out with friends, and even went as far as taking a weekend road trip to D.C. We were slowly becoming an item, but trying at warp speed. Feelings were developing on both ends, but Basket's indestructible, and sometimes invisible wall, kept them apart. Things were good, but they also needed a lot of work. We were having fun, but we weren't moving forward. Her ex was an issue, but mine caused its own problems. I quickly went from losing a relationship, to being lost in one, to being forced to make a decision.

As I mentioned, I was free of any educational obligations that summer. But September was approaching, and I would soon be returning to Gellen University for another semester in the graduate program. I decided the best way to prepare for the year, and resolve my problems with Basket, was to do some research. I looked back on our time together, came up with three principal, yet unresolved issues, and then analyzed each one until a final resolution was attained. Class is in session.

Basket Case Study #1: There's a Werewolf in Your Pants

Upon catching wind of Basket being a potential love interest in my life, Short Torso, a close friend, presented information to me that was slightly disturbing, yet bearable due to the timing of the event. On his account, Basket and Pookie returned to our friend K-Rock's apartment, after an alcohol induced night in New York City, in need of "shelter." Shortly past arrival, Pookie disappeared into one of the bedrooms with one of K-Rock's roommates, while Basket retired to the third bedroom with the third roommate. The following morning, sex stories were exchanged, and through the grapevine, Short Torso passed onto me the one about Basket having sex with our friend, Werewolf.

At a bar in NYC, Basket and I sat at a table exchanging pleasantries and libations. In passing, Short Torso gave word that K-Rock and Werewolf were stopping by. I chose to be juvenile and use that information as an opening to discuss Basket's love affair with my friend. Basket, however, acted like she had no idea who or what I was talking about. I initially credited her response to embarrassment, until Werewolf greeted her like they were besties and the curtain was drawn back.

On Basket's account, no sexual intercourse took place. There was kissing of the French nature, but that was the extent of their romantic escapade. Soon after, Basket began chastising Werewolf's name, and the integrity of my friends, swearing the paint off the walls in the process. I told Basket that Werewolf no longer attended sleep away camp, and therefore didn't need to lie about getting girls, but it also wasn't a big deal because it was an episode of the past, a past I was not a part of.

Basket's defensive demeanor subsided, but a self-conscious one took its place, providing new details to the story. While tongue dancing, Basket claimed she fell ill, and in a moment of panic, blew chunkis munkis' in her sock. She proceeded to make her way to the toilet, but said she stayed there for the remainder of the night. Basket professed that unless Werewolf raped her, he is a liar with pants of fire.

Basket's blow up was typical of her erratic behavior, but why did she lie about not knowing who Werewolf was? Or, were my friends lying to me for some unknown reason? Was she genuinely embarrassed of admitting to a random one-night hanky panky, or was the embarrassment stemming from her projectile version of the night? On the other hand, I thought Basket was grieving and painfully urinating over the loss of her ex during that time period? Furthermore, who throws up in a sock? Honestly.

Basket Case Study #2: Highway to Hell

About an hour into our drive to the District of Columbia, Basket checked a voicemail on her cellular telephone. It was her ex-boyfriend, Rubber Room. She didn't relay the contents of the message, but she did loudly declare he was a person who slept with mothers. I again suggested she try cutting off all communication like I had done with Rachel, but Basket went in a different direction. With blinding rage and devil-like fury, she returned his phone call and tore a hole in more than just his eardrum. Once again, I thought she was going to kill me.

A week or two after our road trip, I received a phone call from Pookie. She notified me there was an emotional Basket at her house in desperate need of cheering up. I found it peculiar that Pookie was informing me of Basket's problems, but I went over anyway to see what was wrong, and if I could help. When I arrived, it was obvious Basket had been crying. She had bags under her eyes that looked like scrotums. Oddly enough, she was wearing a smile. I hoped one had nothing to do with the other, but since Basket shut me out, all I had to go on was speculation.

Not long after that night, Basket actually opened up and called me about another problem... drinking too much during happy hour and missing her train home. I was still unaware of what caused her previous meltdown, and I knew it was more serious than figuring out how to kill an hour, but I took it as a small and positive step in communication. Amidst my suggestion to go back to the bar, a friend of Basket's took the phone and told me he'd take care of her and get her on the right train. I thanked Ryan Atwood for his chivalry, assuming he meant a choo choo train, and then asked him to put Basket back on the line. When she returned, I offered to pick her up from the city and take her to dinner. Basket insisted she'd be fine, and would call me when she got home. Twenty-four hours later, she apologized, claiming she'd passed out the second she hit her bed.

It didn't take long to discover Basket's fiery personality, but there reached a point on the drive to D.C. where it felt like I was driving south of Earth. I wondered how many personalities she really had. Was she a compulsive liar, or was I thinking the worst? Was she still seeing her ex, or was I thinking the worst? Or, was she just the worst?

Basket Case Study #3: Will the Real Slim Shady Please Stand Up

Italian O hosted an unbelievable eighties party. It was one of the best I'd ever been to, and been to many I had. Everyone was in costume, the music was jumpin', the bass was pumpin', toes were tappin', fingers were snappin', and behind the bar, dressed as a punk rocker but serving and entertaining like Tom Cruise, was I. The party eventually slowed down in the wee hours of the morning, which was when Basket decided to drive to Pookie's house to pick up a bag of clothes. Since she was returning to the party, I went with her. However, inside Pookie's house, we took a ride of different proportions (no kissing). After the humpty dance we returned to the party, but soon after that, Basket called it a night.

The following day, I received a late afternoon phone call from Sir Tucksin Shirtsalot, delivering the unfortunate news that he and Basket made out at the party. I expected my stomach to instantly collapse like it had when Rachel delivered similar news, but it was surprisingly fine. More than anything, I was annoyed, seeing how it happened under my nose. There are always two sides to every story though, so I decided to listen to both before pointing fingers.

Sir Tucksin Shirtsalot gave a very vague synopsis of what happened. He said that at one point while I was bartending, he, Basket, and Pookie were hanging out in the living room. Pookie eventually relocated, leaving the two of them alone. Sir Tucksin claimed he got off the couch shortly after, declaring he felt uncomfortable. Basket stood up as well, but kissed him before he

326

left. Sir Tucksin Shirtsalot pulled away stating, "Are you out of your mind! Jon is in the other room. Aren't you guys together?"

Basket responded, "I don't care."

When I called Basket to deliver Sir Tucksin's account of what happened, Basket blew up and refused to tell her side of the story. She said she would be wasting good fuckin' oxygen, because there's no way in hell I would believe her over a close friend, regardless of the truth. She insisted I trust Sir Tucksin, and forget she ever existed. I chose to meet her the next day.

I picked Basket up after work from her local Long Island Railroad station. I expected her to be closed off, but apparently she had a change of heart and sung like a canary. Basket also said that she, Pookie, and Sir Tucksin were hanging out in the living room, but claimed Sir Tucksin Shirtsalot was being inappropriate by continuously touching her and trying to sit on her lap. She said that was the reason Pookie had rolled out, but when she went to do the same, he pulled her in and kissed her. Basket admitted to not instantly pulling away, out of instinct, but said she did so quickly enough. Basket then said to him, "What the fuck are you doing? I'm with Jon."

Sir Tucksin responded, "I don't care. I had to kiss you." He continued, "Come with me to Montauk tomorrow. We'll take the boat out and we can worry about it then."

"You're a piece of shit!" Basket implored. She said that's when Sir Tucksin Shirtsalot recognized he had made a mistake, and covered his tracks by threatening to tell me Basket was the Frencher and not the Frenchee. He added, there's no way I would believe Basket over him.

I no longer knew what to think, but I did know how to test Basket. Every time she talked about her mother, she would confess mild hatred for her, but never her father. She said she loved him more than anything in the world, and sincerely felt like she wouldn't be able to live if he wasn't in her life for years to come. I decided to use that to my advantage and ask Basket to swear on her father's life that everything she confessed to me was the absolute truth. Basket paused, but then looked me square in my baby blues and said, "I swear to you on my father's life, I'm telling the truth. May he be struck dead if I am lying."

I found it hard to believe anyone would wish death on their father over such an issue, unless of course they hated him, but that wasn't the case with Basket. Sir Tucksin Shirtsalot was a close friend of mine for many years, so siding against him was also very difficult. Then again, he was always unusually close with Basket, to the point where he appeared to have a crush of his own. Had Sir Tucksin not called and told me what happened, I wondered if Basket would have said anything at all. Then again, she could have been waiting for me to provide her with ammo before responding, like she had. I also couldn't ignore the fact that Basket and I bumped uglies after the incident. So, was I to assume Basket went about her night normally because the kiss meant nothing and she didn't want to stir an unpleasant pot? Was anyone really to blame, or was the entire event just symbolic of our "relationship?" Or, very simply, was Basket a whore? Italian O's eighties party was incredible, yet when I reflect on it, every memory is tainted. *That* is what really pisses me off.

A silent week after Basket confessed her honesty, I went to visit her in the hospital. She was having her tonsils taken out. The operation was in Jericho where Jacquelyn works, so I called in a favor and asked Mom if she could check on Basket from time to time, meet her parents, and ring me when she was out of surgery. Being the star she is, Jackie did all of that and more.

I came to the recovery room with a large bouquet of assorted tulips in one hand, Basket's favorite flower, and an adorable teddy bear in the other. Her face lit up when she saw me, but her voice was too strained to talk. Instead, I stood by her side, held her hand in silence, and eerily felt like I was somewhere else. I didn't know how long I was gone, but when I returned, I knew exactly what I had to do. I leaned over Basket, kissed her moist forehead, and pressed my cheek against hers as I whispered in her ear, "I'm going to walk away now."

Basket and I never developed a real relationship, but the effort to at least try was there (obviously more so on my part than hers). I could easily blame myself for rushing into things, or trying too hard to replace lost feelings, but I could also blame Basket for fucking Werewolf before we met and lying about it, fucking Rabbison in Montauk and not saying anything, fucking her ex-boyfriend while we were together and lying about that, and of course, lying about what happened with Sir Tucksin Shirtsalot, sentencing her father to death in the process. What can I say? She was a classy one.

I believe we were doomed from the start, though. The things we shared in common, the music, the writing, the *Converse*, etc., I saw all of them as signs telling me we were brought together for a purpose. Ultimately, I was right, but not in the way I thought. *Basket* was actually my sign, and even though it took a while to recognize it, I eventually understood why.

I missed Rachel. I missed everything about her in every way possible, but worst of all, I had missed my chance to see her. The new school year was underway. Unless Rachel dropped out and became a Hare Krishna, she was back in D.C. I'd gone nearly an entire summer without speaking to her, but it felt like I had a lifetime worth of words to say. I wanted to tell her I met someone. I wanted to tell her that someone turned out to be crazy. I wanted to tell her I was sorry, but what I really wanted to tell her was it all made me realize how much I loved her. I knew it before, but I wanted Rachel to know I meant it for always.

"Well hello there!" Rachel answered.

I smiled the moment I heard her voice. "Hey."

"I didn't know ghosts could talk," she sarcastically joked.

"Just the Catholic ones; it's a perk for believing in life after death."

"I'm sure it is." Rachel already had enough banter. "To what do I owe the pleasure of this phone call?" She quickly added, "Before you answer, keep in mind I hate you."

"Hate's a strong word," I laughed. "What I think you meant to say is, I understand."

"Yeah, we'll see," she said, pretending to be tough. "Start talking; or was that it and I don't get to hear from you for another three months?"

Wow, I never thought I would actually miss someone busting my balls.

"Yep, that was it. I just wanted to say hi and let you know I'm a ghost... boo!"

"Not funny, and I'm waiting," Rachel strongly declared.

"Well, I'm not exactly sure what it is you're waiting to hear, because I think you already know why I stopped talking to you."

"Nope." Rachel was now pretending to be clueless.

"Allow me to refresh your memory," I said. "You made plans with me, you watched the Yankees get their ass kicked, you came back to New York City, and then you blew me off. Sound familiar?"

"Maybe," she lied.

"Right, well, when you called twenty times that week and I didn't pick up, I figured you made the correlation."

"Yeah, I did." Rachel almost sounded embarrassed. "I'm sorry."

"Listen, I don't think it's any surprise that you handled our... separation better than I did, so there's no need to apologize. That night just made me realize even further it was time to move on. If I was going to sincerely try though, I had to keep you out of my head as much as possible," I explained.

"So you forgot about me," Rachel implied.

"I'm afraid that's impossible, but as much as it killed me to read your text messages and not respond, or dial your number and not press send, it helped me see the world without you."

"And...?" she waited.

"And... it was empty."

I could feel Rachel through the phone. I could see her curdled up in bed, sitting with her back against the headboard. I could see her eye mask on the nightstand and Oprah on the television. I could see the world's most kissable cheeks and her life-changing lips. I could see her beautiful eyes and I could see myself lying next to her. I could see our world.

"I have a boyfriend."

That I did not see.

"I didn't know how to tell you. I was going to mention it earlier, but..." Rachel didn't finish her sentence.

"Is that why you never came to see me?" I couldn't believe I was asking a question when it felt like someone was repeatedly kicking me in the nuts.

"We weren't boyfriend and girlfriend yet, we had only hung out a few times before then, but yeah, that's where I was... with him." Rachel was speaking softly, trying to mind my feelings.

"You don't have to talk like someone died..."

Me.

"I'm happy for you," I lied.

Ecstatic.

"I met someone, too," I said, pretending to be okay. "That's actually why I was calling."

"Really?" Rachel's voice woke up. "What's her name?"

"We broke up."

"What happened?" she laughed.

"You know, boy meets girl, girl turns out to be crazy, the same old," I downplayed.

"Wait, was she really crazy, or are you just saying that?"

"It's a long story," I dismissed. "I interrupted you anyhow. What's your boy..." I vomited in my mouth and swallowed the word. "What's his name?"

"Spencer."

Asshole.

"I take it he's a replica of Preemie?"

"Maybe," she laughed. "They don't look alike, but I guess they have the same build and style. Although Spencer is obsessed with shoes."

Say Converse and I'll fuckin' kill him.

"Apparently there's this whole underground shoe world. It's crazy. He calls them kiks though."

Oh, so he's gay.

"Don't make fun!" Rachel jumped on me before I could say anything out loud. "He's really nice."

"How old is he?" I continued.

"He's a year younger than you."

"What's he do?" I asked.

"His father owns a chain of shoe stores throughout the city, which he wants Spencer to run and eventually take over, but right now he works in finance."

"You've got to be kidding me?" I chimed.

"What?"

"A rich Jew with a similar family business to fall back on; he's Mitch's wet dream."

Rachel laughed, but decided to sprinkle a little salt on the wound. "He's Orthodox, too."

And I'd heard enough. I couldn't pretend to be happy anymore while painfully falling to pieces.

"All right, Ray-dog, I'm gonna go. *Sportscenter* is about to come on." I collapsed into my bed.

"Okay," she said, sounding disappointed, yet knowing what was wrong.

"Goodnight, Ra-Ra."

"J-dog?"

"Yeah."

Rachel took a moment. "Please don't stop talking to me again."

I quickly pulled the phone away from my face so she wouldn't hear me break.

"Jon?" she whispered.

I swallowed the boulder in my throat and put the phone against my ear. "I wouldn't dream of it," I said.

"Good."

"Night, cutie."

"Jon?" she called out again.

"Yeah."

Rachel paused, but I could hear her sniffling this time. "I miss you."

I closed my eyes and let a single tear fall through the phone, hoping she'd feel it. "I miss you, too."

"Goodnight, J-dog."

"Goodnight, cutie."

I love you. I love you, too.

The Last Song

Rachel,

Three days before Jesus' birthday (not the Mexican one), nine days before mine, and yes, the year 2006, you and I stood side by side in my kitchen, smiling at each other while scraping vegetable lo mein off our plates. When we finished I offered you a fortune cookie, to which you opened and read something insignificant and Asian. After that it was my turn, but I was too awestruck to read Fate's message aloud. You did the honors, and then silently stared at me with equal disbelief.

Stop searching forever; happiness is just next to you.

I joked around and gave the microwave a hug, but deep down I knew it was another sign. A realist would say it was a coincidence, but a romantic would say, "Of all the fortune cookies, in all the towns, in all the world, she had to walk into mine."

That night I got to see the sincerity behind my parents' words. They no longer had to say what they were supposed to, or say what I wanted to hear. They simple looked at their son's smiling eyes, and followed them in your direction.

Amusingly different from the past, we spoke through silent

exchanges. Our hug at the door, a kiss on the cheek, playful shoves and pretend sadness, were all excuses. Every touch was like an electric shock, charged only by our connection.

Good or bad, I don't believe we have an off switch. I'm not sure it's possible for us to detach. You've managed to drown yourself inside me, and *that* is how I know our love will last forever. My only question is, do you remember?

August 2003 – We did it! We lasted all summer! I don't know what was going on in my head that I thought we wouldn't. These last four months with you have been unreal. You make me so happy and filled with love. You have become my mind, my heart, and my life. I feel like I have known you forever, yet, every time you touch me, my heart beats like it's the first time. You are all I think about. Well, you and us. You make everything so much better, from watching TV, to eating, to shopping, to going "out, out." *You* are what make these things so amazing. Two weeks of preseason isn't that long, but to me, every minute without you is a challenge. However, I think it will make us appreciate each other even more, and when we finally see each other, it's going to be incredible. I'm on the plane right now. I want to take you on a plane with me. I want to be the one who makes you calm and comfortable. I want to be there for you, for everything (I also want to see what you're like when you're nervous, hehe). I love you, I love you, I love you! We are so lucky to have what we have. Love always and forever... Rachel.

September 2003 – I love you. I love you, and in a weird way, I knew it from the first day we met (don't say I'm lying). Maybe not the first time I saw you, but after the first time we really spoke. I think we both felt something, and as time went on and we got to know each other, that something turned into love. Okay, I have to stop writing now because I need to save stuff for future anniversaries (hehe). I heard this on TV and immediately thought of you. "I loved you yesterday, but not as much as I'll love you tomorrow." This truly sums up how I feel about you. My love only grows stronger as the days go by. Love always and forever... Rachel.

October 2003 – These past six months have been surreal, like out of a movie. I went from thinking you were, "Not even remotely attractive," to thinking you're hot, to treating you like a boyfriend, to hating you, to being the luckiest girl in the world! I think it was when you got me the roses at formal that I knew you were genuine, and I saw the true side of who you are. When I am with you, I feel so good, so happy, and so safe. When we kiss, I feel tingly all over. I want to make love to you every minute of the day, and no, not because I'm *horny*, but because nothing beats that feeling of closeness... Rachel.

October 2003 – I think love has a lot to do with accepting someone for who they are. We are definitive proof of that. We are perfect compliments for each other, and I hope we never change. If we do, it better be together! I will love you for always and forever... Rachel.

November 2003 – I always think about how I lost my virginity to you so fast, yet I don't regret it at all. It just felt right. You made me feel so ready. I gave a part of myself to you, so now you are bound to me forever! (I like that) You're probably smiling right now. I love when you smile. I like seeing how happy you are, especially when it's about me. I hope you always feel what I feel when I'm with you. I think you're so beautiful (inside and out!) and I feel so lucky to be yours. I do thank g-d for you. I must have done something really good to deserve you. Wow, I just read this letter back and instead of it being an anniversary card, it's a Rachel is praising Jon card (hehe). Happy seven-month anniversary baby, and many more! Love always and forever... Rachel.

January 2004 – When I am with you, I feel lucky, and special, and happy, and loved, and perfect. I think we are a perfect couple and I think we share the power to keep each other happy for the rest of our lives. If I got to make one wish on your b-day, it'd be for us to spend *all* our birthdays together. Baby, I wish you were sitting next to me right now so I could kiss you, and look you in the eye, and tell you I'm deeply in love with you and it's not going away. Love Always And Forever Even After Death Does Us Part... Rachel.

January 2004 – Jonathan Andrew, what do I say to my love, to my life, on his twenty-second birthday? I hope you get everything you want, always, because you absolutely deserve it. Honey, I'm truly speechless. When I look at you, I see the sexiest man alive. I see a man that I can picture myself waking up to every morning for the rest of my life. I see a man that I want to have children with, a man that I know will keep me laughing forever. I see a past, a future, and a confusing present. We both know that dating guys who weren't Jewish wasn't an option for me... until I met you. I saw something that made me want to get to know you, no matter what. "I took the road less traveled by and that has made all the difference." (I love that line. It's Robert Frost. I hope you know that my little English major.) I took a chance and I fell in love with an amazing guy. We have so many good memories together (formal, the bath, the roses, Yeshiva University, going out in the city together, eating a lot of pizza and *Subway*, the first time we said I love you, me trying every non-kosher food, all the air mattress nights (sorry, I'm out of order), the first time we saw each other at PC after pre-season, *Sportscenter* and no *Lifetime, the O.C.*, my Aunt's Surprise Party, the list, "beautiful but far too critical," the time you told me you didn't want to hook-up with other people, and last but certainly not least, NEW YEAR'S!). I love you, and I hope we continue creating amazing memories together. Love always and forever... Rachel.

February 2004 – It's pretty crazy that I didn't know you this time last year, because I feel like in the past ten months, we've gotten to know each other better than anyone could in a lifetime. I love you, Jon, the negative parts and the positive, when you're happy and when you're sad. I couldn't imagine spending this Valentine's Day with anyone but you, because if I did, it would be anything but perfect. Love always and forever... Rachel.

March 2004 – I was never such a weak person. You are my true weakness. I've always had the upper hand in relationships until I fell so hard for you. I wish I could tell you to hook up with other girls and I'd be fine with it, but we both know I wouldn't. If I were, this wouldn't be true love. I'm looking at you right now and all I want to do is hug you and look into your beautiful blue eyes. I look at you and think of my children. How can I be okay? Love always and forever... Rachel.

April 2004 – I don't want to, nor could I ever, picture my life without you. We have so much fun together, whether we are out or just doing nothing. I can't believe I'm going to lose my best friend and the love of my life. I'm going to miss you every day I am without you, and I am going to count the days till I can be with you again. If you think I write you a lot of letters now, just wait till next year (get excited, hehe, you're going to need a bigger shoebox). Anyway, I just wanted to write you this so you know that I do appreciate you and that I do notice when you treat me well, and when you treat me like I'm the only girl in the world (that's the way I want it. I like a dat!). Baby, I cherish all the moments I have left with you and I never want them to end. Be with me forever. L.A.A.F.E.A.D.D.U.P... Rachel.

I want you to be happy, Rachel. I want you to be genuinely and truly happy. There is nothing in this world that makes me feel better than seeing you smile. I can look at you and feel alive for days. The only problem is, my heart was set on a lifetime.

You and Spencer have been together for about a year now. You've managed to make a long-distance relationship successfully work, and this summer, you'll be joining him as you move into the city. I think it's safe to say he's not right for you. He's Orthodox. I'm Catholic. He's wealthy. I still buy *Natty Light*. He has a family business to take over. I have a gymnasium. He lives in a Manhattan apartment. I live in my parents' basement. *E-harmony* will disagree, but on paper, compatibility means nothing. Your heart fits in mine, my heart fits in yours, and *that's* what matters.

I'm not asking you to choose, Rachel. I'm not looking for a verdict or leaving you with an ultimatum, I'm simply placing one last bet. I'm putting everything I have, all of me, and all of us, against Fate, Cupid, Luck, Destiny, Religion, and every other odd, and betting on you. I'm confidently betting on the love of my life.

The night we shared our first kiss is the most flawless memory I will ever have. It's the one I will use at the end of my life. Wisely, I stole the moment. I knew I'd want it forever. You breathed out, I breathed in, and my heart fights to never let go. I love you Rachel, always and forever, till death do us part.